PRAISE FOR *THE BOY* *~*

"With sensitivity and grace, *The* hidden lives of a previous centu ows and immerses them in the tic ~~~~~ ~~~~~~ ~~~~~ Cowell writes with addictive momentum and passion as well as a keen eye for the telling detail."

-Christopher Rice, *New York Times* bestselling author

"*The Boy in the Rain* transports us to another time and place in this powerful, sensual and lyrical novel that literally took my breath away—the love is so visceral, the pain so deep, the beauty so real, and the danger so palpable!"

-*New York Times* bestseller, M.J. Rose, author of *The Last Tiara*

"A masterpiece of longing, love, and empathy."

-Lauren B. Davis, author of *Even So, The Empty Room, Our Daily Bread* and others

"Shadows of E.M. Forster and Oscar Wilde haunt this tender, moving novel of illicit passion and enduring love. I was captivated by both the self-discovery of young artist Robbie and the redemption of his lover Anton, tormented by past regrets. A vividly immersive portrayal of the heady joys of youthful romance and the heartbreaking cruelties of Edwardian England."

-Myrlin A. Hermes, author of *The Lunatic, the Lover, and the Poet*

"A tender and immersive love story such as you've never read before… Cowell evokes the glamor as well as the underbelly of Edwardian England, a place rife with prejudice and social injustice, where the book's protagonists—a working-class artist and a well-born socialist crusader—search for love, meaning, and redemption. The characters, the story, and the landscape are utterly immersive, utterly compelling."

-Barbara Quick, author of *Vivaldi's Virgins* and *What Disappears*

"Poignant, engrossing, and evocative. I know of no writer who captures place, period, and emotion better than Stephanie Cowell."

-Mitchell James Kaplan, author of *Rhapsody* and *Into the Unbounded Night*

"At its core *The Boy in the Rain* is a sweeping love story—complex, bittersweet—reminiscent of *Wuthering Heights.*"

-Janet Goldberg, author of *The Proprietor's Song*

"*The Boy in the Rain* is a poignant love story about two Englishmen set at the beginning of the twentieth century when homosexuality was a crime. As Robbie tries to launch a career in portraiture, Anton fights his demons to give voice to his socialist beliefs. How they collide, come apart, and try to rekindle their romance against forbidden yearnings, kept me turning the pages."

-Martha Anne Toll, winner of the Petrichor Prize for Finely Crafted Fiction, and author of *Three Muses*

"*The Boy in the Rain* is a novel I hated to put down and was sorry to see end. It's rare for that alone, but it's also an important novel about injustices that linger on today. Stephanie Cowell is a wonderful writer."

-Sandra Gulland, author of the internationally bestselling Josephine B. Trilogy

"Stephanie Cowell's *The Boy in the Rain* centers on two young men, worlds apart in experience, navigating a passionate, once-in-a-lifetime romance against the backdrop of England in the first decade of the twentieth century. Their love unexpectedly mirroring both the ecstasies and the agonies of a world on the brink of momentous change."

-Lance Ringel, author of *Flower of Iowa* and *Floridian Nights*

THE BOY IN THE RAIN

Stephanie Cowell

Regal House Publishing

Published by
Regal House Publishing, LLC
Raleigh, NC 27605
All rights reserved

ISBN -13 (paperback): 9781646033492
ISBN -13 (epub): 9781646033508
Library of Congress Control Number: 2022942693

Cover design © by C. B. Royal
Cover images by John Singer Sargent, 1908

Regal House Publishing, LLC
https://regalhousepublishing.com

The following is a work of fiction created by the author. All names, individuals, characters, places, items, brands, events, etc. were either the product of the author or were used fictitiously. Any name, place, event, person, brand, or item, current or past, is entirely coincidental.

Printed in the United States of America

for Russell

October 1906
From: Forest's End, Nottinghamshire, England
To: Holborn, London

My dearest Robbie,

Now that we've said goodbye, I must begin to accept that you won't come back. Still, I look for you, useless as it is. I prowl our rooms in the farmhouse, and every corner says to me, He's not here. I go into the bedroom; you're not sleeping under our quilt, covered to your eyes. I walk from room to room with a candle, searching wardrobes and attics, find nothing, nothing. I walk in the woods, not feeling the cold for a long time, and can't bear to return here.

When I climb our stairs, I remember how you first climbed them to find me that October night. You were wearing that ridiculous coat, and I said, "Don't come in." But you wouldn't go, no matter how the risk made you hunch your shoulders. I can still see your anxious eyes and hear how you stammered for words. I should have known you would eventually leave. You wanted to paint, and you are painting now, and everything I predicted will come true for you.

Still, things will be more dangerous in London. You know it. Be careful whom you trust. Don't be a young fool. If you fall into trouble, write me.

My darling, I'm sorry for the things I did and my silences. There are things that happened to me I can never tell anyone, and now I'll never be able to tell you. One thing I am proud of: I kept the promise I made to you. And now I must keep the one I made to myself.

You won't answer this, but perhaps you'll read it. Is it too much to add that I'll love you always? Or as my Italian grandmother would say, *Ti voglio bene, caro ragazzo mio!*

You should burn this, perhaps?

Your Antonio

BOOK ONE

1

THE JOURNEY

November 1900–August 1901

Robbie discovered the farmhouse the second day after he arrived to live in Nottinghamshire near the village of Forest's End. It was a few minutes down the path from the vicarage, just past the wooden bridge which crossed a narrow stream. Not far away was a large barn that smelled of damp and mice; it had likely not been used for decades.

He returned to the house, walking around it. He saw it was built of warm brown brick and that several chimneys rose from the low-pitched slate roof. The window frames needed painting. He tried the door handle on impulse and found it locked. Robbie went around to the back door, which was also locked. He found a well and fields of grass. To the left was another path that led into the dark thatch of conifers marking the beginning of Nottingham Forest. There was a weather-worn sign indicating the direction.

He had always been curious about other people's houses. Sometimes when he couldn't bear to be in his uncle's house, he had walked the streets for hours, looking into windows, behind curtains, wondering what it was like to live there. He supposed that someone inside those rooms loved someone else tremendously.

The November wind blew under his collar.

Robbie put his hand on the farmhouse door, his palm flat against it. He thought, I would have liked to have drawn this. I won't anymore, of course.

For a moment he felt drowned in sadness.

He turned away back to the vicarage, hands now in his pockets, head down, kicking the stones. The wind followed him.

Late yesterday afternoon he had boarded the train from the small manufacturing city of Newark-on-Trent, one hour away. In his reflection in the compartment window, he had seen a slender and ordinary young man of somewhat more than medium height. Under the thick brown curly hair, which fell tangled halfway down his neck, his ears were small. He had worn his usual brown trousers, a short jacket, a heavy coat, and his brown wool cap, which he had pulled down as much as possible over his face so that no one could see he had been weeping helplessly.

It wasn't done when you were eighteen.

Darkness had not yet fallen when he heard the porter's call for Nottingham station and gathered his luggage. Just pushing open the compartment door, he glanced back at his artist's portfolio on the seat, then bit his lip and snatched it up against him. On the platform he was buffeted about by crying children, rushing porters, farmers in caps. Trying not to bump into anyone, he emerged onto the street.

"An elderly clergyman will meet you," his uncle had said coldly. "And for heaven's sake, try to behave decently or he'll chuck you out as well. And then where will you be, boy?"

The vicar's not here, Robbie thought despondently. I'm all this way and he's not come.

Still, when he looked through the small dispersing crowd, he made out a two-wheeled gig drawn by a black horse edging toward the station, driven by the clergyman wearing a white collar with its linen bands tucked half into a thick muffler. "Robert Stillman, is it?" the clergyman called in a ringing bass. "I'm Mr. Langstaff, your tutor. You received my letter that the local train to the village is not in working order; track repair. Drop those bags in the back and never mind the bale of hay. Come up on the seat here. Blackie will take us home."

As they drove along into the countryside by the gig lantern, Robbie gazed listlessly at the shadowy houses. Heavy, moist leaves hung down from the trees over the road. The sound of the wind merged with the soft clop of hooves on dirt. He glanced at this unknown Mr. Langstaff by the light of the gig lamp. Where was he going? And who was this broad not very tall clergyman in a coat that smelled old? Robbie quickly took in the heavy lower lip and the mostly white hair ragged almost to his shoulders.

They were passing a dark stone church seemingly pressed down by the trees and sinking into the earth. "That's St. Michael's," the old man said. "I've been vicar there thirty-five years. It keeps me busy with the needs of the parish. We're almost home." The gig rolled past the church under more trees and in less than a minute stopped before the stone vicarage.

Robbie pulled his carpetbag and portfolio heavily from the gig seat as he followed the priest through the door. Until this moment he had managed to remain calm but now his heart began to beat faster.

Inside the vicarage, slowly removing his coat, he looked around the parlor, noticing many crammed bookshelves and still more books piled on the stairs. On the large rolltop desk sat one of those new black typewriting machines which fascinated him. An upright piano was piled with music. To the side, with its own door, was what he supposed was the vicar's office.

He dropped his carpetbag and rubbed his hand from the weight of it. He would not put down the portfolio.

"Tea?" asked the vicar, taking off his coat and collecting a tray from the kitchen. "My housekeeper's just gone out, but she's left meat pie."

"Please, sir," said Robbie, sitting on the edge of a chair.

George Langstaff poured the tea. He said, "Well, here we are. Must be strange for you. Have you been away from home before?"

"No, not to stay."

"Your uncle wrote me that you're here to be tutored for your university entrance examination. I've had boys here to tutor years ago but not in a time. We'll have you up on Latin and history before you know it. It's your own wish to go up to university?"

The bit of mutton before Robbie suddenly looked impossible to put between his lips. He murmured, "Yes, sir."

The vicar's narrow eyes studied him intently. They were eyes not easy to lie to, but Robbie had done it. He lowered his gaze to the carrots on his plate and hoped he wouldn't be asked more questions.

Filling the silence, the Reverend Mr. Langstaff said amiably, "There's preserved cherries and custard for pudding. You've hardly eaten a thing."

"My stomach's a little unsettled, sir." Now his situation was plain to him. He had been sent away like some unwanted parcel. He had been bundled out the door. Not that he hadn't desperately wanted to go for years since his mother had died.

After the plates were cleared away, Robbie slowly climbed the stairs to his new bedroom with his luggage, locking the door behind him with the large iron key. By candle, he made out the sloping shadows of the room and a single bed with a mended blue coverlet. Sinking to the bed's edge, he allowed himself to breathe deeply.

His portfolio leaned against one of the bed legs.

He lifted it tenderly and untied the ribbon. It fell open. Perhaps… His breath came faster in hope that something had changed, that time had turned back before that day but the portfolio was empty. Robbie dropped it, rolling to his side on the bed, burying his head in the pillow.

It was only a week since it had happened, yet it seemed years.

He had left school after failing again and his uncle with whom he lived had put him to work in the drapery and tailoring business he owned on the ground floor of their house on a city street of shops. There Robbie had to sit behind the counter before the capacious shelves of wool fabric ten hours a day waiting for customers while his uncle tailored men's apparel in the back room. "For you must do something," his uncle had said. "Forget about your everlasting drawing. It will bring you nothing." The words between them were worn and bitter.

"Pay attention," his uncle had said.

But no customers came that rainy morning, and after a few hours, Robbie silently slipped out a piece of stationery from the drawer and began to sketch with pencil. As he worked, that gentle feeling that all was well began to fill him. He drew the shop sign painted on the wet glass window, reading backward the words, *Henry Stillman, Draper and Tailor to Gentlemen,* only dimly aware of the sound of the sewing machine in the back room.

He did not hear his uncle's footsteps. Without warning, that fat stomach was leaning over him, sputtering, "Damn you, boy! I've been calling you. What are you doing? That's it! I've spent my life seeing you didn't turn out like your featherheaded mother, my miserable sister. And you're just like her!"

His uncle snatched the drawing and tore it to shreds. Robbie shouted and tried to gather them from the floor, but his uncle grabbed his arm, blurting, "I've warned you for the last time!"

Suddenly the shop journeyman and the house cook rushed through the door, seized his arms and forced him down the steps of their house to the basement kitchen. There, laid on the kitchen table near the bowl of turnips, was his large leather portfolio.

"You asked for this!" shouted his uncle in triumph. "Hold him! So, you prefer drawing to work, do you, nephew? Turn his head. Make him see." And his uncle opened the portfolio and stuffed handfuls of pictures into the oven door, showing his teeth, saying, "There, there!"

"Son of a bastard, I'll kill you!" Robbie cried. He struggled against the others' grasp until he felt his arms would break. The oven door was open; the edges of paper seemed to reach out for help before being drawn down to the flames. All of it, all he had made and kept during his life—the drawings in pencil on scraps of paper, the watercolors of the streets, the pen-and-ink sketches, the only pictures of his mother. *Help me, darling,* she seemed to cry as her picture curled to ash.

His free hand stretched out to save it.

"Drawing is for girls!" his uncle shouted. "I'll make you into a man if it breaks you."

Locked away in his room, Robbie pounded at the door until he could do no more. When they finally released him at night, he ran down to the shop and slashed into several of the bolts of wool with a knife.

After this was discovered, his uncle was afraid to beat him; for once Robbie saw fear in his eyes. "So, you'll make nothing of everything I've given you and destroy my goods as well?" his uncle sputtered. "I'll not keep you here. I'll remember my late sister's wish and send you away to be tutored for university. The money she left for you will pay for it. But you're like her, not in your right mind, and now you have spoiled a hundred pounds of wool."

And everything changed.

Robbie was no longer in a tradesman's city house but in a vicarage somewhere under the trees.

Before he slept that night, he lay a long time staring into darkness, his plans for the future beginning to form. He would never live with his uncle again. He would go to university and then, the very day he was twenty-one and came into his inheritance, he would study art. How you did that he had no idea. His town was full of shops and little culture. He had never been inside a museum but had heard there were art schools in London and Rome. That was all he wanted from life. Until then, he would not risk drawing again.

Lessons with the vicar began the next day at the table by the window facing the garden. The Latin textbooks appalled Robbie; he slid against the back of his chair to put some distance between them and him. Gradually his shoulders softened; he felt he must be crafty to follow his plan. He allowed a declension or two to slip into his mind. He sensed the vicar was a patient, sometimes funny man. Robbie liked the cleric's thick, blunt hands, the roughly cut nails and his frayed, ink-spotted shirt cuffs.

As the weeks passed, he began to understand that nothing would really bother him here. The small household was warm and cordial, managed by the housekeeper, Nellie, an ancient woman who walked with a limp and had the most fascinating swollen nose. For hours every day, the vicar disappeared into his study, where he spoke with men and women who sounded humble, friendly, and respectful. On the Sabbath, Mr. Langstaff conducted the church service, preaching without the fire and brimstone his uncle's church had favored.

Robbie liked the peace of St. Michael's with its worn memorial plaques to centuries of the dead; he liked the hymns. When they walked home after, he remembered some words of the liturgy and asked the old man if loving one another was really the second great commandment. "Of course, it is," George Langstaff said.

That the vicar was a little tipsy before bed didn't bother Robbie. Langstaff was a mild-natured clergyman, quite the same from one day to the next. He was a patient teacher though he would audibly sigh and settle his heavy hands on the table at times.

Then Robbie could no longer contain his need to draw, which welled up in him, and one day he walked to the empty farmhouse down the path and sketched it on the blank back page of a novel by Dostoyevsky which he found on the vicar's shelves, with its worlds of guilt, greed, sorrow. He felt the emotions of the book enter his drawing.

After that, wherever he went, his right fingers, hidden in the safety of his pocket, felt for his pencil. He kept it secret. Sometimes in the evening, the vicar played Beethoven sonatas on the peeling piano keyboard, mostly the slow movements in which he could manage the notes, and Robbie sat silently on the stairs to listen, clasping his hands about his knees in their wool knickerbockers. The deep music made a confusion of feelings inside him and one January night, he went upstairs to his room to bring back paper and draw his teacher.

When the vicar had done playing and heaved himself up with one hand on the keyboard frame, looking with some longing at the whiskey decanter, Robbie walked shyly down the stairs. "For you," he said, holding out the drawing.

George Langstaff put on his spectacles, which he had slipped into the pocket of the shapeless jacket he wore at home. He looked carefully and began to smile with the corner of his mouth. "Why, it's me," he said. "It's very good. No, it's rather remarkable. I do hunch when I play. There's the line of my back. I had no idea you were an artist, no idea at all. Your uncle never mentioned it. Will you show me more?"

Robbie stared bitterly down at the discolored keyboard. "I can't... There was an accident... They... Keep the drawing. I want you to have it."

"An accident! How terrible!" said his teacher. "Are you sure you can spare this? I'll send it to my sisters. I've six of them, all unmarried. An artist. How marvelous. I can't draw a teacup."

After that, Robbie began to draw everything. One day, brushes and ink appeared on the dining table with two sketchbooks. Another day, he found watercolors. The vicar said former students had left them in the attic. The old man had rummaged up there, knocking over things, and come down with dust on his coat shoulders and hair. He had to brush it off; a young couple was stopping by for marriage counseling and he couldn't look like a dustbin.

Some of Robbie's work remained in the sketchbook and some was slipped into the portfolio. He tied the ribbons up quickly to protect them. Hours passed unheeded as he struggled with watercolors, despairing, rejoicing. Two of those he tacked up on his bedroom walls. Whenever he walked, whatever path he took, he found new things he wanted to capture. The winter had been full of gray skies and often snow. Now it was summer, and the sun danced through the trees onto his thick, curly hair and his hands as he worked. He began to master watercolors better. He wanted to paint the whole world so he would never lose it.

From memory, he painted his mother and her pale, sad look.

The girls who came to church liked him, and after the service, when everyone else stood about drinking tea in the parish house, he drew them and gave them the sketches. As he walked home with the vicar after the last tea was drunk, the old man said, "You have a radiant smile when you're happy."

Some days Robbie accompanied the vicar on his parochial visits. Across the tracks a few miles away were pockets of shabby houses and families with too many children who always looked hungry. Robbie saw the yearning beneath the faces. Everyone wants love, he thought. Everyone wants what others are most unwilling to give…tenderness, approval.

He painted the farmhouse down the path in watercolor at the height of summer, when roses grew wildly from the bushes in riots of red and pink, and some sensually dark. Their fragrance filled him. He painted easily now, his back against a tree. By this time, he knew that the house belonged to the vicar's friend who had been away for a while.

He was upstairs dressing one morning when he heard a man's voice in the parlor but when he came down, buttoning his jacket, he found only Langstaff there, smiling broadly. A strange brown valise with the initials AH stood by the door.

"Ah, you just missed my friend!" Langstaff said. "He's come suddenly. He's left his valise here. Bring it to him in the house down the path, will you? And introduce yourself. Then come back for tea."

Robbie walked slowly, idly noticing bees above the roses as he brushed his hand against the petals. The leaves before the house were still unswept since last November, when he had discovered it, and for the second time, he laid his hand against the front door before trying the handle. This time it opened.

The hall smelled of damp and dust. Through the open double library doors on his left, he saw a large room, full of books, whose chairs were covered with sheets. On his right stood a coat rack, empty but for a worn mackintosh.

Footsteps sounded on the floorboards above.

Past the turn of the stairs, with its large empty vase on a side table, came a stranger wearing a brown tweed jacket over broad shoulders, knickerbockers, and riding boots. He wore a dark, full-trimmed beard and mustache and his skin was slightly dusky.

The man said briskly, "Hello, lad. You must be George's new pupil. Anton Harrington here! Shake hands? Pleasure to meet you."

Robbie walked back slowly to the vicarage. As the morning went on, he felt a warm disturbing sense in his body, as if the day were too hot.

At lunch, he asked casually, "Sir, how do you know Mr. Harrington?"

"I've known him since his father moved his family here when he was very young. He was just six or seven then; his father had bought the old house."

"Were you his tutor?"

"No. He was too gifted to need a tutor. He needed a friend, especially the way things went forward there. So perhaps I've known him more than twenty years. He's been traveling for his work, and he always writes, but the past few months, I've heard nothing from him, which worried me. I'm so happy to see him again."

In his room, Robbie heard the tall clock chime from below. It was five-thirty in the afternoon. He must dress, the vicar had told him casually before, for they were going to supper at a neighbor's with the man who had just returned. But when Robbie had brushed his hair and descended, he found George Langstaff sorting papers at his deck. The vicar said, "A headache's come on. My friend will be by the gate in ten minutes. Go with him to the supper. You'll like him, lad."

"I'd rather stay here," Robbie said. "I'm a little shy with strangers."

"No, go. You're too much alone with me."

The vicar walked slowly across the room the way heavy older men do, heading to his comfortable upholstered chair with the whiskey decanter beside it. Robbie stood perplexed, hands fingering the music pile on the piano. He was indeed shy with strangers, but perhaps he should go. By the end of the evening, he could find out a little more about why this man was dear to Mr. Langstaff.

Things he preferred not to remember passed through his body.

He stood by the piano still, shivering a little, as the clock struck six.

2

CONVERSATION

August 1901

Anton Harrington was standing by the gate, hat in his hand, a tall, lean shape in the slanting late-day sun. He turned as if his mind had been elsewhere and said, "There you are. It's Stillman, is it? Well, it's just us for the dinner, then!" His accent was high English, with no hint of the thicker, rumbly speech of the county. Neither did he look like a local man with his fine wool coat.

They set out over the bridge. Robbie carried the unlit lantern to see them home later, and Anton threw his walking stick into the air and caught it again and again. The summer light glittered. Fields stretched beyond them, full of wheat. They passed through a small, forested area; trees closed them in.

They were almost the same height; Robbie was perhaps an inch shorter.

Oh God, thought Robbie. He says nothing. And what shall I say?

Finally, when they passed a slender young oak tree, Anton seemed to remember Robbie was there. He said with a charming sudden smile, "So Langstaff decided to take a new pupil? All his old boys love him, send him cards, though he hasn't taken a new pupil in years. So, it's university examinations for you, eh?"

"Yes, sir."

"Pretty dull. How long have you been here?"

"Perhaps ten months."

"Ah. How old are you, Stillman?"

"Nineteen in October."

"Are you? When I was your age, I didn't much give a damn about anything."

I don't give a damn about much, Robbie thought. He wanted to keep up the conversation but feared he would sound young and stupid. He wanted to ask, "Who are you?" That he couldn't begin was his own fault.

By that time, they had made their brief walk to the neighborhood of large, pleasant houses where the more prosperous local industrialists lived.

Mr. Hayes stood in his doorway with his pipe. Robbie always saw him in church, where his pew was toward the front and labeled with a small, polished bronze plaque. He greeted them, shaking Anton's hand and saying delightedly, "There you are! My wife and children have missed you so much! Hello, Stillman. Lessons going well?"

Robbie shrugged. Always the same ridiculous question.

At least ten people were gathered in the heavily furnished parlor with its upholstered chairs and fireplace. A woman in a blue gown glanced at him and smiled. One of Robbie's moments of dreaded shyness descended upon him, and he pressed against the wall as Anton moved confidently into the room, kissing the women and shaking hands with the men.

Robbie retreated to a corner again and examined the books. Fortunately, when called to the long dinner table, he found himself seated across from Anton.

Robbie studied him quickly, as if he were sketching something that might move. He took in the thick, dark eyebrows and full mouth, the lower lip so rounded it looked almost bruised, the full, short, impeccably trimmed beard. By the right eye was a short scar. Ah, so there he is a little, he thought. He expanded his chest and felt his coat buttons pull. Over the past few weeks, the coat had become too small for him.

Anton noticed Robbie's gaze and smiled briefly at him. Robbie felt a rush of warmth. He looked down at his plate of carrots and potatoes, which the maid had served.

Mr. Hayes stood at the head of the table carving the mutton.

"So, you've been away working for a branch of the Bank of England in Switzerland, Harrington?" he said, throwing out his jovial voice. "Can't say I've ever been so far. My children admired the postcard you sent. Climbed the mountains when you were there?"

"A bit, yes. The Mönch, near the Eiger, is not too difficult to start. I would have gone on to the Jungfrau as well if I'd stayed."

Silverware clattered and people bent over their plates. "Well, you must find us very provincial after Switzerland," Mr. Hayes said, serving the last plate. "The truth is, we're old-fashioned. Gas lamps and candlelight in the country, while some of London's lit like the night sky with electricity. We live the same as our grandfathers. No change here unless you note, of course, that the poverty's worse."

A man near him spoke suddenly, loudly. "Lazy bastards, all of them. Never satisfied with their wages." Robbie turned to look at the speaker, an older man with thinning red hair and a flushed face who seemed to rise from his seat as he spoke. "Your father knew how to manage such people, Harrington. He was an admirable man. Some of us remember that miners' strike years ago, which he broke."

Anton touched his fork but didn't lift it. He said, "They had no choice. They couldn't go on with those conditions."

The red-haired man laughed cuttingly. "Still the socialist, are you, Harrington?"

"Ah now, no politics, please," Mrs. Hayes said gently.

The diners' murmured conversation, which had been broken, resumed uneasily. Anton said nothing more, but his face flushed with anger. He still didn't take up his fork, though other forks and knives scraped discreetly on other plates, and glasses of ale were refilled by the household maid. Robbie also ceased to eat in solidarity. On his knee, his fingers moved on the wool trousers as if to draw the profile across the table.

After the plates were cleared, Mr. Hayes called cheerfully, "Harrington, our vicar told me you were home to stay. I suppose you'll find work in the Bank of Nottingham."

"No, I may not work in banking for a time."

"What? You rose so fast. First in London… Perhaps you'd think of buying into some other sort of business. My wife claims there's nothing you can't do if you set your mind to it. Isn't that so, Elizabeth?"

Robbie looked down at Anton's hand; it was broad and lay slightly open on the tablecloth. He imagined Anton sliding it under Robbie's hair and pausing gently at the nape of his neck. The thought made him draw in his breath. He put down his spoon. He didn't eat the pudding but sat quite still. Perspiration gathered under his armpits.

He wanted to go home now but couldn't. There was the musicale to come.

The adolescent Hayes girls played the parlor piano, and other people he didn't know recited parts of Tennyson. Anton sang and played. His baritone voice was so clear and strong that all murmurs ceased, but Robbie could still feel his anger. Finally, the parlor clock struck ten and Anton was suddenly at his side. "Shall we go?" he asked with a slight urgency in his tone.

Robbie was relieved to give his courteous thank you and then slip with Anton into the blissful silence of the path and the evening darkness.

The lantern he held made strange shadows of the trees. Suddenly Anton stopped and burst out, "My God! Why did they speak of the mines when they knew how I felt about my father's breaking the strike? A long time ago and still it hurts. The miners have a hard life! Tell me what you think of the issue of profit versus human profitability."

Robbie replied, "The vicar says it's…wrong to take cruel advantage of one who has less."

Anton rubbed his short beard. "Do you believe that?"

"Yes, I do, truly," said Robbie.

"That bastard, Carter…he was close to my father. Hard men, both of them. Pays as little as he can to his workers. Hayes is a good man. We met as boys."

Anton raised his cane and slashed a few times at slender tree branches, but not hard enough to make them fall, as they continued to walk. He said, "Tonight I asked myself a few times: Why in the name of hell did I come back here with all my memories?"

What memories? Robbie asked himself. He said, "Perhaps you came back for the vicar, sir. He missed you."

Anton said intensely, "I can't get on without him. I know he's waiting for me. I played and sang tonight. I do want to be back. And I remembered they liked my songs."

"Your voice is wonderful. What kind of songs were they?"

"Sailor tunes. Well, I'll walk back there tomorrow for my mare. Hayes kept her when I was away to exercise her. I've missed her. Now I want to just stay home and think about what I'll do next. My house needs work. I'm good with my hands, though my wife thought I should do something better with my time."

They were now on the small wood bridge, and the water rushed beneath them. Robbie stopped so quickly that he almost tripped. "Your wife, sir?" No one had mentioned anything about a wife, not even the vicar. "Where is she, sir? In Switzerland?"

"She's in London."

They were walking the dirt path, which passed the vicar's house, the white gate glistening faintly in the dark like something otherworldly. Robbie could see the parlor oil lamp no longer burned. "Same old habits," Anton said fondly. "Langstaff always turns in early. Walk over to my study for something to drink."

"Oh, that's most kind of you, sir," said Robbie.

They continued along the path and to the farmhouse, up the stairs, and through the small bare foyer to the door of Anton's study. Robbie looked about.

A worn brown sofa sat before the fireplace, but the wallpaper was added more recently and only slightly darkened here and there with fire or lamp smoke. On the mantel were some sepia photographs. Books were grouped in low piles about the floor by the sofa. Robbie made out Tennyson's *In Memoriam* and

Shakespeare's *Winter's Tale*. The desk was covered with a great deal of mail. A blue plaid dressing gown was thrown over a chair, and slippers huddled beneath it. It was such a plain, masculine room that Robbie couldn't conceive of a woman living within it. Curious, he gazed around for some photographs of Mrs. Harrington but could see none.

Anton stripped off his coat. He said, "My former housekeeper Mary was here today dusting. I'm glad she had time for me. Look about! There's my pipe collection. I missed the ones I left. By the by, you should smoke if you haven't begun. I did when I was your age, though I got the devil for it."

"My uncle didn't like it. He's my mother's older brother, my uncle Henry."

"Didn't he? It seems he oughtn't to be trusted as a source of wisdom, this uncle of yours."

"I don't trust him, sir. I don't like him."

"Ah, then you must have reason."

A thousand reasons, Robbie thought, but he was silent.

Anton pulled on his dressing gown and knelt to make a fire. He said, "Night chills here from the forest. May I offer you a glass of port?"

Robbie shook his head. He would have gladly had some, but he had once drunk a lot in school and said things he wished he hadn't.

"Oh, very well then," said Anton, standing and dusting his hands. "Bring me the decanter and suit yourself. Thanks. You'll find the glass on the bedroom washstand. Don't trip on the rug. And don't call me 'sir.' We're both Langstaff's lads."

"He said you were friends."

"He's the only one who..." Anton said no more.

The adjoining bedroom was in shadows. On either side Robbie could make out what seemed to be massive wardrobes, and, against the far wall, a high oak poster bed half hidden by hangings. Anton came behind him with the oil lamp, shining it on a painting of a ship in a storm over the marble washstand.

"Langstaff says you're an artist. What do you think of this picture?"

"I think…the ship's well done, but it's awfully dark."

"You're right. Ever seen Turner's work?"

Robbie shook his head.

"Really? You must go to London and see it. It's remarkable! This is commonplace, but you know, it's mine. It wouldn't fetch a shilling at an estate sale, but it was in my nursery when I was a child, and I used to imagine I was a man on that ship. I think perhaps a sort of pirate. My grandmother came from Livorno in such a storm…only Italian blood I have."

Robbie remembered the name the vicar had used once: *Antonio.* He felt the sound of it on his tongue. "Then I suppose you speak Italian."

"Italian and schoolboy French. I took Italian up again when I was home for a time after my marriage ended."

So, there was no more marriage, Robbie thought. He didn't know how that could be. You couldn't get out of it, could you?

He was aware of how close they stood and that the faint sweatiness he had felt most of the evening had increased. He felt it under his armpits and inside his trousers. He hated it. He experienced the sort of excitement where he might blurt out the wrong words. He felt shamefully young. Even his voice lost its depth and sounded younger when he felt like that.

"Come back to the fire," Anton said. "Did you really enjoy yourself tonight? I felt clumsy."

Robbie sat on the very edge of the long sofa. "You didn't seem it."

"I've long taught myself to hide things."

"May I ask—are you a socialist, Mr. Harrington?"

"I was briefly at your age. Then I understood how powerless we were. Langstaff's a socialist as well. Say nothing: a priest must please everyone in his parish. He's a complex man. Are you sure you won't have some port? No? To your health!" Anton leaned back and for a moment absently stroked his right wrist with the back of the forefinger of his left hand. "So, have you been here long?"

"Nearly nine months, since November."

Anton said thoughtfully, "When I'm here, I read a lot. Do you like reading? I thought you did. What do you like?" Anton took a long drink of his port. "Poetry? Novels? If you read through Langstaff's books, come and begin on mine."

"Oh, may I?"

Anton smiled as he held out the glass, and Robbie took it. He put his lips near where Anton's lips had been and tasted tobacco along with the port. It went to his head almost at once. Within three minutes, he felt it touch his knees. He drank again. It made him feel bolder.

He said as clearly as he could, "Could you tell me something about Switzerland, if you don't mind?"

Anton hesitated a moment. "Switzerland, yes. Perhaps one day you'll go there and paint it. I went up the mountain with a guide where there's nothing but rocks…and some snow that's high and bare the way you suspect the soul is when stripped of everything. I've never seen myself so clearly as I did in my last weeks there."

Robbie thought, Why does he say such things? Perhaps it's because his wife's gone. Did he love her, and does he miss her? It must be awful to love someone and have them go off. Perhaps he's lonely.

He asked, "Do you have children, Mr. Harrington?"

"No—a pity, and I wanted them desperately. So did my wife. The vicar doesn't have children either. You look surprised. You didn't know he was married for ten years? She died young, and he keeps her things in the attic; he never wanted anyone but her. So he's fatherly. He takes in boys to tutor. They write him years after."

Leaning forward with his hands on his knees, Anton said, "Your mother must miss you."

Robbie looked at the worn fringes of the rug. "She died a long time ago."

"I'm so very sorry. Langstaff didn't mention it. But your father—"

"I've never met him. They weren't married, you see. People say it's shameful."

"No, it wasn't if they loved each other. What's sad is when people go away, and we miss them horribly."

He means his wife, Robbie thought.

Anton had laid his hand on Robbie's arm. Robbie felt the warmth of the palm through his coat and for a moment didn't speak. It was just as warm and soft as Robbie had imagined it would be. Then Anton moved; he let his hand fall to his knee, palm up and still open. By the yellowish lamplight, Robbie thought he saw a fairly recent scar on the inner wrist.

Anton's voice startled him. He said cheerfully, "And now you go on to university soon? The old man's fond of you. He'll miss you."

"I'm going only because I must, to get away from my uncle," Robbie said, his voice suddenly deep. "What I want is to become an artist."

"You must follow your heart—you must, Stillman!" Anton rose and, with hands stuffed in his dressing-gown pockets, made his way to the window. "I've talked a lot of nonsense," he murmured. "Better to you than to myself, of course. If you think I've had a bit too much port, do keep it between us. It worries the old fellow. I worry about him, and he worries about me. We're a pair, he and I, both of us tipplers. I presume you knew that. Since his two old friends died. But I'm sometimes more than a tippler. The glass is a wonderful way of forgetting. Good night, Stillman. It was good to have your company."

Robbie returned to the cottage, swinging the lantern as he mounted the dim steps to his room, his head spinning a little from the port. The whole last hour had been so strange, so enchanting. Anton, he thought with wonder. He felt as if something very important had happened to him, and yet he couldn't define it. He was not good with words, only with pictures.

He had wanted to put his lips to Anton's hand and the scar on his wrist.

No, more. He had wanted to touch his finger to those lips beneath the soft mustache.

Here behind his locked door, he could admit it to himself. He had never fallen in love with a girl, as tenderly as he felt toward them. His whole desire had been toward men. In the school hall a few years ago, one of the older boys had come up to him, pushed him into some curtains, and groped Robbie's crotch. Robbie had instantly become hard but turned away. But of course, it was wrong. Every way inside him was wrong.

He had felt a heartsick love for three schoolmasters. To have something of them, he stole from them. Nothing of great value: a pen, a handkerchief, a packet of chocolate, which he never ate or unwrapped but kept in a box and looked at. Before coming here, he had thrown these things away.

Such things were not only immoral; they were also against the law.

He had heard two masters speaking in low voices behind a study door. Some London courts had made laws punishing intimacy between men by two years' imprisonment with hard labor. A famous playwright had been caught and sentenced. Robbie had looked for it in the local newspapers but found nothing. It had faded away as if it had never been. He was quite young when he heard it.

No one spoke of such things in his town. They fretted over apple crops and factory production and the loneliness of the old. Under their trousers was a prudent formality. The things that thrilled his mind and body obviously did not touch theirs. He was once again that thing he'd been blamed for most of his life: different.

Still, it depressed him; it was one more real thing in him he must never show. Even with his private longings, Robbie knew the truth of the world and what it had in store for him. You became a man and worked at something you despised; you married a woman and did moist, clumsy things with her in bed. He could see no further. He could only imagine wearing his bowler and going to some work with ledgers. Not a draper, of course. Something else deadening. He would forget art.

Yes, he must forget it. It was impossible. That was life, wasn't it, never saying what you really felt or wanted? Yet hadn't the man he had spent the evening with said to him, "You must follow your heart"?

Robbie listened to the faint stir of branches against his window, the almost perfect silence of midnight this late-summer eve. Standing before the large oval mirror in the corner of his room, he removed his clothing and dropped it piece by piece upon the floor until he was naked.

So—this was himself: rather upturned nose, a mouth caught in surprise and a chipped front tooth. Taller since he'd come here. A body in early manhood. Shaving every few days, for his beard was slight, though a thick gathering of curled hair descended from his navel to his groin.

As he approached his reflection, his whole body was as open as if he had been running happily toward someone he loved. His penis hardened; his body ached. He stared at himself, furtive, flushed, defiant. And about him in shadows in the air of the little room were the Renaissance paintings and ancient sculptures of naked men he had seen in books which so thrilled him. Men were beautiful things: Why could God create such things and not allow them to be touched? Wasn't it natural to touch a beautiful thing?

To fulfill that might end in a prison cell and, after that, eternal hellfire.

Still, the vicar when tipsy one evening had told Robbie that hellfire was a medieval concept to keep people in line. Hell, George Langstaff had said, was separation from God. Robbie was warned not to repeat this. A few members of the congregation felt the need for a real hell of some sort. It kept a sort of world order. But burning your finger for a moment on a hot kettle was bad enough; an eternity of it for the whole body was not to be conceived. And supposing the preachers in the church he had gone to with his uncle were right: one slip and you sizzle.

Footsteps across the hall and a knock made him leap into the bed. From outside the door, the vicar whispered, "I saw the light under the door. It's past twelve. You ought to be asleep, you know."

"I was just in bed."

"Antonio kept you out late."

"We talked awhile."

"Excellent. Did you have a pleasant time?"

"Oh yes.... Good night, Mr. Langstaff!" Forcing a nonchalant yawn, Robbie turned out the lantern and lay in bed, desire growing to a painful throb which must be fulfilled. He did, stifling any sound, wretched with longing, and lay in the darkness and was ashamed.

The vicar was already reading his newspaper and drinking his tea when Robbie walked downstairs for breakfast the next morning. Hands thrust into his pockets, he took a moment to look out the parlor window. The garden was soft with sunshine. I can't let the old fellow look at me or he'll know what I felt last night, he thought. Old people don't feel such things. Perhaps Anton Harrington will go away soon, and I won't have to see him again.

That evening, he went down to the farmhouse kitchen and searched the laundry basket until he found a shirt that smelled of tobacco and the musk of clean sweat. "Anton," he whispered, "I was wrong. Don't go away just yet. Stay a little, Anton, please."

Burying his face in the shirt, he carried it carefully back to his own room, where he fell asleep with it cradled in his arms.

3

NIGHT THOUGHTS

September 1901

Anton was falling from the southeast ridge of the Swiss mountain. He had tripped on the descent and fell endlessly; he tried to grasp at the rocks and couldn't. The guide had disappeared, and his body scraped against stone. The rope that had held him was gone. He shouted, and it echoed to the valley, which went on forever, but no one replied.

He sat up suddenly in bed in the middle of the night, heart pounding, looking about his bedroom in the house under the great trees that had been his father's. He heard someone crying, perhaps his mother or his father, and he was running and running and there was no escape.

You'll come to nothing. Christ, why did he never stop hearing those words? They disappeared sometimes for whole months, and then a sadness or a silence came, as clear as his father's voice had ever been and as insidious in his ear. *You'll come to nothing.*

He had shouted in his dream, waking himself, and he was no longer abroad but home in his room in his house.

He covered his face with his hands. Even the dark dusting of hair on his arms trembled. It will all come out right, he told himself. He had climbed the southern ridge of the Mönch, he and the guide, and had seen the snowy peaks of the Jungfrau and the Eiger. He had had no problem with the descent. The dream was nonsense. But one bucolic day, when he was preparing to climb the Jungfrau, which was harder, he returned from supper and found that letter with its unforgiving news waiting for him.

After that he did not write to George, who loved him like

a son, the only utterly good person he had ever known. He had stayed away two months more, returning here only a few weeks ago to find the dreams had followed him. The devil with it! Anton would never let anyone know what he had learned in Switzerland and what he had done. He would push it deep down inside himself where one day it would dissolve to nothing. He pulled the quilt over him. Finally, he slept

When Anton awoke in the morning, the dream of the mountain was gone. He felt warmth all through, as if somebody loved him. He put his hand inside his shirt to his nipple and then to his stomach as if making sure he was there; his fingers passed through thick chest hair. He pressed the strong muscle of his right arm and looked around, a little bewildered. There was a feeling of well-being as if he had been through some dark rite, yes, as if he were cleansed.

He had climbed and not fallen in his time in Switzerland; that had been a nightmare. He was strong and agile, and his father's voice was gone.

Within moments, he thought of his life, compressing it to the space of his palm. The brilliant university career, his several months in India, then home again to manage his father's affairs. A funeral in the rain, wet shoes, consoling voices, his violent desire to kick the earth onto his father's lowered coffin, to wrench up other gravestones with his bare hands and hurl them into the open hole of wet earth so that the dead might never arise.

Then escape to London with his large inheritance, newly married to the beautiful Louise and employed by the Bank of England: an office, letters, ledgers, huge sums of money, investments, that London world where he knew that what he had become was what he had willed himself to become. *Yes, Mr. Harrington. Certainly, Mr. Harrington. Very good, sir.*

The weight of his old life lessened in his hand, became nothing.

Anton lay back, staring at the dark fabric canopy of the bed, which he had bought when he'd moved back here from London with his wife. He had sold almost all the furniture in this rather ordinary old house that his father had owned, buying other used, common, comfortable things to make this into the warm home he had always wanted. He had taken up his tools and repaired and renovated the house, which had been neglected for a long time. The only new thing was the green-covered eiderdown quilt which he had sent from Switzerland. Beyond its folds, he saw the washstand with its pitcher and bowl and the shape of the window frame. Outside, a little away, lay the forest.

Since his return to his house in the midlands of England, he had traveled here and there to see what work might interest him. He'd seen old friends and had been given referrals to places of business. The bank in London where he had first worked wanted him back. He had an offer from Zurich again, but he couldn't go back there. He had to stay here until he found out what he was meant to do.

He must make a time to have one of his long discussions with George Langstaff when the night grew late and they had both drunk a little too much and he had courage to say, "Where do I belong? Show me how to live my life better. George, show me. Christ, George. In early spring, I'll be thirty."

4

Beginnings

September–October 1901

The problem with loving someone secretly, Robbie thought, is you can no longer speak to them casually. The smallest sentences—an invitation to supper, a refusal of that invitation, an impatient look—are fraught with hope or pain. But the love that began in the privacy of his heart remained there as all his previous crushes had done. He said not a word. Anton Harrington was seldom about, and once when Robbie hurried in and found him in the vicarage parlor, he was so moved, he could speak no word of greeting.

They met outside on the path now and then, and Anton always said, "Hello, Stillman! So, are you getting on?" Sometimes he seemed cheerful; sometimes he barely looked up and then something dark crossed his face and he went on with his hands in his pockets, beautiful and unapproachable. Sometimes he wore dark brown fine-wool suits and linen shirts with white cuffs and gold cufflinks with little dark gems; the cuffs extended over the edges of his hands. His clothes were London tailored for certain.

The backs of Anton's hands held a faint dusting of hair.

Robbie wished he could kiss them. He felt he would give all he had for that kiss.

He drew Anton from memory: the small dark mole which was not quite obscured by the mustache above the full lips; the straight part in his oiled hair; the teeth slightly stained from tobacco. The front teeth were crooked, and it gave him a workman's smile. Robbie thought, Ah, that's it!

He knew the momentary pleasure of the artist who has succeeded in capturing some deep truth. And he felt, as he always had with his drawings, that what he had put down on paper was somehow his.

He slipped some of his favorite work into his portfolio, continuing to fill it. The days were free once his halfhearted lessons were done.

For some weeks after the dinner party, Anton was often away. Even if Robbie had had a chance to speak with him other than their brief encounters, what could they say to each other? Anton could ask, How are your studies? and he could reply, Oh, well enough. Ridiculous, infuriating. They had spoken a lot that one night, but it was over like a door that had been open before and is suddenly bolted.

Once, on a Sunday when Anton was home, Robbie saw him standing in the back of Mr. Langstaff's small church, St. Michael's, coming forward for Communion with bowed head. He heard Anton's beautiful deep voice amid the hymn singers. Sometimes when Robbie was working in his room on translations, he would hear Anton speaking from the vicarage parlor. One rainy afternoon, he walked softly to the landing, leaning as far as he could over the banister without being seen. He could just make out the deep brown rose-patterned carpet.

Anton and the vicar moved into the dining room and closed the door. He hated that he couldn't hear what they said. An hour later Anton emerged alone, his head lowered. He touched the edges of the sofa and chairs as he walked somewhat unsteadily to the door and went into the rain.

Robbie returned to his room and sat at his desk, studying his drawing of Anton again. It wasn't good enough. He looked away from his drawing with a sigh, heel of one hand on the desk edge. How could he understand why Anton seemed troubled? Robbie was young. It seemed a fault.

Later, when he came down the stairs to the empty parlor, he found Anton's little gold-embossed pocket copy of Tennyson's *In Memoriam* on the floor by the soft chair where it had fallen. Inside the front cover was a small bit of paper and, tucked within it, some strands of shiny rust-gold hair. He took the book up, holding it first to his lips before he slipped it into his pocket.

To his surprise he realized he was very happy. He knew by this time how much he could get away with, and his studies sank while his cheerful typing of the vicar's scholarly papers (he had quickly mastered the mechanism) and willingness to run errands increased. George Langstaff was rarely gruff, and the sound of his careful footsteps ascending to bed each night with a little whiskey in him was reassuring.

The letter from his uncle took away his happiness. He sat on the piano chair to read it, repelled even by the handwriting.

"Oh dear, is it bad news?" Mr. Langstaff asked, looking up from the sermon he was writing at his desk, pen held above the paper.

"Yes, awful! My uncle's getting married in three days, and my aunt-to-be wants me to come to the wedding. How can he marry? He's never loved anyone." Robbie played a few notes on the piano. "I don't want to go," he said.

The vicar put down his pen and wiped his fingers. "I'm afraid you must," he said. "Your suit must be altered; you need a new one, but there's no time. Walk down to Mr. Oates's this afternoon and see what he can do. You'll be back quickly."

Robbie closed the fallboard. "Do you think he'll demand I stay?"

"I doubt he will, lad. I'd miss you if that happened, and so would all the church ladies."

"Oh, the church ladies!" Robbie laughed. "I make them pretty when I draw them, but some are very pretty indeed."

He boarded the train to Newark-on-Trent in his suit that, in spite of Mr. Oates's attempts at alteration, was still too tight across the shoulders. The trousers had been carefully lengthened with matching cloth to accommodate his new height. His curly hair, though he had brushed it, was wild about his face. The old sense of heaviness crept into him before he entered the door of his former home, next to the closed drapery shop.

Robbie opened that door to loud exclamations. "There he is—look how he's grown—he's become so handsome." Relatives he had seldom seen rushed up to kiss him, and he realized with a start that he had truly grown some inches since he had last been here; it felt strange now to stand above the bobbing, capped heads of three or four women. Then they forgot him and returned to rushing about laying the long tables with large platters of food.

But who is the bride? he wondered.

His chest tightened as his uncle approached him, though it hardly seemed like his uncle, in so small a suit of his own making that his flattened buttocks were squeezed together, and his belly strained the waistcoat buttons. "There you are, nephew," he said. "Two hours later and we'd have been to church. Why is your hair so long and hanging in your face? Is that what scholars do?" He lowered his voice. "Your new aunt wished you to come."

A heavy woman some years older than his uncle came up to him affably and kissed Robbie's cheek several times.

Robbie attended the church service, singing the hymns, following the prayers, watching the bobbing silk flowers in the bride's hair. Outside the house he felt calm and confident, but once he was through the familiar house doors again, the tightness in his chest returned.

The reception was a supper and a very long evening. Some people Robbie liked came up to him. "My, you've grown handsome," a young neighbor said, swaying before him in her blue dress. He could not decently refuse to be her partner once table and chairs were pushed back and dancing was called.

One by one the guests left, and he volunteered to help the maid clear away. When he returned upstairs to his old room, he heard murmurs and giggles behind his uncle's bedroom door. Oh God, he thought. The wedding night! It was appalling, and he lay down uncomfortably by the window, which looked out on a street of city houses with pitched roofs.

In the narrow bed, which was now a little too short for him, he crossed his arms tightly over his chest, feeling his old sullenness return like a sickness. He felt his mother's ghost, pale and silent, walking the rooms. I've become as invisible as ever she was, he thought. Leaping up an hour past dawn, he stood by the window looking over the shops and brick houses.

Hunger made him dress. Robbie wondered if there was food downstairs or if he must wait for the wedding breakfast. He was coming from his door when his uncle emerged from his marital room, buttoning his coat. Perhaps such a breakfast was not planned.

"Time to be up and working!" Henry Stillman said. "She's still sleeping. We had two problems with the shop yesterday when it was closed. You haven't asked me if there's a bit of work you can do, as usual." He looked at Robbie closely, baring his large, stained teeth a little. He added, "I locked the shop door last night. If you slash my fabric, I'll call the police. Will you?"

"No."

Robbie studied the old directory on one table. *Newark-on-Trent Places of Commerce 1844* it said. It was more than fifty years out of date, and almost everyone mentioned within long dead.

Henry Stillman finished buttoning his coat, consulted his pocket watch, and said, almost tenderly, "I still haven't given up on you. Think of it from my point of view! I worked my fingers to the bone to care for your mother after our parents died, and what did she do but desert me to run off with a penniless artist she had met in our local art school? And what did he do but desert her as soon as he found out you were in her womb?"

Now his uncle's voice had reverted to aggravation. "Yes, and she came home and spent the rest of her sickly life instilling this nonsense in you about the golden life of the artist. I worked to support you both while she hoarded her small estate for you. We never heard from the man again. He had no use for us. I took care of you and her. No one could love her as I did."

Oh God, not that story again! Robbie thought.

He stood with his hand on the banister, unable to move though he could hear a few women below preparing for the wedding breakfast; there would be one after all.

His uncle straightened his cravat, looking directly at his nephew. "It doesn't matter," he said. "It will all end as I've predicted. You'll end up a draper's assistant."

"Why did you ask me here?" Robbie asked, not minding how his voice carried. "I loathe being where I'm not liked."

"Being liked is a luxury in this world. I did my best with you to teach you your duty."

"You never wanted me."

"You ruined her life by your birth. She wouldn't listen to me, and neither will you. It's pounds and shillings that matter; it's the food on the table that matters. Not that I could ever knock any sense into your head. What are you fit for without me?"

"I don't want to listen to you anymore."

"Oh, listen, you will when you've forgotten your studies and scribbled your life away. You'll listen if you want bread to eat."

"Enough!" Robbie exclaimed. He glared at his uncle, fists clenched, until Henry Stillman stepped back and rapidly descended the stairs. Robbie's eyes filled with the old impotent tears of frustration. He ran up the stairs and found the key to his mother's old room in a vase on the hall table and slipped inside, locking the door behind him.

At least he had not been followed.

Here in that bed, she had died. He had been eight years old.

Those days, even now in his mind, retained a peculiar gray light in which the shop bell seemed muted, and he found paper and sat on the cold attic stairs to draw flowers in patterns which became a motherly shape. But she had no shape: she was white cotton gowns on white cotton pillows, not much more than a heaving chest trying to breathe. Then she died, and it seemed as if nothing changed. Slowly the curtains were opened, but the house still seemed dim, and he tiptoed past her room because he believed in some way she was still there in that bed, trying to grasp at the air.

Now the drawn curtains were heavy with dust, and the damp spots upon the wallpaper unchanged. Bureau drawers creaked as he reverently opened one after another, gazing at her chemises and night dresses; the wardrobe creaked as well when he opened it and ran his hand over his mother's frocks. His uncle had changed nothing; it was as if he expected his sister to return.

Standing quite still in the silence, Robbie could yet hear the sound of her pitiful weeping, and his uncle turning the handle of the locked door, whispering, *Alice, Alice! Alice, my only love!*

Robbie shivered. "There's a plan for you, Robbie," his mother had told him years before. "You'll find where you belong one day, and your drawings will lead you." Stuffing his hand in his pocket, he felt the little book of Tennyson, which he had kept with him.

He straightened.

Yes, he understood now. It was all quite clear.

He would never come back here as long as he lived. He would return to his room in the vicarage. He would find some way to resume the beautiful, perfect closeness he had felt with Anton that night he had gone with him to the supper party and drunk the port. They could give something to each other... but what? It had to be reasonable. Friends to be sure, somehow even though he was young. Could he make himself good enough to be Anton's friend?

What he needed most was to be in that little pocket of Nottinghamshire with its hedgerows and enormous trees. And then all his life he would live in the vicarage, calmly drawing, bringing happiness to those around him, teasing the old housekeeper, Nellie, listening for Anton to come whistling down the path.... This state of permanent happiness.

He gathered his things at his uncle's house and, without saying goodbye to anyone, left and walked about the city all day to calm himself and then to the rail station. At Nottingham he caught the local train, which left him somewhat more than a mile from the vicarage, and from there walked home. There was no hurry. He thought Anton had gone to London.

In spite of the oil lamps which shone comfortably from Mr. Langstaff's windows, Robbie didn't turn into the garden but continued toward the brown brick farmhouse. He could sense from his shivering that a fever was coming; he felt a slight disconnect from his body, as if he had to order it to move. It's nothing, he said to himself. Then he went on because his heart was singing.

The farmhouse was dark. Empty, he thought.

To make sure, he knocked, waited, and knocked again.

He looked at the brass doorknob, which he had touched for a moment, and felt the shape of its embossed roundness in his palm as if he had already made his entrance into a place not his. The door was unlocked.

I can't go in there without an invitation, he thought. But it's quite all right! If he should be there, I'll say I came to return his book.

He opened the door and walked into the hall. He called out, but only his own voice echoed back from the rooms. Robbie lit one of the candles from the hall table and ascended the stairs to the first floor. Floorboards creaked; his shoes padded softly on the wood. He passed the study, lightly caressing the doorknob. If Anton should come out! He hoped for it and feared it. What would he say to him?

He again called Anton's name. His voice drifted down the dark hall and gave no echo in return. Of course! Anton was indeed in London and the housekeeper had forgotten to lock the house door.

Robbie entered the other rooms on the same floor, where doors opened to reveal beds stripped of all coverings. For some time, he tiptoed about, finding a box of toys in the corner of one room. The wooden animals of a Noah's ark, their paint worn away, gazed up at him.

Putting his candle on the floor and kneeling, he soundlessly extracted the ark, laid it on the floor, and for a time tried to match the animals until he felt silly. He put the figures away and ascended the steps to the attic. Here were many trunks, and the silence was forbidding. He could hear nothing but his own breath, and the very brush of his coat sleeve against the wall made him start. A cradle rocked slowly at his touch, wafting dust.

There were ghosts here as there were in his mother's room.

He found a small formal photograph in an oval frame; the faces of three little girls looked back at him from behind broken glass. Who were they? Why was the glass broken? And then a few piles of books covered with dust. He sat down and looked at them: books on socialism, abolition, the lives of the poor. Newspaper clippings: a grainy photograph of what must be a young, beardless Anton and the headline "Fifteen-Year-Old Son of Local Businessman to Speak at the Nottingham Socialists' Club." He remembered the conversation with Anton that time when they had walked home from the dinner party.

Now he recalled things about it that the vicar had told him one evening weeks ago when Anton was out late. "Anton began to speak on the responsibility of the well-off to care for the less fortunate very young. He was brilliant. People came from everywhere to hear this shining schoolboy pour out his words. But his father Edgar Harrington was a bitter and violent man. He put a stop to Anton's speaking and— But that is enough. These are not my secrets. There's such sadness there, lad!"

Robbie returned the things he had looked at to the attic shelf and slowly descended the stairs. Yet if the house had felt empty before, it was not now. Candleholder in his hand, he sensed something behind the closed doors of the library.... No, not something, someone.

Quietly, he opened the door. He was right, for Anton was there. The light flickered across the large room to the sofa where he was sleeping. Robbie saw the rise and fall of Anton's chest under his shirt. He's been here all along and I didn't know it, he thought. Will he be angry if he knows I've been looking at his rooms?

Anton murmured, "We can't... We must... Bess!" His voice was different: younger, startled, almost frightened. It might have been the voice of the boy in the picture.

Who was Bess? Robbie wanted to rush forward but didn't dare, only called, "Hello, are you well?"

"Who is it?"

"Mr. Langstaff's student, Robbie Stillman."

Anton struggled to sit up, feeling for the side of the sofa to steady himself. His shirtsleeves were rolled halfway up his arms, and his suit coat had been thrown over a chair. He found his voice and asked, bewildered with sleep, "Stillman, why are you here? God help us, is George sick?"

"No, he's well! I've just come from the train from my uncle's wedding."

"A wedding? What time is it?"

"Past ten. Did you hear the clock chime before?" Robbie noticed a decanter on the carpet beside the sofa and an overturned glass. How much had Anton Harrington been drinking? Was he drunk? Robbie's mind was full of the image of the young speaker who had spoken so brilliantly and then stopped. He wanted to ask a hundred questions.

He said, "You dropped your Tennyson the other day." He put the book respectfully on the table. "I borrowed it to read and then I thought I should return it before I forgot. In case you were looking for it."

"You came at this hour to return a book?"

"Before I forgot. I'm bad with books."

Anton looked at him with those deep eyes, shining so wonderfully by only the candlelight. How enchanted it was, the room in deepest shadow and only the bearded face of the man and the vague shapes of objects flickering here and there. It made him wonder if only the two of them existed in the world.

Anton said, "I had an awful dream; I'm glad you woke me."

Robbie began to perspire. He felt he ought to go and leave this man with his shirt open to his neck. He held on to the back of a chair and said as casually as he could, "I'm glad to find you here. I wanted to ask you if we might...if you're home and have nothing to do...take a walk together as we did after that dinner party."

"Ah, that dinner party!" Anton said wryly. "I was glad to have you there. Sit down. I'm still half asleep and here you are."

He rubbed the back of his neck. "Yes, let's walk!" he said. "There are trees over six hundred years old in the forest, did you know that? You could bring—what do you call it?—your drawing book. Even though the forest's not what it was a hundred years ago. So much has been cut down. They cut things down, the bastards."

Robbie sat on the edge of the chair. He lowered his head a little to prevent the desire to rush forward and throw his arms about this slightly smiling, candlelit man who had already lived such a rich life and now had accepted the idea of a walk. "Yes, Mr. Harrington," he said. "I'd like that."

"Good. Let's say tomorrow at around six. Meet me at my door. And call me Anton, will you?"

"So late!" said the vicar, rising from the piano stool when Robbie came in the vicarage door. "Did you walk from the local station? Lad, you look feverish. Come here. Off to bed with you. If you're not better in the morning, I'll go for Dr. Eliot."

"I'm quite all right," Robbie replied sharply; he was filled with a private happiness so intense that he couldn't bear to have anyone look at him. He couldn't wait to be alone in his room and under the quilts with his dreams.

Call me Anton. Meet me at my door.

The humble love tokens he had collected of men in the past few years (the pen, the comb, the chocolate bar) were nothing next to what he felt now. Everything was nothing to this point.

Hours passed. The vicar slept, and then there was no sound but the wind in the trees, the leaves drifting down to the windowsill, and Robbie's body turning on the sheets. Quite late he heard hoofbeats. He rolled to his side and heard horseshoes striking the boards of the bridge. Anton was going away on his gray mare. Robbie hurried to the window, but Anton was no longer in sight. Tomorrow at six, Robbie thought. He'll be back; he'll be waiting for me.

The morning rain stopped, yet the sky remained gray and heavy. Langstaff had decided the doctor was not needed but that Robbie should stay in bed most of the day. After their tea and pork pie, when the vicar walked out to visit an elderly schoolmaster, Robbie rapidly laced his shoes and hurried down and out the door. The hour was six.

But Anton had not returned to the farmhouse.

Shadows crossed the house, and twilight came and after that early darkness. He crossed the small bridge and walked a little down the path that was bordered by low stone walls. Under his hand, the stones grew familiar. He ran his fingers along them, experiencing the peculiar disorientation that always came with his illnesses and fevers.

Darkness folded in upon the path and field; rain was coming. The trees dipped slightly. We can't walk if it rains, he thought, now standing by the house door. Perhaps we'll sit by the fire and talk. I'll take two glasses of the port if he offers it. I'll sit close so that the back of my hand will graze his. But he mustn't see I'm sick or he'll send me home.

Robbie had no idea how much time had passed, because it was too dark to read his pocket watch, an old one that his uncle had given him which was forever stopping and therefore not reliable. It had been a few hours perhaps. Then he heard the horse's hooves striking the wood slats of the bridge.

Anton was coming at last.

Robbie waited near the door as Anton pulled his mare into the stable. He came forward stumbling a little toward his door, and Robbie emerged from the shadows and burst out, "Hello, here I am."

Anton stared at him, feeling for the door, swaying a little, reaching out to grasp the wood. The stare was bitter. Robbie thought, Oh God, he's drunk. He had no idea what to do.

And then Anton turned his back and muttered, "What the hell are you doing here? Go back where you belong and stop following me."

Robbie turned suddenly and ran toward the high grass behind the house.

Thunder came from far away in the deeper parts of the forest, and he ran toward it. Now it had begun to pour, and he ran on, stumbling on the roots of a tree and falling, bruising his leg. He was crying hard. The rain beat at him, soaking his shirt. He thought, I'm never going back, never. Not there or to Langstaff. I don't know where I'll go, but never there again.

He could hardly see where he went; he stumbled again. By the lightning he made out a half-fallen stone cottage that he had climbed about a few times. Most of the roof was gone long ago, but a fragment remained, and he crawled to that corner and huddled there. He shivered so hard, he thought, I'll probably die but then I don't care.

He was a fool; it was like that master who he thought liked him—he had gone to his office door and the man had stared coldly at him and said, "What do you want, boy?" After all the gentle teasing Robbie had been given! All those signs that said "Come here" meant nothing then and nothing now. He remembered now what he never wanted to recall.

He might have slept, but he was next aware that the thunder had moved away, and the rain fell more softly. Through the darkness came the gleam of a wavering light. Robbie gazed through the broken windows. He didn't see the face of the man coming toward him through the gaping hole of a door, but he knew him anyway. "I thought you'd be here," Anton said wearily. "I used to hide in this place. I'm more sober. Come on now, you young fool."

"Don't you call me that! I wasn't the one who…"

Robbie rose haltingly to his feet and struck out at Anton's chest and shoulders, his fists hitting the slick rubbery mackintosh. The lantern had fallen to the ground, and what he struggled against now were the arms which pinned his own by holding him closely. He shouted, "Don't touch me! Let me go!"

Anton said, "You'll knock us both into the mud; we're wet enough here without that." He slowly removed his arms, opened his mackintosh, and pulled half of it over Robbie. "Christ!" he said. "You're sick as hell. The old man's half lost his senses worrying over you. I have to try to light the lantern once more. Walk with me, lad. It's all right."

It's not all right, Robbie thought. It will never be now.

They slipped several times going back through the field and didn't speak one word until they finally reached the vicar's gate. Robbie lifted the latch and walked alone through the garden to the cottage, where his tutor was waiting for him.

5

NOTTINGHAM

October 1901

Anton Harrington awoke the next morning aching.

He had gone to Nottingham the night before last and stayed with his closest friend, Tom Burrows. The next day he went to a pub and drank until he couldn't walk straight, mounted his horse, and rode home in the darkness. He wanted only to reach his bed and pull the covers over his head alone, but George's lad had been waiting for him, and what Anton said he was too drunk to remember. Sometime later he woke to George shaking him, saying, "It's Stillman! He's gone somewhere." Anton managed to get out of bed.

Now he swung his feet to the floor, every part of him aching. He dressed in yesterday's corduroy and flannels, which had dried by the fire, found a pair of heavy dry boots, and lumbered down the steps past his housekeeper Mary, head lowered, still feeling the drink in him. His hair was wild from last night's rain and half fell into his face; his cheeks were stubbly, and he had not washed. He felt filthy all over, as if the grubby sawdust and bitter beer from the public house were seeping from his pores.

The thick sky pressed down against the tops of the trees, from which leaves and branches had been ripped. He tossed the fallen branches aside from the path. The last of the rain came down on the ravaged flowers of Langstaff's garden, pressing them into the earth. Petals scattered on the soaked bed.

He opened the door to the vicarage parlor.

Stillman was asleep on the sofa near the fire, covered with quilts.

Anton walked across the rug, pushed back his flannel cuff, and rested his wrist lightly on Robbie's forehead, wincing at the feverish skin. He looked down, bewildered, as if he had never seen him before. There was light stubble on his upper lip. Anton remembered how he'd found the boy just sitting in the rain as if it would pummel him down until he became part of the sodden earth and dissolved beneath it. Such despair a man learned to keep inside. And then came Stillman's rage and his fists.

Anton leaned forward, resting his arms on his knees. Who was this boy inside?

A quarter of an hour passed. The housekeeper shut the kitchen door and Robbie opened his eyes. He felt for the quilt to cover himself to the chin.

"My room's cold," he whispered hoarsely. "Mr. Langstaff put me here."

"How are you feeling? We should speak of last evening. I was unhappy; I behaved badly. What did I say to you, anyway?"

Robbie looked toward the bright fire in the grate. "Nothing much. We were going to walk together, and you changed your mind."

"I think you remember. We should talk perhaps."

Robbie was silent.

Anton stood and wandered about the room, every now and then touching a book or the typewriting machine. He stopped by the rolltop desk. He tried to sound cheerful though his head ached badly. "I thought I bored you silly that evening some weeks ago after the dinner party when you came to my room. Yes, we're neighbors; we ought to know each other. Let's talk then. Do you want to tell me something more of you? No? I could tell you something of me. Banking's worse than deadly. Family stories then. Are you sure you want to hear?"

Robbie looked down at the carpet and nodded almost imperceptibly.

Anton thought, Good God, he must be lonely if he wants such stuff.

He rubbed his hands together, the nails dirty from slipping in the mud last night. "My maternal grandmother was Italian—I told you that. She's long dead. She left me her house in Tuscany, now empty, which a neighbor manages. Maternal grandfather was English. When my grandmother came here as a maid, she married him, and they opened a saddler's shop in Nottingham. A workingman, he was." He paused for a moment, arranging the pens in the cracked marmalade jar on the vicar's desk. "They had one daughter, whom they adored. She grew up to fall in love with my father and run off with him."

"Were they happy?" Robbie croaked.

"Not in the least. My father was a rough man; he came from the worst poverty, a dozen of them in a room, but was determined to be the richest man in the county. He and my mother had four children, me and then three little girls. The girls all died of diphtheria one winter's week...in one week, in one week when the snow fell. They were young. I was eight or nine. Grief was thick for me. I adored them. The house was so silent!"

"The little picture I saw in the attic of the three children?"

"You were there?"

Robbie nodded slightly. "Sorry."

Anton studied him, hands in his corduroy trouser pockets. Was the boy sorry about the death of the girls or about exploring the attic and finding the picture with its broken glass frame, which Anton had hurled across the room one day when he was home from university? And why would anyone want to go there? He avoided it like hell.

Robbie half sat up, leaning on his elbows; he looked at the carpet. Anton let his hand run over the typewriter keys. "The deaths—something ended in both my parents then. I felt I should somehow make it right, but I couldn't."

Anton bit his lip. Why was he talking about these things?

He said, "My father's gone now, the girls, my mother when I was just twenty...though I didn't lose her as young as you lost yours. You wonder why some of us get to go on and the others are stopped."

The house door opened, and the vicar crossed the room with his arms full of flowers, looking for an empty vase. "Ah, so you're here, Anton!" Langstaff said. "You look tired. If you would, when you feel better—the roof's leaking. I suspect a lot of slate needs replacing. If it's bad, the water will go through the attic into the lad's room. Will you ask old Miller to look at it?"

Anton straightened. He said, "I can do it. I'll see what I need. This desk needs some wax; the tambour's jammed." As the vicar climbed the stairs, Anton walked over to Robbie and put his hand on his shoulder. He said, "I wanted to say that I'm sorry for whatever I said or did. When you're better, we'll have that walk. I'll be about a lot. I'm not returning to banking." But he was not sure he meant he would walk, and he knew by Robbie's turning away that the young man had put it aside. He also realized that the reason Robbie had climbed to the attic was to somehow find out about him. That interest was also apparently gone

Anton went back into the wet garden with his hands again in his pockets.

He kept his word. The next day he climbed up to look at the roof and found that a portion of it needed to be replaced. Some nails had rusted and slipped, and he found them in the roses with some shattered slate. It took him a few days to buy the materials, and by that time Robbie was as healthy as ever but strangely subdued, as if the events of that night in the rain had not entirely been settled. Well, what can be done about that? Anton thought. He'll be off somewhere soon and forget me.

Even as he put down the hammer, he felt the warmth of the boy's shoulder when he had touched him. It was so real that he examined his bent fingers as if there were some physical evidence of it.

Autumn was coming. Dressed in his corduroy trousers tied with a cord at the knee, whistling, Anton stood on the ladder with the sun on his hair, nailing the last pieces of slate. When it was done...well, he could build other things. He could keep building things. He rehung doors in his house and made a new bookshelf. Now and then he saw Robbie about; there was still a sense of hesitation between them, though he came to celebrate Robbie's nineteenth birthday and gave him several books of poetry and travel. By this time, he understood that Robbie had put off his university examinations from last spring to this coming one. George didn't mind how long he stayed and turned a blind eye to how little his pupil did. The old fellow's lonely, he thought, that's why. And as far as depending on me, I've been gone but I'll do better now. I swear it. I'll be here for him.

Anton thrust his hand through his hair; it had been more than a week since he had bothered to wash it or oil it down. His clothes smelled faintly of sweat.

He climbed down from the ladder and was walking out through the garden when he saw the vicar and his student crossing the bridge. He strolled closer and said with casual charm, "Morning, vicar! Rob, have you seen the posters about? The annual Nottingham Goose Fair opens tomorrow. Care to join me? It's in Market Square. Our vicar finds it too noisy."

Robbie rubbed his boot in the dirt. He was silent for a time. Then he said, "I'd like that." His smile was tentative, but he had agreed.

Anton had loved the Goose Fair as a young boy. He had danced there. He had boxed and won, one glorious afternoon years ago. No matter what was happening in his life, the Goose Fair held only happy memories—with greasy food and warm bitter ale on his lips, he wandered, tall, confident, and happy, among thousands of pushing strangers.

He was going back then to that memory.

Whistling, he harnessed Blackie to the gig, and Robbie climbed up. They both wore knickers and plain wool workman's caps. As they came closer to Nottingham, the crowds on the road walking or riding grew thicker. As always, children with switches drove geese to be auctioned. There was the familiar sound of honking, and the mild October air was full of floating feathers under the yellow-leaved trees.

Robbie said, "My mother told me she came here once with my father."

Once inside the Nottingham streets, they found a boy to

mind the gig and horse and walked rapidly toward Market Square and the bands. Turning the corner, a vast sea of colored tents spread as far as they could see.

Robbie exclaimed, "Oh, look at that! Where shall we start?"

"Anywhere. You take the lead."

For a few hours they wandered about, hearing the criers for the tents of comedy troupes, acrobats, and jugglers. When they were hungry, they bought a large meat pie and shared it, eating with their fingers. They also shared an enormous pewter mug of bitter ale. Anton felt the warm beginnings of drunkenness in which any tension fell away from his body.

Robbie knelt by two mangy monkeys owned by the organ grinder. Anton knelt beside him. "Look at the little fellows!" he said. "Darwin felt they're as sentient as we are, and now look at them, here away from all they know. You've read Darwin? His book's in my room. They're friendly. Have you any crusts left? What a pity...."

Robbie's profile was serious; his nose was a little sloped, and freckles spattered across it. Anton lightly rested his hand on Robbie's back, but the young artist seemed too absorbed to notice. "Oh yes, I want to read that. I wish I could buy them."

His look was so intense that Anton felt he had drunk more. He stood up, dusting off his knees. "What, keep them in the stable to scare the horses?" He laughed. "Come on! There's the arcade. For a penny you can shoot a pellet at moving wood ducks and win some stuffed animal as a prize."

Robbie leapt up, smiling. He said, "Let's go there! I'm a good shot!"

"Show me."

They paid the pennies to the woman at the stall and eyed the wobbling wood ducks with their worn-away roughly painted feathers. Robbie raised the gun carefully to his shoulder. He looked until the last second and shot, and the duck fell in surrender. Anton tried three times until he put down the pellet gun, shaking his head. Robbie said, "You can do better than that," and Anton replied, "Perhaps but you tried harder, wanting that stuffed mouse." The truth was, he had shot carelessly and knew it.

Robbie tucked the small mouse into his jacket pocket.

"You're going to keep that thing?" Anton asked.

Robbie was about to answer, but they heard the sudden burst of violins, horns, and accordion. "The dancing's started," Anton exclaimed. "Come on!" They hurried together through the crowded walkway between the rows of stalls and tents that opened suddenly to a large country-dance circle. Men, women, and children joined hands and stepped toward the center and out again. He stood lost in memory and hardly heard Robbie's voice.

"Let's," said Robbie.

Anton felt the warmth of Robbie's hand grasping his hard. He didn't have that hand long; partners in the circles changed, and he found he was dancing with a girl in a straw hat with autumn daisies pinned and trembling on its brim. She was whisked away as well, and an old man grasped his hand with rough worker's fingers. Everyone stepped to the center and back again.

He glanced at Robbie across the circle, his shirt open at the top buttons and his head uplifted in laughter. When the music stopped, he sprinted across to join Anton. "We didn't dance much at home," he panted. "They were fools not to go to fairs. I want it to go on and on."

"Not tired?"

"No. I'm sweating." Robbie wrinkled his nose and felt his shirt, moist under the arms and down his back. They stopped to watch a girl walking a rope high above them, her lace parasol held above one thin arm.

Robbie said, "We need something to drink. Lemonade. Do you like it?"

"I could drink a quart, I think. I wish we had time to come another day."

"Why can't we?"

"Because I'm going back to London...soon, perhaps tomorrow."

"How long will you stay?"

"A week; I'm not sure. I just decided. They've been writing me."

"Oh, the bank. Is it dull?"

"Very. You'll draw."

"Perhaps," said Robbie, suddenly quieter.

They found the lemonade tent after a few minutes, but the drink was weak and a little sour. Anton felt the disappointment of it. As he stood with the empty cup in his hand, he felt the slow draining away of the joyful day, and all that he had found so enchanting seemed to fade as if it had never been. Why had he said he was going up to London? The letter had come, but he had planned to refuse.

"Time to leave," he said abruptly. "The roads get very crowded later."

They said nothing as they walked back to the place where they had left the horse and gig. Anton swung up to the seat and they turned from the city. The streets were littered with paper and feathers. They rode past the castle down the road, first past houses and then fields and hedgerows.

Finally, Robbie burst out, "I wish you weren't going. At least we started to become friends today. We did, didn't we?"

He sat looking straight forward, his hands curled on his knee. Anton felt something in his chest expand. He reached out to squeeze Robbie's hand.

"We're friends," he said.

For the rest of the journey Robbie sat with his head down saying little. The descending sun fell on Robbie's fingers, which seemed somehow burnished. Robbie looked at him suddenly, warily and yet adoringly. Anton pressed his lips together hard.

There was trouble with a wheel. It was almost dusk when they reached home.

6

FALL IN THE COUNTRY

October-December 1901

They stopped in the vicarage and shared a cup of beef broth and a plate of sandwiches which Nellie had left for them. As soon as he could, Anton escaped back to the farmhouse and spent an hour trying to find his copy of Darwin.

He woke in the middle of the night, pulled on his dressing gown, and lit the oil lamp. His stomach ached. He thought, Ah, that old thing again! I'll drink some whiskey and perhaps sleep more.

His feet were cold, and he threw a few more coals on the fire, found a pair of socks, and opened a new novel but didn't read it. After a time, the clock struck three. The whiskey made the aching stomach better. On the way home, when they had driven through the now dark and secluded area of trees on the road, he had wanted to stop the gig and hold Robbie against him so tightly that nothing could come between them.

He had wanted to kiss him.

He remembered something from a long time ago.

He had been at school and fallen in love.

Stephen was his name. He was sandy-haired, freckled, admired by everyone, cheered at football, and expected to be head boy next year. They fell on each other in sport, and then in private. Finally, they didn't pull away, and Anton had looked down at the boy pinned beneath him and kissed him. Clumsily, experimenting, they became lovers.

They took chances to be together. They heard the school chapel bell and the footsteps of the boys below walking to service and moved off to the shadow behind a hedge and then to their secret place in the barn. It was more than sexuality; it was like coming home to himself.

Then one afternoon as they lay together in the hay, Anton had blurted out what he had never told anyone: He was humiliated and mocked by his father; his mother had not left her room for several years and spoke to him only through her closed door. Once he began to talk about his home, he couldn't stop. He said that he should have died instead of his darling little sisters, and that he was exhausted being strong.

After that, things changed between them. Once Anton had confessed his unhappiness, he withdrew. He turned cold to the boy. Only success mattered, proving how good he was.

Now in his dark study, Anton breathed deeply, hand around his glass of whiskey. He thought of those few months in the school when he had told himself, It's better that it's done. Mother would never believe it, but my father suspects and despises me.

"You'll never be a man; you'll come to nothing," his father had mocked him, and Anton set out to prove himself to the world. He was very successful in all work he chose. He courted women and slept with them when he could. He knew he had pleased them. He was the sort of man women dreamed of, or so one girl had told him. He married.

Yet at times through the years, he would notice some young man looking at him carefully across the room. The boy in Oxford, that blond fellow he had met in a Zurich wine cellar at one of those long tables, and the banker who assisted him in London. The last was the most difficult.

Behind the closed door of his office, he had covered his face with his hands and prayed, forcing his body tight until all feeling left him. "Hold my hand," Anton wanted to say, but he remained silent.

He woke to the October sun coming through the curtains past one in the afternoon. He spent some time looking over his post, but after he'd picked up the same envelope twice, and couldn't

remember which pile he'd reviewed, he threw down the letter
opener. I need to see him, he thought. There will be no more
than that. I have not allowed it since school. It's friendship I
need. Oh God, I need that.

Anton walked cautiously to the vicarage and found Robbie
slicing apples in the vicarage kitchen with Nellie. The young
artist's face had somehow changed since they had said goodnight. It no longer held the joy of their time at the fair; even the
freckles on his nose seemed faded and his mouth was severe.
He raised his eyes and looked at Anton. "Mr. Langstaff's away
for the next few days," he said flatly. "Are you going up to London today?"

"No, I'm staying here. Such beautiful weather! Do you want
to take a picnic to the forest with me?"

Robbie's face brightened; he breathed deeply. "Of course, I
do!" he exclaimed.

Anton found the wicker basket and packed it quickly. He
also took a brown picnic blanket and snatched two wine bottles
from the low cupboard. He wanted them both in the forest
before Robbie could change his mind.

Outside, the air smelled of apples from the few trees behind
the house; windfalls lay at their roots. Tall, sturdy sunflowers
arched toward the sun.

Within ten minutes, they had reached the old forest with its
carpet of burnt-orange leaves. As they walked down the path
under oak and maple trees, Robbie leapt to touch the branches.
Anton took his arm; the crook of it felt warm. Robbie smiled at
him. He likes me, Anton thought. I knew it the way he looked
at me last night.

But that can't mean anything.

A squirrel rushed halfway up a walnut tree and stared at
them defiantly.

They walked on until Robbie called urgently, "Here's the
pond! Let's stop." Leaving Anton behind, he climbed easily
down through the thick wild grass, knelt, rolled up his sleeves,
and dipped his hands into the water. Anton gazed at his bent

neck and the hands in the pond. They were not large hands. Robbie turned, squinting against the sun, which had sunk lower in the sky at this midafternoon hour.

"The water's so clear here!" Robbie called excitedly. "There are turtles."

"How does an artist draw water?"

"Oh, by the way the light bends and distorts what's below, ripples and crests. Do you have a pencil and paper, Anton? I'll show you."

Anton stood with arms folded on the bank and shook his head. "I haven't brought a pencil. If a poem came to me, it would never be expressed, but there are no poems coming today."

"Do you really write poetry?"

"I have."

"I never knew it."

"I never told you."

"Does Mr. Langstaff know about the poetry?"

"He used to; he kept it when I gave it to him."

Robbie was looking at him; then he bit his lip and turned to the water again. For a moment there had been that look of reverence. Their silence was broken only by a spotted wood-pecker whose calls sounded like it was taking small, sharp bites of the air.

Robbie stood. "There, on that branch," he said softly. "You can see his red tail feathers." He climbed up, balancing with his arms, and came close to Anton. He said clumsily, "I wanted to ask you. I found some strands of hair in your Tennyson books. Are they your wife's?"

Hazel eyes, Anton thought. He said, "No. I'll tell you one day. By the way, I saw the portrait you drew of me on your wall when I was replacing the broken slates on the vicarage roof. I looked in your window."

Robbie bit his full lower lip. "You don't mind that I drew you?"

"No, I don't mind. I look rather intense."

"I think you are. It's not a very good drawing."

"On the contrary, I liked it." Anton looked about at the pond where turtles splashed; the happiness of yesterday was returning. He said playfully, "We should make a bargain! If I tell you something of me, you'll tell me something of you."

"You first then," said Robbie, eagerly.

"Let's walk."

Anton picked up the basket and they went on. After a time, he said, "I was in Rome once quite alone; it was after my grandmother died, before I went to Switzerland. And I felt myself the only person in the world in the midst of crowds. I wish you'd been there. It would be nice to show the city to you... the ruins of the Forum where the emperors walked, the Sistine Chapel in the Vatican."

"I want so much to see Rome."

"Rob, it's your turn to say something of you."

Robbie stopped walking and frowned. "I need some time."

"Do you? Then let's go on," Anton answered. They walked a few minutes, Anton holding on to Robbie's arm. He kicked a heap of leaves under a tree and Robbie laughed and kicked another. Then Robbie stopped.

His shoulders hunched. He murmured, "Must I say just one thing about me, or can it be more than one? Though I hardly have the courage for one."

"It can be as many as you like."

"You won't be bored?"

"Not at all."

"Very well then! I've walked to that pond many times. I want to paint it in oils. I'm saving for them, but I'm a little afraid of them. They're hard to use. There were wild ducks here when I came. I wish I could study art, but my uncle wouldn't allow it."

Anton replied, "Ah yes, your righteous uncle! Did you always get on badly with him?"

Robbie's voice became tighter. "As long as I can remember. He didn't want me born. My father gave my mother three art books, thick ones with beautiful reproductions. She and I would pretend we lived in a world of artists, a better world. We pretended we lived in Florence or Rome."

"What happened to the books?"

"I brought them with me. There's a picture in one, a Titian." He went on describing it in detail, suddenly lost in the awe of the art. Every now and then he hesitated and looked anxiously at Anton.

Anton thought, I need to take his arm again or forget about the whole thing. Why is he talking of art? Why am I here?

He set down his basket under a tree and said, "Come, sit down and have some food! It'll be dark in a few hours." He spread the blanket and knelt to uncork the wine. "Sit," he ordered, over his shoulder, and poured them both wine. Robbie dropped to the blanket, suddenly shy.

Anton drank his wine almost at once which went straight to his head. "Drink yours!" he said, as he placed cheese, bread, and ham on the plate before them though his stomach recoiled at the thought of food, so aware was he of Robbie's hand close to his on the blanket.

He said bluffly, "You know, I could buy you whatever paints you wanted."

Robbie turned to him with his face full of wonder. "Would you do that?" he asked. "I'd pay you back when I earn money. I'd give the painting to you if you wanted it."

Anton poured another glass of wine for himself, looking down at it, swirling it slightly. The sun had now disappeared entirely behind some clouds, and the wine seemed a dark, strange thing. He glanced at Robbie, who had hunched his shoulders, cradling his wineglass protectively in both his hands. Was he pulling away? He had moved a few inches apart.

But Robbie only murmured in a deep voice, "This is what I really need to say about me, the truest thing. I want things too much. If only feelings didn't run away with me."

"Then you wouldn't draw."

Anton hesitated and then slipped his hand under Robbie's hair, finding the nape of his neck. He could feel the shiver that went through the young artist. "Do you mind, Rob?" he asked softly.

Robbie swallowed. "No, I like it," he said.

"Now tell me more about you."

Robbie arched a little toward the hand. "Well then. I care about things too much. I wish I didn't. I want to be needed too much. I want to be anyone else but me."

"And who would you like to be like, eh?"

Robbie looked up from the wine, and his eyes were so dark, only a sort of longing could be seen in them. "I'd like to be like you," he said.

That was it then. Anton pulled Robbie to him and kissed him. He lowered Robbie to the blanket, feeling the chipped tooth with his tongue. Robbie wound his arms tightly around Anton and kissed him back as if parched, bringing his leg around Anton's to force him closer.

Anton's heart pounded faster until his chest was so tight, he could hardly breathe. He turned his head and muttered, "God! Whatever possessed me! Enough, Rob."

He tried to disentangle himself, but Robbie held him tightly, crying, "Don't go! Please don't go."

Anton rose to his feet. Robbie scrambled to his knees, trying to catch his hand, saying, "Don't, don't—" But Anton suddenly held up his hand in warning. Robbie rose to his feet, looking in the same direction through the trees.

A man and woman in their middle years appeared on the path, walking closely, both carrying baskets full of sweet chestnuts, the burrs of some of the top ones burst to reveal the nuts. Their clothes were old and limp, their shoes broken.

"Oh, good day, sirs," the man said, reaching up and lifting his wool cap respectfully.

"Good day," Anton said. His voice hardly sounded like his own.

"Been nutting. A lot will still fall."

"Yes," Anton said. "Until December sometimes. I used to go nutting."

"The day's lovely for it now. Well, good day, sir."

Anton glanced at Robbie who was paler beneath his freckles. They both stood motionless until the footsteps were far off, and the voices faded away down the path.

Robbie murmured, "Oh God." He walked slowly through the crinkling leaves to Anton and lowered his head to Anton's shoulder.

"They nearly…it…" Anton stood straight. He gently urged Robbie away and lowered his voice. "What happened before…a moment of madness. I have no idea why… You must forgive me. Best forgotten." Suddenly he threw the remains of the lunch into the basket and poured out what was left of the wine from the glasses into the tree roots. "Just take up that blanket any way. I'm due back at the house. I must go."

He turned and began to hurry back on the path. His stride increased until he was almost running. As he came from the woods, he stopped and looked back, but Robbie was nowhere to be seen, nor was the couple with their gathering of nuts, who had gone another way.

He took the stairs two at a time at home, locked his study door behind him, and flung himself down on the couch on his back with the pillow over his face. After a while, he heard his house-keeper leaving through the kitchen door and cycling down the path. Darkness came swiftly, and he rose to find matches and lit the lamp and the fire.

Anton ran his hand repeatedly through his hair. He thought, I kissed him and—God!—he kissed me back. And then the second thought: We were nearly discovered. But that man and woman might have thought we were larking about if they'd come then. If they remember us, it will be, "We met two gentle-men in the forest—picnicking they were, with wine in a bottle and food on the plate."

That was not the issue. The issue was the kiss with Robbie.

Anton walked around the room, touching the pencils and fountain pen on his desk, the edges of his books, hunching his shoulders, folding his arms across his chest, his heart beat-ing strongly. For thirteen years I've run away, he thought. I've turned my head and denied what I wanted. I came home to be safe, and oh God, what I longed for was waiting for me.

He looked from the window at the darkening day and the

empty field and straightened his shoulders. Then he thought, Why shouldn't I? No one would know; he'd never tell anyone. I wouldn't hurt him. I'd take care of him. He's so damn lonely; he wants me. I can see that he wants me. To touch every part of him, how beautiful it would be! He kissed me back. Tomorrow I won't go away. I'll see him tomorrow. He's gone away in shock.... No, I left him. He didn't leave me. Perhaps he'll run off again. I'll find him wherever he is, I swear I will.

But it must be here, in this house, where we are safe.

Someone was coming up his stairs.

Anton heard the soft bootsteps and then the low knock; he crossed the room in a few strides and opened the door.

Robbie stood in the dark hallway, enveloped in a large coat like a traveling peddler, fists clenched as he shoved them in and out of his pockets. He must have gone back to the vicarage and taken one of the extra coats that hung there. "Anton," he said. He swallowed as if searching for words. "Aren't we going to be friends anymore?"

Anton folded his arms across his chest. He said as casually as he could, "Why shouldn't we be? Look, I'm sorry. I don't know what came over me. I suggest you go back now. A fine mess it might have been."

"I thought when you—"

"It was the last thing you could have expected."

"I liked it. I don't want to go back."

"Go wherever you please then. You're my friend's student and he trusts me. I don't care what you feel about this. You must realize what we did can't even be spoken of before good people. Good night."

Anton shut the door and returned to the sofa. There was silence in the hall; he didn't hear footsteps or any sound at all. It was as if Robbie had vanished into the dust. Anton opened a book, but the words blurred. He watched the clock, hearing the tick as the hand moved from minute to minute. He thought, But what do I want with him?

A profound loneliness began to permeate every limb of his body, until every part of him ached with the weight of it.

He thought, Oh, the hell with what anyone thinks!

Just for now, just for this hour.

He flung open the door again. Robbie was standing where Anton had left him, head lowered, as if he had planned to wait the night.

"Didn't you hear me tell you to go?" Anton said.

"I won't go."

Anton gestured inside with his arm and said, "Very well, come in for a glass of port." He turned back to the room, where the fire was still burning, hearing the footsteps following him softly. Robbie touched his arm; he turned. Robbie threw his arms around him and kissed him. Anton felt the hair on Robbie's upper lip. He still wore the oversized coat, fragrant with light sweat and the smell of the newly cold air. He panted under his shirt.

Anton pulled off Robbie's coat and shirt and kissed his neck. But this isn't me, he still thought. This isn't the man who lives in these rooms.

Still, he didn't stop. They dropped to the hearth rug, and he pulled off Robbie's trousers. Robbie's mouth was on Anton's shoulders and chest. "You'll disappear," Robbie gasped. "You'll be a dream and go."

Anton forgot everything then. Kisses weren't enough; he wanted to be inside that warm, beautiful body. He murmured, "Do you know about this, what men sometimes do?"

"I never did it. I want you to. Wait…stop. I'm a little…"

"Not if you don't want to, Rob. Christ, did I hurt you?"

Robbie kicked out with his strong legs, pushing Anton back, and ran to the bedroom, though he didn't close the door. Anton stood in the center of the carpet, wearing nothing but his shirt until he took that and hurled it across the room, snatching up his dressing gown to cover himself. He walked slowly to the bedroom though it was his own. He hardly dared walk lest he make a sound. He was now the intruder.

Robbie was standing by the washstand with the knitted blue blanket from the chair wrapped around him. His eyes were wet and frightened. He blurted, "I'm sorry. I just—"

"Lie down with me. I couldn't bear it if you went off now."

"I'm not going."

Anton lifted the feather quilt, and Robbie hesitated before climbing into the bed. Anton slipped in beside him. He touched Robbie's cheek with his knuckle and whispered, "Let's hold each other for a few minutes, and then you can get your clothes."

"Would you mind kissing me again?"

"Just that."

"You could do what you tried before."

"Are you sure?"

"I'd like you to do it. I really would. I was just scared."

"Never of me," Anton said.

Robbie's words turned to gasps as he stuffed his face in the pillow. "Yes," he said. "Yes." After, he turned and threw his arms around Anton and clung to him with an intensity Anton wouldn't have thought possible. The room was still, as if the absolute, sudden peace between them had extended to everything within it. Robbie kissed Anton's shoulder softly. "I'm loved," he said, and Anton answered, "You are."

Yes, Anton said to himself with sudden calmness as they held each other. This is him. This is me.

They walked out every day. And then November came, and the trees were stripped bare by the wind. One day they spent the day in bed talking and then the whole night together. Langstaff was away, as was his housekeeper, and Anton's housekeeper was also on holiday.

That night winter came. When Anton pulled back the curtains, he gave a whistle at the snow-covered path and gardens. Snow increased: each tree was white, each branch and every twig, and still it tumbled from an endless white sky. They rushed outside; they chased each other to the field. Robbie ran with his arms out until he could run no more and then fell on the ground. No one was about, but if anybody had been, they'd not have noticed anything more than men larking about like mates.

They turned on their backs and saw a few birds, dark and shivering on the thin white birch branches. Then they were so cold they hurried inside, chasing each other up the stairs, shoving and laughing and falling into the bed, pulling the green-covered quilt over them both.

Even before George Langstaff had returned, Anton and Robbie conferred together. The vicar must know nothing, nothing, of course. They had become closer friends, that was all. They talked it over, huddled by the fire, foreheads touching, hands tightly entwined.

In the white light of a December afternoon, they cut down a small tree and carried it back to the vicarage to decorate with nuts, berries, cornucopias, lace angels, and little white candles. The village singers came caroling outside the vicar's door, accompanied by a few badly tuned violins. Toward midnight, Anton and Langstaff and Robbie walked out under the stars. "A happy Christmas, vicar," Anton said. He touched Robbie's shoulder lightly and walked off alone down the path.

Tomorrow was Christmas and the church service. Robbie and Anton would both be there, singing the hymns to welcome the birth of Jesus. The liturgy was from the old prayer book: "We beseech Thee, O Lord!... This is the second great commandment: Thou shalt love thy neighbor as thyself." Anton would stand by Robbie's side. He would pray, "Accept me, O Lord," as fervently as he had as a boy.

He could pray it now; he was happier.

Mounting his stairs to his rooms, Anton made a good fire and set out seedcake and ale. The tall clock from the hall struck two when he heard the creaking of the front door below and the slippered feet on the stairs. Robbie rushed into his arms.

After, Anton held Robbie's head on his shoulder until he slept and then lay awake a long time in the dark with his arms about the slender, breathing back, the rise and fall of mysterious, tender life within him.

Anton thought, It can't be forever. He'll go on and I'll go on. But for these days, dear God, don't let it end.

BOOK TWO

7

WINTER IN THE COUNTRY

January–February 1902

Robbie had slept late on New Year's Day 1902 and now stood in the Reverend George Langstaff's parlor by the table munching cold toast with marmalade, lovely greasy bacon with a not very hot cup of tea. The daily delivered newspaper lay open on the table where his tutor had dropped it. The editorial predicted it would be a year of great prosperity, but Mr. Langstaff had said angrily, before he left to visit a sick man, that they always reported such nonsense while the rich would grow richer and the poor more desperate. What could the church do?

Robbie looked around at the thickly packed bookshelves, the portrait of the venerable, widowed Queen Victoria in a black oval frame; she had died the year before and still gazed severely down from where she hung on the wallpaper over the piano. Robbie always felt she would shake her head and say like a disapproving old woman, "What shall you make of yourselves, Englishmen? What will you do with this glorious empire I've left you?"

Edward VII was now king, and people hoped for a more enlightened ruler after his old and ill mother. His name was linked in gossip to many beautiful actresses, though he had a wife; Mr. Langstaff always shook his head. But these things seemed as far from Robbie as if they took place at the other end of the world, though London was only about a hundred and ten miles away. He could not begin to imagine it. Aside from his uncle's town and here, he had never been anywhere.

These days his own world absorbed him entirely. He would wait until spring to sit his examinations. Not that he cared about them; he had even largely forgotten his drawing. Still, the reliable presence of the Reverend George Langstaff in his wrinkled black coat, from which threads dangled like unfinished thoughts, was one of the most important things in the world to him. Now and then he asked himself with dread, "Does he know? Does he hear me creep out at night? And if he did, what would he do?"

Robbie looked at his old tutor carefully; the vicar knew nothing.

The most difficult thing for Robbie then was to conceal his overwhelming happiness. Fortunately, Langstaff was busy. Robbie helped with every sort of errand. He took soup and socks to the needy and read to old women. People called him the vicar's lovely lad.

January was still and cold upon the house and land. Each evening, Robbie waited sleepless until the vicar's snores sounded through the hall, and then he slipped from the cottage, making his way in darkness down the path. An owl called, and above him the trees moved in the cold winter winds.

He and Anton rode out now and then on one horse, and once even tried a neighbor's unbroken stallion, which plunged and bucked in the field while Anton, who rode in front, shouted, "Grip with your thighs, lad! Hold tight to me"—Robbie's own arms about the more powerful chest and stomach, the body that bent gracefully and reared back to shout with joy. Both were thrown to the earth in a heap, unhurt except for Anton's aching wrist, and beyond them the stallion galloped, slowed, and looked about curiously. "Damn the beast," said Anton, laughing. Thoughts were later exchanged like gifts, and then intermingled until they couldn't recall who had begun the subject.

Robbie knew a few of Anton's friends, though he never entered the library when they were there but heard them talking through the door. There was that balding man Burrows, who belonged to a socialist club and stammered to express his complex ideas. Mr. Hayes came, and older men whose trouser hems were ragged, and shoes worn, and who said, "Anton," not "Mr.

Harrington," and several young girls and a matronly woman called Mrs. Cullen who always arrived with newspapers. A few men drove down from London, well-dressed, wearing good hats, and later Robbie asked, "Who were they?" and Anton laughed and said, "They want me to come back to work in the bank," and kissed him hard and said, "I won't. I want to be here with you."

Off the library were two doors, one leading to a formal parlor and the other a large dining room. There was never a fire in them, and they were never used. Like the unused empty rooms above, Anton seemed to shut them off from his life.

They read to each other; they bought bicycles and traveled about the countryside. They rode the river path. Then Anton taught him chess, and quickly Robbie began to win; unexpectedly, he was the better strategic thinker of the two. They sat over the chessboard, foreheads close, fingers entwined. He was surprised that Anton became a little flustered when he lost. Robbie had not expected his strong lover to be like that. Very slowly, Robbie began to know the hidden corners of Anton. He wanted to heal the hurt ones. He wanted to discover them all.

Robbie was studying in his room on a late January day when he heard the sound of a horse and at once rubbed away the frost from the window to look below. He could see only the retreating wheels of carter Harry's wagon. He waited what seems a long time to him and then pushed away his copy of Cicero's *Di Officiis (On Obligations)* and hurried toward the farmhouse without his coat. Who had come?

The library doors were closed but from behind them, he heard Anton's voice and a feminine, softer reply. He was about to knock when Anton thrust open both doors. "Robbie, there you are!" he said softly, closing the doors behind him. "My wife's arrived unexpectedly, and I'm having an awful time explaining why I didn't answer her letters. She's staying in that hotel in Nottingham where you and I had tea last week."

"Your wife!" Robbie whispered. "Why should she come here?"

"She's urging me to finalize our divorce. I forgot to sign some papers. Come meet her. Her name's Louise, and she's a nicer person than I am." Anton pushed back Robbie's curls from his forehead and said tenderly, "She knows nothing about us, of course."

Robbie shook his head. "I'd rather not. It's awfully odd."

"Come, she's heard us talking!" Anton pushed him from behind, squeezing his bottom hard, and Robbie half-stumbled into the room trying to suppress his laughter.

She was sitting on one of the chintz-covered chairs before the fire. Robbie took in her tight gray bodice with the little jacket, her tiny waist, and the kid glove she still wore. He had seen pictures of such women with their great dipping hats in the *Illustrated London News*. Oh God, he thought, she's so lovely and small. Then he told me true; he has a wife. But he never said she was so lovely.

He approached her, and she put out her hand to take his. Her eyes were wet; she had been crying. She said, "Hello, I'm Louise Harrington. You must be the vicar's student, Robbie."

"Yes," he murmured, his mind rushing. There had been between her and his Anton an intimacy—but that he could not consider without blood rushing to his cheeks. Anton had explained to him one night how women were made and how satisfaction was achieved with them, and Robbie's breath had come faster with disbelief. An image passed before him of this pretty little woman in a chemise (he did not in his mind undress her further) removing her stockings; he felt slightly faint. Ridiculous, he thought. Impossible!

He straightened his back, sensing his own potency.

Her hair was darker than the strands inside the Tennyson book. He glanced at Anton, who was looking sideways at the carpet with his arms folded across his chest.

She said, "You draw; Anton told me."

"Well, a little," he answered gruffly.

"Please show me your work. I so love art."

He fetched his thick portfolio and, when he returned, heard low, agitated voices, which ceased when he came in. He glanced at Anton but could read nothing. Still, he was touched by how respectfully she turned the pages of the drawings and watercolors.

What the devil is happening here? Robbie thought.

"You have a real gift," she said at last. "If you ever come to London, you must spend days in the galleries and museums. Have you ever seen the Impressionists?"

"No," he muttered. "A few photographs in black and white in magazines. That doesn't show them, I think."

"No," she said. "Not Monet, certainly not! Anton, take him at once! Really, he reminds me of my brother." For a moment, her face darkened. He excused himself then, and an hour later, from his bedroom window, saw the carter taking her away. Good riddance, he thought.

Snow fell again, lazily, drifting against the windows some days later, but in the farmhouse study the fire burned brightly. The vicar was out with parishioners.

Anton was writing letters at his desk. Robbie sat cross-legged on the rug before one of the crammed bookcases, wearing only Anton's second dressing gown. The carpet was warm under his bare legs as he pulled out one volume after another.

"What have you found now?" Anton murmured, and Robbie said, "Elizabethan poetry. Marvell: 'Had we but world enough and time!' You have so many books. *Outlines of Psychology*. Did you read it?"

"Yes."

Robbie pulled out more volumes. He called, "Your books on socialism are here! You must have brought them from the attic where I saw them." He read the spines. "Karl Marx, Engels, *The Life of Lord Shaftesbury*...Jack London, Rowntree. And really old ones. When did you move them down?"

"One afternoon I felt I wanted them with me again. Old friends, so to speak. Voices of my conscience."

Robbie was aware of the closeness between them though they were several feet apart. He felt it like warmth all over him. After a time, he pulled out a thick portfolio of loose pages from the bookcase and opened it. Anton's writing was looser than it was now, as if written in a great rush. The subject was the low wages of farmworkers which left a family malnourished and weak with one garment, if that, for each person and no shoes. He read on, appalled, remembering the conversation about poverty in England from the time they first went to dinner together.

He called, "Anton, did you write this?"

Anton looked a little tired. Sometimes small lines appeared on the sides of his eyes, which Robbie always wanted to kiss. "Yes, I did," he said. "I began it years ago. I meant it to be a book. I haven't thought about it in a while."

"It's awfully good. The writing's like poetry and at the same time, it's severe. People must know these things. Mr. Langstaff took me to a few of the wretched little houses a few miles from here. I drew several pictures, but they're never good enough."

"They're very good. I saw them."

"But people shouldn't go hungry. We brought them a basket of bread and cooked bacon and they tore into it."

"I know. There are hundreds of thousands like them all over the country. We had great reformers in the last century; progress creeps forward and is lost. I worked a little for a time. One drop of water in the bucket."

"Why don't you finish your book and publish it? Aren't you a reformer?"

"Not anymore. So much happened between the man I was then and the one I am now. If I ever publish a whole book, I'd like to use your illustrations."

"Really?" cried Robbie, rising on his knees.

Anton said seriously, "I mean it. Read Engels' book on the wretched conditions in Manchester. They're the same in most industrial cities. The book's there among the others, all underlined. Entire families live in one small disgusting room, ten of them, a hole in the floor for a privy. I was so idealistic."

His eyes were downcast, and he ran his palm against the side of the desk as if measuring something. "You know, though, I see it in you, Rob…that idealism. I don't talk about these things much anymore. It seems we're talking now. I'm comfortable with you. I'm not sure why you don't judge me."

"I never would! I love you. I can only think good of you. So does Mr. Langstaff."

Anton moved his palm to the pile of papers on his desk. "I didn't quite say the whole truth. I published part of this book as articles in socialist publications, very shabby little things. I still write them when the injustice of this country leans against my window like a ghost and I fling them to the wind. But I don't sign them. I know what happens when you put your heart in the world. You're abandoned."

Robbie said firmly, "You'd never be abandoned; there's me. You could sign your name to a thousand articles, and I'd be here."

"The world's very big, Rob."

"But that doesn't matter. Don't you believe me?"

The words had become too intense, and Anton looked away. Robbie held the portfolio against his chest. He asked longingly, "When will I have read and seen as much as you?"

"When you're almost thirty too. No, by then you'll have read much more."

"You're not thirty until March 4th. We'll celebrate."

"Yes, absolutely."

"Who are you writing to? Can I come over to you now?"

"I'm writing about investments, very dull, but now I'm losing concentration. Put that wretched book away and come here at once."

Robbie tucked away the folder and leapt up. They had made love intensely a few hours before, when he had first come in, and he could still smell it on his body. About the room were intimate signs of both: his own toppled boots, his hose and knickers in a heap, Anton's white shirt tossed across the sofa. Robbie walked seductively across the carpet on bare feet, dressing-gown sash trailing, gown swaying open. When he came close enough, Anton pulled him, and Robbie resisted. They struggled playfully.

"I'm almost as strong as you," Robbie said.

"When I let you be."

"When I want to be."

"Whatever you want to be, Rob." Anton's voice was husky as he stroked Robbie's hair, fingers resting at the back of his neck. "You," he said.

"You," said Robbie. He laughed. He shouted, "Race you!" and hurried into the bedroom, throwing off the gown. Now he had forgotten all the books. Anton followed and stood above him. "Wait," he said, "I want to wash."

"Don't."

Still, he watched as Anton dropped his own dressing gown and stood naked washing under his arms before the mirror. The muscles of his back down to the buttocks and thighs were rosy in the light of the oil lamp. Robbie's breath came quicker. He squirmed down in the soft mattress and called, "I want to be one person with you... No you, no me, only us. And you're doing that so I can just long for you horribly."

"Exactly. Long for me."

Anton dropped the cloth into the basin. He fell onto the bed and balanced on his arm above Robbie, kissing him hard again and again. Smoke from the wood fire in the next room drifted through the door, its pungency mingling with the freshly washed scent of Anton's chest and beard.

He felt Anton's body pressing against his and then that great, wonderful warmth filling him, moving deeper and faster until he began to gasp. "I wanted to make you wait longer," Anton said after, stroking Robbie's cheek. "But you couldn't, could you? I like to see how long you can wait. Each time a little longer, eh?"

"Anton, I'd die of feeling."

"Oh God, there's nothing more lovely in the world than making love to you."

Anton dropped back with his hands behind his head and gazed up at the canopy. Robbie rested his cheek on Anton's chest, his arm about him, feeling the gradual slowing of his lover's breath, which was so beautiful to him. The heart beating... *thump, thump,* and slower. He kept its count with his fingers against Anton's nipple. Again, the smell of their sweat mingled.

"What was it like…your marriage?" Robbie asked. "I've thought about it a little." He began to extract small feathers from a hole in one of the pillows and let them drift down on them.

"I imagined you'd think of it," Anton said. "But now you've met her. She's a kind, intelligent woman. Kept down by her mother, but I wanted more for her. After we married, she began to study painting and singing and to campaign for the women's vote. Once she was arrested, but I got her out. We had married shortly after my father died. I bought a London house and began happily but… We came back here for a few months, but she didn't like it. She returned to her friends. I remained. The ending of things is hard. The fault was never hers, all mine. I'll tell you more one day. She wanted children. They didn't come."

"Have you signed all the divorce papers?"

"Nearly."

They lay in a heap together, listening to the crackling of the fire. Anton reached out and ran his hand through Robbie's dark hair and down his shoulders and slender, naked back.

"I'm famished," Robbie said. He jumped up and returned to bed with several biscuits in his hand, which crumbled over the green quilt. "Want one?" he asked, his mouth full of crumbs.

"I'll feed it to you."

"Thanks, I'd rather have port."

"No, you need food. Open your mouth. Mr. Langstaff says you mustn't drink too much."

"He drinks too much himself; you've noticed, I suppose. I would too if I had to keep harmony between everyone in his parish. He tells them about Christ's love and two hours later, they've forgotten every word. Poor fallen humans. Stop! Where are you going now?"

Robbie had finished the biscuits and was now pulling on his long wool underwear. He felt suddenly anxious and said, "I've got to go back, Anton! He may return."

"Then tell him you were helping me sort my books. He

knows we're friends; he can't know more. He couldn't dream of this."

Robbie climbed back into bed with his long wool combinations half buttoned. He wound his arms around Anton and threw his leg over his. They lay in silence, Robbie feeling the moving chest under his hand and tracing the full lips beneath the mustache with his delicate fingers.

"Anton?" he said softly. "Who was the last man you liked most?"

"Someone I worked with in the London bank, but I never told him."

Robbie's long fingers moved to Anton's chest hair and rested there possessively. "Was he older than me?" he asked.

"My age, I think."

"Did you go to bed with him?"

"No."

"Why did you choose me? Would you still choose me?"

"Yes, darling."

"You're thinking deeper things, Anton. You frown a little and your eyes go all dark. Tell me."

"I once had a child."

Robbie sat up on his elbow. He asked, astonished, "You had a child with your wife? I thought you said—"

Anton raised his eyes and, taking Robbie's hand, slowly kissed each knuckle. "The child wasn't with my wife, my darling," he said. "It was long ago. Come back when our vicar's asleep. Promise me or I won't let you go."

8

LATER WINTER IN THE COUNTRY

February 1902

Robbie woke three days later to the sound of hoofbeats on the path and looked from his window, to see Anton riding rapidly toward the bridge, heavy brown coat buttoned and topped with a thick muffler. For a moment he wondered why his lover had rushed away without throwing a pebble to his window, as he often did.

He dressed and hurried down the steps. Mr. Langstaff was kneeling by the desk drawers, his head pulled back to read a document. He had misplaced his reading glasses the day before. His small traveling bag was by his side.

"Are you going somewhere?" Robbie asked.

"I am, lad," the vicar said, taking Robbie's hand to stand again. The old man's face was heavy with sadness. "A wire's come that my eldest sister's quite ill in the north. Poor Matilda! I must be on the afternoon train. I'll be gone about a week at most. Anton stopped by early, and I told him the news. He'll be there if you need anything. On the desk there's the list of the sick and elderly I'd like you to look in on."

"I'm so sorry," Robbie said, and yet in his mind, the luxury of free nights with Anton filled him with joy. A week! He asked casually, "Do you know where Anton went so early?"

"He didn't say. He said he'd be back soon."

The snow continued to fall in disorderly flurries as they climbed to the vicar's whitewashed bedroom after breakfast to empty the trunk, in which extra books were stored. A week's clothing was packed. Mr. Langstaff added, "My address is on the desk if you need me."

Robbie and his tutor moved up and down the steps remem-

bering more things the old man needed to take until the parlor
clock struck one. Then Robbie hitched Blackie to the gig and
climbed up beside the vicar, taking the reins. They rode quickly
to the station, but no train was in sight down the long, snowy
track.

The vicar, who was heavily wrapped against the cold, asked
anxiously, "You did remember to only pack my socks without
holes, Rob? Otherwise, my five healthy sisters will feel they
must come here at once to take care of me!"

"Oh yes."

"Dear lad, what a blessing you are! I don't know how I ever
managed without you."

The horse placidly bent his great nose to some dry grass,
while a few leaves rustled on the branches as they waited for the
train. Robbie pulled at a thread in the bottom of his trouser leg
and said casually, "Anton said he had a child once."

"Did he tell you that? Then he must trust you! A small number of us remember. A sad affair, Rob, one of the saddest I
recall."

"Will you tell me, sir? I think he doesn't want to speak about
it."

Mr. Langstaff hesitated for a time. "I'd rather you knew the
truth than some rumor. The girl lived with her mother in a small
hamlet of wretched houses in a field some five miles north;
Squatters' Field, they called it. Half a century or more ago,
tenant farmers had lived there, and when they were no longer
needed, they were forced out and a few dozen wretched poor
moved in. No one bothered them for a time; the owner was
gone. Some of them made a little money in crafts and sewing
and laundry. Anton was sixteen then, and we'd visit them and
bring them food. There was a girl called Bess, a lovely young
thing."

Robbie nodded; he kept his eyes on a hungry sparrow peck-
ing around the dried grass. The vicar shifted his weight and
sighed. "Things were bad for him at home, really bad. Sometimes he ran away and stayed some hours with me, sometimes
nights with them, sleeping on the floor. It was the year he was

speaking for the socialists. Well, Anton got Bess with child. When her belly began to swell, she ran away."

"Horrible! Was he in love with her, sir?"

"I don't think he was, but he was honorable and wanted to take care of her."

Ah, the strands of hair in the book, Robbie thought suddenly. They're hers. Oh, my love, my love. He blurted, "But why didn't she write him?"

"She couldn't write, never learned, but she could have gotten word. I don't know why she never did."

"And what happened to him?"

"His father went to the Nottingham Socialists' Union and dragged him out by the arm. His good friend Burrows tried to intervene and was thrown to the floor. The girl was gone and Anton ceased to speak for the Union. He turned away as if it had never been. He got on with his life. He was a star at university; anything to which he turned his hand he did well. Languages, poetry, essays. He learned wrestling and boxing. Again and again, he defied his father, yet in the end he always went home. I don't know why—he was very unhappy. He's still looking for the girl, but it's been more than twelve years. Something happened to him in Switzerland before he came back here. He won't say. But he seems happy now, more than I remember, as if he's settled something."

Langstaff sighed. "Enough. What came over me, lad! I've spoken too much perhaps. We must keep these things between us. There's the train in the distance; I hear it."

The conversation moved Robbie deeply. It was a physical sensation, as if he were drunk. After the vicar had boarded his train, Robbie drove straight to the farmhouse. With cold fingers, he unharnessed Blackie, tended to him, and stalled him near the gray mare. Anton had returned, and Robbie hurried across to the house door and walked inside.

He stopped by the coats hanging in the vestibule, hearing voices from behind the closed library doors. He stood biting his lip, understanding that the pretty woman Anton had married was in there with him. Perhaps it was the last signing of the divorce papers. Then things would be safe. He and Anton would go on in secret happiness. He would somehow stay on here, drawing. He would throw away any pretense of studying for university, and one day they would travel together. The rest he could not see, but that would come. Anton would manage it.

Quietly, he left the house and bicycled to the village of Forest's End, where he bought stale bread from the baker and fed the birds. He stood on the bridge looking down at the cold water rushing over the rocks. He counted the minutes until he felt he could go back. When he finally returned, he found Anton standing alone by the fire in the library.

"Why, where've you been?" Anton asked, turning to him. "I was almost going to look for you."

"I was only walking," answered Robbie. "And I had to take the vicar to the train to see his sister." He wound his arms around Anton's neck and pressed his mouth into the soft mustache, tasting tobacco. Yet the vicar's story had moved him so much, he couldn't begin to ask all his questions or expostulate on his plans.

He said, "He's gone, so I can stay all night with you. We haven't done that in a while. Why was your wife here again? Anton, I don't like her here. It's complicated enough as we are."

"She only came to settle things." Anton kissed him back and took him by the shoulders before breaking away and dropping into one of the armchairs by the fire, hand to his lips.

Robbie sat on the chair's arm, hesitating. He couldn't ask about the child now; he would wait for the evening. He would find some delicate way to approach the subject. When Anton was sated with love, he said all sorts of things, speaking words into darkness as if it were safer that way.

He also had no words to ask about the complexities.

Robbie lifted Anton's hand and kissed the wrist with its odd scar several times. "What's this?" he asked suddenly. "You never said."

"I had a nasty cut on a rock when I was climbing in Switzerland."

"You weren't hurt?"

"I bled, of course."

Robbie's stomach felt queasy. He blurted anxiously, "Even if you were sad, you would never do something to yourself?"

"Of course not!"

"If anyone ever hurt you, Anton, I'd kill them."

"No one can hurt me. What are you talking about today?"

Robbie flushed. Ah God, he had asked things clumsily, wrongly. He only knew he wanted to go back in time and make everything better for this man he adored. Now the years between them lay heavily on him. There was a space also, perhaps from the words he couldn't say. It had happened several times since they had become lovers. If he were only six years older, seven years older. If only they were equal, but Anton was so far ahead of him. He was a man of the world. And Robbie needed to close any difference Anton's years had made.

He remained on the chair's edge, his hand on Anton's shoulder. Then Anton said quickly, "Damn it, then, I almost forgot! Our friend Hayes has an extra ticket for *Hamlet* tonight in Nottingham and asked you to come. You've read it ten times. You should go. Look at the clock, Rob. He'll be here in twenty minutes."

Robbie shook his head. "I'd rather stay with you," he said. "I'd rather be with you and talk. We're alone. And the last few days I don't feel you've talked to me much. There's things you don't say."

"If I don't tell you everything at once, it's because it's difficult for me, but I always do eventually. I can't tell you what I don't tell myself first. Don't frown. Go change your clothes or you'll be late. I'll be waiting when you come back." Anton shoved him gently and then harder and still playfully to unseat him from the chair arm, and then stood. "Hurry now. You'll miss the first appearance of the ghost."

"I don't want to go."

"But damn it, I said you'd come, or he would have given the ticket to Joshua Wilkes's brother. It's quite sold out."

"Oh, very well," said Robbie. "Wait for me."

The play in the old theater seemed endless: Actors strutted in and out, and the Hamlet was a fellow of sixty with a big stomach. Between acts, a frail young woman sang sentimental songs with her hands clasped before her. Anton had taken Robbie to touring theater companies four or five times in Nottingham and discussed them on the way back, reciting lines they remembered. One day they planned to go to London and see theater every night. George wouldn't mind. Again, Robbie looked at his pocket watch.

At last, it was done, and he climbed into the gig with Hayes and his two daughters. The girls gazed at Robbie flirtatiously, giggling; they were not more than fourteen. He tried to be patient.

He looked up to see the gig turning to the west and the village. "You can leave me here," he said, beginning to rise. "We're going the wrong way. Thank you very much, sir."

Hayes pulled in the reins so that the horse moved more slowly. "Why, you're staying with us," he said. "My wife's warmed the spare bedroom. Harrington said you'd go home in the morning."

"Staying with you tonight? He couldn't have said that."

"He did indeed."

"He meant a late supper at your house."

"Perhaps he did."

"Thank you, sir, but I'd rather go home. It's not far! I can walk," Robbie said, his voice rising a little.

Hayes shook his head then, and answered, "Well, a misunderstanding! Sit down, lad, sit down! There's no moon. You can't walk without a lantern, and I've not got an extra. I'll take you back."

Robbie fell silent, turning his face to the dark trees. At the bridge he jumped down and hurried as fast he could to the farmhouse. From his pocket he took the large iron key, inserted it in the lock. The door creaked. Without stopping to light a candle, he felt his way to the stairs and mounted up. By the time he came to the top, he could make out the shadow of Anton's closed door. He put his hand on the knob and turned.

It was locked.

Robbie stood motionless in the hallway, listening to the ticking of the Worcester clock from below, the creaking of a branch that moved in the wind and knocked against the roof. He could feel the beating of his heart under his thick wool coat as he put his hand on the knob once again. "Anton," he whispered. His light voice cracked a little and then broke.

He called, "Anton!" It echoed up the steps to the attic and down again to the vestibule, where it died away. He shouted again, calling out Anton's name repeatedly. Then the door opened suddenly, as if Anton had expected a stranger.

"Rob, what are you doing here?" he whispered. "You were supposed to stay with Hayes. Let me take you back to your room."

"My room? I don't want to go there. I want to be with you. Why did you lock your door? You knew I was coming back. What made you ask Hayes to—" He stopped speaking because his voice had become shrill, to his shame. He glanced desperately through the open door to the darkness.

He whispered, "Is someone there?"

"No one's there, but I need to talk with you."

"We could make love first. I want to make love so much!"

"Let's go to your room. Nellie's not there? Good." With his arm around Robbie's shoulders, he urged him gently down the steps and out the door. Wind blew the folds of his dressing gown. Robbie kept turning to look at Anton's thick dark hair also tossed by the wind.

Holding hands, they climbed the steps together to Robbie's small room. After closing the door, Anton pulled Robbie against his shoulder, stroking his back. Robbie could feel the shape of Anton's body beneath the dressing gown; he wore only that over his pajama bottoms and was shivering. His bare feet were pale with the cold.

A few slight spasms passed Anton's chest. He murmured,

"I've something to tell you: the most difficult thing I could ever tell you."

"You're going back to the bank?"

"It's not that. It's about Louise. My wife."

"I don't like it when you call her that, because she's not that anymore."

"Robbie, please listen to me."

"Tell me then."

Anton swallowed. He said, "Louise and I want to try to mend our marriage."

"Anton, you're teasing me."

Anton shook his head.

At first Robbie could find no words and when he did manage, he struggled to keep them steady. He asked softly, "Did I do something wrong? Don't you love me anymore?"

"I do…I do," Anton murmured. "Try to understand, darling. What happened between us couldn't last. I want to be a husband and a father. It's what men do. I want children. You will too when you're older. What we have together is so beautiful: the most beautiful thing I've ever known. But I want to go back to my wife and stop this secrecy. What we have can only exist in the shadows."

"Will you go back to work? You hate banking. You want to work for the poor."

"That was a dream."

Robbie pushed him away and stared at Anton's averted eyes, the dark lashes that were so long and seductive. He cried out, "Oh God, Anton! Is *she* there? In your rooms? Did you lie to me?"

"No, I couldn't have her there after… What do you think of me? She's in the Nottingham Arms."

"Send her away! Anton, please."

Anton shook his head. "I can't, Robbie. She still loves me a little, and what's between you and me is wrong. I thought I'd put it away. I thought that part of me was buried. Then you came and it returned. I allowed myself to give into it."

They sat down on the edge of the bed. Robbie seized Anton's hand and kissed it many times. "Anton," he begged.

Anton said, "To hurt you kills me.... It kills me. I came back earlier this afternoon to ask Langstaff to take you with him, but he had just gone. Then before you returned, Hayes came by with the ticket and I thought perhaps, if you stayed away with him, it might be a calmer time to discuss it in the morning."

"Stay with me here tonight and we *will* talk about it in the morning!"

"Rob, damn it! You know we'd make love if I remained. Even now I want you, but...I need you to understand."

Robbie's voice broke. "I understand that yesterday you wanted me, and now you don't anymore! I understand that you told me you never wanted to be without me, and now...you're ashamed." Robbie's wet mouth pressed against Anton's neck.

"You deserve a better person than I am."

"What about your book? I was going to illustrate it."

"Look, go to Rome to study. I know a painter there and his wife. I'll arrange it; I'll pay for everything. You'll be famous. You'll fall in love. You'll forget me."

Robbie shook his head. He said to Anton's neck, "I won't go to Rome without you. You said you'd take me. You said we'd go together. I don't give a damn about art without you. I don't want anyone else but you."

"Let me go, darling. Please let me go. I'm sorry, I'm sorry. I'm going away from here. I shouldn't have returned. I'll write when I can. Please."

"Do you promise?"

"Yes, I do. Please. You'll hear from me."

Robbie rolled limply aside, his head buried in his pillow. He felt Anton's slow kiss on his hair and then heard his footsteps as he went away down the stairs.

Robbie didn't sleep that night but lay awake listening to the wind. The next morning, he rose at dawn and wandered to the farmhouse as near as the big tree and stared at its dark windows.

No one came in or went out. Robbie thought, He'll look out the window and call me up any moment.

The truth returned and dissolved again in the confusion of his mind. He would forget what had happened and then would remember. He didn't understand where he stood or what hour it could be. His pocket watch had stopped.

What had happened in the three days before the vicar had left and Anton had sent him off to see the play? Anton had been moody; a few times he was lost in thought. He had disappeared at times for hours; then, returning, he would explain, "errands" or "business." He had drawn Robbie against him on the study sofa and kept him close, and when Robbie wanted to rise for some water, Anton had said tenderly, almost pleadingly, "No, stay here." In what hour then did the reconciliation with his wife occur?

There was silence in the farmhouse.

Some rubbing and banging came from the kitchen. He found the housekeeper Mary polishing the kitchen grate and asked as lightly as he could, "Have you seen Mr. Harrington?"

Her honest, round face looked at him. "But surely you know, Mr. Stillman," she replied. "Mr. Harrington's with his wife in the Nottingham Arms."

"Ah yes, of course," he replied. He and Anton had always been careful before Mary, the serious, lanky, and round-faced local girl who came twice a week. She smiled at him; she guessed nothing. But how had Anton gone away? Both horses were in the stable. Had Anton walked to the city suddenly, furtively, softly on the leaves?

There was no use staying here. Robbie left the house so heavily he could hardly continue down the path.

That night, he couldn't bring himself to undress. Yet after he had managed to fall asleep for a few hours, he woke with the thought, Well, it can't last, because it's me he loves. By tonight he'll be back.

In the morning he drew Anton from memory by the rainy light and then buried his head in his hands. By dinnertime he began a letter to his uncle saying he wanted to come home and tore it up. The bit of kidney pie hardened at the edges, the tea grew stewed and cold in the pot, sugar congealed in the plate of apples.

The promise to visit the sick neighbors and shop for them never entered his mind. And no letters came.

On the third day he woke from a late-afternoon's exhausted sleep and knew he must go to the city and bring Anton home again.

He had bicycled to Nottingham several times with Anton. He knew the hotel, a heavy early-Victorian building with its bricks already darkened with city dirt. Inside was the plush restaurant that served such a large, comfortable tea.

Robbie jumped on his bicycle and rode past the familiar houses. Darkness was coming soon this winter evening. He felt the cold sting his neck. Perhaps in a few hours he and Anton would both be home again.

At last, the ornate hotel rose up before him. He parked his bicycle and hurried to the hotel desk to ask for Mr. and Mrs. Harrington, though the specific words made him sick to say them. "They are expecting me," he added to the clerk. "I'm Mr. Langstaff's pupil." Everyone knew Mr. Langstaff. The clerk nodded and gave him the room number.

He mounted the two flights of stairs and made his way down a narrow, carpeted hallway. Number 24, he thought. He stood before the door. He had planned what he would say. He would be calm; he would be gentle. He would try to take her feelings into consideration. He would say, "I'm sorry, ma'am. It's not your fault. It's just it's me he loves now."

He knocked. There was no answer. He knocked again. The echo of his knocking on the locked study door a few nights before haunted him, but this time no one came out.

Robbie stuck his hands into his pockets and made his way down to the lobby again and the desk clerk. "Ah, young gentleman, so sorry!" the man said. "It's been a busy day. Mr. and Mrs. Harrington left an hour ago."

"They couldn't have," Robbie said.

"Yes, they did."

"Where did they go?"

"Why, they were leaving for the train station. I believe I heard her say London, then Paris. Imagine, so far away."

But in the station the train to London had left.

Robbie grabbed his bicycle again. He was crying so hard he could barely see. He rode into the vicarage garden, leaned his bike against the wall, and ran up the stairs into his room, where he seized the floral water pitcher and basin, shattering them into a hundred sharp fragments against the wall. Water seeped into the carpet and across the sketches he'd tacked around the dresser mirror. He took Anton's shirt from the bed and ripped it to shreds. Then he locked the door, holding the bits of fabric in his arms and rocking them.

Nellie's call rose querulously from below. "What clatter! Lad, not a bite of supper?"

He gritted his teeth. Blocking the door with his body, he pulled the quilt from the bed and lay down on the floor.

After a time, darkness came.

9

GEORGE LANGSTAFF

February 1902

It was the gray, wintry light which woke him, and he started up and looked around him trying to remember. Several of the drawings tacked to the wall were so streaked with water that they sagged, charcoal trees blurring into the paper. The blue ink of a girl's face leaked downward as if she were dissolving. Across the rug, Anton's shirt lay in torn fragments, buttons huddling next to the shards of the broken water pitcher and basin.

It was not just one of his terrible old dreams. It had happened. He had thrown the water and torn the shirt. He had been left by the person he loved most. He had slept all night on the floor.

But perhaps it would be all made up. It had to be. Supposing Anton had returned from London and was even now walking down the path, his long legs thrusting in front of each other as if he begrudged the time it took for even so short a way? Could Robbie forgive him? Would Anton weep? The thought was frightening though satisfying. Then the drawings would be whole again and the shirt returned to its usual hiding place beneath the mattress.

But there were sounds below: a door opening, footsteps, murmuring.

Robbie stood awkwardly. His clothes, which he had not removed, were wrinkled. Despite the winter chill of the room, he felt sweaty. A few small cuts on his right hand from the basin shards were just beginning to scab with dried brown blood. His watch still did not go, but the clock below chimed eleven. He opened the door, trying not to let his footsteps sound on the wood, came to the top of the stairs, and looked down to the parlor.

In the dull light, he saw Mr. Langstaff seated by the window in his traveling clothes, face turned toward the garden and carpetbag by his side. "Come here, lad," he called wearily. "I think we need to talk a little."

Robbie descended slowly, holding on to the banister. He made himself cross the carpet to his teacher, who had not turned to him but remained looking through the window into the bare garden.

The vicar said, "My sisters have no telephone, of course, so Antonio called from the Nottingham train station to the hotel near them. The hotel boy came to fetch me. I heard from Anton's voice that he was drunk. He said something terrible had happened and it was his fault. I thought at first you were hurt. He said how dear you were to him. He said it several times. I could barely hear him. He said he loved you."

Robbie was stunned into silence.

George Langstaff turned and stared at him, biting his lip. "I began to think...I couldn't conceive of such a thing. I count on you to tell the truth. Was there something between you both... of a physical nature? I've turned it over in my mind so many times. He couldn't have meant that."

There was no use hiding now. "There was," Robbie said dully. "Why did he call you? Why did he have to tell you?"

Langstaff's weary face, not even shaven today, his clerical collar crooked, looked at him in astonishment. He seemed to rise a few inches from the chair and then slammed his hand down on the arm, shouting, "In the name of the most holy Lord, I can't believe it; he was never that way. I wouldn't have let him near you if I'd thought that! I never suspected. Did he force you?"

Robbie spoke softly to the fading pattern in the rug beneath his feet. "No, I wanted to be with him."

"And how long has this been going on?"

"Nearly four months."

Mr. Langstaff let out his breath with a harsh expiration.

Robbie sank into a chair and brushed away his tears with the heel of his hand. He couldn't bring himself to raise his eyes from the carpet, whose dark roses now danced before him. Lamps and books, the piano, the lace curtains, the unfinished manuscripts on the desk, all seemed to condemn him.

The voice of his teacher drifted toward him in a tone of bitterness he had never heard before. "I see. So, this was why you wanted to remain here. Now I understand your strange outburst last week when you asked me if I'd become your guardian because you felt you belonged with me. That you'd found a home here with me. And I was moved, truly. I was a fool enough to be moved."

Robbie exclaimed, "I meant it. No one's been to me what you have."

"Lies! You meant it so you could continue this thing. It's a schoolboy madness, and schoolboys are justly punished for it."

But Robbie jumped up. "Is he going to Paris? Do you know? Will he stop in London first? He must have stopped there; he wouldn't take the channel boat at night. I've got to find him. He's made a terrible mistake. I can talk to him. I'm the closest person in the world to him. I understand him. I can manage him."

"What are you saying? No one can manage him. No one has ever managed him."

"I can."

"Sit down."

"He needs me even if he doesn't know it. Do you know where he is?"

"I wouldn't tell you."

"Please, you must. I love him too."

"Love!" said his teacher scornfully. "Love! What do you know about love, Stillman?"

Robbie had never seen his teacher so angry before; he swelled with it so that his shoulders and chest seemed to expand under the wool vest and jacket. Even then, Robbie shouted back, "Why do you think I don't know it? People love. You loved your wife."

"My wife died of consumption, and I've mourned her all my life. But love between a man and his wife is blessed by God, and what Anton led you to do is unnatural. Were you aware that it's against the law? A criminal offense?"

"I wanted to forget it. Some say love between men is morally wrong, but that can't be. It's pure. It's good. I know it."

"Thousands of men have been arrested. Perhaps you don't know about the playwright Oscar Wilde, who was convicted six or seven years ago under the Gross Indecency Laws."

"I think I heard it mentioned once, sir."

The vicar grasped the arms of his chair and leaned forward. "Did you know they sent him to prison for two years, with solitary confinement, and that for several months he could have no visitors or speak to a soul? One of the most brilliant men in England not allowed to read or write! The warders shaved his head and dressed him in convict's clothes. He slept on a plank; he ate such poor food he sickened. Only one hour a day he could exercise in the yard with a hood over his face. The hard labor almost killed him. His family fled the country. He never saw his beloved little sons again. He died a few years after he was released."

Robbie folded his arms across his chest to contain his panic; he vaguely remembered his schoolmasters speaking of it when they didn't know he was near. His mouth was dry with confusion now. He touched the back of a beloved soft chair for assurance; he had often flung himself into it during deep talks with George. He asked slowly, "Do you approve of those laws, sir?"

"No, of course I don't," the vicar said impatiently. "They're barbaric. But schoolboys lose interest in one another and go on to marry. I don't know what possessed Anton. Fortunately, he's mended his marriage. He and his wife are on their way to France. He told me they were going."

Robbie slumped. Then everything was over and suddenly he belonged nowhere; no speck of dust behind the piano legs was smaller than what he had become. When he could speak, he said in an almost inaudible voice, "I won't go back to my uncle. I'll go off alone. You'll be rid of me. It doesn't matter what happens to me."

George Langstaff held out his thick hand and shook his head. "No, stay here. Listen to me. I care very much what happens to you. Anton may never want to come back here again—he said that. And as for you, don't try to find or write him. Forget this. Promise me, Rob. Come here then. Take my hands and swear as you love your God. How you've both hurt me! How happy your friendship made me and what a fool I was!"

Robbie stumbled across the carpet and felt for Langstaff's hands. He tried to speak, but his voice broke, and he ran from the house and stood shivering in the garden without his coat until the vicar brought him inside and gave him hot broth, watching as Robbie tried to force it down. "No more words about it," his teacher said. "It's over, it's done. You're not the one to blame. You were always so starved for affection since you came. But Anton! I've believed in his moral goodness. One of the dearest things in the world is broken for me."

There was no one at all in the farmhouse. Not even lanky Mary came. The windows were shuttered, and the same leaves remained unswept on the step.

Strange how life went on with the service as usual on the Sabbath with its hymn singing and beginning of Lent and the cold air seeping through the unheated wintry church and the murmured supplications from the prayerbook: *From all inordinate and sinful affections; and from all the deceits of the world, the flesh, and the devil, Good Lord, deliver us!*

The vicarage was friendlier. The parlor books on the shelves seemed to hold some of their old affability and the piano was warm to his palm. There was post, a rare letter from an old school friend, as if from a life no longer his own. And through it all, Langstaff's unfailing kindness, his blessing, his tactful silence.

It was as if it had just begun. He had come here to study,

to get away from home, and he was still here. The rest was a dream. Yet as he stood slightly apart from rooms and books, Robbie felt he wasn't young anymore.

A few weeks later, he found George Langstaff reading in the parlor in his soft chair with his feet on the hassock, and said, "I want to go up to London to study art, sir."

The vicar removed his reading glasses and studied him for a moment. "Yes, of course," he said. "Yes, you must. But you can't live alone. Let me think about this." A few days later he knocked on Robbie's door with a plan. He said, "Friends in the city know an artist and his wife who'd board you and look after you. Thaddeus J. Wippell's a good man, a churchwarden, a portraitist. You could study at the art school. I wrote him and sent those drawings you gave me. He suggests the Royal Academy of Arts. Your uncle must give permission. He's still trustee for your inheritance and holds your money."

Robbie bit his lip. "It's beyond a dream to go to The Royal Academy! Will you persuade him, sir?"

"We'll visit him."

They rode the train to Robbie's old town together. His new aunt hid upstairs but his uncle who greeted them was unchanged, with his bony body, bloated stomach, and the old suspicious anger about his mouth. He and Robbie and the vicar sat in the parlor before a plate of stale biscuits.

His uncle listened to everything in silence and then sneered a little. Finally, he said, "Very well then. You may have a small bit of your inheritance for expenses now, nephew, the rest when you turn twenty-one. One day when it's all gone, you'll crawl back to my door."

Robbie jumped up. "You'll wait a long time for that," he exclaimed.

Two things had cushioned him. One was Anton's love, which was gone now, and the other was the sleepy countryside in Nottinghamshire and the old man who was better to him than he deserved. That he had to keep. If he lost both, he knew he would be unable to go forward. He turned suddenly as they left his uncle's house and kissed George Langstaff's hand.

"If your uncle had said no, I would have sent you to study," said the vicar. "God has made you an artist. Now you will thank Him by using that gift well."

Though Robbie knew he was breaking his promise, he had to do it. On the evening before he left for London, he walked down the path. He had kept his key to the front door of the farmhouse and now opened it and stood listening to the silence which filled the rooms. He walked up the stairs and into the unlocked study.

He had a hard time deciding where he would leave his note but finally settled on the desk. It said only: "Please don't forget to write your book. Don't forget who you are. Don't entirely forget *me*…and send me a letter as you said. R." He put a small stone on it before leaving the room. He had chosen the stone carefully.

10

THE YOUNG ARTIST IN LONDON
March 1902–January 1903

On a cold, dreary night, Robbie arrived carrying two suitcases at King's Cross Station, whose high glass-and-steel dome glittered by electric light. At once his bags were snatched by a porter. He climbed into a cab as a refuge and stared from the window as the horse trotted along. The driver called out the sights, moving the horse and carriage past hundreds of others. Robbie sank back into the seat upholstery at the overwhelming noise of the crowds.

There was less congestion as they moved southwest of Regent Street. "We're near Hanover Square," the driver said. "That's the house, there."

Robbie climbed the few steps to the town house. He pulled the bell, and a servant girl answered, leading him up two steep flights of stairs. He sat down on his bed, his arms clasped around him, and stared at his bags. This cold, narrow room! No wind from the forest, no path, no bridge. What have I done? he thought. Why am I here?

After a time, he rose lethargically and walked to the desk. There was no stationery, but he tore a page from a sketchbook and unpacked his own pen and ink from a side pocket of his luggage.

Dear Mr. Langstaff,

I must write you before I sleep and ask you the thing that's in my heart. Can you forgive me that I've let you down after your great kindness? You said it, but it nags at me. I don't care what the rest of the world thinks as long as you still see some good in me. I want you to know this always and forever: I did want you to be my guardian. It wasn't just the other thing.

Yrs respectfully,

Rob Stillman

He slept with the pillow against his chest, and when he awoke the next morning to the raspy call of the muffin man and the clatter of milk cans on the street below, he remembered for the first time in a while to pray. And then he dressed and climbed the last flight of steps to the studio where the portrait artist Wippell was waiting for him.

The small, elegant portraitist with the waxed gray mustache shook his hand and then slowly turned the pages of Robbie's sketchbook. "You have some talent and many bad habits, young man," he said at last abruptly. "Don't pay too much attention to what you feel about what you see, only what's there. Those who feel starve."

The portraitist closed Robbie's sketchbook. "Art is a craft, and for those who make it more, I have no patience. You've been accepted as probationer at the Royal Academy on my recommendation."

Robbie nodded. Some of Wippell's own portraits were displayed on the wall and easel. They seemed to be insipid and have no individuality. But who was he to criticize? Wippell was famous; Robbie was only a beginner.

At breakfast he met Mrs. Wippell, who was heavy and had a worried, unloved face. They had no children. But the worst thing was that Robbie had been in the city less than twelve hours and already suspected that he had no talent at all.

Write me, he said to the invisible Anton.

Some day this week, let there be a letter.

And then, carrying his sketchbook in one hand, a small, prepared canvas and a bag of some paints in the other, he stepped, blinking, into his first day in London.

After some wrong turns, he was pulled into the chaos of Regent Street on the bright, cold winter's day. The noise was deafening. Underground trains roared beneath his feet. The air was thick with coal smoke.

At last, he found the huge classical Burlington House, which held the Royal Academy of Arts below the exhibition rooms. Some of the greatest masters of the last two centuries had studied in this place. I'm here, he said to himself with awe, walking inside and touching the walls to make sure. I'm here. For a moment he felt nothing else.

All down the halls artists hurried to this class and that, young girls with hair loosely piled on their heads, great loose skirts sweeping the chalk-stained floors; older bearded men marching defensively as if to shield their work; and everywhere the talk of art clattering to the high ceiling gaslights. Everything was shabby, dusty. Windows were murky with city dirt. There were the expanses of easels across the great rooms, the smells of pipe smoke and coal braziers, charcoal sticks and pencil shavings and oil paints. Most of the students were older than he.

Robbie pushed open the door of the life drawing class.

He hung his coat on a hook, taking a smock which held the scent of some stranger, kneeling to unpack his pencils and paper. He leaned his sketchbook on a board and raised his face to the model who had just stepped onto the platform.

She was naked with full breasts and little nipples and red hair. So, this was what a woman looked like in real life! Could Anton have preferred…? Robbie bit his lip hard. He mustn't think of that.

For a few hours he struggled with the shapes of her breasts and hips. My uncle would die if he could see this, he thought. He ate something from a cart outside the school and drank bottled ale, which made him a little tipsy.

Then he found the painting class taught by the famous Augustine DuChamps. DuChamps paced up and down between the easels on long thin legs. He was perhaps forty; his narrow shoulders drooped. Robbie had seen some of his portraits and landscapes hung in the hall and was amazed at his gifts.

The students were to paint a vase of yellow hothouse flowers. Robbie carefully watched what the others did to prepare a palette. After an hour he felt DuChamps standing behind him. "First time with oils, eh?" said the teacher. "They are huge to learn, and once you start, you'll go on learning all your life. But you will learn. I saw the pictures Wippell sent to me. You're gifted. How long have you been drawing?"

"I was very young."

"Well then! Have you been to the National Gallery yet? It's just at Trafalgar Square. You must go; you'll see what can be done."

The next morning, Robbie walked into the National Gallery alone. For hours he wandered, staring at the dark portraits of Rembrandt, the Dutch masters who evoked their world miraculously and meticulously in the light on a kettle or a fish on a rough board, the country scenes of seventeenth-century Flanders. The great religious art shook his soul: pale white medieval Christs with round bellies from which drapery modestly slipped, and Marys ever kneeling by the Cross with uplifted eyes.

Another day Robbie went to see the new French artists, to gaze at the exquisite rosy flesh of Renoir and the luminescent gardens and flowers and beaches of Monet. After all these encounters, he felt shattered.

"What am I compared to those?" he burst out to Master DuChamps the next day after class was over and the others had left. The master had seated himself on a high stool near Robbie's easel. "I'll be a hundred before I can do what I want. I can see, but my hand is stupid."

"My dear Stillman, I'm sure you'll be elected to the regular students and stay here for years. You're living with Wippell? He's a terrible artist. For God's sake, don't listen to any of his advice. And give yourself time. In six months, you will develop a great deal. It's between you and your hands and the canvas, and then so much determination. Even now when I paint, I struggle to capture what I see. Every time. All our lives."

Robbie was so happy when he left the school, he felt certain there would be a letter waiting for him at home. There was not.

He wanted to cry. Still, he knew in his soul that Anton would write soon. Even if he was in Paris, Anton would send a letter. But it was only the faithful vicar who wrote.

My dear Robert,

Of course, I've forgiven you! Didn't you believe me? I miss you terribly, but I'm so proud of you. You honor the gift God gave you. Learn and make art, and time will reveal more clearly how you'll use your talent.

Langstaff

Dear Mr. Langstaff,

I've been here several weeks and am always missing home. I know many people, and sometimes we go out for dinner, but I smile and laugh and somehow feel *withheld* inside me. After I'm done with studying, I'd like to return to Nottinghamshire to live with you again. Would you mind? I ask myself who I am as an artist, not as a person. I ask myself where I belong. But I must stay here a time and make you proud of me.

My dear Rob,

Of course, you can come back here if you wish, but I'm sure by the time you graduate, you will have made another life there. The house is empty without you. It is odd indeed to play my sonatas without a listener, as Nellie is now almost completely deaf. The sketch you made of me in the winter hangs above my desk. I never sent it on to my sisters. I cannot bear to think of taking on another lad to teach, but the girls are doing very well in their school by the church, and one may go to university to one of the new women's colleges.

Months passed; the city flowered into spring and Robbie walked and painted in the gardens. He worked fast, but he wanted to work faster. Summer was hot; he painted the Thames. Autumn blew in and he turned back to portraits of anyone who would sit for him. He used pencil, charcoal, pen and ink, and oils. He painted the parks again, starving for trees and the country. Walking through the leaves was the worst. He picked up a few and slipped them gently into his pockets. And he had friends, of course. He just didn't let anyone know him.

His closest friend was Annie.

Robbie first saw the tall young woman in late winter, when she had joined the oil-painting class, working with a stern fierceness as if no one dared interrupt her. She was very thin, with a long neck, and wore her hair loose in a spilling mass down her back to her waist; she had little breasts and didn't wear corsets. He met her after class one day outside, and they began to walk past the gorgeous Georgian houses of Mayfair to her flat in one of the older streets in Chelsea, crammed with derelict mansions.

"Wait here; I need to go up and bring bread to Mother," she said. "We live together, just us." Flatly she added, "Father's gone, brother's off in Australia. Mother's always ill, but she writes fast novels, bless her."

Later he found out that she supplemented the small household income by taking in sewing, and in between she took classes. "I'm going to be a great artist," she said proudly.

He loved her long, loose dark hair.

Once, she admitted she was hungry. He took her to an eel pie restaurant, and they gorged themselves. He also lured her to the colorist shop and bought her many colors of oil paint. He had to use some of the money he had hoarded; he didn't tell her. For the first time, she cried. He put his arms around her in a doorway.

"Whatever I manage to do in art, I'll show you the way."

"You'll be famous."

"I've hardly begun."

"You go straight forward," she said, and they stood in the street for a long time talking.

He told her many things about himself but nothing of Anton. Somehow, he felt she knew. And always at the end of their time together, he became anxious and thought, Perhaps he's written me. Perhaps there's a letter at the Wippells'.

But there still was none, though he willed it to come.

In eight months, there had been nothing.

It grew to a hot longing within him mingled with shame, anger, and bitterness. He was drawn to some men he saw in school and in the streets, but he did not know whom he could approach. Approaching the wrong man could mean the end of everything: arrest, prison. He remembered George Langstaff's warning. And no one he knew seemed to be his way.

Some autumn evenings, he locked his bedroom door in the home of the Wippell family and, balancing the sketchbook on his knee, drew Anton from memory. Once he drew him naked from the back washing under his arms at the blue flowered china basin on the washstand. The drawings became erotic. Outside, the darkened roofs of London slanted away to the streets as midnight came to the great city. After he slipped into bed, he touched himself and, when it was done, felt so alone.

He thought, I will be alone always.

Still, he thought, Master DuChamps was right. I can paint a little. I have begun.

One day in class he approached the red-haired model and asked if he could make her portrait. He thought he would enter the Student Portrait Competition. Suddenly he had a goal.

They were standing before the teapot and heavy white cups in the social room; other students lounged about on old soft chairs, and art hung on every inch of the wall. He looked into the gold lights of her eyes.

"I could come to your rooms, Rose," he said. "I'd like to paint you in your home."

She asked mockingly, "Where I live in Whitechapel? No gentlemen goes there except to sleep with the girls. Even the coppers don't go there. No one has nothin'. Babies found in ash bins. It's where that murderer chopped up all those girls a time ago."

"I want to go. I'll pay you."

"Well then, suit yourself," she said, leaving him with a click of her heels.

He set off one afternoon after his painting class, telling no one where he was going.

The omnibus took him first past once fine houses turned to boardinghouses; then the streets grew smaller. He gazed through the dirty window as they led into narrow alleys not four feet wide (so dark you couldn't see the sun) and spilled out again into shabby shops: a butcher's with one carcass of a pig hanging, stalls of limp rags, stalls of stale bread, innumerable public houses. Women hurried home with a bit of food in their aprons. The stench from the gutters made him feel a little sick. Something in him said, "Turn back," yet he would not.

Cautiously descending the omnibus steps at the street Rose had given him, Robbie wandered lost until one old man indicated a brick house above a laundry. Two women with babies cooed at him and said, "Come to pay for what a girl has, are you now?" Their sharp laugh followed him as he mounted the broken stairs with a small canvas under his arm, a box of oil paints, and his light folding easel. He went carefully because there was no light. The chorus of women called up after him from the street.

Rose stood in shadow in the fourth landing with crossed arms, waiting for him. "Didn't think you'd come," she mocked. "Saw you from the window."

"I told you I would."

"Please yourself, then."

She opened the door and he walked inside.

The one small room was almost entirely filled by a heavy bed with a wood frame and a neatly folded quilt. A sour smell rose from a chamber pot or from the floor. "Did you expect a palace?" the girl mocked. "Can't afford it. I'm the only one wot earns. There's me mum and two sisters. But your sort lives in mansions."

"One day you'll do better."

At his words, her mouth softened to that wistfulness he had seen in her. She said, "We could have tea. Hot water costs a penny. They sell it below. And another penny for cake."

He gave her the coins and she ran off and he soon heard her breathing harder as she returned up the stairs with her cannister. She made tea, pouring the water over used tea leaves. No stove of any sort, he noted. A fireplace not used in some time. "Do you fancy gin in your tea?" she asked, looking up brightly.

He shook his head. The impressions of the place were overwhelming. Everything—the cracking walls covered with torn magazine prints, the thin quilt, and the beautiful girl in the midst—formed into a painting in his head. He had to paint this; it was a physical ache in him.

"Tea first," she insisted. She winked and poured gin into a tin cup.

It went to his knees at once. Still, he set up his light easel and canvas and began to prepare his palette. He had to sit on the bed; there was only one wobbling stool, and Rose had taken it.

She leaned forward and sideways and pressed her mouth against his. "You're handsome," she said. "Oh, what a darling it is!" She sat beside him. He felt her small hand creeping under his vest and between the buttons of his shirt.

He shook his head and took up the brush. "Stop!" he said.

"Why, what? All the students want to sleep with me."

"Do you let them?"

"If they're nice. If they buy me something."

"I want to paint you, that's all," he said. "I'm here to paint your face and your room and the window behind it. It's because there's such longing in your face…something I once told an old friend. Everyone wants love; everyone wants what others are most unwilling to give…tenderness, approval. Most of us hide it. But it is what it means to be human."

"What stuff you talk! Three shillings to paint me, and I won't charge a penny to unbutton your trousers."

"Only the painting."

"Then I want red shoes too. With heels and ribbons."

"Red shoes then! Be still—let me work," he said. He already had sketched her in pencil and now painted fast. He feared it would all go before he caught it.

An hour passed. From the window behind him, which overlooked dozens of sagging ropes weighed down with wet wash, the light was beginning to fade. "Don't talk; your mouth changes," he said impatiently. He was fighting the moving hours and the remains of gin inside him and the strange way her tickling hand felt against his cheek.

He picked up another brush. "Just half an hour more," he said. His hands were cold; there was no heat in the room and the first days of November were upon them.

After three hours, Robbie carefully secured his wet portrait in its protective frame. Rose insisted walking down to the street with him and once there, stuck her arm in his. "My shoes!" she said suddenly. So, they descended broken stone steps to a dusty shop, and he bought her the red shoes.

Outside the shop in the twilight, he felt the last of his passion for his work drain from him. His shoulders sagged from weariness. Oh, Anton! he thought. He looked down the street. He knew then. There was no letter waiting for him where he boarded. Eight months had passed and there would never be one.

She sensed his sadness, looking up at him, now touching his arm gently. "Oh, that's it," she said softly, for women with children and men coming home from work pushed past them, their bodies brisk and warm. "Oh, that's why! You're a nancy boy. Anyone else would have had me skirts up! Such a pity! I could love you. I suppose you go to the Crown to meet men. Our neighbor used to go there. It's a public house on Charing Cross Road. Coppers don't touch it; someone pays them to turn their eyes."

He was speechless.

She stroked his arm. "You go there," she said gently, almost motherly. "Take care. There's someone nice for you perhaps."

As the omnibus pulled away, he saw her looking after him and though the light was gone, he made out her small red-heeled shoes on the broken cobbles.

Robbie left the Wippell house on a late November evening and walked to Shaftesbury Avenue to the top of Charing Cross Road. There he saw the lights behind the window of the Crown public house. He walked up and down the block to calm himself and almost went away again before turning back and pushing open the door.

He had never been to a pub of any sort alone, only a few times in Nottingham with Anton, and the feeling of men together away from their wives for the night had been very different from this. He felt his way carefully between the strangers, past the thick smoke of cigars and pipes, aware of the warmth of an arm or someone's back under a rough tweed coat. No one noticed him; smoke rose and circled about the dim gas lamps. He walked to the bar and asked for a small glass of gin. Like Rose's special tea, it went to his head at once.

After a time, he became aware of an older man with a worn, wary face watching him. Robbie could feel his eyes. When Robbie turned his head, he saw himself in the scuffed mirror as the man might see him, a young man with a sloped nose and unkempt curling hair who badly wanted to be touched and no longer cared what he had to do to get it.

The man said, "What, here all alone? A nice young fellow like you?"

"Yes, alone."

The stranger called for another small glass of gin and offered it to Robbie, who drank it quickly: it burned all the way to his stomach. Perhaps I'm not nice, he thought. Liar, bastard, and in my hands there's art but I don't give a damn about that now.

"I'd like to get to know you better," said the man. "This is a noisy place to talk. Suppose we go to my house. It's not far from here, you know. What do you say?"

They walked over the cobbles, now wet from rain, and found a hansom cab. Robbie looked at the puddles from the window and people coming down the sidewalk laughing as sweat formed under his armpits. This is not me, this is not my world, he thought. But it's just for tonight. Tonight I need anyone. They mounted the carpeted stairs of a private house into a beautifully furnished bedroom.

"Now," said the stranger, shutting the door, "let's know each other better? Your jacket's wet; won't you take it off? You're new at this, aren't you?"

There was the fat hand under his shirt and against his belly, and then in the front of his trousers.

"You'll like it very much, you know," was the whisper. Then there was the stranger's mouth against his groin. Robbie threw back his head and at the end shouted. Afterward his knees shook so he could barely stand.

"Ah, you're lovely," said the stranger, and he folded some bank-notes into Robbie's hand and took him downstairs to put him in a cab. Robbie didn't understand he had the money until he was on Wippell's doorstep. Running upstairs, he bolted the door to his room and looked around. Here was his ordinary life waiting for him: his soft pressed clothes, his art supply bag, his sketch books. Once more he glanced at the desk, hoping, but no letter had come. Still, he would never go to that place again. Never.

His resolve lasted one week, and then his need drew him to the public house once more, where he met the same man, who didn't recognize him at first. They returned to the house. "Ah, you're lovely!" said the stranger again, and stroked Robbie's thighs. Robbie never looked at the man's face and after that forgot him. One night the man didn't come to the public house, and Robbie went home with someone else.

When he walked into painting class the next morning, everyone gathered about him. "You've won second prize in the exhibition with your *Girl from the Slums*," they exclaimed. "The youngest artist ever to have won." And his teacher DuChamps asked him home to dinner with his family.

They walked in the early winter evening, down streets with

small townhouses filled with writers and artists. They passed the British Museum and then continued under the heavy trees of a park. Thoroughly lovely, soft lamplight shone on benches and then gates. As they walked, Robbie felt nothing but gratitude for the news of the day and that this teacher who had taught him so much. Gratitude burned within him; he could not say enough.

They walked through a square down another street and DuChamps said, "There it is!"

Gaslight showed the dark redbrick house with white window frames. They passed a perambulator and ascended one flight to a room with paintings covering most of the walls, two or three dogs, and what seemed like at least four children; the two smallest girls, under five, gathered around him. Mrs. DuChamps hurried inro the room wearing an apron and gave him a hug.

At the dinner table everyone talked at once. After the meal and coffee, Robbie sat on the floor with the girls and built magical things with blocks and told them stories of princesses and elves. He felt a comfort in them. Here's life, he thought, this warm place...and I am safe here. I'm the safest since I came to London.

At the end of the evening as they returned the blocks to their box, Mrs. DuChamps said thoughtfully, "Robbie, my husband says the artist you live with is a difficult man. No one in the art world thinks much of him."

"He doesn't like me."

"He's jealous," DuChamps said, taking his pipe from his lips. "Look, dear fellow! Why don't you come live with us after New Year's? We have a spare bedroom. Mina and I would love to have you, and my girls hardly will let you go home tonight, as you see."

Robbie walked all the way home from Bloomsbury, thinking, If I can do that, I'll be good. I'll never go home with strangers again. I'll find a new life. I'm twenty now. Old enough not to take silly risks. He was so happy that he did not wonder if a letter would be waiting for him.

There was one on his desk, but it was only from the vicar.

He picked it up, loosening his collar and draping his coat over the chair with his other hand. The lamp left pockets of shadows about the room. He turned over the envelope before untying his shoelaces, then dropped it in the drawer with the many other letters from his old teacher which had come before. The truth was, he had hardly read them all. Now after he put on his pajamas he stood looking down at the envelope in the open drawer. It was likely news of the parish, people who sent their regards, but never, never the news he wanted most. The vicar had never written one word of that.

Robbie sank into the desk chair and opened his letter. Yawning, he skimmed the paragraphs of the first two pages. Dear Mr. Langstaff! he thought. I'll write him about the prize tomorrow. I'll tell him I'm moving to a wonderful place in Bloomsbury with my teacher's family.

He brought the page closer to the lamplight. It was when he was skimming the third page that he noticed the word "Antonio."

He breathed slowly. He smoothed the paper. The name danced in the light.

The old slight trembling in his thighs and stomach began almost imperceptibly.

> I should tell you before rumor reaches you that Antonio has been home for a time. His marriage sadly had ended, and he's taken a position in a bank in Nottingham. I hope this will not keep you from coming for Christmas in a few days. He'll be away in Scotland then. He mentioned he's thinking of marrying again.

Robbie read the page several times, trying to rearrange the words. He lay down in bed on his back still holding the letter, folding it into smaller and smaller pieces. His whole body was trembling down even to his feet. Anton doesn't ever want me again, he thought. He divorced and still he never came back. He's marrying again. I should go on.

Turning on his side, he was too stunned to move for some time. The trembling was so intense now he felt that he would fall apart. He lay awake for hours and woke to find the lamp had sputtered out and left the smell of burning oil in the dark room.

A few days later, Robbie wrote the vicar a brief letter saying that he was too busy to go home for Christmas and later, sent him several jars of marmalade and a book. Late Christmas Eve, he slipped out of the house and set off to the Crown on Charing Cross Road to find someone to hold him. He never asked the man's name or looked at him. The next few nights he went as well.

Annie was standing at the Wippell's door when he came down the next evening just as darkness had fallen. "Where were you off to?" she asked.

He spoke nonchalantly. "Just a walk."

"I was coming to see if you'd take me to dinner," she said, shivering before him in her light blue coat. He bit his lip, repentant. The truth was that for the past week or so, he had forgotten her.

She took his arm, and they walked for a time and then turned into a shop for fish and chips, bare uncovered tables furnished with bottles of vinegar and jars of salt. It was full of working-class men and women and smelled of old cooking oil.

The food came and he touched his fork but did not lift it. She had taken several ravenous bites and then noticing him, ceased to eat.

"You're eating nothing," she said. "Tell me what's happening."

He turned away a bit to study the chalked sign board with the menu on the wall. He shrugged. "I don't like myself, that's it. That's all."

"Are you proud that you won a prize?"

"I don't know."

She took his hand and kissed the knuckles. "Mates always," she said. "You can tell me anything."

Tears filled his eyes. When they left each other on the windy corner, he wound his muffler around her neck and shouted at her when she tried to give it back.

Five days after Christmas, he left the pub with two men he had never seen before. Even as he mounted into their carriage, he had an uneasy feeling he had made a mistake, and yet there was a darkness inside him that made him mutter recklessly under his breath, "I don't care."

One man was perhaps forty, his face half hidden in his muffler; the other was older. Robbie noted that they went past Oxford and Mortimer Streets. The younger of the men wore thick glasses. When he noticed Robbie watching the streets, he pulled down the leather shades over the windows. "I want to get out," Robbie said suddenly but the man grabbed him hard and covered Robbie's eyes with his hand.

They climbed the few steps of a house, and the older man muttered something and seized his arm. A door was opened, and he was pulled down some steps to a basement. The man's hand was no longer over his eyes. He could see.

His heart was rushing. The words tangled in him: I shouldn't have come but I don't care.

He looked about.

The large room was furnished with dilapidated red velvet chairs, on which sat several boys under the age of sixteen; they were astonishingly beautiful and wore women's lace chemises over their pale, narrow chests, and long, extravagantly layered petticoats. Their eyes, darkened with kohl, looked disinterestedly at him, and their mouths were painted deep red. A child about ten years old walked with a faint sway like a miniature imitation of the girls in the variety shows, with a dipping of his bony white shoulders.

Who are these children? Are they kept here to be used? he thought. They look as if they expect it. They have no feeling. I need to help them and don't know where I am.

He thought, When they come for me, I'll knock them sideways. I'll run up the stairs. Then somehow, I'll find the address and bring help.

But no one came for him, and to calm himself he sat in a corner and drew the painted child on the back of a music-hall notice he had found on a table. In the smallest letters possible, he wrote, "Child prostitute, London, late 1902." He carefully folded the drawing and slipped it into his pocket.

"What are you doing here, old fellow?" asked the child with painted lips.

"What's your name?" Robbie asked.

The child was coyly silent. "He's not to tell," another boy said. "They beat us if we tell. They gave him a new name but he can't remember it."

Robbie heard rapid footsteps, the door flung opened, and the two men came into the room. He tensed his arms to fight, but they overpowered him. One of them shoved a cup to his mouth and said, "Drink this." His head was tilted back, and he was forced. He tried to spit it out and was punched in the stomach so that he fell. They held him again, and what tasted like whiskey was forced down his throat.

"Goodbye, old fellow," said the child wistfully.

The men dragged him upstairs and then up another flight and into a room with a bed covered in a worn, stained quilt. He was flung on his stomach and his trousers pulled down. Someone mounted him and thrust down inside him. He felt he was being torn in two.

"Stop!" he gasped.

Then all he could do was bite the stained cover to stifle his screaming. One man finished and the other began. Robbie twisted and fell off the bed; they pulled him back by the leg. His punches fell limply through the air; whatever he had drunk was drugging him. He stood and fell. "I'm an artist," he tried to shout. "I don't belong here." This is the end for me, he thought. What have I done?

He heard their laughter and knew nothing.

Robbie woke hours later lying on the street against a wall at first light; a ragged worn woman was shaking him. Above him was the side of a theater with its pasted posters on the brick. He felt his body and his greatcoat buttons. Someone had dressed him. He remembered what had happened and began to shiver. His rectum was in a fire of pain. He stood and cried out. He fell and rose again. He tried to make his way toward the Wippell house, trying to remember the streets and turns. At one point he went careening into a milk cart and was cursed. Tears ran down his face and people looked at him strangely. Two girls approached him, but he waved them off.

He kept to the walls, his shoulder hugging them. A policeman approached him and said, "Here, are you sick? Has there been trouble, young gentleman?" Robbie's coat, though dirty, was of fine wool, so he was treated well. The benign face of the youthful officer looked after him as he went on. "Set upon? A fight? Up all the night drinking? Move along now. Go home to your family."

The world was filling with light of day.

He felt blood ooze down his leg under his trousers.

When he reached the door of the house, he found his key and limped up the steps to his room. It sounded as if no one was yet awake. Something in his jacket pocket crinkled; he took out the folded drawing.

He washed, leaving the water in the bowl pink with blood which he dumped out the window to the alley below. How sick am I? he thought. Now his heart jerked about in his chest. He knocked into books and sent them tumbling. Will I die?

He slept all day, managing to leave a note on the door that he was ill.

When he finally rose from bed, he found a letter from DuChamps slipped under the door. He had to focus his eyes to read it. "Where are you, Robbie? Why weren't you in class last week before we closed for the holiday? I hope to see you on New Year's Eve. Some artists are coming who want to meet you, and we can make plans for your stay here. My wife is delighted."

Robbie didn't answer the letter; he hid the drawing.

The pain lessened over three days, but he dreamed he was being torn apart and woke sweating with fear. His lungs burned.

"Dear, are you ill?" Mrs. Wippell asked when she came to his door with a tray of food. "My husband's away."

He felt that either the world was disappearing to him, or he was disappearing to the world.

He went out into the cold bleak day.

He couldn't understand what people were saying. He couldn't judge the height of curbs and was afraid of falling, and sometimes he thought the houses on the square were tumbling toward him. He saw no one but a fellow student. "Do you know where Rose is?" he asked hoarsely. "The model with red hair."

"No, haven't seen her in weeks. Where have you been, Stillman?"

Robbie shook his head and returned to the house, climbing up the stairs, and sat on the edge of his bed.

On New Year's Eve he didn't attend the gathering at the DuChamps house. Instead, he went to the Crown on Charing Cross Road, though he knew he would never dare go home with anyone again. He found a stranger who kissed him gently in the alley near the street outside the pub. A carriage rolled by and a man in a top hat stared at him from the window. A woman sitting next to him said, "Disgusting! Ought to lock them all up."

He had come inside to warm himself by the fire when the door suddenly flung open, and the Crown was filled with rushing police. Robbie ran through the back doors into the alley, knocking over ash cans, hearing something crash. No one followed him, but when he reached the Wippell's family's street, he found the portraitist waiting for him in dressing gown and slippers, a lamp in his hand.

"You!" he hissed into Robbie's ear. "I said it couldn't be true. My good friend saw you not half an hour ago in an alley in embrace with...a...he knew it was you. He drove at once to tell me. So that's where you go at night. I just was in your room. What are those disgusting drawings of men?" Wippell wiped his hands furiously. "You're one of those *unspeakables*. They ought to send you to prison for hard labor and give you a sound whipping. I'll keep silence on this matter, or my name will be ruined. And you were recommended by a clergyman!"

"Leave me alone! Do you care about the children? Does anyone?" Without explaining, Robbie ran up the steps into his room.

On the morning of New Year's Day, he left the house. He walked out without coat or hat and wandered around the city until he reached the King's Cross train station, but he didn't have enough money to buy a ticket. When he returned to the artist's house, he found that Wippell had gone from the city again and Mrs. Wippell let him in against her husband's orders. "What is it, dear?" she asked again and again.

Robbie mounted to his room and locked the door, refusing to allow the physician she had sent for to enter. After a while, he heard DuChamps's voice as well, as his painting teacher banged on the door. "Answer me, Robbie!" he shouted. "What's happened? Annie's with me. We care about you. She's crying. Robbie! We can help you."

No, you can't, Robbie thought. No one can.

He lay in silence with his knees drawn up against his chest, shivering, fully dressed under two quilts. But the voice he heard the next day made him go to the door. George Langstaff, in his broad-brimmed hat and white collar beneath his coat, was standing in the hall.

The vicar pulled Robbie against him. "Ah, dear God!" Langstaff said. "Your teacher telegraphed me. You're very sick, lad. I'm taking you home."

12

Convalescence

January 1903

Bitter winter rain was falling when they arrived in the village late that evening and climbed into old Harry's wagon, protected by enormous black umbrellas. The gig's single glass lantern threw shadows on the path. As they drove past the houses, everything blurred for Robbie. All he heard was the rain on the umbrellas and the crunching of the wheels on the boards of the bridge over the stream.

Mr. Langstaff opened the vicarage door. "Now up you go slowly," he said. "Lean on me." Robbie climbed the stairs supported by the vicar and stumbled through the door. He dropped to the bed's edge overcome with coughing and chills and fever, which came in waves as Mr. Langstaff lit the oil lamp and shoveled coals into the squat portable stove. Robbie moved a little to allow the vicar to warm the bed sheets with the copper pan, and he stood up as his clothes were unbuttoned. Once tucked into bed, he saw the same dresser and the window and the curtain hanging lopsided as always. His room. He heard the vicar's voice on the stairs telling Mary she must run for the doctor. I'm home, he thought. I'm safe.

Then he knew nothing more.

Anton had been writing letters at his desk all that cold, rainy evening, head resting on his hand. The study had changed little over the past year, but books were now also piled on one of the chairs. He was writing to a college friend whom he had seen in London; he didn't hear the rapid footsteps on the stairs at first or the impatient knocking.

Mary stood with the rain dripping from her short cloak.

"I was at the vicarage to help and about to go home." She hesitated and lowered her eyes, feeling the pocket edge in her apron as she did when searching for words. Her wet laced shoes moved in place uneasily. "It's only that Mr. Langstaff's brought Mr. Stillman home and the doctor's just leaving. I thought you might want to know, sir. He's not been here for so long."

"My God," said Anton, "Stillman's here? What do you mean, the doctor's come? Is he ill?" He stood quickly and found his knees were weak. He hurried past her, down the stairs, and ran out without coat or umbrella into the winter rain and dark path.

A light shining through the white lace curtains of the parlor window allowed him to make out the stout figure of the vicar in his long, old-fashioned coat. He hesitated a moment and then turned the door handle without knocking.

"I see Mary told you," Langstaff said dryly. "The lad's come back with pneumonia in both lungs; it's bad. His eyes can't bear light, another problem. Mr. Eliot's been here and given him something to sleep."

"I want to see him."

The vicar's face grew stern. His voice seldom rose in anger, but it did now. The words sputtered. "You promised me you'd stay away from him."

"I have to see him! I won't wake him."

The door of the small bedroom had not been fully closed; Anton made out the narrow bedstead and the coverlet under which Robbie slept. He approached soundlessly and looked down.

Robbie's breathing was heavily congested and his hair moist with sweat. His eyelids wrinkled slightly, as if he feared his dreams. Anton pulled up the single chair and sat down by his side. After a while he pushed away Robbie's hair from his forehead and ran his fingers across the cracked lips. He had to stand for a few moments at the top of the stairs before descending again.

He asked, "George, in God's name, what happened? He's so thin."

"Mrs. Wippell told me she saw him eat almost nothing for

the last two months, at least not at their table. He was supposed
to come at Christmas when you were away. He never said he
was falling ill."

Anton nodded, opened the door, and went out once more
into the rain. He thought, I've no right to be there after what
I did, no right at all. And yet he felt strangely alive under the
rain, and his heart sang, and he said to himself, Even if Rob's
so sick, he's here.

He felt a life stirring in him he had not felt for some time and
walked quickly. He leaned against a tree in the rain, all coming
back that he had not allowed himself to grasp in eleven months.
He stood fifty feet from the vicarage garden in the dark with
the rain running down his face. His throat swelled with feeling.

Robbie slept, woke for moments, and slept again. He had talked
incoherently all the way home from London, bundled in two
coats, crying now and then. He had wept of his loneliness, of
his failure as an artist, of his father he had never known and his
mother dead so young, but each time the smallest hint of the
strange men who had touched him would force itself to his lips,
he gasped, turned away, and thrust it deep inside himself to the
dark place where all the things remained that he would never
say. That much coherency he had.

His body was in a fire of pain; every time he breathed it was
worse.

Over the next few days, the doctor's sister, long-faced Margaret Eliot, brought basins of warm water and alcohol to wash
him, and tall Mary from the farmhouse sometimes sat by his
bed knitting what appeared to be always the very same sock.
Candlelight and shadows on the wall dipped and moved. His
hand closed slowly, as if to feel a paint brush within it.... Si-
enna brown, he thought. The painting was of the streets of
Whitechapel, and he was struggling toward it, or it was inside
him and trying to find a way out. Then he was in the little room
again, with the sound of Beethoven rising up the stairs. I'm
here, he thought. The rest was a dream. I'm the vicar's student
again.

Snow began, and he lay in his bed watching the large flakes peacefully fall against the window and gather on the tree branches. Then he was on the parlor sofa with all the books gazing down upon him. Oil lamp flickering, the sound of a pen scratching.

Mr. Langstaff was reading the *Nottingham Evening News*, his feet on the footstool. The papers rustled, and the low voice of the vicar reached him from across the room. "Are you awake, lad? Mrs. Jordan from the parish brought you raisin cake."

He whispered, "Is Mr. Jordan well, sir?"

"Bless him, yes! He's four and eighty! I don't know what else I wrote you, lad, of news here. Everyone missed you."

From far away, the vicar's voice floated to him past the oval frames and the stuffed furniture. "My Nellie died—you know that; she was buried before Christmas. Life has such loss!" After a time, Robbie closed his eyes again and eventually heard the soft sounds of the first movement of Beethoven's "Moonlight Sonata" drift across the room. He thought wretchedly, My darling old Nellie. I forgot that the vicar wrote me she was gone.

Weeks passed. Parishioners came and went through the side door. He heard funerals processing to the churchyard from his window. It was all apart from him.

When his eyes hurt less, he skimmed through old copies of the *Army and Navy Catalogue* with the taste of Scott's Emulsion of Cod Liver Oil in his mouth. He lay on the sofa gazing at the walls of the small parlor and at the photograph of the Reverend George Langstaff as a young minister: scrawny, an awful, stiff collar around his neck, and his thick hands on the Bible.

Alone in his room that night, he looked at his reflection in the oval mirror. It was not quite the face of the boy who had gone off to London to study; it was more serious, and it seemed to him that the gentle lines at the sides of the mouth showed the sort of man he would be at thirty.

DuChamps had written; he had not yet answered the kind words.

Robbie asked Mary to cut his curls. "You look the proper soldier now," she said at his now close-cropped hair.

Finally, he began to draw the simple things about him: the upholstered chairs, the fire screen and copper coal scuttle, and the vicar with his back turned to him at the typewriting machine. One evening, he destroyed most of his erotic London drawings and forced them from his mind as quickly as he was forcing all other events of his life there from his memory. He thought, *Anton*—warm arms enclosing him, a comforting body pressing into his, that delicious weight above him and inside him. His own sighs and cries of pleasure. Lost somehow. The crackle of the fire, snow falling. Loving each other until the last bit of feeling was shared. "Do you like it a little, Rob?" He was too weary to mourn.

He would be all better again; the doctor had said it. Then perhaps he could remember the sequence of things and understand them. But for now, there was no London. There was no Anton. There was only art.

13

Late Winter in the Country

February-March 1903

Anton saw Robbie the first Sunday the young artist walked down the path to church with the vicar. He followed them, staying out of sight. He waited and then entered the church after the service had begun and sat in the back. He sang softly, and yet he knew at one moment that Robbie had heard him. He saw Robbie's shoulders stiffen.

But Robbie was not prepared to see Anton. Weeks went by, and all he had heard was Anton's voice. It was as if they were invisible to each other. In the middle of March, the cold lifted suddenly, and he came into the sunlit garden to draw, heavily wrapped in sweaters, seated on a stool. In the center was a bird bath; the ice, strewn with old leaves, had melted. A bird alighted on the edge.

He raised his head at footsteps as Anton came down the path.

Anton said, "I've asked about you every day. I hear you're better."

It took Robbie a time to find his voice. He said, "I am, thank you."

"George told me you're not returning to London."

"No, I'm staying here."

"You cut your hair."

"Why not? I'm not the same."

Robbie looked down at his drawing, which he had liked but which now seemed mere lines some fool had scribbled. He could feel his breath as it was trying to emerge from his throat. All the old natural things he used to feel! I could run to him, he thought, and throw my arms around him. It would be as if nothing had ever happened.

But he was silent; he sat heavily on the stool, motionless, swallowing, staring at the edge of the paper as if he had nothing to do with it.

Finally, he heard Anton's soft voice. "You don't look at me. Do you hate me so much? Yes, you would, of course."

Robbie flinched and slipped his pencils into his pocket. "You're not the way I thought you were when I first knew you," he said. "You're not honorable at all." His throat swelled. He could say no more.

He rose slowly and walked back to the vicarage. After a time, he managed to climb to his room. From his window, he saw that the path was empty as if no one had walked there today.

The following day, Mary came down the stone backstairs of the vicarage when he was boiling water for tea to hand him a note. He leaned against the great iron cooking range and roughly broke the seal. Bits of wax fell on the stone floor.

> My dear Rob,
>
> It's much warmer today. Would you like to take a walk? I'll be at the garden gate at two and will wait for you. Say yes, Rob.
>
> Anton

"I won't go," Robbie murmured under his breath. But the vicar was out, so there was none to advise him against it. At ten minutes past two he put on his coat and cap and opened the vicarage door. Anton was standing outside the gate.

Robbie felt as if he stood by the vicarage door for endless minutes before he went forward.

"We won't go far, Rob," Anton said. "Perhaps a bit past the old barn."

"Don't you have work?"

"Not today, no."

They set out toward the fallow field. Anton was wearing a

worn green flannel shirt and an open coat he might have bought at a church rummage sale, buttons missing or mismatched. His pipe was tucked between his teeth. Any sign of the elegant man Robbie had first met was gone.

Anton swung a basket of wine and food at his side; it was the same basket they had taken for their first walk. It seemed long ago. "Field's full of rabbits here now," he said clumsily. "I should sell it off, but I don't want strangers farming near, and I always mean to do something with it. The rest of the roof on that wreck of a stone cottage went last summer in a storm. I suppose you don't remember how you ran off in the rain one night and I followed you there."

Robbie didn't answer.

He saw the opening of the forest, the trees thickening suddenly, the sun sporadically finding its way through the thick, empty branches. It had been a year since he went away, and nothing had changed. The forest stretched before him: the English elms, the walnut trees all gathered as one, broken nutshells sheltered near tree roots. A conifer branch brushed his shoulders with its long, slender dark-green needles.

He heard the woodpecker.

"Is this too far for you?" Anton asked.

"I'm perfectly well."

"I went to see that very large oak a few weeks ago. It's been there for hundreds of years. Do you remember it? They say it can take an oak over thirty years to produce acorns, perhaps much more."

They walked into the cooler shade now; Robbie felt the damp from the earth and shivered once.

Anton asked at last, "So, did you learn a great deal in London?"

Robbie kicked a branch. "What do you care what I learned or didn't?"

"I do care. I think about you all the time."

"Did you have time when taking your pretty wife for walks? Oh, that's right, you're divorced. I don't know why I came out with you today."

He could feel that Anton hunched his shoulders a little at the words and tried to remain steady. "Well, then, why did you come?" Anton asked.

"You invited me."

"Is that the only reason?"

Robbie stared at the dirt path ahead. He muttered, "There's no sense avoiding you. You're here, or perhaps you won't be when you remarry. George said you're thinking of it."

Anton stopped and stared at him. "That's not true; I thought of no such thing. He lied, the bastard."

"Well, whether it's true or not, you've done enough."

"Rob, I've missed you."

"You drove me away." Robbie had also stopped in the path. "You chose your wife, even though you loved me best. Well, I soon forgot you. I slept with enough people to forget you and her."

"Oh, did you then? Fellow students I suppose."

"No, strangers. I went home with strangers."

He stared at Anton's stunned face and raised his voice. "Yes, that's what I did after you left me. Why shouldn't I throw myself away? You didn't want me! I accepted how worthless I was." A terrified squirrel ran up a tree and stared down at them. A late clinging brown leaf drifted down to Anton's shoulder.

"It can't..." Anton began. "It can't be the truth. Christ in heaven!" His voice rose and his eyes burned. "You damn crazy little fool. You could have been hurt or killed. Look at me. Didn't you know what might have happened?" He violently kicked a few branches fallen across the path.

Robbie shouted, "I didn't care. It was as if I wasn't there."

"You idiot, you little bastard! I'd rather you'd found someone else to love and I never saw you again."

"I didn't want someone else. Don't you understand? I wanted to stop longing for you. You said you'd write!" Robbie's voice rose in rage. He hurled himself toward Anton, punching him wildly, shouting, "You said you'd write, even after the thing you did...and I loathed myself longing for you. I still do. You said...you'd write...you said..."

Anton had raised his arms to cover his face but otherwise didn't move to defend himself.

Robbie said then, "I can't." He bent over with coughing.

Anton caught his arm. "Stop it—you'll hurt yourself."

"Let me go, you bloody bastard! It's not me I want to hurt."

"You need some wine."

"I don't want wine or anything from you."

"Robbie, sit down."

Robbie sat, feeling for the earth, as Anton knelt and held a flask of red wine to Robbie's mouth. Robbie gagged and spit it out, covering his mouth with his arm and leaving a wet dark stain on his coat. Slowly he sank against the tree. The bark was rough against his back and all the soil about him hard, full of dead grass and knobby roots. "Oh, the devil with it!" he sputtered. "Do you think you can still do as you want with me?"

When he looked up, he saw that Anton's eyes shone with tears. It shocked him, and he wrapped his arms around himself and clung close to his anger.

Still kneeling, Anton covered his eyes with his hand. He said at last, "I found out where you were studying, not that the old man would say a word. I went to London. I saw you, but you didn't see me; I hid behind one of the columns before the Academy when you came out of your school with your friends. I thought you were happy. I could have reached out and taken your hand. I had no idea what mad thing you were doing. I came home and accepted a local position, but since you've returned, I'm a shadow there. Every hour I think of you. The past week I haven't gone at all. Do you want to hit me again?"

"No." Robbie looked at the roots rather than at Anton, running his knuckles over their roughness. He was now chilled through, but he wouldn't say it. "Tell me about your time with your wife. What did you speak to her about, Anton? In the middle of the night, what did you say? When you went without me to Rome?"

"We never went to Rome. We talked a little. We tried to speak."

Robbie looked at the dirty hair hanging down Anton's forehead. There was nothing formidable about him, only something a little lost. "But you slept with her; you slept with her."

Anton slowly sat beside Robbie, making sure their knees did not touch. He said, "We never did; I couldn't bear it. I told her about us in Paris, Robbie, two nights after we went away. It was horrible for both of us. I went to Switzerland for a time alone and climbed a bit. I saw her again when I returned to London to sign the divorce papers. She told me she had guessed about you."

Robbie did not move. He had a moment's desire to put his hand on Anton's arm but forbade himself to do it. Instead, he arranged a pile of dry leaves with his long fingers and murmured cautiously, "So you're not marrying again?"

"No. I want you. I'm a little lost, Rob. There's something in me that doesn't know who I am but for loving you. Rob, be with me! You can paint all the time. I'll build you a studio. I'll watch over you; you'll never be alone again. I'll love you my whole life, I swear it. I'll give my life to you, whatever it's worth. I'll give you all that I am."

"I wish I could believe you."

"Let's go back. Give me your hand."

He stood and took Robbie's hand, helping him rise. Robbie took Anton's arm and they fell into a slow walk over the hard dirt with its twigs. Over wild grass, he saw the roof and chimneys of the farmhouse.

"We could have some hot tea," Anton said. "And meat pie and custard. That's best, I think."

"I'd like that. I'm cold."

"Take my coat."

"No. Anton, what did you do when you were alone?"

"Nothing much. I saw friends. I wrote to you."

"I never received any letters."

"I never mailed them. I couldn't. George wouldn't give me your address."

"What did they say?"

"That I was sorry."

"Were you, Anton?"

"Need you ask?"

"Did you really come to London and not speak to me? You didn't know how things were with me then."

"I never knew. Oh Christ, I never knew. And you wrote me and left it on the desk under a stone. I found it when I came home alone. I read it so often. Sweet words, Rob! Wise ones. I had no idea who I was. I never worked on my book. I never forgot you."

Upstairs in the study, after tea and a fragment of meat pie by the warm fire, when Robbie finally stopped shivering, their lips met, and they moved apart. Robbie took refuge by the shelf of books, the Darwin, the Shakespeare, the volume of old English poetry. "You spoiled it, you spoiled everything," he gasped. He shoved Anton so hard that Anton fell. Robbie dropped to the floor between the sofa and desk beside him; they held each other. "I'm sorry, I'm sorry," Robbie said. "I can't. You've got to make it the same. You've got to make everything go away."

He first slept on the sofa and then came into the bed, where Anton was awake. He wanted to be touched; he shrank from it. They finally went into each other's arms. In the darkest part of the night, they made love, clinging to each other. They were starving then and ate what was left of a tin of stale biscuits. He let himself be rocked in Anton's arms and buried his face into Anton's chest, his fingers threaded through Anton's tangled chest hair while outside the wind rose and the whole world seemed to blow away with it.

BOOK THREE

14

STUDY OF A HOUSE IN OILS

October 1905

On an October afternoon just a few weeks after his twenty-third birthday, Robbie walked rapidly down the path under the drooping branches, a small easel gracefully balanced on his shoulder and his paint box in his hand. A soft brown mustache touched his upper lip, and he wore a loose brown tweed jacket. He turned the curve toward George's medieval church.

Robbie set up his easel and canvas. Stone saints were carved in the door, their faces long eroded by the years. They had been worn when he came.

The heavy branches of the autumn trees danced shadows across the grass. He felt the light inside him move with his breath and began to paint. Still, when he stopped a few hours later, he thought: Why is it that the moment I've done my best, I no longer believe it's my best and there's more to reach for? What is there in me that makes it this way?

Anton had spent the afternoon in Nottingham arranging a transfer of some of his affairs to London. As usual, he wore corduroy knickerbockers, high socks, a loose jacket, and cap. His hands were calloused and his nails always a little dirty. In his jacket pocket was a packet of screws and two new screwdrivers he had bought in the dim light of the supplies shop. He whistled and sang an Italian folk song from years ago under his breath. *Bella ragazza dalle trecce bionda...*

He didn't need to hurry; he had no regular work. He had left the bank when Robbie returned.

He mounted the gig and told the old horse to walk on.

When his grandparents had lived here, the street was good,

but now it had degenerated into poverty, leading past the new, cheaper bulk grocery to the enlarged workhouse, with its old people staring belligerently at the world that had ceased to need them.

He turned to the side street toward St. Agnes's Church and stopped the horse in front of steps leading to the undercroft. The worn painted sign, reading Nottingham Socialists' Union, which he had known when he first discovered this place at sixteen, had been replaced by a newer one with the words Independent Labour Party.

Just then the door squeaked open and a heavy woman in her sixties appeared, her half-gray hair pushed up into a bun. Her dress was brown, and she still wore the same thick-lensed spectacles. She smelled of vegetable soup. "Mrs. Cullen," he said joyfully. "Mrs. Cullen!"

"Why, my heavens, Antonio!" she exclaimed, climbing the steps, and reaching up to grasp his hand. "I was thinking of you just the other day. I came to see your garden. The vicar's student keeps it beautifully." She gestured down the stairs. "Come down to our meeting room. It's not too tidy. We've just finished handing out soup to those who come. A lot today; we need to make more tomorrow. Did you know your old friend Mr. Burrows is now our president?"

Anton said, "Yes, he stopped by the other day and as always talked and talked. He's hoping to have a Labour man elected to the Nottingham city council. I know you've been trying."

Just then Burrows trotted up the steps carrying a few hundred flyers and a hammer; his jacket pockets bulged with a large wood box of nails on one side and a jar of paste on the other. His thin face opened with happiness seeing Anton; it was a face that usually looked as worried as it had when they'd met at the club as boys. He lived on a small side street with his aging widowed mother, as he had then.

"Antonio!" Burrows exclaimed. "Surprised to see you here! Just off to tack these posters up over the town for our next meeting! Mother was asking about you. I was going to bicycle over to you tomorrow. Regards to your vicar."

Still seated on the gig seat, Anton watched his old friend hurry down the street, stopping at one horse post to tack up a notice with two firm taps. He turned back to Mrs. Cullen and asked, "What are the chances of your Labour man winning the seat?"

"Small, but we must keep trying. The well-off get richer and the poor go hungry in this city. The nature of man's a hard thing. Yet one day perhaps we'll have enough votes to even send a Labour man to Parliament."

"I always wished that."

"I hoped always it would be you."

"Me? That was a long time ago, Mrs. C.!"

She looked at him closely. "Come for tea," she said. "Come help us. I used to feed you bread and honey when you were a boy. Do you remember? You always looked hungry."

"Kind, as always! Another time."

The air was fragrant with the coming of the fall, the dust from the wheels on the unpaved road settling slowly. Leaning forward, he let the reins dangle. Harvested fields spread on either side of him, and he clucked softly to the old gelding. His beautiful gray mare had died the previous spring, and he still missed her. Old Blackie patiently drew the gig. When he and Robbie didn't have to carry much, they used their bicycles.

Jiggling on the seat by his side were several packages for Robbie.

Robbie.

When the young artist had returned to him two and a half years ago, Anton had been so full of love, he hadn't known what to do with it all. He wanted Robbie to see the world and had taken him to Italy for a few months. Robbie's encounters with the works of the Renaissance in Rome were intense. They had traveled to Tuscany and found Anton's grandmother's farmhouse, now rented to tenants. They had visited Paris as well and searched out museums and shops for the works of the Impressionists. Then they had happily come home.

Now they had joined a local dramatic society, in which

Robbie was presently playing a deceived husband. Anton was teaching Robbie a little Italian, but not very often. Robbie also went two or three times a week to Nottingham to take lessons with a painter there called Angela Tippett, a widow who had studied with his London teacher DuChamps. Robbie said he was learning every day.

He and Anton woke in the mornings in each other's arms; in the summer they swam in the pond and in the fall wrestled each other in the leaves. They were intensely passionate together. For the sake of Mary, who came to keep the house three times a week, Robbie kept another room on the same floor whose bed linen he judiciously rumpled now and then. He was still a little less than six feet, but the slender gracefulness of his body made him seem taller, as if he were always reaching up. He moved quickly except when dreamy, and he was often dreamy. His face was stubbly by the evening or for days when he was too busy to shave. He had a small gathering of tangled brown hair on his chest.

They were peaceful but for Robbie's nightmares, which woke him shouting and thrashing. Anton would hold him and soothe him. I did this, he always thought. If not for me, he would not have been so desperate in London.

Anton moved the gig to allow a low, sputtering motorcar pass him on the unpaved road. After the village, he turned east toward the church. Early twilight was falling amid the trees, and Robbie was just slipping his easel and painting inside a little church door for safekeeping. Even drawing near Robbie, he felt the pull of him and that beautiful deep thing between them that they called *us*.

With a leap, Robbie mounted the seat. "Ah, there you are!" he exclaimed. For a moment they joined hands, and then pulled fingers away. "Did you buy apples? Give me one, will you? Did you go to Nottingham? Did you remember the paints and brushes?"

"Yes, and yes, sweet." Anton held up an apple. He said playfully, "Come, fight me for it." Robbie rammed his head into Anton's shoulder and grabbed for the apple. He shouted as Anton pulled his hand away. They struggled close, Anton feeling the young hard chest through Robbie's shirt.

"Tell me where you were today!"

"This morning I've been trying to shore up Mrs. Baggon's side wall, the one near the pump. Her husband's dead and she hasn't a penny."

"Ah, the lady we brought soup to last week."

"She sends her regards."

"I think you're shoring up half the houses of the poor in the county."

"It makes me happy. And then I went to Nottingham for errands."

They turned over the bridge and drew up before their farmhouse. They unharnessed and stalled the horse, then opened the doors of the old barn.

"I want to show you what I drew yesterday," Robbie said.

In this weather-worn structure, unused since Anton had moved here with his family as a child, he had built a studio with a comfortable sofa and tables and a model's platform with its soft chair. When they lit the three brilliant hanging lanterns, he could see the hundreds of paintings and sketches tacked everywhere. Large skylights reflected back the lanterns, their black glass glimmering though the edges of the room that remained in deep shadow. In the day it was flooded with light. On the easel Anton saw the nude portrait of himself drawn in brown ink from the back, hands clasped behind his head. He had sung sailor songs while modeling for the many versions of it, all the tunes he knew.

On the table lay two new drawings of a woman in a ruffled cap and apron looking into the distance. "Mary held still for me," Robbie said. "I made her stop working, and she grumbled. I'm giving her one of them. She hasn't chosen yet."

They held each other around the waist as they did when apart for some hours. Anton studied the drawings. He said, "How you see people...there, by her eyes.... And her mouth is impatient."

"What else did you do today?"

"I visited where my grandparents used to live. I also stopped by the branch of the Independent Labour Party in a church undercroft and saw my friend Mrs. Cullen. She wants me to join them again."

"You should, Anton! Mr. Langstaff says you were the best speaker."

"That was half a lifetime ago, my love. I'd prefer to be unnoticed except for those close to me. Now more so."

Robbie raised Anton's hand and kissed the knuckles. He said, "Did you send out that article this week on mining conditions to *The Socialist*? With my drawing?"

"I did. I asked them not to print my name. Yours is there. R. C. Stillman."

"Why, Anton? Aren't you proud of what you write?"

Anton said suddenly, "Robbie, I can't speak before people or sign my name after some of the things I've done."

"What things?"

Anton shook his head, and Robbie exclaimed, "We're so close, and there are still ways you keep me at a distance. You say things and won't say the reasons behind them."

Anton couldn't speak for a time. Then he said, "There are still things I can't face. I'm sorry." He drew Robbie against him, so they stood chest to chest.

He said, "Listen to me, love. Do you know before you came into my life, I used to want to go off with a bag over my shoulder and leave everything the old man gave me, every penny? But you changed that. Now all I want is to be with you, reading and walking and singing in George's church choir. Making sure you can paint. I have enough money so we can live like this until we're old. I want to take care of you. I'm happier than I've ever been in my life. Don't you know that? And we're safe. No one dreams of anything between us around here. They remember my years with girls. They suspect yours will begin soon."

"At least George is speaking to us again. Don't go off."

"If I do, I'll leave you everything."

"It's no good without you." Robbie paused. He murmured, "Anton."

They still stood close, though Anton had relaxed his arms. Robbie said cheerfully, "Let's spend tomorrow just us. Ride our bicycles into the forest. Find that medieval chapel with the frescoes. We have to be back by six for the church dinner."

That night for the first time in a few years, Anton dreamed of the Squatters' Field.

When he had discovered it at sixteen, it had been full of tumbledown houses, some old stone, some wood. A group of family and friends had recently settled there, with hardly a penny to their names. The women grew little patches of flowers under the drooping lines of wash. Some men had work and shared their earnings; women knit, kept chickens, and grew vegetables.

Through the wild grass outside the houses one day, a girl had come running to him, long golden hair down her back. She had listened to him, she had adored him, he had walked hand-in-hand with her. It was that confused year when he had turned from the boy he loved in school and had begun to speak on socialism. In a sunlit grove in the forest, he had tried to teach her to read. Instead, she climbed on top of him. And then one night she had walked all the way to his house, and he came down in his night shirt.

"There's a baby in me," she had managed to say, sobbing softly.

In that moment his life changed. "I'll marry you," he said. "I'll find work."

But when he returned from school again, she was gone. No one knew where. And then eight years on, the houses of the Field were torn down, and the people scattered.

The Field lay five miles to the north.

Anton never went to see it.

He realized he was awake in his bed and that there were tears on his face.

15

Autumn Days at Home

October-November 1905

The division between them and George Langstaff had begun to heal only last spring, when Langstaff fell seriously ill with a chest infection which moved to his lungs. Letters and visitors from about the county came for the vicar. As Robbie read aloud to the convalescent man a few hours each day from the psalms and from detective stories, he leaned forward a little to silently ask for understanding. By the time the vicar was well enough to work in the garden, an unstable peace had come between them. It could never be more than that, it seemed, for the vicar had muttered, "Whatever's between the two of you will bring you nothing but unhappiness."

"Well, damn him then!" Anton had exclaimed. Flinging himself down to the sofa, he had said, "It seems like happiness to me. You he partially forgives; he thinks it's all me. He doesn't understand a bloody thing about it."

"Don't, Anton," Robbie replied. "We broke our promise, didn't we?"

"A promise of what? To make myself into what he feels I should be?"

Robbie hurried back to the vicarage, went in by the kitchen entrance, and, embracing the startled old man in the parlor, begged, "Can't you understand? Isn't there anything I can say to make you understand?" The vicar had waved Robbie away and ascended the stairs. Now fragment by fragment, Robbie began to bring back the trust between them.

The sound of the heavy black typewriting machine tapped in

the air as he walked through the garden this bright October day, a magazine under his arm. Inside, the usual books and newspapers were heaped on both sides of the desk. Robbie closed the door behind him, watching the vicar raise himself a little to bend over the machine and scrub with an eraser at some error.

"If you're typing up your sermons from manuscript, I could do that," Robbie said. "I'm faster than you and you've got other things to do."

"Yes, I've always a great deal to do. Visiting takes longer. I may take your offer to drive me in the gig now and then and for some of the typing."

Robbie bit his lip to hide his smile that his offer had been accepted. Watching the clergyman rise from his chair, he knew George's legs were in some pain and felt the bewildered compassion of a young man who ran fast down the path looking back at an older man who had always been his strength but was now a little slower each year.

He dropped the magazine on the table. "Here's the newest Holmes mystery story, George," he said. "Also, I've come to tell you something." Robbie folded himself in his usual armchair and tried to speak lightly. "You know, some people have been suggesting I exhibit in London. Master DuChamps from the Royal Academy wrote me about it. Anton's booked a private gallery. It's in six weeks, in December, but to tell the truth, I feel I'm just beginning and there's so much I have to learn."

The vicar regarded him thoughtfully. "I'm so proud of you," he said. "But how can you learn and grow? Antonio keeps you as if you can't do anything for yourself."

"He does not."

"That's half of what concerns me. What does he do for himself besides watching over you? He was excellent in his profession. Now he spends his time shoring up old houses for five miles around to be a good neighbor. Widows, orphans, the unemployed, the elderly. Strange for an educated man in the prime of his strength and intellect."

Robbie replied, "But we like the way things are. We're happy.

Whatever else he wanted to do, I'd cheer him on. I wish he'd become involved with the socialists again, but he says he can't go back now. He shuts off when I mention it. I avoid saying things that make him shut off, because then I can't reach him, and it scares me."

He folded his arms over his chest and flushed; he knew he should not speak of the emotional intimacies of his relationship with Anton, and yet sometimes he wanted to shout, "But damn it, vicar! You're the only one I *can* ask!"

He continued, "But, George, about the art exhibition. It's just suddenly I'm afraid I'm not ready, that I'll disappoint everyone. And London has bad memories for me."

"You were homesick and ill there." The old man still did not know all that had happened and never would.

Robbie dropped a kiss on the vicar's broad forehead. "Please allow me to come back in a few hours for that typing. I'm also glad to drive you anywhere. We both are."

In the three weeks following the conversation, Robbie didn't go near his studio. By early November, he knew he couldn't delay choosing which work would be displayed; someone was coming to escort the paintings and sketches to London to be catalogued and framed. They had been sent copies of the newspaper release stating that Robert Christopher Stillman, who had never exhibited before, would show landscapes, portraits, and still life paintings in mid-December at the Winchester Galleries in Drury Lane.

The thought made him sick.

Cold wind bearing the scent of coal fire set drawings fluttering from their tacks as he thrust open the studio doors once more. His paintings were stacked against the wall. He paced, hands clasped behind his back. Then he sat on the single high stool to stare down his work.

There were the oils of the shadows of trees upon the field, the roofless cottage, kitchens, the bridge with a cart and horse plodding slowly across; sketches in brush and ink, the vicar at his piano, and Mr. Langstaff's oldest living sister, Matilda, a pristine woman in a black bonnet. Robbie had drawn it last spring during the vicar's illness when she had come to visit.

Robbie folded his arms over his chest. It was all an outpouring of undisciplined love, but whenever was love disciplined? The predictable was constrained. He could recall all the hours he had spent in awe in London museums and galleries. A Rembrandt sketch of a bridge and cart, landscapes from the Netherlands, those of Corot...he couldn't make light shimmer like that! This was all greatness, while he stumbled on the very beginnings of his talent.

My God! he thought. I need four or five years more, yes, that's what.

He leaned forward with hunched shoulders, clasping his hands together between his knees. He thought, I need to somehow study more, then roll myself up and out anew like dough for bread until I'm more ready. I can't go now! No, we must stop this at once, have them say in the papers that it's canceled. People do become ill, die perhaps, cancel things. If I died, they'd have to cancel, wouldn't they?

It's not all I can do, he thought. I'll make an oil of the house, the way I approached it and found a world inside it. I never did it in oils. We'll carry it down ourselves, he thought, and at least that one will be good.

Opening the doors, he carried the easel to a soft pile of leaves, then changed his mind and bore it about here and there for some minutes until he decided on perspective. Within a few hours, he was so involved, he knew nothing more.

He almost didn't hear the wheels of the wagon on the soft path. Brush in his hand, he saw the carter Harry at the reins, shoulders bent and bony, unshaven as always. Besides him sat a slender young man as lovely and insouciant as an entitled heir of the wealthy. Robbie noted the pale face, the blond mustache. He might have stepped from the pages of an illustrated magazine.

"Good day," the young man said in a light Irish lilt, descending.

He shook Robbie's hand. Robbie noted the nails were pale and perfect buffed while his own were rough-cut and stained with paint.

"Mr. Stillman?" the stranger inquired. "Keith Donovan here. I'm the manager of Winchester Galleries, come to pack up your work for your exhibition."

Was he really? Robbie found words. "Come this way. It's in the barn."

The young man walked about looking closely at the work which was lit by the bright sky through the skylight. He walked slowly, hands behind his back. Finally, he said, "These are very good indeed! We never know what to expect. Where have you studied?"

"Royal Academy. Augustine DuChamps."

"Ah, of course!"

Together they selected the art to be exhibited. Robbie had already decided against the nudes of Anton; they were too personal. He also thought of including the small sketch in pencil he had made in the boys' brothel years before but couldn't face it.

He and Donovan slipped the last canvas and paper into two large portfolios. They discussed the specifications for framing. And then the work was loaded into the wagon and gone. Robbie, who was watching the cart disappear, was startled to hear Anton's voice beside him.

Anton said, "Rob, I thought we could stay in London for a few weeks after and go to theaters."

But Robbie's mind was elsewhere. The picture he had begun before called to him and blurred all else. He worked until the descending sun began to throw cool shadows over the house and land. Then he brought it into the studio and lit the lamps to study it.

Outside, acorns fell, leaves blew, branches rustled against the barn roof. He thought, Why, it's almost good! Perhaps I could do it.... Yet too dull, somehow, all browns and grays! It needs only something red, like a wheelbarrow.

He took up his brush. It was an hour more when he heard
Anton come in and say, "Supper's long set! Didn't you hear my
call?" and Robbie put down the brush. For some time after, he
was distracted, smiling vaguely, pulled so between his work and
his longing for food and sex that he was not quite sure where
he was.

16

Winchester Galleries

December 1905

He finished the portrait of their house on a December morning as the cold mist rose from the ground. On the bottom right corner of the painting, he wrote the words *Midlands Farmhouse near Nottingham Forest, 1905* with a fine brush and under it signed his name, R. C. Stillman. The paint was still not dry, and they had to pack it carefully.

They brought it with them on the train ride to London.

The huge, luxurious lobby of the Savoy Hotel on the Strand overwhelmed Robbie. The bellman ushered them into their two-bedroom suite, whose parlor overlooked the ancient River Thames. He could not wait until the man left them.

Anton had collected more acceptances to the exhibition from the lobby desk and sank down on the sofa to read them. "Here's Peebles, Rob!" he called. "We were at college together. He has three sons now. I'm so glad some of my old friends are coming. He wants to take us to dinner tomorrow night. Then he'll come to the exhibition opening the following evening."

Robbie dropped down on the sofa, looking at the unknown handwriting. He said moodily, "What shall we tell him we are together? Anything but the bloody truth."

"I would like to say that you're the love of my life, but I can't."

Robbie stood rapidly and walked about the room, past the vase of hothouse roses and the dish of chocolates. "Then what am I?" he asked. "The vicar's artistic student, I suppose; that's a respectable enough thing to be." He opened the drapes to the river further and said moodily, "So we'll sit with your friend for a whole dinner and lie about ourselves. At least the portraitist I lived with as a student died last year, poor old Wippell! He can't come forward and denounce me. Anton, you shouldn't have taken these rooms. They're likely horribly expensive."

"You mustn't mind it: I'm wealthy enough. And you've changed the subject."

"I wanted to change it."

They found the Winchester Galleries the next day in Drury Lane. In the window, a poster board announced Robbie's name. Inside, he saw most of the work he had sent to London beautifully framed and hung. They appeared to be the work of a stranger.

He bit his nail and glanced at Anton, who was looking at the framed pictures in the second room. Keith Donovan, the gallery manager, walked briskly from the office, followed by a workman in a wool cap. "How good to see you again, Mr. Stillman," Donovan said coolly. "We've a few more to hang. Do you like your two waifs in this corner? Your early work, by the date."

Robbie watched the pale, thin hands as they directed the workman exactly where the remaining pictures would go. They indicated, they hardly touched. Even papers were picked up by only the tips of those fingers.

Donovan said over his shoulder, "The gallery sent two hundred invitations to critics, the art world, society. Newspapers printed notices. We should have a crowd. The catering's excellent. There! Now all the work is properly hung, don't you think, Mr. Stillman?"

Standing together, they spoke more of the position of the paintings. Then Donovan paused. "If you're not busy tomorrow night," he said, "I could introduce you to some friends later, all artists. It might be a bore. I'll be here until eight, if you care to come. Mr. Harrington is welcome."

"Very kind of you!" said Robbie. "I'll ask him."

But Anton said he would join his friend Peebles as promised. "Go and meet some artists," he said as they left the gallery. "You'll like it, Rob."

The exhibition rooms were dark when Robbie returned just before eight the next evening, but the door was unlocked. Only a small electrical lamp burned in the office where Donovan was just closing. He turned his mild, round face and said, "Ah, there you are! Come on, then; it's in Holborn. Working class. Clerks and garment workers and poor artists."

"I know it; I studied here for a year."

"That's right, you did. Then you have a lot of artist friends in London."

"Some. It was a bit of a solitary time for me." He tried to make his voice gruff, but it came out wistful. Then his words brightened. "I knew a lovely girl, Annie. She's coming to the first night of the exhibition." That cheered him; until then, he had looked back at those student days with a darkness he wished to forget.

He and Donovan left the gallery and walked out into the evening. Through a restaurant window he saw people laughing, women in lovely taffeta and long white gloves. The sound of a violinist came through the opened door. They turned north.

"Have you studied in Paris?" Donovan asked as they allowed one of the new gleaming black motorcars to pass down the street before crossing.

"No, only visited there."

"Ah! I lived in Montmartre for a time to study and sat across from the great artist Toulouse-Lautrec once. We talked a little. An ugly, short man, quite deformed, but a genius. Is it worth being a genius to be so ugly? And now he's dead. Alcoholism and syphilis."

"I wish I'd met him. So, you're an artist as well. I'd like to see your work."

"Perhaps later you could walk to my rooms."

They passed Lincoln's Inn Fields and continued to a dark, narrow alley until they saw the light of the Old Mitre Tavern. Robbie heard the roar of voices before the door opened. So much smoke filled the air that even the light from the hanging lamps was dimmed. He remembered coming here with some students on a night he had been very lonely. A group of young men and women hailed them from a corner and waved them over; the lamp above the table cast shadows on the faces of the girls and the oiled hair of men. Robbie leaned over mugs and glasses to take their hands as they called, "Pleasure! Charmed! Take a chair!"

A scent of ale and fried fish hung in the air. One girl gathered her paisley shawl about her shoulders and said, "Keith says you're exhibiting at the Winchester. But don't they charge a fortune to rent the gallery? You're lucky you can afford it."

Another girl looked at Robbie as if measuring him up. An amateur actress in the local theater troupe at home had flirted with him last year, and he hadn't noticed it until Anton told him. This girl said, "Do you have a sweetheart?"

No one waited for an answer; they all plunged into the discussion of art. He was fascinated by the girls' loose clothing, as if it had been drapery wound about them on a whim, accented by their colorful beads and falling hair. It was the new look. In the reign of this more liberal king Edward, artistic women threw away their corsets. The young men were shabby and had dirty fingernails, and everyone raised their voices to be heard. Robbie drank a large beer too quickly. He thought, Why, this is the genuine life.

But after an hour, the noise was too much for him. "My head aches," Robbie whispered to Donovan. "Can we leave and perhaps go see your work?"

Together they turned down shabbier streets full of small brick houses that had once been private; now they were broken up into flats accommodating people who managed to cling to the lower middle class. Donovan's house was much the same. The vestibule was dark, and they took a candle from the table to light their way down steep cellar steps. When the gallery manager finally unlocked the door, Robbie saw it was cluttered with the detritus of a sculptor: the tools, and clay ground into the heavy cloths thrown over bare floors. The easel was empty; it was a room where no one had painted for a time. Some stationery for the gallery sat on the table, and there were notices of other exhibitions, a teapot, a biscuit tin.

Off this were one small bedroom and a fragment of a kitchen.

"My palace," Donovan said wryly. "Or rather, my half of it. A temporary reduction in my usual manner of living. My family has a house on Stephen's Green in Dublin; they have a lot of money. I grew up there. I shared this place with a sculptor who left owing me rent."

"I like it here," Robbie said. "In the cellar, hidden away."

"There's no light and no fire. You should keep your great-coat on. Whiskey and water and biscuits? I've little else. Do you like it mixed half and half?"

"Mixed with water, thanks." Robbie sank down to the small, squeaking sofa, and Donovan loosened his cravat and put it carefully aside. He poured the whiskey and sat down with a sigh. He said, "You're fortunate to have your exhibition in our gallery; it's one of the best smaller ones."

Robbie ran his finger around the rim of the glass. He said moodily, "I heard that young woman's comments. The gallery was hired. Perhaps that means I have no talent?"

"Nonsense! You have so much talent, you don't know what to do with it all; it comes from you, I think, in a volcanic way— or rather, you don't so much have it as it has you. My friend at the restaurant only spoke that way because she's jealous and she wants to sleep with you. She sleeps with everybody. I suppose I should show you my art now before I lose courage."

Donovan cleared the table of stationery and brought the lamp closer; he took a sketchbook and a portfolio from the wardrobe and opened them. Robbie rose to stand beside him. There were no paintings, only drawings, a great many nudes and women and men in evening dress. Robbie thought, But it's like a fashion artist who sees only what's elegant. He doesn't see the rest or is afraid to see. My old teacher Wippell would have liked it.

He murmured kindly, "This one's so fine. I like them."

Donovan said in a flat voice, "They have moments here and

there. With a little more work, I could be… But it's not like you, pouring out and out."

"Simply keep working. I keep trying."

"With you it's worth it." Donovan's face looked bleaker. "I've no talent. It's all I ever wanted, and I don't have it and I can't face it!" He began to gather the work, but Robbie felt Donovan's devastation as if the room were suddenly cold and shapeless.

Donovan laughed sharply. "Oh, who cares?" he asked. "Does it matter? Let's not speak of it!" He shoved the portfolio and sketchbook back into the wardrobe under the neat hanging clothes and threw himself back on the sofa, pouring more whiskey into both their glasses.

But he rounded his shoulders and did speak of it. His light voice grew heavier. He said, "For three years, it was nothing but art for me. I had some money from my family in Dublin and went to Paris to study for a time. When I first came here, I had spent everything, and I met someone wealthy. He was rather taken with me. He couldn't keep from me. He said he'd stand behind my work." He lowered his eyes, and Robbie saw how soft and long Donovan's eyelashes seemed.

This was how you said what perhaps should not be said, going deeper into an unknown lake, uncertain.

Donovan continued, rubbing his finger on the rim of his glass and looking into the whiskey and water. "You see, the truth is, I was in love with him, and he made me many promises, but then he tired of the whole thing. Then I lived with that fellow who works in clay. We were fond of each other for a while, but after a time, we avoided being in the same room."

The gallery manager sighed. "There you have it. Everyone's personal life is shabbier than when you first see it, Stillman. No, I'll call you Robbie if you don't mind. That's what *he* calls you, doesn't he? I saw at once what was between you."

The cold corners of the room touched them, and Robbie glanced once or twice at the narrow, solitary bed in the corner. For one moment, he envisioned this pale young man stepping from his unbuttoned underwear, and how the shadows of the small buttocks must curve under the hip bone. He hastily drank more of the whiskey and water.

Donovan said, "Tell me about your life in the country."

Robbie leaned forward with the glass held on his knee and tried to explain his world, but when he mentioned Anton's name, his face felt warm. Donovan lit a cigarette and drew in the smoke. He said, "May I say something? Your Mr. Harrington's like many men with money who haven't had to struggle. He bears himself so proudly."

"He's not proud and he does struggle; there are more ways to struggle than money."

"Do you love him?"

Robbie nodded. "Yes, very much," he said.

Donovan flicked his cigarette. "You may be gifted, dear, but you know very little of life. Why do you think he chose a younger man? He controls you with his love, and you will never become your own man until you break from him."

Robbie stood. "What's the matter with you that you say such things?"

"Don't go! I was rude. I'm sorry."

The room now seemed colder and more uncomfortable to Robbie. A half-formed clay bust of a woman in the shadows appeared like someone who had died a time ago, and the sofa hurt his back.

They drank more and ate biscuits, and Robbie turned the conversation back to the art world of the city. They had not noticed the hour until the clock chimed softly from behind the vase of feathers on the shelf near the door. "Ah, one in the morning," Donovan said.

Robbie stood clumsily. "He'll be worried for me. Look here, Keith." His words were unsteady, as was his balance. He laughed a little. "I can help you with your work. Will you let me?"

"Perhaps," was the low response, and then Donovan rose, his shirt wrinkled and his eyes a little dull. "There's a cab stand on the corner; let me walk you there." Still, they remained indecisively within the door of the flat in their greatcoats without moving. Then Donovan said, more simply than he had said anything before, "Help for my work's not all I need now. A kiss would be lovely. I'm rather in need of a kiss. Have you forgiven me?"

Donovan's mouth under the little mustache was soft, small and erotic and alluring as it was pretty. At once, the image flung itself again upon Robbie of his host's body in shadow, now turning, shape of knees and limp penis, the declivity of backbone. He took Donovan by the shoulders and drew him closer, kissing him several times. How slender he was! Almost as if he could be blown away with the wind.

Robbie broke away with an embarrassed laugh, wanting to wipe his mouth but not doing so.

Donovan threw back his head. "Oh, you sweet boy!" he said. "No wonder you're so loved."

In the end, Anton had not gone for a glass or dinner with his old friend but walked over to the Old City for a lecture in the ancient Guildhall which had been listed in the paper. When it was finished, he stayed until a charlady came to sweep and put out the dim electrical lights. As he left at last, he passed under the flags of the various London guilds, which spoke of the history of workingmen in London centuries before: The Worshipful Companies of Fishmongers, Ironmongers, and the Scriveners, the first booksellers. Darkened stained-glass windows broke the stone walls. The exquisite stone vaulting of the ceilings rose high above him.

For centuries, trades had banded together to protect themselves.

Now the wealthy, seldom the workman, took the profits.

He walked away, hearing some people singing from a pub. He had gone impulsively to this lecture by one of the greatest socialist speakers of his time. That was all that mattered.

He passed the small, ancient streets which filled this oldest part of London, approaching the great bulk of St. Paul's Cathedral. Shadows moved around the cathedral steps, people with heads hidden in blankets. He turned down Fleet Street, dark and quiet, into the Strand.

Anton reached the Savoy Hotel and took the elevator up to his floor, opened his door, and called, "Robbie!" But the rooms were empty; he saw Robbie's gloves, which Robbie had forgotten on the table. In one of the two bedrooms, Robbie's suitcase lay open, and tomorrow's formal black frock coat was draped over the clothes horse. The lampshades were fringed with little hanging glass beads.

Anton ran his hand through his hair, looking about. His chest tightened in this sudden loneliness. He had been far away; in his coat pocket, he still had the latest issue of *The Labour Leader*, which he had taken from a newly printed pile.

He sat down and read every word. Then he looked at his pocket watch once more and saw it was past two.

He was standing by the window in the hotel room over-looking the river when he finally heard the door open; then he strode across the carpet, knocking his newspaper from the chair arm to the floor. Robbie slipped into the room, slender and tall in his tailored suit. He had removed his blue silk tie and folded it in his pocket, but most of it had escaped and hung down his coat. By the way he walked so carefully, Anton knew he was a little drunk.

Robbie stood smiling slightly, swaying a little.

"Rob, where were you?" Anton stooped to retrieve Robbie's loosened tie, which had slid to the thick carpet.

"Donovan and I talked late," Robbie said. "We met a lot of artists. I forgot the time. How was your time with your friend?"

"I sent regrets. I went to a socialist meeting."

"Tell me about it," said Robbie, at once very interested and pulling Anton down to the sofa. "My evening was middling. Donovan's a bit of a bore. I wish I'd gone with you."

But Anton suspected Robbie did not feel as calm as he sounded. His palms were cold and his cheeks a little pale. It's nerves for tomorrow, he thought.

17

THE EXHIBITION

December 1905

Robbie's patent leather evening shoes had already begun to pinch him when they arrived just before five o'clock at the Winchester Galleries. It didn't matter. His body was filled with memories of the lovemaking between him and Anton last night. He sighed and thought, I am utterly, utterly happy and fulfilled. I don't give a damn about anything but him and me.

And there was Keith Donovan, his face and voice without emotion, saying, "My word, Mr. Stillman, you've dark circles under your eyes! Evening, Mr. Harrington. The champagne and caviar have arrived in ice, and the waiter is in the office. Let me just take your coats and hats and I'll put them aside for you."

Robbie looked about, startled. It was real; this truly was the first night of his art exhibition with his paintings on every wall. Yet why did they seem remote to him? He felt the need to walk away somewhere and think. If only his shoes didn't pinch! But there was no time as people began to pour through the door.

He pressed the hand of an ancient lisping woman, who was wrapped in enormous layers of fox with fox heads hanging down over her shoulders. Some men he didn't know pumped his hand sincerely. Anton introduced them, but Robbie forgot at once because the young artists he had met last night rushed through the door with the clank of beads and jewelry, all outshouting each other. "Oh, how splendid!" they exclaimed. "Cakes and champagne! Lobster on toast! Oh, marvelous!" Many more people came in.

They said, "So here's the artist! How do you do?" and he answered many times, "So glad you've come!" He drank one glass of champagne and then another. Yes, it was his art on the wall. There was the painting of the house he had made over the past weeks; there were the children, there was the housekeeper; but none of it seemed to have any relationship to him.

Near him a few men walked up and down before the pictures with hands behind their backs, muttering of *the artist's use of perspective and shadow.* Another man in black stood motionless before one painting, taking notes.

Then a soft hand rested on his arm, and a musical woman's voice said, "Robbie, it's Louise." He could smell the heaviness of rose perfume.... Louise, who was Louise?

The lovely young face above a pale green shimmering dress. Surely it could not be…

The only time he had seen her, she had been huddled in a chair in the farmhouse on a winter's day, fighting back tears, saying complimentary things to him about his work. He remembered bicycling madly to the Nottingham train station to find that she had gone away, taking Anton with her forever.

Of course, it had not been forever but still…she was Anton's wife or had been.

Under his waistcoat, nausea nudged his stomach.

She touched his arm again and he stepped back, bumping into the ancient woman with the fox fur. "It's Louise," she repeated. "The former Mrs. Harrington, very former to be told. You showed me your work. Now I see by your face that you remember. Dear Robbie! What a splendid evening, and how gifted you are! I knew this would happen to you one day."

Dear Robbie? He wanted to hurl her from the door. How could she behave so charmingly to him when he was the cause of…?

He was too appalled to find words.

Mercifully, someone else was calling his name, and he turned to answer a man who had taken notes on the paintings. Then a breathless girl with hair braided about her head wearing a loose paisley dress rushed in, and he cried, "Annie!" His dearest friend from his wretched student days was here as promised. They had written each other on and off for the past few years. She had told him she was still living with her sickly mother in the one huge room in a dilapidated eighteenth-century mansion.

He flung his arms around her.

"I'm so proud of you," she said.

"I'm so glad to see you! Are you painting, Annie?"

"I'm still not back in classes. I want to, but—"

"Oh, you must!"

He so wanted to speak with her, but someone pulled him away for questions. Now he could no longer see Louise, for it seemed all the people on the Strand had come here and were fighting to get by each other with cries of "Excuse me! Are all the delicacies gone? Please do not tread on my shoe!" Anton was nowhere to be seen and Annie had also disappeared. He had wanted to pull her to one of the small velvet sofas and tell her everything. If there was a sofa free. . .

He began to perspire.

Robbie nudged his way to the back of the gallery, ignoring voices who called him, pushed open the heavy door, and stepped into the cool night of the alley. After a moment, he began to breathe more slowly. He looked about with relief at the blackened bricks of the rears of buildings, the iron ladders, and as far as he could see, the endless sky.

The door squeaked opened and he saw Anton standing in his evening coat with the light behind him. He said, "Rob, everyone's looking for you."

He burst out, "Louise is here, Anton! Your... Don't tell me you asked her."

"I didn't. She saw the announcement in the papers. Don't look like that. She doesn't want me; she's happily engaged to a musician. Ernst Hauptmann."

"A musician? Really?"

Anton walked over and pushed back Robbie's hair. He said gently, "Ah, look at you! Don't drink so much. You're not used to it. Come back. Your old painting teacher's wanting to see you."

"*DuChamps is here?*" Robbie rushed past Anton into the gallery again. DuChamps was standing by the door as if trying to understand which way he could walk. His face looked tired as always.

"There you are!" his teacher said above the noise. "How your work's grown, the little I have managed to see of it from here. The two in the window are exquisite."

Robbie muttered, "It's not rubbish, is it?"

"You never have made rubbish. These solo exhibitions are very difficult. Everyone who has one worries so. Where are you staying? I'll telephone to make a time for you to dine with us while you're in London. My wife has missed you, and the children.... Thank you for writing."

At seven, guests began to retreat from the gallery. Louise had once more found her way to him, and said, "It's lovely there will be a dinner now! Anton just told me. Some people are walking. Will you walk with me?" And he thought, Oh God! Anton must have arranged a dinner and not told me. I want only him and Annie and my teacher and perhaps Keith Donovan. There are too many bloody people. And now she is coming also?

Robbie opened the door to a small room with a desk, type-writing machine, and piles of announcements. Again, his name stared at him from a poster taped to the wall. He took it down and, folding it, looked for a place to tuck it.

Keith was closing the account books. He said, "Well, the evening didn't go badly."

"Look here, they're taking me to dinner! Café Royal, I think. Come with us."

"Do you really want me there, Mr. Stillman?"

"I'm Robbie. Did you forget? Come with us. I want you there very much."

"Then I shall oblige. Go ahead then. I'll see you there."

Louise and several others were waiting for him on the sidewalk. She asked shyly, "May I take your arm for the walk? I was so proud of you tonight. My fiancé had a rehearsal or he would have come."

He gathered himself together into the gracious young man,

though he was increasingly anxious. "I'm pleased to hear of your engagement," he said, lowering his voice. "You're so kind. I want you to be happy." He tried to laugh and brought the back of his hand to his mouth. "I still feel strange when I think of all that happened."

She looked up at him and said simply, "I gave you a lot of pain, but I never, never meant it. But all's well now. Perhaps one day we could be friends." She lay her gloved hand on his.

"Friends?" he asked incredulously. He wanted to shake her off but was too polite. Instead, he gave her his arm and they began to walk.

He heard Anton's voice from behind him as they passed several closed shops. Sooty fog hung over the evening, bits of coal dust drifting down about them. How strange it all was! Still, he softened as she chatted on about the exhibition and her anxiety in meeting him again. He was feeling a little drunk and suddenly happy that it had gone not badly.

They turned a corner, and he caught his breath.

He stood on Charing Cross Road.

He dared not look more for he knew just some doors down stood the pub called the Crown, where he had run in loneliness to give himself away to anyone a few years before. How long had it taken for nightmares of it to cease? Robbie stared into the faces of men coming toward him on the street to see if they would be the same ones who had taken him. Old voices murmured in his head. *You, boy! Why, I know you. Remember where I took you and what you let me do to you?... Off with your trousers, boy.* I must not drink anymore, he thought.

Louise still held fast to his arm. "What is it, dear?" she asked, and he muttered, "My shoe pinches. It's just that. You're so kind to ask."

The small party moved through the doors of the Café Royal and once inside, were surrounded by statues of naked nymphs near huge vases of ferns and feathers. They passed from room to room. He heard crowds of chattering, laughing people and the strains of violins soaring over their talk. Popping corks made him start; waiters sailed by with enormous silver platters.

Robbie felt himself unwillingly pulled along. All that he really wanted was eel pie and a pint in a slip of a shop where he and Annie had once talked their hearts out, and to forget the street he had just seen.

At a round table, he found himself seated between Anton and Louise. She was close enough to make out the individual curls of her hair and her breath moving in her throat. How lovely she was! What was it like to be that small and delicate with such little wrists, such little breasts? Robbie could see the crevice of them. Had Anton kissed them? Jealousy filled his chest so intensely that his shirt buttons strained.

He reached for a glass of wine and took Anton's by mistake. His lips touched where Anton's lips had touched: for one second their eyes met. He sought Anton's fingers under the table, feeling the rough place where the saw had broken the skin a few weeks ago. Anton had shouted, "Where's the sticking plaster, Rob?" The private marks on Anton's body: the scars on the knee, one on the mouth, and some across the shoulders, the peculiar, jagged cut on the right wrist…yet they never discussed those, never, never.

He really wanted eel pie.

He drank his glass of wine in a few swallows.

All the people at the table had been at the exhibition, though he could not remember their names. But where was his teacher? Where was Donovan, who had promised to come? Damn Donovan with his cool independence! Where was Annie? He remembered now. His teacher had a sick child at home and Annie's mother also was not well. Perhaps Donovan would still come.

He drank more wine. He tried to follow conversations; he lost them. He leaned half across the table and pulled a rose from the vase and gave it to Louise. "Why, you're so courtly!" she said. "I'm giving you my card. Here's my address for letters."

A waiter set an unknown meat in brown sauce before him, and he began to eat rapidly, nervously. All the voices about him were babble. He sensed the warmth of Anton's shoulder near him. Desire rose. He imagined lying back on the table in the middle of the flowers, unbuttoning his trousers, and having Anton make love to him then and there. His penis hardened.

Oh my God, I'm very drunk, he thought.

You boy came the remembered voice. *Come here, boy.*

My God! Robbie thought. Here we are in London at my own exhibition, and we don't dare even to... If we were a proper couple, we'd have calling cards printed with both our names, and ask people to supper parties, and publicly share our happiness. Perhaps they would read, "Mr. Stillman and Mr. Harrington request the pleasure..." He wanted to rush off to the printers and have them done immediately and hand them out.

He turned because Louise smiled at him, gazing fascinated at the rosy crevices of her breasts, the hint of chemise lace, the depths of rose perfume and powders. He asked, "When shall we meet and talk?" I'm jealous, he thought. I'm jealous that she's engaged. What's happening to me? I would rather be in a shabby shop with the menu on the chalk board. She could come.

He had long given up following the conversations, or rather he went from one to another, coming in too late to understand the topic, drifting away in his mind before it could be concluded. He frowned and tried to focus. Under the table he again sought Anton's hand.

Anton's hands were clasped together on the table. So, no hand.

Robbie leaned toward the conversation between Anton and his two friends, whose names he could now not remember. "What you need, Harrington, is another wife," one of the men said. "I have a cousin in the city and could arrange a luncheon with her tomorrow at Simpson's. Bring Stillman. He'd like the roast sirloin there."

Robbie glanced at Anton, who had leaned back in his chair with a smile, and his heart began to beat fast. He muttered under his breath, "Tell him he's a bloody fool, why don't you, Anton?" He didn't realize that his voice rose. "Tell him he's a bloody fool, Anton. Tell him."

A few people had stopped talking and stared at him.

Holding on to the table, Robbie stood. "I would like to clarify matters," he began. "There are some misunderstandings here. How can we be honest friends without it? Mr. Harrington and I…" He sought for words, and they seemed to come out backward. Despair rose in him. If he found them, he couldn't say them. He reached out and knocked over his full wineglass and overturned his plate. Sauce and wine flooded the white cloth. The men rose to their feet, and the women gasped.

All the diners throughout the restaurant had stopped speaking to stare at him. Even the musicians ceased to play.

Nausea shot relentlessly through him. He felt for his napkin to cover his mouth but found it sopping with wine. He ran for the door, and in the cold night of the street, he began vomiting in the gutter.

Anton reached him before the others.

"There you are!" Robbie gasped. "I'd like to go home now. Is it too late for the train to Nottingham?" He was aware that Anton was trying to get him into the door of a motorcar, but he fought him. "I've changed my mind," he said. But by then he had been pulled inside the cab.

The smell of cigar smoke and petrol made him sick again as they moved through the evening city traffic. Someone was continuing to shout in rage, though Robbie did not understand it was himself until he felt Anton's broad hand over his mouth. "God, you can't drink like that," Anton murmured. "We're going back to the hotel for now. Try to be a little still. *Calmati, caro.*"

18

SQUATTERS' FIELD

December 1905-March 1906

Robbie was sick again in the marble hotel bathroom with its gold spigots and voluminous soft towels. He sat on the edge of the enormous bed with the blue silk tasseled pillows and tried to drink from the water glass Anton held. "I'm sorry, I'm sorry," he gasped when he had managed to say some of what he felt. "You wanted to make something beautiful for me and…it's you and that cousin."

He fell to his side on the bed, and Anton knelt beside him stroking his hair. "Did you ever think I would? Robbie, Robbie. *Calmati, caro.*" But his voice was very tired and a little unsteady.

Robbie mumbled, "You might be persuaded, and then you might like her."

"I love you, sweet."

"Then why can't we tell anyone?"

"You know damn well why we can't."

"What's the matter with me? I keep crying."

"Many things…the exhibition, meeting Louise, drinking too much. I never meant to take you to a place near that street which had such awful memories for you. But that was then, Rob! I wanted… I tried. It was as much as I could do."

"It's all my fault. I want to leave this place. I want to go home where there's just us."

They canceled all future dinners and theaters and took the late-afternoon train back to Nottingham and then the local with its hard seats to the village. At home, Robbie tucked away their opera clothes, top hats, and soft linen shirts in the wardrobe.

He wanted to wrap the beautiful ordinary quality of their lives around them again: the house beneath the trees, the green quilt on the bed, the creak of the floor, the wind against the windows, the smell of the forest, the concerns of neighbors and parishioners, and George, and the marvelous communion of their lovemaking when they became one person. Robbie felt he needed to say with his body, "We are one; nothing has changed."

As Christmas came, they cut down and decorated a tree as always for George. They followed him to church on Christmas Day and came home to a lovely dinner and a few presents under the tree from each other. Langstaff drank gin punch with them and told tender stories about his spinster sisters, which made them all laugh. Neighbors and parishioners stopped by with cake and small gifts.

Donovan wrote once, only to give a tally of expenses and pictures purchased. Both Robbie's self-portraits at age nineteen had been sold; the two different buyers had paid in banknotes but remained anonymous. Donovan remembered a pretty woman with curled hair, and a well-dressed gentleman in his fifties with an expensive silver pocket watch. Robbie guessed the woman was Louise. He had no idea who the man could be. Several other things were sold too. The remaining work was carefully packaged and returned where it was stuffed somewhere in the studio.

The exhibition had lost money, which depressed him.

He spent much time that January tramping over roads and woods alone, sometimes walking as far as the more distant villages, carrying food in a satchel over his shoulder. In his dress suit coat, which he had worn to the exhibition, he found Louise's card with her address. No thank you, I won't write, he thought. He was ashamed that he had made such a fool of himself.

Annie sent a letter from London. *I hope you don't mind a few of the reviews as much as your letter to me said you did. Sorry I didn't come to the dinner. Problems at home. See you again, dear?*

But he did mind the reviews; he had brooded over them too. A few said he was very gifted. One wrote that he was immature and to present his work by itself at his age was ridiculous, but anyone could do anything with enough money.

He tried not to think about that one.

That late winter, Robbie bicycled three times a week to Nottingham for lessons with Mrs. Tippett, who lived on the upper floor of a house overlooking the huge City Council Chambers. Afterward, he stayed for tea with artists who dropped by. A few hoped to go to London to study. She was a good teacher.

Sometimes the artists had supper together, and Anton came once.

But Anton had returned from London troubled. He was disturbed by seeing Louise, whom he had made so unhappy; he had always vowed to write her but did not. He felt he had made Robbie miserable. And he could not forget that speaker he had heard in the London Guildhall, that brilliant Scotsman, son of miners and a miner himself until the age of ten, who was changing men's hearts with his fierce words about how poverty could be wiped out in England.

Anton thought of the deserted Squatters' Field miles from the house. One February day when Robbie was at class, he bicycled to see it for the first time in years.

His breath grew short under his cashmere overcoat and wool muffler as he approached. There were some wild hedges, and then, having dismounted and walked his bicycle past them, he was there. The winter day was mild, and the surrounding trees were bare.

He walked about.

Several years had passed since the houses had been torn down. Parts of stone walls remained. It was still but for birds and rabbits that poked among things abandoned by the people who had lived there: a corroded pot lid, a bit of a dress, a card of thread so long in the mud that it had lost color. He picked it up and wrapped it in his linen handkerchief before putting it in his pocket.

He remembered how he would bicycle over with a basket of food stolen from his father's kitchen and all his pocket money. The people had been his friends. Where Anton now stood in his fine leather boots had been a house where he had fled from his father a few times, given straw to sleep on in the corner, the woman of the house whispering so as not to disturb him.

He remembered all their faces as he stood there: the old, the young, and the children running bare legged in the grass: some thirty people who had made a home there for years, and Bess, who had seduced him. But the land had been bought by his father's friend. One day when Anton was twenty-two, the friend and his men and Anton's father had torn the houses down and forced the people to go.

Anton stood in the ruins as if memories wouldn't let him move. He looked around slowly. "Big John," he said under his breath. The old fellow on crutches who once had been a skilled blacksmith was gone. Three had gone into the workhouse. God, he loathed those state-supported institutions, which rose all over the country! People went there when they had no place left to go in the world nor bread to feed themselves. All possessions were confiscated, even their clothing. Families were separated. Women, men, children would shuffle bewildered through the halls. They were given work to do for the state in return for their keep: knitting or weaving or breaking stones or picking ropes apart.

He thought of old crooked Sarah, who had turned to begging for a living. Months after the houses had been torn down, he had found her gathering dandelions in her apron by the road for her supper. "You promised to protect us," she had shouted, and spat at him.

She had soon after gone to the workhouse too and died.

He bicycled home. The air was cold and still and through the windows of the library he could see Robbie lying on the sofa under a light wool blanket, his arm behind his head, reading a book. Anton walked inside and sat down in one of the armchairs. He began to speak of what he had seen today and remembered. He spoke mechanically, keeping down his emotion. Robbie had put aside his book. He sat up and was listening intently.

"You must write it down," Robbie said. "And one day it will be part of that book you wanted to complete. Let's go back now, and I'll sketch it. Now when you feel this way. And you write it this evening."

"Snow's coming."

"Then we must hurry." Robbie was in the vestibule, pulling on his coat. He slung the art satchel he brought to lessons over his arm.

They mounted their bicycles and set off into the day as the trees by the path seemed to huddle by the weight of the thicker sky. Anton took the lead.

Once there, Robbie sat with his back to some fallen stones, opened his sketchbook and placed the ink in a small bit of scooped earth. High dry grass dipped to his pen. He worked quickly. Above them, the clouds grew heavier until the grey-white light sighed and gave up its first flakes of snow.

"Done," said Robbie. He blew on the ink, held his muffler over the page until it dried, and then closed the sketchbook and put it in the satchel. He and Anton watched the thickening flakes cling to the tumbled rocks and the grass and the handlebars of their bicycles. In a moment they were mounted and racing each other down the whitening path.

The branches of oak before the house were white as was the roof below it. They hurried inside and lit the lamps. As it grew dark, Anton sat at the book-piled library desk and wrote the story. The snow did not stop, and the burning fire cast a soft light on the upholstered chairs. The short day faded outside the windows, and they had tea and meat pie

Robbie read the article. "It's the best you've done," he said. He looked up from the pages, the freckles on his nose faded in the winter, and added, "You must post it to that magazine you like. Anton, I think that's the field where the girl lived who was carrying your child."

"Ah, you know that story. George told you, I guess."

They lay together on the sofa as full darkness came. "Once a branch broke from the weight of the snow," Anton said softly. "Years ago, when I was small, the night my youngest sister died."

His body grew heavier with memory as he bicycled off with the good copy of the article the next morning to the post office in the village. The sun had melted the snow and he was careful, though it took more effort to pedal. Neighbors called to him, and children ran from the houses but the memories which rose from the copied story in a briefcase in his basket cried louder.

They shouted at him; he saw the old faces.

When he returned some hours later, he turned into the library. The cold tea from the morning still sat on the table; no one was home, and he had no energy to boil water for more. Instead, he walked to the desk and violently ripped up the article's rough copy, dropping it into the embers of the fire, stirring them up. Then he lay down on his back on the sofa, his arm over his eyes.

Shortly after, he heard the front door open, and Robbie come in with a whisk of cold air; he rested his portfolio by the chair. "All posted?" Robbie asked.

Through the wool of his shirt sleeve, Anton muttered tonelessly, "Not posted. There's your drawing on the desk. You can hang it at your next exhibition."

Anton felt Robbie sit down heavily on the sofa's edge. "Why not posted?" he asked unsteadily.

"I tore it up and threw it in the stream. The rough copy's also burned."

He heard Robbie's silence and then his burst of words in a voice which cracked. "You destroyed both copies? Why? Anton! How could you? It was our article."

"I broke my own promise to myself to never speak of it."

Robbie demanded, "Why? Tell me."

"Because I could have stopped them tearing it down," Anton said, sitting up, and hurled a pillow across the room. "I trusted where I should never have done. I made compromises that came to nothing and hurt people. You'll likely ask about and hear many sides of it, but I know the truth. Go asking if you want to make me wretched, Rob. I don't need the tears in your eyes. I can't manage them. I can't console you this time and I don't need any of your cheerful words, if you have any. And I don't want to write any more articles."

His voice rose harshly and echoed back from the windows as he buried his face in his hands.

That week, Anton dropped from the church choir and the community theater. He said he needed time to think. There was a darkness coming to him that he couldn't put into words. He knew it; he had experienced it in college, in his marriage, in his months in Zurich when everything ceased to have meaning for him.

"You'll come to nothing," his father had always said, and Anton thought two things: One day I'll kill my father; or secondly, One day perhaps, I will be perfect enough so that he will love me. Both desires melded in him so that he could never separate them.

He and Rob began to quarrel, one night so badly they hardly slept. Robbie would not even go to art class the next day until he felt it was settled. "Because I can't," he said, his words half choked.

And Anton cupped Robbie's face and said, "Go to class. I love you."

He sat at the small library desk again a few weeks later in March, rolling a pencil between his fingers, trying to think clearly. Recently, he had felt he couldn't; perhaps today, with Robbie off to a lesson and the house quite empty, he could begin.

This morning, he had been determined to tackle his unanswered letters, and now he stared down at the ones on the desk amid the clutter of other things, some read and retucked into their envelopes, some unopened.

The truth was that something had changed in him since they had returned from London.

He had seen some of his old friends there: Peebles, the others at the restaurant. He would have seen more of them if he had not gone home so quickly. Looking back, Anton saw that they had gone on paths not unlike his own had been years ago: to marry, to find a place in good society. Of course, they had no idea. His life had gone the same way as theirs and then diverged so sharply.

At one point he had been able to talk a little to Peebles: no more. There was that one thing that had to remain unsaid: the gifted, sensual artist at his side who was his world. If you can't tell a good friend who you love, what use are the dinners together? Still, Anton must write him something.

He frowned, studying the shape of the pencil as he rolled it and his not-too-clean fingernails. Robbie was off in an ecstasy of painting; Anton was here alone in the house. Recently everything that had seemed so rich was empty. He had lost any desire to repair roofs or walls or windows for his poorer neighbors.

He rolled the pencil and did not begin the letter.

There were the horses, of course. He had suddenly bought four from a neighbor who was moving away, beautiful creatures. He stood and walked to the library window, pushing the dark curtains farther back, looking across at the paddock.

He was tired, that was all. He was not sleeping much. When Robbie left to meet friends to paint, he tried not to say, "When will you be back?" When Robbie returned, Anton listened to all his stories but more to the sound of his voice. Was he happy, was he disappointed? And then at night, he stayed awake and watched his young lover sleep, his hand on Robbie's back. He would close his eyes and let his fingers move down the bare flesh, feeling the intimate path of the backbone and the muscles he knew so well.

But one by one all his other interests left Anton. He felt inside him something he had not since his married days: a dark thing, as if something was clawing to get out. Robbie needs me, he thought and then again, he asked himself, But does he? For Robbie seemed to have put the art exhibition behind him and was bicycling off to paint with the other students so happily.

And Anton would never tell him how he lost he felt, never, because he was the older one, he was the stronger. He had to maintain that position. He felt at least some steadiness there.

No, he would never meet cousins, work in London, have convivial glasses with friends. He would breed horses; he would be a good neighbor. He would stay awake at night to watch Robbie sleeping deeply with his palm on Robbie's back to feel his breathing and know that somehow their world was whole. He needed no other reason for living; it was here.

19

THE HOUSE OF THE GREAT-AUNT

Spring 1906

Robbie found the letter on the vestibule table one late afternoon when he ran in from his bicycle ride, his sketchbook under his arm, some meat pies he had bought wrapped in newspaper against his coat, his pencil case held in his teeth. The letter had been wedged in the pages of the newly delivered *Army and Navy Catalogue*. Putting down his things, standing by the hanging coats and galoshes, he opened it.

> I'm sorry I never came to the dinner. I walked as far as the street of the restaurant and couldn't make myself go on, for reasons you may or may not understand. I write only because I may be coming to Bridgeford outside Nottingham to visit my great-aunt, and if I do come, I would like to see you. It's a mile from your village. Give regards to Mr. Harrington if you wish.
>
> K. E. Donovan

Robbie stood quite still with the letter in his hand, his other fingers scratching mindlessly at some candle wax on the vestibule table. Brilliant yellow daffodils, which he had gathered yesterday, crowded their vase on the table and reflected in the hanging oval hall mirror.

He heard Anton's voice with a friend from the library. For the past few days, Robbie and Anton had been quite close.

They ate the pies for tea, talking distractedly about their days: a new model for the class, George's cough. Robbie had stuffed the letter in his pocket, and when he changed jackets, he forgot it.

A month later, when he looked through his post again on the vestibule table, he found another letter from the gallery manager saying that Keith was now in Bridgeford with his great-aunt and things were dull. He would be at the Sparrow Inn tomorrow for lunch at half-past noon if Robbie wished to meet him.

Robbie slipped the envelope into his jacket once more, bringing it forth several times that morning to look at it. He woke the next day to a vague sense of uneasiness. Anton was out, and he left a note saying that he was bicycling to the village for the vicar's cough tonic and raced off in a flurry of dust, turning at the few graves by the tree.

He stopped before the Sparrow Inn, leaped off, and went inside the cool darkness.

Coming from the brilliant street, he could at first see the gallery manager only as a slender shadow; then as he came closer, the sharp chin and sweet, reserved smile. In the little dining room, they ordered steak pie and beer. Old photographs cut from newspapers were carefully framed about the walls, including one of the acrobats at the October Goose Fair, where he had returned with Anton last autumn.

"My great-aunt's giving me some money so I can draw for a time." Keith's voice came through his thoughts. "I wanted to see you. I wasn't sure you'd come."

"That's wonderful about the money! Of course, I'd come! How's the gallery?"

"I left; I'm returning to study art in London, perhaps Paris. Spending time with friends. They ask me about you." There was some silence. "Wondered if you would come back to London. Well, I'm staying here for a bit to give Aunt Elizabeth company out of obligation, you know. The money will keep me a year if I'm careful."

They sat over lunch for three hours. "Come to tea tomorrow at Auntie's," Keith said, rising. "We'll draw together."

It was a distraction he needed; he didn't understand what was happening with Anton. He asked and the answer was always gruff. "Nothing, nothing." For the first time in their lives together, he hesitated a little when going home. He craved the laughter of the other artists and their hours together in some pub, not the one Anton went to nearer Market Square.

So, he didn't speak of his visits, neither the first lunch in the inn with Keith nor the subsequent tea with the deaf great-aunt. Then one day when they had been drawing a church altar side by side, Keith suddenly buried his face in his hands and said, "It's not fair, your being so gifted. You're better, and always will be."

"Stop. I'll show you! Try again."

"No, damn you…no. I wonder what you would be without your lover standing behind you. Could you be anything on your own? No, I'm sorry."

Robbie dropped his sketchbook, drawing the gallery manager against him. They kissed as if they couldn't bear to stop, breathless and hungry. Robbie broke away and rode home on his bicycle with his heart pounding.

Anton and the housekeeper's ten-year-old niece Maggie were chasing each other around the library, and when she saw Robbie, she rushed straight into the artist's arms, banging her head against his midriff. "Oh, you pretty lass!" he said. She had been about the house for a time. Later, Robbie drew faces on acorns with ink and a fine brush for her to keep. All evening he chattered about nothing to Anton while through those hours and into the night came the great silent reproach of his new desire.

He burned with shame; he thought, Never again. Still, two days later he met Keith in the little bedroom at the great-aunt's while she had gone for a walk. The room smelled of candle wax, lavender, and soap. Keith thrust his hand inside Robbie's shirt and then under the buttons of the long underwear. He kissed Robbie with a soft, open, hungry mouth.

Robbie made love to him at once, holding him down, entering him. It happened fast. Though he felt the greatest tenderness, he also once or twice would have liked to hurt. Dimly came his power to hurt, poured out by so much he had withheld, though he wouldn't hurt anyone. He only knew that he was the stronger of the two by far, which was a thrill to him. Then he fell asleep as if he had been drugged.

When he woke, his arm reached at once for the familiar hangings of his own bed. He whispered, "Oh God! What have I done…what have I done?"

Outside the window, the cool spring night was brilliantly lit by the full moon, so much that he could make out that the large hand of his pocket watch read just eleven. He imagined Anton walking downstairs sternly and bolting the door against him. He wouldn't, of course; he would never. Keith was still sleeping. Robbie crawled about looking for his scattered socks and clothing and for a long time couldn't find his right boot. He washed in the basin.

Tiptoeing downstairs, boots in hand, he mounted his bicycle, wheeled away down the path past other silent cottages. When he reached home, the Worcester grandfather clock was tolling midnight.

He removed his boots before climbing the stairs to the dark study where he stripped to his skin, shivering, and walked into the bedroom, his limp penis moving gently. He slipped into bed beside Anton, pressing his cold chest to the warm, broad back.

From his near sleep came Anton's whisper, "Awfully late! Worried—let me know next time, dear?"

I'm unworthy to be loved, I'm unworthy, Robbie said to himself. He remained staring into the darkness with his chest constricted in grief and his arm around Anton's shoulder.

If it had ended there, it might have been forgotten, a shameful hour in his mind put behind him. He didn't leave the house for three days, but in each of those hours, the slender, cool body of his new friend passed like a vision before him. I belong to myself, he thought defensively, not to Anton.

He did go at last to Keith who was still there, and they quarreled over the length of time Robbie had stayed away and then escaped upstairs to make love again. He forgot art, he forgot Anton; he wanted only that, that.

20

RESOLUTIONS

Spring 1906

Mary was not there that day, so Anton bicycled to the village of Forest's End to buy dinner. On his way back from the shops with the food in his basket, he passed a young woman from the artists' group, bicycling with one hand on her hat to make sure it didn't blow away. She recognized him from the evening he had spent with the group in the late winter.

"It's Flora," she called. "Where's Robbie? We've not seen him in days. Send him my love. He's probably off wandering, painting alone. Why don't you come to any of the parties sometime? We'd all like to see you."

"I will," he said.

Rob had promised to be back by seven from his afternoon with Mrs. Tippett's little group of artists, but the hour had passed, and he still didn't come. As Anton sat at the small table looking at the cloth with which he had covered the food, he began to put the last weeks together. He was very still.

His mind almost ceased to think, as if it had come to a wall and could go no further. He ate nothing and finally went to bed.

Past ten, he heard the closing of the door below and the pause as Rob came to the landing past the Worcester clock, where he stopped always to reset his pocket watch by his candle. The study door opened. Anton heard him undressing, dropping his shoes on the floor. He closed his eyes as Robbie entered the bedroom and slipped into bed.

Then he sat up abruptly and lit the oil lamp. He shook out the match and said without turning, "Well, dear?"

Robbie remained silent and Anton turned to look at his

love's profile against the red hangings of the bed. Anton said unsteadily, "Where have you been this week, Rob?"

The mattress groaned as Robbie turned heavily to his stomach and buried his face in his arms. Anton could see the declivity of his beautiful back.

The reply when it came was low and muffled. "Don't ask me, Anton."

"Damn it, look at me!" Kneeling on the bed, he turned Robbie and pushed away the bare arm covering the face, which seemed to belong to an elusive stranger. Taking him by the shoulders, Anton shook him once or twice, and then harder. "You will tell me, Rob!" he shouted, his voice ringing to the bed canopy. "You will tell me, damn it!"

"I can't."

"You're with someone else."

There was a silence, and then Rob nodded, his face once again covered. Anton tore the arm away roughly again and stared down haughtily at him, trying to find his voice. There were very few times in his life when he had felt faint, and now he lowered his head. His heart pounded so he felt his chest would burst.

"What have I done?" Anton whispered when he could speak. "What have I done to deserve this?"

Robbie rose to his knees and tried to pull Anton against him. "You're everything to me!" he said. "I did something very stupid, horrible. I'm sorry, I'm sorry. Please lie down with me again…please, darling, please."

Anton lay down once more.

Everything had drained from within him; he felt he was skin only and nothing beneath it but an echoing hollow. He allowed Robbie to lay his head on his chest, an arm cautiously around him; he felt the tuft of chest hair, one small cold nipple. He felt the emotionless weight of the arm. They lay like that for some time more, not speaking. Anton said finally, "It's that Irish fellow, isn't it? That gallery manager. I thought I saw him once in Bridgeford. He came after you. You went with him. Oh God, Robbie, Robbie, why?"

Robbie moved a little closer. Finally, he said, "Because I'm lonely. You're miserable and you won't tell me. You don't talk with me. We don't laugh anymore. Oh, I don't know. I don't know."

Anton lay awake for a long time and when he woke in the morning, Robbie was gone. There was no note. George knew nothing. "I suppose he's with friends," Anton said with a shrug, and the vicar blinked and sat back in his chair and asked, "Doesn't he tell you?" And Anton was sorry he had come and walked back to the farmhouse.

Every time the floors creaked, Anton started up with his hand against his chest, heart pounding. The child and Mary were gone to visit the child's mother, Mary's sister. He walked out to gaze across his own field, over which butterflies dipped through the dazzling trees in sunlight. He was enlarging the fence in part of the field so the horses could have a greater area; he had felt suddenly he couldn't bear their smaller enclosure. Hands roughened, nails cracking, he worked wildly, splitting and cutting the wood with a violence that left him gasping. A lad came with a delivery of wire and other things, and he shouted at him, "Not there, not there, bring it here!" The bewildered boy took the coins and scurried off with the empty wheelbarrow.

At teatime, Anton walked upstairs. He wanted a drink more than he had in a long time, but took instead two glasses of water, draining them with one hand on his hip. He remained in the center of the study carpet, as if the decision to turn either toward the desk or to the sofa were too difficult for him. At last, he pulled off his shoes, hurled them across the room, and flung himself facedown amid the sofa cushions, which smelled of fire smoke and tobacco, breathing in a deep, slow way as if it hurt him. One hand trailed to the carpet, touching the edges of the unopened post. Peebles, another friend Hawkins, catalogues of materials for home improvements, a parcel of books for Rob from France, undoubtedly art. Later the bill would come, and he would pay it. He breathed hard and steadily, thinking of the things he ordered for Rob to please him.

Three days passed.

Toward the end of the third long afternoon, he heard the door open below, and footsteps on the stairs. Anton was lying on the sofa. Vaguely he recalled that he had not bathed or changed his clothes in three days, sleeping in them. Then he compressed his mouth and said, "Damn it!" He rolled from his stomach to his back with such a sudden gesture that the sofa quivered, and rested there with his arms behind his head, long legs in corduroy trousers stretched out.

Robbie was pale when he came through the study door, his clothing also rumpled as if he had worn it a long time, his hair dirty and unbrushed, his face unshaven. He looked as if he had not slept much. Stopping some feet before the sofa, he gazed about with the same boyish shyness as when he had first entered this room.

Anton drew in his breath; he bent one leg warily and his hands tensed.

Robbie moved slowly as if dazed, touching the edge of the mantel and the back of a chair, every now and then glancing back at Anton for some sign that he could come closer. Stopping for a moment by the edge of the desk, he murmured in a low, hoarse voice, "I'm back."

"So it appears, Rob. How's your lover?"

"He's gone. I told him it was over. I stayed with an artist friend from my class. I didn't sleep, hardly at all."

"What makes you think I still want you?"

He could see Robbie was taken aback. Robbie hesitated and then said, "I thought of things. I thought of a lot of things."

"What did you think of exactly?"

"That tone! As if you know so much more than me! I think I should go away, go back to London to study. I'm tired of being your boy."

"But you liked it."

"I'm tired of being the younger one; I'll always be. The way you treat me. In bed, you came inside me from the first and I loved it, but when I wanted you that way, you said no."

"It's only that thing. I couldn't."

"Don't you know I felt humiliated because I loved you? That's all I damn did was love you, adore you."

"You loved me? Past tense?"

Robbie walked into the bedroom and began to pack his suitcase. He threw in his shirts and suits, his shaving brush and soap and razor.

Anton followed him to the bedroom door, staring at him. This could not be happening. He'd said the wrong things, but he was so angry. But what could he do? Perhaps Robbie should go, and he'd be back within a day or two. They'd begin again. How could he snatch the spoken words from the air and throw them into the fire?

He fought to keep his voice steady. "It's silly to leave. It'll be dark in three hours. Wait until the morning. Perhaps we can talk. Where the hell will you go? What on earth will you do?"

"Go to the devil."

That was it. Anton strode across the room, took Robbie by the arm, and slapped his face. He shouted, "Of course—you're going to him. I suppose I should be used to the idea that you're naturally promiscuous. Now you can go to pubs and sleep with a different man each night. That's what you want? Isn't it? Isn't it?" Anton slapped him again. Robbie had stumbled backward but rose with a shout.

Anton wiped his mouth with the back of his hand. "There," he said. "Don't ask me to apologize for it. Get out before you have another. Damn you. Why didn't you leave me alone? God, your nose is bleeding. God, Rob."

But Robbie pushed him back and shouted, "Go to hell."

"Take some money at least—don't be unreasonable!"

"I don't want to take things from you, Anton."

"We should never have begun together."

"Take care of George. Promise me!" Robbie strapped his suitcases closed and ran past Anton down the stairs.

He won't make it as far as the train, Anton thought.

He waited until the early hours of the morning, but Robbie didn't return.

BOOK FOUR

21

Spring in Edwardian London

April-June 1906

The problem was where to stay in London. Robbie didn't know any modest hotels. He considered Annie in Chelsea, but she and her mother had only one room. His teacher DuChamps and his sensitive wife read Robbie's every mood and he didn't want them to know how wretched he was. So he rode by motor cab from the train station to Louise's house in Eccleston Square across from the little park.

She pulled open the door herself, lovely in flowing pink silk, her face open with happiness. Behind her, he made out the dining room through an open door and heard laughter and the clink of wineglasses. He had arrived during a dinner party. And he saw himself as she must see him: unshaven, hair dirty, shirt wrinkled and unfit to be a guest.

"Why, Robbie! Well, such a surprise!" Louise exclaimed and then with a puzzled look, glanced down the dark street. "It's nearly nine at night," she said. "Where's Antonio?"

Robbie answered as casually as he could. "I'm alone. I was going to take a room somewhere and not bother you, but I had your address from your letter and your card." He thought of the sweet letter she had sent him, announcing her marriage and saying that he should come to see her anytime.

Someone called her from inside. He murmured, "I should go. I'm presuming to come here." But he was so tired that he leaned against one of the columns.

She pulled him by the hand inside her vestibule. "Oh dear, did you both quarrel?" she asked seriously. "He can be very difficult, I know! No, you must stay with me. Surely, you're not up for dinner-table conversation! Let me show you to a room, and my maid will bring you a tray. Dora!" The maid appeared, curtsied, and took his bag.

The bedroom was lovely, with heavy curtains and an oil painting of flowers over the fireplace. Robbie was almost too tired to undress. He fell asleep at once and woke to the now silent house. He woke again with the sun coming through the curtain cracks and didn't know at first where he was.

When he finally rose, he pulled on his dressing gown and studied the painting, which was signed Renoir. One of those French artists, so lovely. Tears filled his eyes.

Louise knocked at the door and came in wearing her dressing gown, her auburn hair falling loosely down her back. She carried a tray of tea and muffins and placed it on the small table. "Tea?" she asked. "Sugar? Cream?"

"Yes, tea, please," he said huskily. "I didn't eat your lovely tray of food last night. I tried. I still don't know if I can eat. Everything happened so fast at home. The vicar doesn't even know I've gone, or perhaps he's found out this morning." He made his voice gruff. "I'm not going back," he said. "I can't."

"Oh, Robbie! What on earth happened?"

"I don't know—things piled one on top of the other. It was my fault in the end. But I couldn't reach Anton. I wanted to reach him. There was someone else then. I never intended it to happen. And then he said some things to me that stung me so."

He sank onto a chair and looked miserably down into his teacup.

"Robbie," she said, taking the desk chair to sit near him. "I'm so sorry. Stay with us until you make better plans. My husband won't mind if you stay. He's asked after you. What will you do today?"

"I think I'll go out for a time. Walking will clear my head."

"Well then, we'll talk more tonight," she said. "Ernst has a rehearsal with his string quartet. He's first violin. There's a concert next week at Wigmore Hall. We'll have supper."

Robbie walked around London that day, seeing places he recalled from before. Once more he saw a shadow of the lonely boy he had been and shuddered. He walked until his feet hurt. But he reminded himself that he was here for one reason: to make a living in art, to learn to stand on his own feet.

Still, how did you begin such a thing? People were only hired on reputation, and he was merely an artist with one small exhibition behind him that had sold little. Few artists made money, but for the legendary painters whose names were known throughout England and the Continent, the magazine illustrators who scrambled from fee to fee, some newspaper journalists, and a few portraitists. There was of course the American John Singer Sargent, who earned thousands of guineas for a portrait, but he was clearly one of a kind.

He wondered if his uncle's prophecies about him were true and he would end up a tailor's assistant, delivering packages of trousers to customers, taking the measure of inseams, displaying the weights and weaves of different tweeds on the counter of the Newark-on-Trent shop.

When he returned to the house in Eccleston Square, Louise hurried down the steps. "I've been waiting for you," she said. "I've a little reading room in the back. Let's close the door and have sandwiches for supper."

All he wanted was wine and bread; he vowed not to take too much of the former, even though he felt that the best thing in the world was the oblivion of drunkenness or sleep.

They walked into a lovely little room with chairs and a sofa covered with white-and-pale-yellow floral print and a few bookshelves with novels. Closed, curtained doors looked out on a city garden. Sandwiches, wine, and cakes were already on the table, and one of his two self-portraits in pencil hung on the wall. "You bought this?" he asked. "It was in the exhibition. I was a beginner when I made both of them. I was first studying art in London."

"I love it," Louise said. "A stranger bought the second one. You looked so sad in the one he chose; I'm glad I got this."

Louise studied her hands and twisted her new wedding band a bit while gathering her words. "Robbie, I couldn't put this in my one letter to you, but I need to say it, why I understand certain things. It's about my younger brother. He was a gifted artist like you. One day our parents found out he was in love with another man and threw him from the door without so much as a change of clothes. He went out to India and has never written me for ten years. I hear he stopped painting. It breaks my heart."

"Oh, how sad for you to lose him!"

"You're such a dear. I'll always love Anton, but I wanted a man who can love me. I remembered how distant Anton could be. Sometimes with him I felt I didn't exist."

"I'm so grateful you've found someone else," Robbie said.

"I want you both to be happy, and now it seems you're not. I go about in life trying to make people happy and sometimes I can't. Often I can't."

He didn't know how to answer that but with a weak smile.

At her insistence, he unlaced his shoes and put his feet on the footstool, sinking back in the deeply cushioned chair with a sigh of luxury. He unbuttoned his coat and waistcoat and draped his tie over the chair back and reached for the smallest sandwich. They would eat on their laps. Someone had forgotten plates. Crumbs fell to the floor. This informality seemed charming, and he was grateful for it. Still his throat filled with misery.

She said, "First tell me about your day."

He sighed. "It was rather humbling. I'll have to ask people to pay me, and…I've never known how to do that. I spoke to an artist in a supply shop, and he says it's hard to start. I could perhaps try reportage drawing," he added, looking longingly toward the wine bottle. "I can see myself shipping out to the ends of the Empire wearing a canvas hat to record the strife of nations in pen and ink."

"Oh no, dear! Far too hot and dangerous. You can find work in London."

"Who did you think I was when you first met me, when you came to see him at the house about your divorce?"

"Why, the vicar's pupil. It wasn't until I heard Anton in the telephone box at Nottingham station calling Mr. Langstaff when we were leaving for Paris to try again that I understood. I watched through the glass panel how he ran his hands through his hair and his face was in misery. Two days later in France he told me the truth. I said, 'Go back to Robbie,' and he said he couldn't—he was too ashamed. I was in shock, of course. It took me a time to be happy. I was angry at him, at you, at my brother. It all passed."

A silence fell between the two of them. She said at last, "I'd like to tell you how I married Anton, though likely he's told you something of it. May we speak of him? I won't if you don't wish it."

"I don't mind. I think about him every moment."

Louise shook off her shoes and leaned back on the sofa. "Strange," she said with a small smile. "I feel like we're old friends, that we played together as children in a park somewhere. Isn't that odd? Were you wary of me when we first met?"

"Yes, very much." Gratefully he drank the deep red wine. He didn't know what he would hear; at least he didn't have to hear it entirely sober.

She said, "Antonio and I met at a party given by my mother. I was twenty-one and he was twenty-four. When he walked in, every head turned. He was the most beautiful man I'd ever seen—proud, strong, intelligent. He was a gentleman, as I said, but could be playful. He sang songs at the piano; he enchanted everyone."

"Yes, he enchants people."

"All my friends were envious. He took me to the opera, to the ballet. He bought me a diamond engagement ring, the most beautiful thing I ever saw. His father had died several months before, and it was his first freedom. He bought us a house just across the park here. We were happy for months, so happy."

Louise played with a loose strand of her hair, looking away into the curtained doors to the garden as if she could see her story there. "At first, he wanted to go everywhere with me, and we lived a bohemian life, the sort of life I'd always led and loved. We filled it with artists and writers. We'd have readings and concerts in our parlor. In the day, of course, he was at the bank, where they promoted him several times."

She hesitated then and frowned. "Then...gradually in his free time he said his head ached, he needed to rest, he was too surrounded. He said I could have my soirées, and he went for walks. Where he went, I never knew. Or I'd go out to the theater, and he'd stay home reading. He said he felt closed in by the city."

The wine gave Robbie more courage. He said, "It must have been awful for you."

"It was! He wanted a child; we went to doctors. I couldn't conceive and felt somehow defective. Not that he ever said that, but all our first happiness slowly began to dissolve. He loathed his work. And at one party when he did come, I saw his eyes follow a young man around the room and how silent he was when the man left. I felt cold through and through. My perfect, handsome husband didn't really want me. He was like my beloved brother. It broke my heart. Then for a time he avoided any intimacy with me, which made conception..." She bit her lip. "The times were bleak for me. And yet he was so kind."

She stood up and walked to the garden doors, pulling back the curtain. Robbie joined her.

She said, "I think he hides a lot from long ago. He didn't speak much of his childhood. He said his parents adored him, but I suspect he lied. Finally, he said he wanted to go back home to the Midlands, and I went with him. All he wanted was to wear old clothes and rebuild the farmhouse. I love my world here, with its concerts, poetry readings, theater, actors. I lived with a handsome ghost. We separated. He went to Switzerland and came back home—and found you."

Louise suddenly bent over her wineglass, cradling it, smoothing the outsides as if protecting it. She murmured, "That's all, really! He gave me the house in London, which I sold for this smaller one. The divorce is long done. But as for you...listen to me. You'll go back to him eventually. No matter what he said, or you did. He loves you. He'd die for you, Robbie."

"Don't say that. Not after what I did. And his silences. I loathed them. The one thing he wants most in the world he'll never let himself have. He wrote such a deep article about some field and tore it up. I walked out the door and all I want to be is back there…and I can't. I need to find out who I am without him." It was a huge outburst, and his voice cracked at the end of it.

She sighed and was still for a moment. Then she raised her head. "There!" she said. "Quite enough said. We'll ring for coffee and talk about the immediate future."

Coffee came in a silver urn, and they spoke of the city and the museums, and Robbie said, "I was thinking of taking classes at the Academy to get back into the heart of things. That is… if your husband doesn't mind if I stay a time."

"He worries I don't have enough company. I like having you here. It will be lovely. Oh, Robbie, this is just a moment, and you will get through it. Come!"

She hugged him against her. Then he couldn't wait to get away to fight the tears that wanted to well up in him for the loneliness he felt. He barely managed to be civil to her husband, Ernst, when he looked into the room, his violin case in hand.

"I must pull myself together," he murmured when he woke the next day.

That morning, he walked the familiar streets into the Academy. His footsteps echoed on the floors, and he heard the laughter of students and smelled oil and turpentine and the dirt of paint-stained floors; dusty light sifted down upon him from the tall windows like something heavenly.

He was talking with another student in the painting studio when Augustine DuChamps heard his voice and came to meet him. His old master had been elevated to president of the Royal Academy of Arts.

"My daughters are growing up," he said buoyantly. "Eight and nine years old now, imagine. They remember you from your evening with us. Come to dinner again!"

Three students in his class gathered around him as he was leaving a few evenings later and asked him to join them for a meal. At first, he refused, but the next day he agreed, though he was careful not to reveal anything about himself. He was hungry to talk of art; he wanted the world to be nothing but art. To live solely for his work—hadn't Rembrandt done the same in his last years, bankrupt and sketching in brown ink the life of Christ? He recalled the self-portraits of the old genius, the wise, disillusioned eyes.

His anxious breath slowed in his art classes. The conversation of others was a hum in the distance with the occasional opening of a pencil box. Everything about him was still but his hand. The large studio smelled of pencil shavings, which curled on the floor at his feet.

He finally went home with DuChamps for dinner. With the girls clamoring about him, he felt loved as if he belonged to something wonderful. They both talked very late about the art world, and then Robbie returned to Eccleston Square.

He had written to the vicar with his new address and received a return within two days. Perhaps it was for the best, perhaps not, the old man wrote. From Anton there was nothing but silence. Robbie would not write first; he could not separate his longing from his pride. He still heard Anton's bitter words.

It was a lovely life, but as a few months passed, he began to grow unsettled. The violinist, charming Ernst Hauptmann, welcomed him warmly. Still, Robbie was aware of Louise's intimacy with him as the couple mounted the steps together hand in hand, and it made him lonely.

One evening, when she knocked on his door to say goodnight, he told her, "I ought to go. I need to stand on my own feet."

"Oh no, don't go! Ernst and I like you so!"

He looked about the comfortable bedroom, which had been his for these few months, and once more felt like an orphan. She sensed it. "Do you need money?"

"No, nothing. I'll manage," he said, but he thought, I'll not live as we do here with two maids and a cook and fresh flowers delivered every day. I'll have to learn to do with less. I can't just be a student. I must earn a living.

He kissed her cheek. "If I'm in trouble, I'll come to you."

"Will you visit?"

"I promise."

Robbie packed his things: the clothes and books and cufflinks Anton had sent on to him, Anton's letters, which had now begun to arrive and which he couldn't bear to read. He had written George every week. He wrote to the old man from the desk with his packed suitcases about him.

Darling George, you were ill, and I didn't know. Mrs. Cullen told me she'd been visiting you since she joined the church and wrote that you're better now. I send you a hundred kisses on the top of your head and all my love and will try to have the courage to visit soon. I'm moving once more.

All love from your gypsy, Robbie

22

The Boarding House

Summer-October 1906

Through another student at the Academy, Robbie found a room in a boardinghouse in Holborn, not far from where Keith Donovan used to live, which catered to theatrical people, musicians, and artists. It was called Mrs. Steadman's Rooms and was considered moderately genteel.

Above him lodged a young man who played viola at the Gaiety and who practiced Mozart with heartbreaking pathos. Robbie sometimes passed two beautiful actresses on the stairs or at supper. They always wore tight skirts to the ankle and hats with black veils. They were thrilled that he knew *Macbeth* well, and the taller one invited him to hear her play Lady Macbeth in a church hall one rainy evening by yellowish gaslight on a stage with only a few chairs covered with rugs.

Robbie woke in the mornings to the clatter of horse hooves and wheels and the clanking of motorcars and the shouting of newsboys.

He had supper with Annie once a week in a nearby tavern; one night when a little drunk, he trusted her with his secret. She said she had always known. "I've seen you look at men for a moment and make yourself look away," she said.

She carefully cut a small piece of her fish as if to make it last. In a very low voice, he told her about Anton, and she grasped his hand hard on the table, shaking her head. "Terrible," she said.

He did not tell her about Charing Cross Road. Only Anton knew.

He said, "Tell me more about you."

"Me? First, I'm so glad you're back in the city."

"How's your work?"

"I'm trying to earn a living. It's a rich person's game unless you can. I'm painting cards on commission for a stationer I know on Charing Cross Road. Buckingham Palace, Horse Guards, etc., all bought by tourists." She smiled brightly and drank some beer before continuing. "The shop owner tells everyone they're painted by a genuine London artist."

She lowered her own voice now. She said, "I'm in love with someone and hoping he will stay, but my mother's more and more helpless. Love is to be avoided. Friendship is the best."

He always paid for supper though he had little money, having refused any help from Louise; he had only his mother's inheritance. The four thousand pounds invested at four percent, of which he had used some the first time he had been alone in London, had been officially transferred to him by his uncle with a written lecture a few years before. Robbie took the smallest amount possible to sustain him for a time until he decided what he could do. He resolved not to touch the principal except in the worst emergencies.

Keith Donovan was studying in Paris, friends told him. They said he had grown a beard, wore only old clothes, and was in love with someone. Rob winced when he thought of their last meeting in the little bedroom, Keith's pale angry face and breaking whisper: "Well then, goodbye, and damn you, Stillman! I made a fool of myself coming after you. Go and be his kept boy. Wait until you're not so pretty anymore, and he'll be quick to find another."

Robbie had never considered that. "It's not so," he said, but then he didn't know. Sometimes he felt he didn't know Anton much at all.

It was the heat of summer. He took his works to galleries that were not interested. He had still not earned a penny; it was as if he didn't exist.

Then, just when his loneliness grew worse, Louise Hauptmann sent over a note that Hauptmann was playing in Berlin again and she was so alone. Would Robbie come to dinner? Of course, he had gone several times since he left but now Louise had engaged a new maid, and he could only guess what the girl thought when she answered the door to him: husband out the door, another man in. Robbie and Louise escaped to her pretty yellow room, where they broke into giggles.

He had turned over many ideas about earning a living, and as they sat at a supper of cold chicken together, he said, "I think I'll try to be a portraitist, though it can't be easy now with so many photographic studios about. The man who taught me and let me stay with him when I was a student made a good enough living. He wasn't very talented. Some artists are a lot better."

As he poured more wine, she said, "That's what I've been thinking myself, unless you decided to draw on the sidewalks in chalk and collect money in your hat. No, you're perfect for it. You paint people well and you're charming. Women will find you irresistible."

He said, bewildered, "But how do I begin? I don't know anyone. Should I have cards printed, and drop them in mail slots?"

"Perhaps I can make introductions for you."

They spent the next evenings creating a list of people she knew who might want portraits and then writing letters on her personal stationery to them. These were posted on a Monday, and two days later, they had their first response. It came by the new telephone which she had installed in the yellow room.

Covering the mouthpiece, she whispered across the room to him, "It's my old school friend Mrs. Garrett! She has two little girls she wants painted."

"Tell her twenty guineas," he said.

"That will hardly cover your canvas and paint!" she mouthed, and uncovering the receiver again, said loudly and clearly, "He's really very busy these days, but he'll make time for you. It will be fifty guineas. I assure you, Gertrude, he's excellent. You're fortunate he can fit you in."

Robbie walked up and down the street three times before he had the courage to knock at the Garrett family door and announce himself to the butler. The house was grand indeed, with carpeted stairs and formal family portraits from centuries back. Mrs. Garrett, whose enormous bosom sailed before her, led him up the stairs, where he found two girls not more than six years old peering between the banister posts, sticking their tongues out at him.

He set up his easel in the nursery and began to sketch on the canvas, while the children wriggled, complained, made faces, called for water or sweets, or quarreled. He returned three mornings in succession in his best coat and trousers. But they wouldn't be still enough to paint. Sometimes they wouldn't come out from under the bed and the nanny had to pull them out by their feet.

At the end of two weeks, Robbie hadn't progressed with the painting. "But Mrs. Hauptmann said you were experienced," Mrs. Garrett said with great disapproval. "Really, you're exhausting the children. You needn't bother returning."

Exhausting the children! he thought.

He walked all the way back to Louise's house, and when she opened the door, he said, "I've failed."

She pulled him inside and brought him to her little yellow room at once, where she poured him some wine. "Drink it—you need it," she said. "I'll ring for a beef sandwich. That will cheer you up."

"Nothing will cheer me up," he mumbled.

"Nonsense! Everyone knows Gertrude's children are so spoiled they rule the house. It was a bad idea to start you there. The fault's mine."

The next several weeks he obtained no new clients, though he followed Louise dutifully to teas and soirées to find work. Finally, two women said they would try him, but added doubtfully, "You do seem very young."

"I can't help that I'm young," he told Louise.

Robbie walked around the streets of his clients' houses several times before daring to knock; the first portrait in pastel was so clumsy, he hardly knew his own work. For the second, of a Mrs. Darcy, he worked in oils and did better. The client said she would ring when she'd thought about it, and half the evening he waited in the little yellow room looking at the long neck of the black phone as if he could slug it for its silence, and then cursing under his breath when its harsh ring blasted through the room, and it turned out only to be an invitation for Louise. But the second ring was his client, and he heard the woman's voice from the receiver even as Louise mouthed the words to repeat them to him.

"There!" she said afterward. "Mrs. Darcy is so pleased! You did very well. Fifty guineas."

"I wish I hadn't failed with Mrs. Garrett's little monsters."

"Why are you thinking of those naughty children?" Louise demanded. "Mrs. Darcy is recommending you to a friend. She says you made her lovely. Robert, are you listening to me?"

"A little," he said, clutching a pillow against him. "I did it once, but what about the next time?"

He arrived early to his next assignment. His client was shyer than he was, and he gently put her at ease.

Walking home to the boardinghouse reflectively that evening, he found himself under a large oak tree whose roots were littered with acorns. He knelt to gather them. Before he had finished, his pockets were filled, and he had made a sack for more with his handkerchief. When he went home, he wrote an apologetic letter to Mrs. Garrett and asked to try to paint her children again.

Three days later, he walked to her house. The girls looked at him suspiciously, staying on their side of the room. He had set up his easel but didn't approach it. Instead, he sat down cross-legged on the nursery carpet, withdrew an acorn from his pocket, and slowly began to give it a face with his finest brush. He could feel the girls creeping closer, curious.

"You wouldn't be still for me at all," he said, "so I couldn't paint you, but I'm painting your faces on acorns as I did for another child once. Her name is Maggie and she lives in the country. Now, how shall I draw this acorn portrait? How do you feel today? Sweet? Angry? Ready to give me trouble?"

The girls now sat near him on the carpet, watching him work.

"It looks like me," the younger one said, "when I'm happy. Can I have it to keep?"

"Perhaps," Robbie said. "Perhaps I'll even show you how to make them yourself. Let's make a bargain, shall we? For every half an hour you sit still for me for your portrait, we'll make another acorn face. There'll be one for everyone in your family and one for every way you feel. Shake hands. Very well. Here's the first two. When they've dried, I'll shellac them so the paint will stay."

He stood up. "Shall we put them on the bookshelf now to be safe?" he asked, arranging them carefully before the books. "But now you owe me half an hour. Are we agreed?"

They stood in their pinafores, nodding solemnly; one girl slipped her small hand into his for a moment. He arranged them on the sofa and said, "Look at me. Think of how the next acorn shall be. What will it feel? Will it be the sort of acorn that's loved?"

For the next half hour, he divided his attention between his fiercely controlled brushstrokes and teasing them, bantering, sometimes singing sailor songs. Then the portrait was done, the curly heads of the girls together and one with her hand to her mouth as if she were thinking deeply. He received an effusive letter of praise from their mother. The sixty or so completed acorns sat on the bookshelf. He had shellacked them as promised and snipped bits of the girls' hair to paste on the tops of some of them. One had the world's tiniest ribbon fragment in her hair. He thought with some sadness of the housekeeper's niece Maggie at home.

His next commission of children brought the request to also paint acorns. He arrived with them in his pockets and let the boy and girl search for them. He walked back to the boarding-house overflowing with pride and weariness.

He ached to be loved. He was worried about the vicar. He was sick with loneliness. He went to bed with no one. Yet every day he grew in confidence that he could paint portraits that pleased people. Perhaps this is growing up, he thought: learning to be unhappy and alone.

23

MEETING

July–October 1906

Summer came and passed through the house in Nottinghamshire; the fields were deep golden with maize. Anton dressed in
his oldest clothes and took little Maggie to the woods with him
and, when she was tired, carried her on his shoulders. More and
more, he dreaded the hour in which she went home again with
Mary.

Friends wrote him to meet; he deferred. His friend Burrows
had written him twice about having a glass and a meal in the
Old Angel near Lace Market Square and he didn't answer.

In all other moments he was a man stunned with loss who
stood by his own door each night, not wanting to enter. In the
afternoons, he walked to the village and waited by the brick
post office for the postmistress to sort the mail. He always
hoped there would be a letter from Robbie, but there never
was. Then Anton wandered down the street by the stream that
ran from the Trent and home again over the bridge to his study,
where he locked the doors and wrote to London.

> Rob darling,
>
> So many feelings course through me. I write and write to
> you. If I didn't know from Langstaff that you're well, I'd go
> mad. My God, to end it like that after all this time! I wrote
> Louise for your new address.
>
> Aren't we friends? I trust you'll answer me.
>
> A.

There was no response. He began to write again but then
buried his head in his hands. In his rage, he knocked every-

thing from his desk; the ink spilled from the crystal inkwell into the carpet. But surely, one argument couldn't send Rob out the door forever, not even one affair. Surely this was not and couldn't be the end.

I'll go get him, he thought. I'll go to London. Five months is quite enough. I'll put my pride in my pocket. It's time Rob came home.

Anton trimmed his beard and mustache. He chose his clothes carefully: the brown tweed suit with matching vest, a burgundy silk tie. As he glanced in the mirror, his face looked calmer.

When he emerged from the London train station, he found a hansom to take him to the boardinghouse. It was much as he had pictured it: of Georgian stone, the windows neatly curtained. A young man with music under his arm rushed down the steps and passed him. Anton mounted to the dark hall and gave his name to the serving girl. Mr. Stillman was out, she said. Wouldn't return most likely until the evening.

Anton spent the afternoon visiting some small shops a few streets away: in secondhand bookstores with dusty shelves, he bought some medieval history texts for the vicar, though George most likely didn't need them. He bought a hat with flowers for the child but nothing for himself. As the last hour of the early-fall afternoon came, slanting down through the trees with its warm golden light, he sat upon the steps of the boardinghouse with his hat on his knee and parcels by his side to wait. He had eaten nothing that day.

Toward dusk, he saw Rob turn the corner down the street. His jaunty boyish walk was a little weary, and his head was lowered. Anton stood slowly. He was standing with one hand on the railing when Rob came directly up to him, raised his face, and blinked several times. He stood motionless, looking very young. The lamplighter had just come, for this neighborhood was not yet wired for electricity, and the yellowish light shone on the face, which seemed very pale under the little mustache and unruly hair. His white shirt glittered faintly.

Clearing his throat, Anton said, "Sorry to alarm you."

"I'm surprised. I didn't—"

"It's nothing, really. Just come to see how you do."

"Oh, I'm well," was the flustered response.

"You've been away all afternoon."

"I went to the museum and to a client."

"Ah! George tells me you're doing well."

"I try to be as pleasing as I can to people. It's different from painting for myself, what they want rather than what I want. I'm glad to see you, Anton."

"I came today. It's your twenty-fourth birthday."

"You remembered."

"How could I forget? Are you glad to see me?"

Robbie only nodded. For a moment, he looked down to control himself.

Anton thought, This is good. He said, "Well then, may I see your room? I imagine always where you're living. I know you were with Louise and left. And then perhaps take you to dinner?"

"Well, it's not much to see," Robbie said gruffly. "Come up if you want."

Up the carpeted stairs they went, past the sound of laughter and singing behind a few doors. Anton looked about the humble little room, with its stacked books and sketchbooks, its easel crowded against the washstand with its bowl and chipped pitcher, the sketches tacked everywhere. Hands in his pockets, he walked to the window, more to put some distance between himself and Robbie than to see the view. "Overlooks the alley," he said carefully. "How do you get light?"

"I don't work here, and I'll be moving soon. I'm hungry; shall we go to dinner?"

Robbie hurried down the steps in front of Anton, formally nodding at other lodgers in greeting.

The tavern two streets away was nearly empty at this hour, and they slid into a dark booth in the back, where Rob folded his hands upon the table, biting his lip. He looked that way when he first came to me, Anton thought. Desperate to be loved. Undoubtedly, he's had a devil of a time and won't say it.

Robbie asked, "How's George really?"

"He has a new housekeeper, you know. He tells me that he misses you so much, he can hardly bear it. He's proud of you and lonely. I think it's impossible not to be lonely when your friends begin to die. He should have remarried. He had his chances."

Anton hesitated and threw back his head at the approach of the waiter. "But that's not what I want to speak of. Dinner! What do you think of the lamb here?" He lowered his voice and added, "I wish you'd answered my letter, Rob, though I understand you couldn't. I understand a lot about you."

"How are you, Anton?"

"Half there without you. I'm glad you asked."

"I don't want you to be that way."

"I was, I am. I did join the church choir again; they were desperate for a bass. And I'm going to start work on my book again. I try and it stops, but I'll push through."

"I'm very happy about that, Anton. You're a powerful man. I couldn't be the only reason for you."

"I'd given up on myself."

"It hurt me, Anton. Don't you know that?"

The elderly waiter in his heavy apron took their order. Robbie had rested his arms on the table and leaned forward so that his long curly hair obscured his face. The waiter reappeared with two large plates of greasy food and set them down. Robbie said, "You didn't ask for anything to drink."

"I'll have beer; that's all I have these days."

For a time, he and Robbie spoke of small matters, and then, lowering his voice, Anton said, "Everyone asks about you at home, you know. I imagine you're not alone."

Chasing a bit of potato, Robbie murmured, "I am."

Anton pushed away the plate and sat back frowning, his fingers rubbing the edge of his glass. "Are you?" he asked. "I'm alone as well."

"Is Mary's niece still with you?"

"Her mother died and she's around the house a great deal. She talks about you, Rob; she misses you. As I do, of course, so, so much."

Robbie did not reply.

They drank their beers and talked of small village matters and what was new on the London stage. The conversation drifted here and there. Anton said suddenly, "Are you still angry with me? Though why you should be I don't know. This whole thing started with that insipid man, that Donovan."

Robbie's head shot up. "It didn't start with Donovan. It started with you."

But Anton hardly heard the words. He wanted to unbutton Robbie's shirt and feel the gathering of hair on the warm flesh and the hardness and beauty of his chest bone; even this common thing which had been his every day was hidden to him here under buttons and linen and coat.

He gazed at Robbie's hands on the table, which opened and closed nervously. Their plates lay rejected on the side of the large round table, and the students some booths away were laughing uproariously over some music-hall performance. Anton sat back. He murmured wistfully, "Do you love me, Rob? You did a few months ago. I never stopped you from doing anything you wanted. That's why I came today. Come home with me."

Robbie raised his voice. "I can't," he said. "I have to do this on my own. And I can't bear that unhappiness in you. I can't get near you. I think you should...I don't know what you should. Perhaps find someone else to love."

"There can't be anyone else. Do you know nothing about me?" Anton sat back and muttered bitterly, "Of course you don't. You're young, that's all. Ridiculously, stupidly, hurtfully young."

"I'm not so young. You keep me that way. And you! You tore up your article. You tore up what you wanted to be. It was awful to see. Or perhaps it was mainly me. Perhaps I want to be free. To have a chance to go out in the world and find—" The waiter, who was sitting down with a newspaper, raised his eyes; outside of that, the tavern was suddenly quite empty.

Anton withdrew money from his pocket and threw it down on the table. He stood up. "I shouldn't have come," he said. "It's over. Shake hands then. Wish me a good life. Say something kind, you young idiot, even if you don't mean it, even if you're incapable of feeling it."

Anton found his way through the monumental rail station. The train wheels jolted him, and when he came home, no one was there. Even George had gone to bed.

He sat at his desk without moving for some time. He covered his face with his hands as his whole body convulsed with sobs. He thought he would never stop; he put his head down on his arms. When he sat back in his chair again, he whispered, "My God...who am I now? Who have I been?"

He walked up and down for a time and then fell asleep fully clothed.

It took him a week to write to London, and then he tried several times to find the right words to say goodbye...for he felt it was goodbye. Still, he recalled that Robbie's voice had been tremulous at the end, and he had understood the great difficulty his young love had had in pulling away from him. But Anton was also angry; he had had quite enough. He wasn't going to beg, not if he had to be alone all his life.

He told nothing to George, who was leaving on holiday to visit his sisters. A few days later, his housekeeper Mary left to live in York with her new husband and took the little girl.

Then the house was completely silent.

24

ALONE IN THE COUNTRY

November 1906

It was an odd life. He had dinner with Langstaff when the vicar returned. At home he had always made his own fires, though none was needed but for the study. He seldom bothered to heat water for his bath. The rest of the house was very cold and creaked.

He continued to work on his manuscript.

He also began to look through the many boxes he'd shoved away in the attic and the jumbled drawers of his large desk. With the curtains drawn against the earlier November darkness, he read at his desk, resting his cheek on his hand, with the yellow flowered glass lamp beside him.

There were folded letters jammed between the drawer and the desk casing ("To Antonio on your eighteenth birthday from Langstaff. Christ bade us love one another, which must include loving yourself. Advice to one who never takes it."). He found bills of sale for riding boots and the gray mare that had died. From an accounting book fell a postcard of a girl dressed as a milkmaid on a swing, and he realized with a shock that it was a studio photograph of Louise taken just before he had met her. He had written on the back, "Love will make me whole if anything will." There was a mourning ring woven from someone's dark hair and a prayer book with an inscription in a childish hand: "Antonio Richard Harrington, age seven years. God bless me and my parents. 1878." Over that was inscribed in pale brown ink, "To my beloved Dickie from Mama."

A photograph of himself at the university, clean-shaven, grinning, his arms around two friends, ready to go boating on the river. One leg jauntily up on a stone. An oval tinted likeness of a young man he'd known in school who said once he had loved him.

Letters from various banks. "We are pleased to offer you a promotion once more...." The work was not bad; it was just that he had been apart from it. It was just never what he wanted.

He thought again and again of his father. What can you do when love and hate from your earliest experience are inextricably twined? When to please the one person you must please, you must lose your soul, and even in that, there is no pleasing? "No one will ever know the poverty of my youth, the bitterness," his father had said. A factory boy from the age of seven, but one year of schooling. Yet sometime later when he most wanted to hate his father, he remembered being very small and sitting on the carpet with him, marching animals two by two into the ark, making animal sounds.

Anton began to write down his thoughts on scrap paper, on the backs of envelopes, on stationery from various hotels. The clock struck ten, and outside, the snow was falling, and he had found an unused ledger book; he bent over the desk with such intensity that his neck ached with the effort. He wrote slowly. This took letter form.

> So much to tell you, Rob. You asked and asked, and I was silent. I am sorry I never told you about what happened to Bess and our child.

Anton began to rise then and made himself resume sitting on his desk chair. He bit the edge of his finger. Then he hesitated and continued to write.

> I was sixteen when I met her. I didn't love her as I love you. I think through her I hoped to meld with that small community of people who saw me as their protector, young as I was.
>
> I told my father, "I slept with one of the girls in Squatters' Field," and he said, "Good for you, boy!" I was hiding so much from him then, clinging to a little of his love, and didn't want to be that thing he suspected I was, a boy who

wanted to be with other boys. So, I said, "I got her with child; I want to marry her. I'll leave school and support her. I'll work with my hands. I can build." I suppose I thought he'd respect me for my honor. Oh God, the way we see things when we're young!

Anton stopped once more and looked into the fire. He dipped the pen again.

My father dragged me to the barn and whipped me with his riding crop. I remember he was shouting, "If your socialism weren't bad enough! Do you want to bury our name I fought so hard for and live with a whore?"

I finally managed to knock him down. Then I escaped to the vicarage. George took me in. I was supposed to speak at the Socialists' Union that night, and of course I couldn't. I felt my life was ended. I wanted to kill my father, to bash his head in, but George held me back.

I returned to school, and when I came home again in the spring, Bess was gone, no one knew where. I wrote to every workhouse within fifty miles. Her mother had gone to family in Ireland, and I sent money to her until she died.

Then my father wrote he'd help me find her if I'd return from India, where I had found employment after university. The condition was to work for him for a year. I thought he meant to make up things between us. My mother was dead by then. And I saw he was very ill and pitied him. I was tall and strong, and his flesh was melting away.

He wrote now intensely before something inside him should stop him.

My dearest Rob! This is what I did that year so I could find the girl and our child. I dismissed workers who had joined the Socialists' Union; I told people their pay was halved and their work increased. Then there were rumors the landowner wanted to pull down the houses in Squatters' Field. That of all things I couldn't have; I would have no part of it. I told the people there I'd protect them. I swore it still. My father promised me it would never happen; he was good friends with the landowner.

But he sent me to London on business for a week, and while I was away, men evicted the people and destroyed their homes. I came back to rubble. By then my father was in the last of his dying; he didn't live a week. A cancer inside him ate him. He never told me where Bess had gone. He was silent to the end, but you see, he didn't know where she was. He had lied to me. He never knew.

I found out years later.

I was in Switzerland, climbing there, when Burrows forwarded news that the body of a young woman and an infant had been found in the hayloft of a deserted barn. He knew her by the pendant necklace she wore; I had showed it to him before I gave it to her. On the pendant were our initials. I don't even know if the child had been a son or a daughter. Rats had got them. They may have starved. So ended the girl who had trusted me.

That day I cut my wrist with my pocketknife and lay down upon the inn floor to bleed to death. But just then, from outside the window, I heard the call of one of those alpine horns. Something broke in me, and I shouted for help.

For days I lay in hospital. The police came to make inquiries, as they do in such a case. Would they have tried me against myself? I don't know. People don't know how to treat a man who has tried to take his own life. What do you say to him? Are you polite, consoling, indifferent?

Anton bent over his fourth sheet of paper; ink stained his forefinger. Outside, a tree branch brushed against the window.

When I could, I traveled by coach to another inn to be alone. I walked a little. I didn't write George. I couldn't tell him the truth.

In my walks, things I had ceased to notice over the years

of my broken marriage seemed precious: the sun glittering in the flowers and the snow of the mountaintops, even my own body, which had failed with women and longed for men. At night I'd walk through the village, aware of the lights behind curtains. And I wondered if in some strange way, since God had spared me, life would open for me again.

I came home. You were there. You found me drunk on the sofa.

These months I must tell you (though it will undoubted- ly surprise you) I have returned to the oddly personal faith which came to me at other times in my life. I'm at George's church every Sunday. And now and then I go out and repair the roof for some poor family. It doesn't bring back the Field and its people, but it is something.

Life is a precious thing, Robbie. All this is long ago, and I've spent too long mourning over it. In my dreams, my father comes to me and says he's sorry. He's not a big man, as I saw him, but shorter than me and weak, for there's nothing weaker than a bully. But I've withdrawn from my friends and poor Louise and you, and for that I'm sorry.

And yet, though I know I am not a perfect man and the obsessiveness of my love for you stifled you, I know I also helped you and believed in you. I want to change what I can, to do what good I can in the world. We each ask, why are we here? We come up with different answers, but there must be some answer. Without a personal answer of some sort, we are lost.

Who is this man, Anton, whom you once loved so much? I'm not old; I am thirty-five. I can take up what I threw away.

When Anton had finished the last lines, he sat by the desk with the clock ticking and the soft crackle of the fire. He glanced at the many loose pages of the ledger. Some of the writing was so intense that the pen had nearly ripped the old paper, and on the reverse side, you could see the ghosts of the letters.

It was past two and the world was asleep. He walked to the window, pulling back the curtains, and gazed into the darkness. Then after a time he packed away the older treasured things in a box to carry up to the attic.

He wrote further memories of his life and childhood over the next several nights: the rich things, the dark things, the painful things, everything he had not said. He copied a few new chapters from his book about the poor, including his rewritten story of the Field. The pile of papers grew, and he finally enclosed them in a folder on which he had written the words "For Rob." He had no idea if he would ever send it.

He and George drove the gig down the familiar road the next evening. They passed through the village—light in a window from a lamp on a dining table, the high voices of children—and then that was left behind, and they turned to the city of Nottingham. In the shadows a few men were smoking. Some other carts had passed him, and a gaseous motorcar, snorting and smoking.

In the streets, all the shops had closed, the empty bars and chains of their signs moving slightly in the small wind. At the church, he and George climbed from the gig and tied Blackie to a post. Down the steps, he could see, there was a light under the door, though the sign, Independent Labour Party, was too dark to read.

It was the same: the large, shabby room, the socialist posters, the scuffed walls, the tea in chipped cups, the piles of outdated socialist newspapers on a table, the shelves of books about socialism.

Some people stared at him coldly, but old friends left their seats and gathered around him. Mrs. Cullen brought them cups of tea.

His old friend Burrows came forward, his narrow face both wary and hopeful. "Back, are you?" he said. "You'll find us struggling, as always. We're trying to convince men to vote for the Labour candidate for city council. Some businessmen are coming next week. We need a strong speaker about why workhouses must be abolished, and the poor provided for in decent private housing with public funds and money for their needs. The affluent must care for the needy. We can't wait any longer. We can't permit another soul to die of want."

His neighbors came to hear Anton speak the following Tuesday, including Hayes, to whose supper party he had taken Robbie one mild autumn evening when Anton had first come home from Switzerland.

He spoke in the church undercroft. His voice traveled easily to the half-filled chairs and many skeptical faces. At sixteen, it had been the earnest voice of a very young man; now it was deeper and fuller.

Afterward, some people left muttering, and a few shook his hand. His neighbor Hayes walked toward him. "Are you going back to the socialism of your boyhood, Anton?" he asked. "This is an industrial city. Not that we don't give to charity, but we believe it's every man's personal responsibility to rise from poverty. Are you advocating that we give our money away?"

"I'm advocating that the more fortunate help by paying higher taxes," Anton said. "I'm advocating for living wages and old-age pensions. You may not invite me to any more of your gracious dinners."

"I'll invite you. My friends are appalled, but my wife sees things as you do. A small number believe and support this party, mostly of course the workers."

"We need a majority."

Anton let his hand linger on the socialist books on the shelf, which had so astonished him when he had first read them; he felt the strength of the authors seep through the pages to his palm. He saw his life both as he had been then and as he was now. Nothing that had happened in the years between, his interests and sorrows and passions, was more important than this. For these hours and a time after, he even forgot his young love who had left him.

25

FRIENDS AND LOVERS

December 1906–Summer 1907

In December, Robbie arrived at the seasonal gathering at the house in Russell Square owned by the wealthy lover of one of the boardinghouse actresses. Even before the maid took his coat, he already felt discomfited by the heavy cigarette smoke in the air and the dozen people who walked past him, briefly gazing at him as if deciding he was not worth knowing.

He wandered from room to room looking for the actress and finally walked up the grand staircase. He found an actor who was willing to talk to him; Robbie felt a surge of sexuality standing near him and decided against it. He hated the noisy gathering, yet the cold solitary night was not much of a welcome either.

He ended up on the servants' stairs, where he stumbled across a man on top of a seated woman, her skirt pulled up, their eyes closed in ecstasy. Her stockings shimmered pink. He walked downstairs again, took a sandwich from the many plates of food on the dining room table, and turned into the small coatroom for his coat.

Another man was there hanging up his hat; he said, "Stillman."

Robbie said, "Keith!" He had not been so happy to see anyone in a long time. He had heard that Keith Donovan had returned from Paris with an English lord who was his lover.

Robbie kissed Keith's cheek. Was there still anger between them? It was odd to meet again in a place so close and stuffy.

"What, back in London?" Keith asked, lighting a cigarette. "Everyone worth knowing is here tonight. And where's your…? Forgot his name."

"He's not with me."

"Not with anyone?"

"No."

They stood among the coats and hats, hearing the noise of the party. Someone was singing something in French, perhaps bawdy, for people were laughing. "And you," Robbie said. "What are you doing?"

"Painting and falling in love."

The light was very dim, but Keith seemed flushed. Perhaps he had been drinking. He twisted this way and that as he spoke and rubbed at his cheeks. "A little rouge," he said. "I just smeared a bit on. Do you think I look less pale?"

"I think you should wipe it off before you leave."

"Always and still the conservative young genius, Stillman! I know your face too. So, love's not gone right for you? Your heart's broken? I'm sorry. I am." Keith hunched his shoulders. "What's the use of hiding all the time? My lover's powerful. He likes the rouge."

"We read about people being arrested."

"Not likely for you, not being with anyone. Besides, most of us are safe; the ones caught have offended someone in power."

"It's horrid."

"You're boring, Stillman. Still, we should have whiskey and talk some more. Did I tell you my family wants me never to set foot in Dublin again? They're ashamed of me. They're rich. When I'm famous, they'll be sorry. Stop caring so much, Stillman. Life's easier that way."

Robbie stayed a time in the solitude of the coat room, found his coat among many others, and went out into the December night. He walked alone, hearing his own footsteps and the sound of carol practice from the local church. He felt he had been in another world during the few hours of the party.

January turned. He was painting or making pen-and-ink portraits all the time, and his reputation grew fast. His fingers, still smelling of oils and turpentine, sometimes drummed restlessly on the legs of his elegant trousers. His mind wandered to the faces of the portraits he had painted—the hopeful debutantes, the small boys stuffed into sailor suits—and the same need he saw in all of them: to be cherished. He always felt he could do better. He was relentless, horribly lonely. He longed to touch someone.

Almost every day, Robbie fought his way through the deep yellow fog to the houses of clients, his sketchbooks and pens in a stout leather bag, snow on his small mustache and curly hair He was always losing his hat. He left his easel at the home of each client until that job was done. His own boarding-house room was so drafty that water froze in his washbasin, and a small ridge of ice formed on the inside of his window. Bronchial troubles left him spitting hot yellow mucus until he was too sick to go out.

One of the actresses took his note to Louise. He had written in an uneven hand, *I'm rather ill. Could you come?* Two hours later he heard Louise's voice on the stairs. She hurried across the room and felt his forehead. "Really, you're as stubborn as Anton," she scolded. "Please come back with me."

"I need to fight things out on my own."

"Perhaps, but I need you. My husband's touring in Germany again and I'm alone. I miss you."

He remembered then all their long conversations at night, far beyond his work but of what they both wanted in the world. He nodded, exhausted.

He walked slowly to the waiting cab, stopping for breath. Had the pneumonia returned? And then the cab brought them to Eccleston Square, and he climbed slowly up the stairs and once more into his lovely old bedroom. The thick curtains drawn against the noise of cabs and horses welcomed him. Two of Louise's china dolls had been set on his bed, and a fire burned in the hearth.

She must have been determined he would come; she smiled.

The doctor arrived soon and said bed rest and beef broth and nourishing meals would cure him. When he left, Louise sat down on a chair beside him and struggled with words. Her eyes were bright with tears. "I'm worried about you," she said. "And I'm lonely."

"I'm lonely too," he said, reaching out his hand for hers. He said, "What is it, dear?"

"I've miscarried a child again. The second time. Two months in."

"Oh, Louise."

"Ernst would come back at once if I wrote him, but this is such a chance for him. Robbie, here you are! You're such a comfort to me! Isn't it beautiful, though, that we're here just together, the dearest friends? Did you ever think such a thing when we first met?"

A few afternoons later, when he felt well enough to walk downstairs, he found her at her desk frowning over a letter. He said hoarsely and fondly, "You look like one of those suffragettes who pass out pamphlets for women's votes, the ones in huge hats who chain themselves to something and stand on soapboxes to preach."

She said seriously, "No, I'm a sad, childless woman burying my unhappiness in trying to help you. Here are the names of two people who called when you were ill." She pressed the end of her new fountain pen against her lips. She said, "I think we should raise your price to a hundred guineas and see if we can go higher in the spring."

"So much!" He crossed his arms over his chest. He said, "You're taking care of me. I wish I didn't need people to take care of me."

"We all do! And then we take care of others. Besides, you're another brother to me."

"I'm very glad to be your brother," he said.

Sitting in a chair by the parlor fire later that day, he drank hot tea and ate sandwiches. When he had been sick, he had had time to think of many things. It was already February, and there were the friends he had not looked up in months because he had been so busy. Though he had met Keith Donovan at the party a little while ago, he wanted to see him again, acerbic as his friend had been. Not that Robbie blamed him; their breakup the year before had been uncomfortable and hurtful. Robbie wondered if they could take up with each other again. Keith was likely alone. He never kept his lovers long; the Irishman had said it himself. Robbie thought Keith had given him his new address, but perhaps Robbie had lost it.

He was returning from work a few weeks following and had bought the newspaper from a lad on the street. He stood first skimming it, waiting for his omnibus, which was always too full and always late, but he was too economical to take cabs unless he was carrying a great deal. He boarded the omnibus, let the ladies take the seats, and stood balanced by the pole to keep from being hurled about by the abrupt starts and stops.

A small article deep within the newspaper pages caught his eye and the words "arrested for gross indecency and sentenced to two years imprisonment with hard labor." That always made his stomach hurt.

He would have turned the page quickly, but this time he didn't. He reread the paragraph several times until his eyes blurred and the omnibus's jolting threatened to bring up his lunch. He pushed his way to the doors and descended, some way before his own stop.

Robbie leaned against a kiosk plastered with theater announcements, finding the article again, tearing it out carefully. He walked as if half drunk, seeing nothing. Drivers shouted at him as he crossed the street. He had the small article in his fist now, the rest of the paper dropped in a trash receptacle; every time he looked at it, it was more wrinkled and fragile but didn't change.

He walked up the few steps of Louise's house.

Voices drifted from the parlor. He found her there with two actors they knew, and when he saw their stricken faces, Robbie understood they also had heard the news.

Louise stood. She said, "Oh, darling, Jonathan came to tell me. Your friend Keith was lured by some stranger who turned him in to the police. It almost always happens that way. If they have two witnesses, they can do it. People make money from it. Simply a way to earn cash for some. Earn ten pounds and end a life."

Robbie felt dazed as she took his arm, leading him alone to her private parlor with the yellow-flowered wallpaper. He walked across the white carpet and opened the two glass doors to the cold wintry garden and stepped out. He said bitterly, "He was just beginning to draw again seriously, and now they've thrown him in prison for two years for what?"

Louise took his arm to walk among the empty flower beds. "And how he loves beautiful things!" she said. "He loathed not being amid beauty. My God, what happens now: the bad food, the hard labor, the solitary confinement."

They sat down on the stone bench, arms about each other. She rested her head on his shoulder. "You know, Keith and I met at your exhibition. A few months ago, we began to meet for lunch. He needed a friend."

"I didn't know that. Oh God, this will destroy him, Louise."

"Yes, it will. A friend's husband, the father of three and a good man, has also just been denounced and sent to two years hard labor. He has asthma and it will likely kill him. And your aesthetic slender Keith picking oakum with convicts, his head shaved?"

"Louise! Stop! I can't bear this. I don't know what to do with this."

The next morning, he worked badly on his latest portrait; in the late afternoon he walked into All Saints Margaret Street. In a pew he knelt with his face buried in his hands. The devout atmosphere of this famous Victorian Gothic church with its brilliant painted walls comforted him. George always had faith, but where was Robbie's? Stuffed in his pocket beneath receipts and coins and pencil nubs?

Half the time he prayed for Keith; he had written a letter to him last night at the penitentiary saying that any help he could give him he would, that he would find a friend in Robbie when he got out. The other half hour he thought about Anton. *I failed him*, he thought. *It's my fault. He was right; I was too young. And now he never writes. The one person who could really make it all right for me never sends a word. That day when he came to find me, and I turned him away was the end for him.*

God knows now what he's doing at home alone. George's words aren't enough.

But for myself, I can't be alone anymore.

He wanted someone to be sweet to him and make love to him. By this time, he was desperate, though he loathed the memory that he had ever gone to that pub. Then he noticed Louise's actor friend Lawrence, who had been in her house when Robbie found out about Keith and who appeared later at one of her dinner parties. Lawrence was beautiful, thin, aesthetic, and Robbie's height, with a way of distractedly pushing back his blond hair when he spoke and a shy smile. He was twenty-five, just Robbie's age. His eyes were pure blue. He tended to lean a little backward, hand on one hip.

After the dinner party they left discreetly and hailed a motor cab; as they sped northeast from Eccleston Square over the bumpy streets, they spoke in low voices about theater and art, though that was not what either of them was thinking. When they reached Lawrence's flat on the fourth floor of a street in the working-class district of Clerkenwell, which smelled of sausages, they closed the door and immediately made love on the iron-framed bed.

Lying close afterward, Lawrence stroked Robbie's cheek and said, "I looked at you across the flowers on the table tonight. I've actually been looking at you when I could over these past months."

They sat up in bed drinking wine, and Robbie gazed at the

theatrical posters and one especially announcing the great aging actor Henry Irving at the Lyceum. "I took a small role in that play," Lawrence said. He put his hand on Robbie's bare knee. "You smiled! When you're happy, you have a radiant smile."

"I want to be happy. I'm working hard. Sometimes I just need to forget. Poor Keith! They say he can't have any visitors for three months, that he's in solitary confinement. It makes me want to spend every hour with people I care about. How will he manage? To be alone…that always frightened me."

"Who were you with before?"

"Someone older than me. We grew and changed."

Later, as he lay awake with the actor sleeping in his arms, he wished Lawrence had not asked about Anton, because the thought of him was now so vivid. He remembered the time in the farmhouse when he had talked to Anton all through the night until first light. What would he say to him now? Robbie had another life. He was painting all over; he was invited to artists' dinners or society gatherings. He managed to get Annie her first portrait commission, which paid as much as two months of hand-painted cards for tourists.

He liked Lawrence but he didn't love him; perhaps he would in time. He had shut up his heart, especially since Keith's arrest. He felt he didn't even know what was in his heart. He didn't want to talk; he wanted to lose himself again in the sweatiness and dizzy glory of sex in this cluttered room full of theatrical posters.

He would have known nothing of Anton's activities back in the country if it had not been for George's letters, which he sometimes read carefully and sometimes didn't. But it was a damp, wet night when he came home to another one. No one was in the house but the maid. He stood in his room looking at the rain pouring down the windowpane and then read. Anton was speaking in the church undercroft on socialism tomorrow night.

He didn't tell Louise where he was going; he told no one.

How strange to be in Nottingham again, which was so much darker than London and at night so much quieter. When he walked from the train station, he saw the leaflets on lampposts; someone else was handing them out. It was not very far to the church, where people were going down the steps. The banner, which flapped in the light wind, read, *Fair wages and housing for all. Meeting at 7.*

The room was full; there were a lot of women, some with children. He found a chair in the back and looked around, suddenly sitting forward on his chair. On one wall hung three of his unframed pictures. There was Sarah Elders, age seventy-eight, laundress; she had laughed when he had drawn her and showed her few teeth. There was a drawing of two haunted boys with thin, angry faces, and the third picture was of a little girl who had a slit of a mouth and meagre braids. These were drawn in the days when he had first lived with the vicar. They had not hung in the London exhibition. Anton must have brought them from the studio.

Anton was sitting to the side with several people and difficult to see clearly. Three men spoke fully, and finally Anton rose. His beard was rougher, and his speech was rougher, and his clothes were his old ones and wrinkled, yet when he began to talk, the room grew quiet. His spoke about the need to strengthen the trade unions, to assure fair wages and decent condition and hours. It was the same rich, resonant voice which had called through the rooms of the house: Robbie! Robbie was so drawn into the sound that he lost Anton's words.

He noticed his fourth picture: the model Rose, who had put gin in his tea and tried to seduce him. *Girl from the Slums*, he had called it. Rose, he thought.

At the end, many people stood up and cheered.

Robbie left the church alone and walked away in the darkness across Market Square. But the Goose Fair wasn't around; it was winter, and all the tents were gone. If he lived here, they could go in the autumn again. He had been such a boy; now he was tall and his shoulders full, his walk smooth, his clothes tailored. His arms swung; his hair under his bowler was long and curly again. Lawrence called it his Renaissance look.

Robbie walked across the great square hearing his own footsteps, hands in pockets, shoulders hunched. He reached the train station and hesitated. He boarded swiftly at the last moment.

Two days later, early in the morning, a short letter came. He didn't consign it beneath his underwear in a drawer like the thick envelope of paper he had received from Anton some weeks before, still unopened. This one he read standing in the vestibule of Louise's lovely house. Anton's familiar handwriting jolted him.

Rob, I saw you at the meeting but then you left. Where did you go? I went to Market Square hoping you'd be there, but it's so damn big and then the London train had just departed. I suppose you were bewildered by my speaking. Rather odd to take up again what I left off half a lifetime ago, a long time to put down an important task. I hope it was all right with the drawings on the wall. I didn't have time to frame them but the one of Rose was already in a frame. I sent you a quite thick letter and other writing. You never wrote if you received them. It was rather personal, and I hope it didn't go astray.

I should open the package, Robbie thought, but he almost didn't want to do it, wary of what might be in it. The third day was like most; he painted both morning and early afternoon, saw two new clients about commissions, called for the third time for his fee with another. His unfinished painting of the wife of a member of the lower house now sat on the easel in Louise's little sitting room, a cloth protecting the white rug.

When he came through Louise's house door at the end of the day, he thought, I must go look now.

Robbie climbed to his room and pulled off his clothes, dropping them on a chair, and rummaged in the drawer for the package, slitting it open and pulling out several letters, papers, and folders. When he looked closer, he saw they were meditations and narratives, some addressed to him and others to no one in particular, some composed of many loose sheets folded together. There was also a letter.

He lit the lamp and dropped on the bed to read. With his cheek on one hand and lying on his stomach, he turned page after page. He read the letter and then, very carefully, the newly written article on Squatters' Field; a note on the page said it would be published soon with the drawing. After that Robbie couldn't bear to read any more.

He rose to walk to the desk. At first the words of his own letter were slow, then rushed. The fountain pen leaked.

Anton, I was rude not to have read your letter and written back right away when the package came a time ago, but I just have read it now and I'm shaken. It breaks my heart to think of Bess and your child dead and you not knowing; it breaks my heart to think of what happened to you in Switzerland. And you said so little. You know I suspected since we were first together what caused the scar on your wrist as well as the ones on your shoulders. If I ever find your father's ghost, I'll kill him a second time for what he did to you. Tonight, I want to go inside of you and kiss away every bad memory. I would!

You can go back to what you wanted from the start. I always said it. I always asked. I know your book will be exquisite. Squatters' Field breaks my heart. It's better than the first version you destroyed. I'll read your poetry soon.

Yes, I was there the other night, and so proud I didn't know what to say to you. You were surrounded; I would have had to push through the people to reach you. I felt myself so apart from you. To tell you the truth, I felt a little unworthy of you, a little shallow. I'm becoming charming and fashionable, and what is that compared to what I wanted most to paint or draw? Louise has me wear 1810 John Keats shirts and velvet coats and silk cravats to create a romantic image to earn better compensation. But perhaps my work helped you a little. Perhaps my drawings of the poor did something. The first evening we had together, you asked me what I felt between human compassion and profitability or something like that and I gave a schoolboy response.

Some men I overheard said you will be at the mines and public halls in towns as well soon. I was astonished. It was as if I saw who you were separate from me, and I've never been able to do that before. Do you know, one of the hardest things I ever did was to stop being your lad?

I was so distant when we had dinner months ago. I was a little defended against you. I'm sorry. I don't know where the boundaries of me stop, and you begin. Do you? I will seal and send this before I lose courage.

Another letter came in a few days from Nottinghamshire.

Yes, you guessed about the scars, but these things are over. The important thing is, I've returned to the work I love, as humble (and humbling) as it is, and feel for the first time in a while that I have a purpose. Burrows and friends are always around. We talk of nothing but the Labour movement.

You have your art and gatherings and I imagine you'll fall in love again with someone who loves you; it's your nature. I understand it now. You fell in love with me because I was there to love you. Just be careful, that is all I ask of you.

A.

Robbie wrote back impulsively, *Is there anyone for you? Man or woman?*

The answer came back simply. *Yes, there's a man, older than me, a miner now working for socialism. We are discreet. I send you my love. Always ask me anything you might need of me.* And then Robbie felt the sudden hot flash of jealousy. Is that all we are? he asked himself. He did not say a word about Lawrence.

Robbie buried his feelings; he had to. He was the rising young artist, and Louise's telephone kept ringing for him. Almost every day, he was meeting strangers, charming them, making them calmer as he slowly observed their uniqueness. He wore his romantic dark red silk cravats. As spring came on, maids welcomed him into elegant houses, taking his hat. A woman or man would come forward and press his hand. They said, "We are very pleased you made time for us, Mr. Stillman."

"Is it my silks and boyish looks they're hiring or my talent?" he asked Annie one evening, and she shrugged and said, "Oh, heavens, don't ask! Simply smile, paint, and kiss their hands. Thanks for the new commission. I have money for a new dress."

"Oh, anything for you," he said.

By June, he had so much work that he hardly could keep up with it. With a shock, he realized that he was doing well, though at night he was too tired to do more than fall asleep. George had continued to write every week, and Robbie didn't expect anything out of the ordinary in the letter that came in the middle of the summer.

> My dearest lad, I would under very few circumstances ask you to come back for a time, but I'm presently doing just this.
>
> Antonio is in financial difficulties. This apparently has been years in the making, and he has been living on borrowed sums for some time and it's all come due. It is as astonishing to me as it must be to you. Now it seems he may lose the house and his beloved horses. I think he will listen to you if he ever has listened to anyone. He cares for nothing except the book he's writing and speaking all over. He's like burning fire, Rob. I have not seen him like this since he was a boy.

Robbie tore the letter, threw it to the floor, and buried his head in his hands. He ran down the steps and walked all over the city until late, arriving at his appointment the next morning exhausted but with a clear mind, though as his brush moved across the canvas, he murmured low under his breath, "What has he done?"

"I don't want you to go back there," Lawrence told him when they were together, holding him fiercely. "Let him go, Robbie; let him go. I'm in love with you. Say goodbye to him now and always."

"I must see what I can do to help," Robbie said. "Don't you see I owe him that? Then I'll come back, I promise."

He withdrew most of his money from his bank, also selling the investments that had made up his inheritance. He tucked the envelope containing the bank cheque into the side pocket of his smaller suitcase and took the train to the Midlands. The newspaper lay on his knees, and he remained silently gazing out the window with his hand to his mouth.

26

BURIED PAPERS

Summer 1907

He stopped at the cottage for only a few moments to greet the vicar, who was with two parishioners.

"Oh, lad, you're back," said the older of the women, who had known him since he had come to live there.

"We miss you, Mr. Stillman," said the grave younger woman, who collected clothing for the unfortunate. "I hear you singing the hymns when you're in church."

Hugging George, Robbie told him he would soon return. Then he took the suitcase and set off down the path.

Before him was the farmhouse and, behind it, the fenced-in field with several horses peacefully flicking their tails. A colt leaped amid the high grass. It was all so beautiful, it didn't appear possible that there could be any trouble in this place. Beyond was the beginning of the forest.

The house door was unlocked, but when he called up from the vestibule, no one answered. He mounted to the study.

Dust hung in the sunlit room, which smelled of tobacco, and the desk was littered with piles of paper. To the right on the table was the same decanter he recalled seeing the first time he walked into this room. It was empty. Robbie almost wished there were some brandy or port, as he needed something himself. Instead, he walked to the bedroom to pour water from the pitcher, trying not to notice the bed. Despite his outer calm, he didn't feel it inside.

Gazing for a time from the window, he saw no one coming up the path, and the horses grazed as if all the peace and summer of the world were theirs. For a long time, he looked down, and then turned to the room again and the littered desk.

The first thing he noticed was the manuscript, now quite thick, handwritten in Anton's large clear writing. *Lives of the Nottinghamshire Poor* was underlined on the front page. How had he written so much? He wouldn't have typed it; he had no patience for typing.

Then there were the bills.

Standing beside the desk, he began to leaf through the papers and then slowly lowered himself to the chair. There were so many things owing: candles, dairy, butcher, but those were the least of them. Beneath were loans at such and such percent; it went on and on. The bank statements from London and Nottingham, the older ones listing large sums invested, others far smaller until there was nothing, the promises to pay, even some of the exhibition bills not settled, and the house put up as collateral.

"My God!" he whispered, his head pounding.

He looked up.

Anton was standing at the door. He seemed a little heavier in his flannels and corduroys, his beard untrimmed. For some moments, they stared at each other, and then Robbie slowly rose. He was sick with feeling to be standing in this old room again with this man he had last heard speak in a church undercroft.

"To what do I owe this honor?" Anton asked coldly. It was utterly unlike the seductive voice of the man who had come to London to bring him home or the tender words of the letter and all the pages he had sent.

Robbie pushed his hair back from his forehead. He said, "I should have written first."

"It would have been decent of you."

"Anton, for God's sake! George wrote me! These bills... yes, I've looked. What are you doing? What has happened? You always said your father left you a small fortune. I can't see what you've done with it."

"I spent it well."

"My paints and exhibition weren't that much. And the travel..."

"It wasn't those things."

"Then what was it? Anton!"

Anton flushed deeply. He was too moved and cornered to speak, and the words came gruffy and defensively as he pulled the bills toward him and roughly gathered them in a heap. "Very well then. I gave the money away."

"You gave it away? To whom? Anton!"

Anton retrieved a few fallen papers and smoothed them into the heap. He smiled crookedly, defensively. "To people who needed it. Little by little. I didn't intend it to be all. Do you know how many people sleep on the streets in bitter winter in this country? I only helped anonymously." His voice rose and cracked a little. "Even working people have nothing. Their children eat bread if that. There's nothing on the bread. It's bad bread."

He urged the pile of papers a little from him and muttered, "I didn't give it myself. My old friend Tom Burrows did it for me. I didn't want it traced to me. Now you know and I don't feel good about it. I feel ashamed. I never felt proud. I couldn't find any pride in me. None."

Robbie had sat back further in the chair as if pressed into it as Anton spoke. His whole instinct was to rise and pull Anton to him. His heart rushed. He said incredulously, "It's strange, it's—"

Anton flung back his head and his untrimmed hair whipped back. He said, "I told you once I didn't want my inheritance. You didn't take me seriously. And what was the point in keeping it when you left? The rest went."

"But, Anton, you can't lose our house."

"Oh, is it *our* house now?" Anton answered, his voice suddenly cold again. "Really, is it? The last time I looked, I was the only one of us living in it."

"Stop it! An old habit of speaking—you know what I mean. Here's money. I earn a great deal these days. Some is what my mother left me. I don't want it." He unbuckled his suitcase pocket.

"You owe me nothing," Anton shouted, slamming his hands on the desk. "And what you owed me, all that I wanted, you took from me—your love—can anything make up that? You come back after all this time to make it up with money?"

"You gave no indication you were thinking of me."

"I gave no indication I wasn't."

"Oh, you very well did. You have a lover. I didn't come here to be shouted at."

"I'm not reduced to needing to be taken care of, Stillman."

"Never, never call me that!" Robbie shouted, slamming his palms on the desk. "Never, do you hear me? If you think I'm weak, think again. Don't you need me at all? Have you ever? For anything?"

"Yes, I've needed you and you're not here."

Robbie stood but clung to the desk; he would do something. He would sweep the papers to the floor. He would hurl things. He would shove Anton down.

Anton dropped to the sofa suddenly. "But you're here now," he said quietly. "And it's lovely to know that."

Robbie sat cautiously beside him. He could see the warm brown eyes and the untrimmed mustache, which touched the upper lip. In that moment, many emotions of regret, fury, and tenderness rushed upon him. He moved his hand to Anton's shirt, and then raised it to the thick hair.

The moment he touched Anton, he felt a wild rush of dizziness and huge strength; he moved closer and kissed Anton's mouth hard. His heart was pounding. He felt so much, he couldn't make a word or a feeling into a sentence. *Lock the door...acorns on the roof... What's that scar? Why did you shout out? Tell me, tell me. If anyone hurts you, I'll kill them.*

They were on the rug now, and still the jagged words rushed through his head, held within him for these months. *Winter's cold! You forgot the... Read to me, hold me, make love to me. Nothing, nothing but you.*

Their mouths and hands were all over each other. He bit, he tossed, he tasted. His arms were pinned. He gave up then. He lay panting on his back, staring at the ceiling and felt Anton's mouth on him saying, "Let yourself." He closed his eyes, his stomach heaving, sweat gathering all over his body and tried to hold back. It was no use. He poured himself out; it took him in spasms.

Then he pushed Anton back on the rug and unbuttoned his trousers and made love to him with his mouth. Still the strange, jagged thoughts came. A *lock of hair… Will you take care of yourself? Goose feathers. Cartwheels and the rising dust. Fill the lantern, lad.*

They lay breathing hard after; Robbie ran his hand down Anton's chest. After a time, he sat up a little, wearing only his shirt. Two of the buttons had been ripped open so fast, they had fallen to the rug.

He looked at Anton. "When you took me to Italy years ago," he said with the old wonder, "I thought some of the male paintings looked like you, the paintings. Titian would have liked to draw you."

"We missed each other by a few hundred years."

"You will keep the money?"

"Yes, darling."

Robbie ran his hand down Anton's inner thigh; he wanted more than anything in the world to kiss and nibble that thigh from the inner knee to the crevice of the hip and then on again. He tried to hold back the feeling that they shouldn't have done this. He was supposed to say what he wanted; and now he was supposed to know what he wanted to feel. And of course, this was impossible; it shouldn't have happened.

He moved up to rest his head on Anton's chest, trying to be calmer. It was not like their nights together when they could be calm because they were both simply there. "I like the sound of your heart," he said clumsily. "How steady it is."

Anton held him close. "Hand, dear," he said.

Their fingers clasped; they lay silent.

After a time, he whispered in Robbie's ear.

"English, please," Robbie said, entranced by the mustache, which tickled him.

"Harder to say in English. *Ti voglio bene…*too tender, I suppose, but I won't translate. You have a lover now. What's his name?"

"I don't want to tell. What's the name of yours?"

"It doesn't matter, but I like him very much. I like being the younger one. Why do we talk of this? Rob, you're my once and forever love. Now you're withdrawing from me. Did you say you saw once what I could be? I always saw what lay ahead for you. Go and be it, Robbie. This is done. You know it."

Robbie remembered goose feathers, a girl on a tightrope.

Anton said, "I heard about Donovan. I'm so very, very sorry. Louise wrote me. If it had been you, I would have died, Rob. No, I would have lived to help you."

Robbie nodded. He put on his clothes and left without looking back.

It was odd to sleep in the vicarage again; his old room was so much smaller than he remembered. When Robbie came down for breakfast in the dining room the next morning, he found hot tea and the vicar waiting for him.

"You saw Antonio?" George asked anxiously. "Did he talk to you about the house? I offered him what I had, and he wouldn't take it."

"The house is safe. I had a little money from my mother's estate; you may remember."

George stirred his tea, his old face smiling. "That's excellent news. Did Antonio tell you about his work? There are those who think his speeches will be enough to get the Labour man into the city council and those who don't. Some despise socialism and Labour and some despise him. Perhaps you'll find some friendship between you, at least that. It wasn't good to separate as angrily as you did."

"Do you care how we left each other?"

"Yes, Robbie, I do." Then he added quietly, "And I need you to stay for a few days. I'm longing to have you about. My churchwardens think it's time I retired, but I won't."

"You never wrote about that!"

"I didn't want to bother you with my nonsense."

That afternoon Robbie telegraphed from the village of Forest's End to Louise to postpone his sittings for several days. He had only brought a few things, expecting to stay one night.

Then he walked back to the field to see the horses and the one colt frolicking.

He slept a great deal that week. He made sure he was never alone with Anton; when on the last day Anton drove him to the train station, they sat on the seating board without touching, like strangers who had not yet been introduced; and still he felt within his tailored clothing that he trembled helplessly with that old, complicated longing, which held so many things.

Anton spoke somewhat clumsily of his work and money.

"I have funds owing me from Switzerland," he added. "I left what I earned there in the bank because I didn't need it then. They also want to hire me to organize the party here, and perhaps they'll be some money for that. I don't want to sell my grandmother's house in Italy, but I would."

"Don't sell it. I could—"

"I know you could."

"None of your old friends here is giving you trouble over your politics?"

"Well, some of course, if turning a cold shoulder when they see me is trouble. Hayes and a number of others are decent, and a few more agree with me. A very few except the workers, of course. Less than two pounds a week for a twelve-hour day in the factories. The children are hungry."

They fell silent. As the train approached, Anton asked, "But how are you, Robbie?"

"I'm becoming fashionable," Robbie said, forcing himself to turn away. "Goodbye, dear." They said nothing of what had happened between them.

27

NEWGATE PRISON

May 1908

A heavy, balding gentleman showed up at the door of Louise's house several months later. He seemed near sixty and his clothes were too small for his weight. There was an air of arrogance about him and then of anxiety as he stood on Eccleston Square at nine in the morning, wiping his mouth with his handkerchief.

Robbie had come out when the maid called him, a cup of tea in his hand. "May I help you?" he asked, bewildered.

"No one can know I'm here, but you knew him. He told me. Your address and some letters were in his room; after they seized him, I found them."

The man looked up and down the tree-shaded square as if someone were watching him. A matronly nurse in a white cap passed wheeling a large black perambulator, cooing down at the baby within. He waited until they passed.

Then he murmured, "You must understand at once that I can't be implicated. I have a wife…and Keith…" Was this the powerful lover Keith had mentioned? It was, then, his old friend's idealistic imagination. Or had that lover gone his ways and been replaced with this man?

Robbie asked impatiently, "Do you have news of Keith? I don't know who you are."

"He's in the penitentiary sick ward. I heard three days ago," the man said, his eyes evasive. "I wired his family in Dublin, not giving my name of course. I have a wife. He was dear to me for a time. I can't go to that place."

"Is he very ill?"

"I should never have become involved in this. Yes, he's ill; he's dying. They say he wouldn't know me anyway."

Robbie left a letter for Louise, seized his money and his hat, and ran to hail a hansom cab. It crawled through Fleet Street and the masses of vehicles and people around the small streets by St. Paul's Cathedral. He cursed the traffic. He had written the prison warder before, asking to visit along with Lawrence, who had known Keith, but both of them were refused.

The guards allowed him to enter the first door of the huge sixteenth-century edifice, so massive in its ancient bricks, its hundreds of rooms, its lower common rooms extant for all these years. The door to the warder's office was unlocked. He could hear other doors from far off, the echo of their closing and the groaning of their opening.

"I'm cousin to a man you have here," he told the warder. "His name's Donovan. I wasn't allowed to come before, but now I'm told he's…dying." He glanced at the piles of paper on the desk and the ledger books. Death and Keith couldn't be in the same sentence. It had to be a mistake. Ill perhaps, but…

"Family and friends may visit now," said the warder impassively.

Guards searched Robbie for weapons and led him through the locked doors and the corridors. Locking and unlocking, heavy barred doors opening and shutting, chains, bolts. I'm inside here, Robbie thought. I'm also locked in.

He heard the sounds of men's voices and tramping from the yard and the voice of a young man shouting, "I did nothing, I did nothing." At last they came to the infirmary, a long room with a row of iron-framed cots with thin mattresses. Two well-barred huge windows let in some light. It was entirely grays and browns. It couldn't be real. The infirmary was quiet. Most of the beds were empty, though Robbie did see an old man in one.

Then he saw someone in the bed by the tall window.

"Bed eleven," the male nurse said. "Fever, bad breathing. Some infection of the blood; he screams a lot when the morphine wears off. We're short on it. The doctor was here yesterday."

"Keith," Robbie said, coming to the bedside. "*Keith?*"

He hardly knew the heavily flushed, swollen face. The hands moving on the covers were not the delicate, tapered hands he recalled but bruised, and the fingertips scabbed from labor. Robbie choked back his tears. He raised Keith's hand and kissed it, and Keith opened his eyes. "Hello, you sweet boy," he said. His speech was slurred. "I'm in trouble, sweet boy. I'm tired. Did you bring any French wine? What day is it? Oh dear, it's so ugly here."

These were almost the only sentences he spoke. His eyes fluttered, he lost consciousness, and then he arched up and began to scream.

"Keith, Keith," Robbie said in despair. He stroked Keith's forehead in a futile attempt to calm him. The elderly male nurse wearing gray came by and gave an injection. Two other attendants appeared. He wondered when he would be asked to leave.

He sat by the bed on a low, wobbly footstool, keeping the hot hand in his. Was he really here with the sardonic Irishman who had been brought to this? His mind flew to other times years before. Keith had arrived at the farmhouse in all his elegant manners to take away Robbie's work for the exhibition. Then they were kissing in a cellar flat in Holborn in a room which smelled of clay and mold; then they were lovers, furtively, in the creaking bed of Keith's elderly aunt. Seductive, yes, and now here.

The sun moved slowly across the floor.

Louise came for half an hour and began crying so hard she had to leave. A few more people visited briefly; the rules were softened when death was coming. But though Robbie looked toward the door again and again, there was no sign of Keith's family. Of course, it would take more than a day to travel from Dublin. It was only late in the afternoon, when Lawrence walked in from a late rehearsal, that Robbie learned the family had sent a telegram saying they couldn't come.

When Lawrence left, Robbie wanted to run after him.

He didn't; he held the hand of the sick man who didn't know him anymore but tried to call him by other names: Isabel, Paul, Alex.

The stale stench of the room was sickening: odorous thin mattresses, unemptied bedpans, spoiled food, sweat. Rats hid under a bed and then scurried across the room, glancing boldly at him, depositing their droppings. A prisoner came in with a pail of dirty water and mopped the center of the floor and left. Robbie glanced at these things coldly, rejecting them. He felt only a desperate, hot hand under his.

"He'll die soon," the elderly male nurse said, coming close. "Maybe tonight, maybe tomorrow. Go home and come back then."

I should take him in my arms and carry him out, Robbie thought. This thing could be turned. But I'm not certain I could carry him, because he's swollen with water, and anyway, I couldn't get through the locked doors.

He grabbed his hat and ran after the nurse. "Let me bring a private doctor," he begged.

"The prison doctor is qualified," said the nurse. "All visitors must leave, sir. I'm so very sorry, sir."

A guard came and led him out, unlocking several doors so he could leave.

Robbie arrived back at the prison at seven in the morning, which was too early for visitors, and paced the yard while he waited, his fists opening and closing. He knew even now his friend could be dead. When they let him in, he burst through the open door of the warden's office. A heavy open book of names sat on the desk. God! Whose names?

As he was led through the doors once more, bile rose to his mouth, and he pressed his handkerchief against it. As the last door to the infirmary was unlocked, he saw that a few more beds were occupied. He hardly dared raise his eyes to Keith's bed for fear of finding it stripped and his friend gone.

But Keith was still there, sometimes silent, sometimes moving his now swollen lips. Robbie once more found the footstool and sat by the bed, leaning over to stroke his friend's face and hold his hands. No one else came to visit.

Robbie's legs were cramped; his back hurt from leaning over. Again, the sun moved across the floor. He didn't bother to look up when the door was unlocked again. Someone came across the floor and stopped.

Anton was standing some feet from the other side of the bed. "I've never been so glad to see anyone," Robbie whispered. "I didn't know you knew or if you'd come."

Anton said quietly, "Louise telegraphed. I thought you needed me, Rob, so I took the train. I know it's been a while since we've seen each other. Eight months or so. I've missed you."

"I did write a little. I've missed you too."

"Not the best time to speak of that. May I come closer? He doesn't need to hear my voice. He can't be very fond of me. Christ, poor fellow."

"I don't think he can hear you."

Anton removed his hat and looked down at the young man in the bed for a long time. "This is a terrible place, Rob," he said.

Robbie was holding Keith's hand an hour later when his friend went into spasms. He arched his chest again and again, harshly grabbing at the air. The breath stopped then and the chest was still.

Robbie grasped Keith's hand harder, but there was no response. Even then, Robbie didn't let go. He threw his other arm over his eyes until he heard the doctor come. "Likely heart failure," the doctor said. "I'm sorry. This is a bad thing to do to people. This is a bad place. They're to tear it down in a few years."

The male nurse covered Keith's face with the sheet. Anton put his arm around Robbie and led him away.

The funeral two days later was modest, some way from the city, where Louise bought a plot; they planned to erect a stone later. Few people stood by the grave. Keith's older lover didn't come; likely he didn't know. Lawrence left after the service, avoiding Robbie's eyes. Anton stayed some feet away. Robbie felt terribly alone. He wanted to say, "Come closer!" but he didn't.

The small group returned by two carriages to the house on Eccleston Square.

Inside Louise's cream-colored parlor with the piano and the many pictures on the walls, Robbie dropped onto the sofa, still wrapped in his coat, staring at the floor. "His family didn't come," he said. "They were notified. We would have taken his body to Dublin if they'd asked. I wrote them again and there was no answer. He was their son." He thought of making love to the slender Keith, who now lay beneath the earth.

Everyone took plates of food. Robbie ate nothing but drank wine quickly. He knew he looked very angry because Louise asked, "Dear, should I fear that you'll knock off the dishes from the cloth?" and added, "Use the pillows, Rob, if you need to throw something; glass shatters and the shards fly everywhere. Antonio, speak to him."

But Robbie answered, "It'll never be all right; he died almost alone. Where were the people who loved him besides a few of us? He was only twenty-eight years old."

One musician said, "We all need to move out of the country to France or Italy, where the laws aren't against us."

"I'm not bloody moving out of the country!" Robbie shouted. "This is my home. I'm a boy from the Midlands…a helpless, stupid boy from the Midlands who's making himself into something fashionable. Wear your hair cut right and they fuss over you; go to the right tailor. They want me in velvets but not in tweeds. Offend the wrong people and you're dead. The world's insane and there's no other one to live in."

Looking at them all desperately, he ran up the steps, closing the door of his room behind him and standing with his back against it. After a minute he heard footsteps and the knock. He opened the door to Anton and then slumped in a chair, still in his coat, still shivering.

"To be in such a place," Robbie said, trying to keep his voice low. "To have your body in the earth without your lover daring to come…no mother, no father. Where were his sisters? To hear the door lock behind you, to have every bit of your life taken from you…"

Robbie rose and locked the door, suddenly beginning to hurl off his clothes. "I want you," he said.

The voices rose from below. "They're expecting us," Anton said.

"I don't care. I'm frightened.... I'm cold. Please."

They came together as quietly as they could; he stifled his gasps on Anton's arm. After, he held Anton against him. "Don't go," he begged. "I'm so alone."

"I won't go. Rob, how odd to make love when we've heard the earth falling on that plain pine box and when we're no longer together. The second time we've done this."

They were both silent for a moment, thinking of the immensity of it.

"Life's not forever, is it?" Robbie asked unevenly.

"It's not."

"You were magnificent when I heard you speak."

"Thank you, darling. I haven't convinced enough people yet for Labour or Liberal in the city council, much less for a member of Parliament. We're closer, I think. Even a little."

Robbie stroked Anton's bare warm arm, the hair on it so soft. He tried to sound casual. "How's your lover, Anton?"

"We don't see each other often. I've too much work ahead of me. His name's John. Now I've told you and you're shivering again." Anton wrapped the blanket around them both.

Robbie said, "There's a rage inside me that scares me. Keep holding me. Tell me things in my ear. Italian nursery rhymes if you like. Keith's dead. I didn't want him to be alive for me but for himself. Oh God. They're calling us from below." He laughed miserably.

Anton rejoined the small mourning group downstairs half an hour later as if something had not just occurred in the bedroom above which had shaken him. He had a hard time concentrating on everyone's agitated words. Instead, he sat with Louise in two low blue velvet chairs by a curtained window and talked. When she was called away, he sat alone for a time, finishing his tea. His head had begun to pound.

Glancing at the stairs, he realized Robbie had not come down to join them. He wondered if the unexpected intimacy had moved Rob as it had him. Darkness had fallen, and he said good night and walked over to sleep in the house of a socialist he knew.

He had planned to return to Nottingham the next morning if Rob had not asked him after lovemaking, when they were turned away from each other to pull on their trousers and suspenders again, "Will you come with me tomorrow to the slums and look for Rose? You remember the girl I painted? I have to find her."

He had said yes and now he was sorry he had. Still, he walked over to Eccleston Square in the morning where he found Robbie waiting by the house steps, sketchbook under his arm.

As the motor cab drove them into the thick of Whitechapel, Anton stared at the tenements and the dirty half-clad children playing in the gutters and young street girls who appraised him coolly. "My God!" he muttered. "Why don't we help these people? Why don't others mind that they're living like this?" Why had he not returned to his real work sooner? No matter how little he could accomplish, it was something.

They descended from the cab and walked, finally discovering Rose's dirty brick tenement with its dark stairs and no candles to light them. "I had gin tea here," he said to Anton as they carefully climbed the broken stairs. But when they knocked on her door, a stranger answered who said he had never heard of her. They asked the neighbors, and one said there had been trouble with the family and Rose and her mother had moved away. What trouble they wouldn't say.

Robbie looked pale and lost as they descended. "She's gone, she's gone," he murmured, and then added fiercely, "I want to draw this street, so I'll always remember. Do you mind? At least I'll have this. I walked down past that alley when I came here to draw. Can you stay and take a later train home?"

"I will."

"People disappear, Anton! They just go."

Anton stood against a lamppost with his arms crossed and watched as Robbie sat on a barrel and began to draw in his small pad. Children gathered around him as he drew the sloping street and the crooked houses. He thrust his hair back impatiently and now and then drew coins from his pockets for the children, looking at them in a sad, bewildered way before returning to his drawing.

Anton sighed, half in anger. It seemed many weeks since the funeral and the small gathering at Louise's house and the unexpected lovemaking. And there was Rob with his raised face so open, his eyes so intense, his hand so steady...a stern, now clean-shaven Renaissance angel, utterly distraught, needing to tell the paper of his grief and disappointments. He remembered Robbie sitting on a tree stump and drawing the high grass and a broken cottage wall in Squatter's Field.

Later, when they were riding away from the slums by the same motor cab which they had paid to wait, Robbie said suddenly in grief, "Oh, Keith!"

Anton pressed his lips together. He thought, But who am I in the end to him? We make love and then he's off in his own world again. This is his life now, with his wealthy patrons and young lover. He has what he wished: He's so far from the boy who I found in the rain, who came to the fair with me. Meanwhile, all challenges lie before me still. One fulfilled, a new one comes. And he's so busy he has no time for me. I'll not be in his bed again. I'm damned if I let him break my heart once more.

"I must hurry," Anton said as they approached the train station. "I'm speaking to some union representatives in the morning. I'll say goodbye here."

"Just like that?"

"I came because of Keith, because you needed me." He let his hand brush Robbie's, and then pulled it away. "Be well," he said, quickly descending with his small valise, holding on to his hat as he hurried through the crowds.

Robbie's dream that night was terrible. They had caught him also and thrown him into a narrow cell for two years' hard labor. The first three months would be solitary confinement.

He felt the walls, he felt the door. The silence stuffed his mouth until he choked on it and couldn't breathe. All he could do was turn round and round the cell. He had seen the open door of one when he'd visited the infirmary, and now it was real. There was the narrow plank bed, the broken table, the stained chamber pot. He shouted and kicked the door. He gritted his teeth and kicked.

This hard bed, this silence.

And what about his portraits? How could he get to his appointment? Someone was waiting to be painted. She would not know why Mr. Stillman didn't come, because this time there would be no news in the papers.

I am in this little space, he thought, and soon they'll send me to hard labor. My fingers will be sore and perhaps broken. I will never paint again. I am smaller than this room. My flesh is melting, my desire, my so-called lovability. My ability to be what people want because I am not what they think I am.

I have ended and still have a mind enough to know it's happened. All I am has ended: that too-ardent boy, the one who said to Anton, "Take me. Make love to me until I no longer exist!" But the law came for me, swinging wide like a great sword. Does it matter who's cut down? Who is more powerful than the law, hewing down anyone before it? Two years' labor.

I am late for my appointment. I was just working on the folds of Mrs. Lodge's blue velvet dress, the best I have ever made with the light which shines upon it. She is waiting at her door, looking down the street. Has anyone seen Stillman? Dear me, the tea's gone quite cold in waiting for him....

You whore, the jailer said, spitting at him.

He thought, No one knows I am here.

No one will ever come for me again.

He woke bathed in sweat. The lovely painting by Renoir still hung above his bed; no one had disturbed anything. He had journeyed helpless months in his mind and had come back here to the feather pillows and the soft blue window curtains. Letters from George were on the desk and a music box from Annie behind it. His leather painting bag sat neatly packed by the chair, ready for the day.

28

The Social Gathering and the Book-shop near St. Paul's

October 1908

Months passed and the worse dreams left. His own life was ordinary, predictable, and safe. He woke late and knew it was Wednesday again and another such ordinary day was before him.

Still in bed, he turned toward his desk and the newspaper photograph of Anton and a few miners in the silver frame. Robbie had bought the paper in Nottingham station when he had gone down about the possible loss of the house. Later, he discovered the grainy picture tucked on the sixth page. The men had their arms about each other, and Anton was laughing. A few months ago, Robbie had framed it and set it on the desk. Once he thrust it in the drawer and then took it out again. Days went by without him noticing it.

Robbie dressed, shaved, and descended to the dining room where the cook had left him hot tea in its floral pot and toast and bacon. No one else was home.

Perhaps after his workday, he would spend the evening with Annie at a studio party. These gatherings were generally up flights of steep stairs, on top floors of old buildings. They were crammed with struggling students and poor artists who couldn't sell their work but were excited by some new vision or argued about technique. Was there such a party tonight somewhere?

There was. That evening as he returned from his day in the early falling dusk, he found her letter on the vestibule table.

Dearest R., Things are dreadful at home, and I thought I was in love but am not. So as usual I have made rather a

mash of my life, though thanks to you, I have another commission. You are my stability. Come to Donald's tonight
and bring wine and chicken if you can! Address below.
Perhaps we can dance again?

Suddenly he so much wanted to be in that huge shadowy
room, pockets of the light around him and someone saying,
"Stillman! Where have you been?" Someone talking about the
interpretation of German lieder, or medieval art, or the young
Nijinsky with the Ballets Russes in Paris.

But just as he had changed his clothes and was taking his
house keys, he saw Louise coming down the stairs in her pink
gown, loose flowing fabric with a wide rose sequined band
about the waist. Her hair was swept up and held a gathering of
tiny pink rosebuds on top of her head. "My dear Rob, where
are you going?" she asked, looking a little alarmed at his worn
trousers, and his coat slung over his shoulders.

He said cheerfully, "I'm off to Donald's bohemian bash.
Come with me, Louise. Annie will be there; you like her. But
where are you off to dressed like that, so ravishing?"

"Where?" she replied in mock horror. "You ridiculous boy!
Lady Morris invited us tonight and we accepted. You must put
on your evening coat and your white tie this moment. It will
be *très élégant*. She is a baroness, and you know she adores the
portrait you're creating of her!"

His mind shifted quickly through his clients. Ah yes! Lady
Morris. He had had only two painting sessions with her and
liked her. He felt her loneliness and had a careful time not to
show it in the portrait. Her daughters had married, and he had
heard her husband, Edward, Baron Morris, was a remote man
estranged from their only son.

Louise took his hand and shook it gently. She said, "She
wants her friends to meet you. We promised. You will get three
new commissions. Now will you please dress as quickly as you
can, or we'll be late! And shave again. It won't do for you to be
scruffy. Wear evening dress."

He seized her hands and began to waltz with her about the

vestibule, through the dining room where the maid stared at them, to her little parlor. "I'm dressing, I'm good," he said.

After looking into the mirror, shaving closely again, and tying his white tie, he rushed down the steps as the charming Mr. Stillman in shimmering black tail coat and black silk top hat. He said, "Transformation! Now am I perfect, my dear? I'll stay until ten."

Their waiting motor cab stopped before a white-stucco Regency home in Mayfair, one of the wealthiest areas of the city. The drawing room was furnished with sofas and chairs from a few generations past and the usual grand piano. He had passed this room before on the way to paint the baroness in the morning room and now saw it more clearly. The paintings on the wall were original fine medieval or late Renaissance. Robbie also noticed many volumes in Latin and Greek in one glass-fronted bookcase, books by Plato, Cicero, Marcus Aurelius, and Virgil. Someone in the house was a classicist.

A flurry of faces turned to notice him, the men in formal coats, the women in chiffon and lace. Several were older and plump. Louise greeted people as she made her way to Lady Morris to kiss her cheek. Robbie joined her, kissing the hand of his hostess.

He took a glass of champagne from a passing servant and drank it quickly. *Careful*, he murmured under his breath and smiled and bowed slightly at the two approaching women. One exclaimed, "Why, you must be the artist! The baroness talks and talks of you. Do tell me, how long have you been painting, Mr. Stillman? Do you have your gift from your father or mother?"

"Mother!" he said, taking a second glass of champagne from a tray. Perhaps it was his father. How would he know?

His head had begun to ache. He ate several pieces of small, thin toast covered modestly with little black pearls of caviar. He so wanted to be at the loft party of artists and musicians. Everyone would argue about what was and wasn't good art. Would the hour of ten ever come? It was not even nine by the clock and he had had quite enough of this gathering, the third or more this month.

Looking around, he saw Lady Morris in her pale gown smiling at him from her low blue velvet sofa. He approached her and said gracefully, "Do forgive me, my lady, but my head aches. May I go somewhere quiet for half an hour?"

"Oh, poor dear!" she said. "Do go up the stairs; there's our library with comfortable chairs. First door at the top. Shall I fetch Mrs. Hauptmann to go with you?"

Louise was across the room by the harp talking to two other women. Suffragette matters, he thought. He shook his head. "No, you're kind. I can go alone."

Robbie gratefully mounted the curved carpeted stairs and then opened the door to the little library. Here was the beauty of solitude. Here was the best room in the house. He closed the door softly, and the sound of chatter from below faded. Any tension fell from his shoulders almost at once, though the champagne made a humming in his mind.

Several bookcases were filled with novels and history, some books in French and many more in Latin and Greek. There was a white fireplace, a large standing globe, and a few soft armchairs. The rug was patterned in dark blue paisley. He saw his weary face in a small mirror as he dropped to one of the armchairs, closing his eyes. He considered removing his shoes and opening the top button of his shirt.

The door opened and an older man stepped quietly inside, a slight, even shy smile on his face. He was tall, terribly slender, and perhaps fifty; his thinning hair was silvery blond. "Forgive the intrusion," he said. "My wife wonders if you need anything else. I am Lord Morris."

Robbie stood at once and shook the baron's extended hand. The hand was surprisingly cold, as if he were anxious. Robbie said, "I need nothing, my lord, just a little quiet. May I ask if all the classical books are yours?"

"Yes, my great passion is for the centuries from the Athenians through the middle Roman period. It was an age of great thought and yet great cruelty. You're welcome to borrow anything you'd like. Do sit down again. There's too much chatter below! For myself I prefer the quiet."

The baron looked at the standing globe in silence for a moment. Then he said, "The truth is, I've been hoping to speak with you privately since you came." He hesitated as if the next words were difficult. "You see, I've seen you before, but you wouldn't remember me."

How the man looked at him! Robbie said, "I'm very sorry, my lord, but I don't recall."

Lord Morris moved to the standing globe, gazing steadily at Robbie. He said, "You presented your work at exhibition at the Winchester Galleries, perhaps three years ago. I was at leisure that evening and stopped in on a whim. I was the one who bought your portrait, the little sad drawing. No particular reason. I thought it was charming. No, there was another reason. Please, be comfortable."

Robbie felt for his chair and slowly sat down again.

The baron lowered himself into another chair some feet from Robbie, still looking at him. He said in a low voice, "We have something in common. We must pretend every moment we're not what we are."

Robbie forbade any expression in his face and replied lightly, "I don't know what you mean, my lord. I'm just as everyone sees me."

Lord Morris leaned forward toward him. He said, "Please listen. It's a matter of some importance to me to say what I'm going to say, and I trust it will stay between us. I need to tell you where I first saw you, Mr. Stillman. It was a few years before the exhibition."

Robbie heard the ticking of the tall antique cherry clock. Some of the books in their leather bindings seemed to look at him.

The older man said, "I used to frequent a certain public house on Charing Cross Road. One night I saw a boy there whose serious face enchanted me. Not a rent boy to be paid for services like the others, but someone finer. I approached more common lads, not this boy. You understand me, I believe. I went back a few nights and saw the boy leave with two men whom I'd heard relished cruelty. I thought to stop them, but I didn't. That boy of course was you. About three years ago I stumbled across your exhibition, saw you standing laughing among friends. I bought your portrait, hanging there in that corner. And now here you are, a rising painter, Mr. Stillman, my wife's portraitist."

Robbie's throat dried so he could hardly speak; his thoughts tumbled.

"What do you want of me?" he managed. "I never did such a thing. You mistake me."

"I'd like to know you better, Mr. Stillman. You have no idea how empty I feel, but perhaps you do or did then. I didn't mean to offend you. Perhaps it wasn't you. Perhaps I was mistaken."

The baron leaned forward, his face kind and longing. "Believe me, if it was you, you have nothing to fear from me. My trouble is to hide my own inclinations. But I'm here if you ever need me in any way. I have a lot of influence. And I should have stopped you that night and I didn't. I heard those men boast of what happened. I've long wanted to ask your forgiveness, but I never saw you again."

Robbie rose and walked to the door. The baron did not follow him but remained in his chair, rocking slightly, saying softly, "Mr. Stillman, I only want to know…"

Robbie hurried down the wide staircase, his head pounding. He almost tumbled into two young women in pale gowns, who exclaimed, "Why, you must be Mr. Stillman! We've been looking for you. We would like to engage you for a pastel—but you're quite flushed!"

Someone took his arm, and he wanted to hurl them off. He drew in his breath. He realized he stood at the bottom of the stairs, and it was only Louise in her pink dress and her gentle face whose hand lay on his coat sleeve. She whispered quickly, "What is it? What has happened?"

"May we leave, please?" he asked, trying to speak calmly. Tears of rage stood in his eyes. "May we leave this minute, now?"

The next few days were among the most difficult he had ever spent. He visited the house and continued his portrait of Lady Morris because he had trained himself to do it. But a few times he saw Lord Morris looking at him from the edges of doorways; the baron passed through the room, kissing his wife's forehead, saying casually, "Morning, Stillman."

"My lord," Robbie answered. He held his brush in the air until the man had left. He willed the memory of their conversation gone. The day was terrible for him. He wouldn't tell anyone. But someone had recognized him, and the nightmare was real. There was only one person he wanted to tell; he wanted to go into his arms and be held like a boy and tell him and perhaps cry, but he would not.

When Anton wrote a week following, Robbie found the letter in the vestibule and stared at the envelope, haughty and disappointed without even looking at the words. The way he was feeling had no room for paragraphs of social reform which, if he were fortunate, would be signed "with love." In his need, he rejected the very stamp. But then he dropped his painting bag on the vestibule floor, sat down moodily in the chair, and opened it.

> My dear Rob,
>
> I have finished my speeches for the week and am completely tired. But I wanted to tell you of a surprise that may please you. I'll send it by post tomorrow with all thanks to you. Without you, much would not be possible, especially this.

The words were warm; they were unlike Anton's dashed notes of odd occurrences in his speaking, and news of Mary and George. Still, there was no warm ending, only Anton's initials with which he signed his political letters. And what did the words mean? He had no idea that the answer lay on Ave Maria Lane near St. Paul's.

Robbie walked over to that oldest area of London with its tangled streets to meet a friend for lunch, and after they had left each other, wandered down a lane of booksellers. He later thought how odd it was that he had passed down this lane and not another. His glance settled on a bookshop window and a volume in green cloth binding on display, open to a drawing of a field with a few broken walls.

It was the sketch he had made in the field a few years ago with Anton.

He remained by the window with his hand on the glass for a time before walking inside the busy shop.

A pile of the same book lay on the center table. He approached it, and everything in the bookstore seemed to dissolve around him as if he and the books were the only real thing there. People brushed by his sleeve; he heard the ring of the heavy black cash register and the soft talk of browsers. He ran his forefinger lightly over the cover and opened the top copy to the front page, which read "*Lives of the Nottinghamshire Poor* by Anton Harrington" and under it, "Illustrations by R.C. Stillman."

He turned the pages carefully. There were his drawings. Delicate tissue paper was inserted before those reproduced in color. My God, he thought, the book's so beautiful. The typesetting was clear, with large initial capitals beginning chapters as if some medieval monk had made them. The pages were creamy and heavy. He ran his fingers down the edges of them.

"These arrived yesterday," the young saleswoman said as she put down several copies of another book. "They're selling well. The author's a socialist politician from the Midlands, I hear."

Robbie sat on the steps of St. Paul's to look at the purchased book, the pigeons poking around him. The choirboys in black capes mounted the steps past him to sing evensong. He read the list of the essays and found "In Squatters' Field" at the end.

Back in his room on Eccleston Square, Robbie pulled out his packet of letters sent to him from the farmhouse and vicarage. He paged through them and stopped at a brief one from George sent weeks before.

> Anton's off again today speaking about the new bill called the People's Budget to give aid to the poor. And what great things are you doing? In all honesty, he misses you as I do. I am so proud of both my lads.

Robbie passed his hand over his lips. Of course, one lad had spent part of the afternoon sitting amid a flock of pigeons on the steps of the great London cathedral while the other was likely standing in the Nottinghamshire mud somewhere taking notes about the diet of farm laborers. And now at day's end, that lad would open the farmhouse door and walk up the steps rubbing his neck as he did when tired, alone. If he was alone. Anyone would want his Anton. He had been snatched up without doubt.

Robbie closed his eyes at his surge of longing.

Why was it so difficult to admit he had been wrong? Or perhaps a decision made a time before was no longer the one he would make now? All he knew is that he wanted to be walking up those stairs beside Anton, one arm around him, leaning slightly against him as they went.

Robbie left the house at ten that night and began to walk through the city, passing places he knew well. The Winchester Galleries. The art school in its majestic building. The shabby little restaurant where he had dined with Anton when he had refused to return, tossing out proud words to defend himself. It seemed another life, all not quite real. He felt only vaguely the boy he had been, running through these streets throwing himself at anyone in the Crown who would love him. Had that been him truly?

He leaned against a lamppost. His eyes were so wet that the statue of Eros above the Piccadilly Circus fountain wavered in the night for him.

In the next three days, he concluded his most pressing work. He sent a long, apologetic letter to Lawrence, who had just left on a week's tour with a comedy, but that relationship had been fading anyway since Keith's death. He talked past midnight with Louise. Her husband was home and had found work in the conservatory and the London Philharmonic. She would not be alone.

"I am very happy for you," she said.

He counted the hours. He counted the minutes. He almost planned a surprise but instead wired Anton the hour of his arrival, saying, "Returning for always," and boarded the morning train to the Midlands.

He was alone in his train compartment. From his window, he saw first the ugly and then the middle-class suburban edges of London until the train passed gradually into the countryside. The smoke from the engine ahead of his carriage moved backward and upward toward the sky. In Nottingham, the local train was there.

When he descended at the village station, Anton was sitting on the driver's seat of the gig, waiting for him. Blackie, munching grass, hardly looked up.

Robbie had difficulty reading Anton's face; he thought Anton was agitated, but it was more complicated. He stood by the small station house, looking across the grass to the road, to his lover on the gig seat. For a moment he couldn't even walk over.

He tried to sound jolly. "What is it?" he called. "Aren't you glad to see me?"

"I didn't see your telegram until half an hour ago. Someone left it in a great pile of letters. There are several people at the house, and I couldn't let anyone see my face when I read it. They were just leaving, thank God. I'm giving a speech tonight, and they're depending on me. City council elections are soon."

He added, bewildered, more softly, "I'd given up on your coming, and now you're here. 'For always.' Do you mean that? How can you mean that?"

"But of course, I mean it!" Robbie turned to look down the now-empty train track with its drying weeds. His voice cracked. "Perhaps I made an assumption," he said. "Because I wanted you, I thought you wanted me. I thought when you wrote me that letter, and after I saw our book in a shop, dozens of copies, that you wanted me back. I'm sorry for every stupid thing I ever said or did. I can wait for the return train."

He picked up his suitcase and walked slowly to the gig, looking up at Anton's serious face. Anton smiled a little. He said, "You idiot, I'm so glad. I can't think of anything I'm gladder of in the world." His voice dropped lower, and he shifted on the seat. "I love you," he murmured uncomfortably. "You know it, damn it. It'll erupt if I allowed it. When did I ever not want you? It's you who went away."

"Two years six months and four days ago."

"You counted?"

"Yes, damn it, I did."

Robbie climbed up and let the edge of his hand touch Anton's sleeve, still looking anxiously at him. Anton said, "Walk on," to the old horse, and they rolled bumpily down the road.

"I am so glad, Rob. I'm so glad. It's only..." Anton was making himself look straight ahead at the road, avoiding a dog which had rushed before them. The oaks bent down, and the acorns strewed the path in the bright autumn day. They had come to the wooded area through which they had walked years ago during their first evening together, when they had gone to have dinner with the neighbors and Anton was only this beautiful stranger who knew everything worth knowing in the world and sang sailor songs.

That faded away to the silent man beside him in his loose, shabby jacket and a muffler with tiny moth holes around his neck. There were deeper wrinkles near Anton's eyes and dark smudges beneath them.

Anton finally stopped the gig beneath the trees. He looked around carefully and let his lips brush Robbie's. They both gazed away, edge of hands touching. Anton mumbled, "I'm weary of walking through my house and never finding you. Never hearing your voice calling me."

Robbie said, "Before…you were starting to say something. You said you were glad I'd come home, and then you said, 'It's only…'"

"Yes, I did say that. I'm terribly strong, Rob. Terribly determined…but it takes everything. If you came back and then left again, it would crush me and all I want to do in this world would end too. Because there's a place in me that's so fragile. You never thought it, did you?"

"I won't go off again. And I'm so proud of the book. I wanted you to write and publish it and me to illustrate it. I wanted you to do what you're doing now, from the very first."

They were near to the bridge. The wheels crunched on the leaves, and a squirrel stopped half up a tree. They turned to the farmhouse, and obviously no one was there any longer. A banner hung from the window with the words "Jobs for the Unemployed."

BOOK FIVE

29

ARTIST, SOCIALIST, AND VICAR

October 1908-spring 1909

Their house was where he had found himself, and now he never wanted to leave it again. The feel of the wood banister beneath his hand, the owl at night and the rustle of trees, the sound of the floorboards creaking under his feet. They walked upstairs together. They made love. There was the wonderful smell of Anton, sometimes sweaty, trapped in clothes, his hair dirty. There was the warm, slightly salty taste of his skin. After, Robbie said, "When we do this, Anton, I don't know which is me and which is you." It was as if their long time living apart had compressed to a few days.

They lounged on the study sofa late the next morning. The crowds in the union hall last night, the many people, moved in Robbie's mind—how Anton had spoken to the hundred waiting faces and his voice had echoed to the ceiling and the balconies. *Man cannot live by bread alone, but neither can he live without bread.* Anton's voice had been uncommonly rich and sweet. Is this him? Robbie thought. And then it was over, and the clapping rose everywhere. From the back, a band began to play, and Anton descended to so many people.

And that was done and here they were. He lay against Anton's shoulder. He ran his fingers down the wool dressing-gown lapels.

Robbie said, "Good news! I meant to tell you at once. Louise is with child."

"I'm happy for her. When?"

"Late spring or early summer. Anton, you know I have to go back to London weekdays to paint? But I'll write every day.

I thought of opening a portrait studio here in Nottingham, but they wouldn't pay as much."

He felt Anton pull him closer against his shoulder. "We'll manage," he said in his deep, sweet voice.

On the day Robbie was to return to London, he woke to sun streaming in through the window. He heard Anton already gathering his papers in the study. Robbie made his way barefoot and sleepy to the study door. "The red portfolio—have you seen it?" Anton asked over his shoulder. His voice was brusque; already he was trying to find a good way to part from Robbie for four days.

Robbie had stayed home for a week and Anton had canceled any speaking. They had taken walks together in the forest. Their laughter echoed to the ancient conifers, whose long, slender needles brushed the cooling air. They touched hands. Few people walked here weekdays. Around the houses and parish, they heard people say, "The vicar's lad's back."

Mary, who had returned to work for Anton when her husband found employment in one of the larger local houses, was frying bacon in the kitchen. He heard the clang of Burrows's bicycle.

"I've got to see George," Robbie said, quickly washing himself from the basin of cold water and dressing. He snatched up the bag he had brought from London and walked down the path. The autumn sun shone on every leaf and rock.

Robbie unlatched the vicarage gate to the small garden with its birdbath and walked through the vicarage door.

George Langstaff had become increasingly deaf, which made him irritable. "There you are, Rob," he said, rising from his typewriting machine. "Just come and off again! It's like you."

Robbie kissed George's cheek. He said, "Believe me I don't want to do it, but wretched money must be earned. I'll be back before you finish that chapter. Oh, I forgot that I brought some things for you from London. Fortnum & Mason marmalade and two of the three books you wanted; the seller never heard of the third. I was going to post them down but came myself.

Here they are." He opened the marmalade. "They put on these lids so tightly, as if you weren't meant to eat it."

The vicar indicated the table and asked wistfully, "Have you time for morning tea? I could do with another cup."

"Very quickly. How are your knees?"

"Arthritis and age."

"You needn't walk. Harry can use the money driving you. Anton or I can when I'm here. No, I haven't forgotten the church supper. I'll draw the one who wins the lottery. Week after this?"

"I never told you about it," George said, shaking his head.

"You did and I said I couldn't come down. Now everything's happily changed."

Robbie listened to some parish stories, toasted bread for the marmalade and drank tea. He kissed George's stubbly cheek again and ran down the path, to wave to Anton before he jumped onto Harry's wagon to ride to the station where he found the local train had already departed.

By the time he arrived at the King's Cross station in London, he was two hours late. Now he pushed himself forward onto the platform and into the crowds and, as he had forgotten to wind the pocket watch Anton had given him a few years before, consulted the station clock. It was half-past two. He had no time to drop off his bag at Louise's house in Eccleston Square. He made his way into the clutter of motorcars and horse-drawn cabs in the street outside and twenty minutes later walked into the town house of the newly married Mrs. Larks, whom he was painting.

The upholstery was silk covered, and the heavy, expensive drapes and costly rugs were a bit of a jolt after the world of the Midlands socialists with their coats often bought from a secondhand clothing shop and two sizes too large.

There was his largest easel with his life-size painting as he had left it in the second parlor, a cloth under it to protect the carpet. He slipped on his cuff protectors and smock, prepared his palette, and then stood back and studied what he had already created. Mrs. Larks assumed her pose. He arranged her blue silk skirt, and as he did so, he tried to tuck away his own life as you throw everything into a trunk and latch the lid.

That evening, he walked slower as he reached Louise's house in Eccleston Square and stopped in the vestibule to page through the engagement diary Louise kept for him in her flowing handwriting. He noticed new clients. The engagements went on for months.

Louise came down the steps and stood on her toes to kiss his cheek. "So glad you're back!" she said. "I kept listening for your voice in the house! I received your letter; thanks for remembering to write. As you can see, the demand for your time has increased. Did you tell Anton that some women here call you society's darling?"

He laughed.

She asked, "How are you and my terrible old husband?"

"We're very happy. And you? How are you feeling?"

"Well and happy! I never thought I'd bear a child!"

"I have plans for mother-and-child drawings. I'll be an uncle. Uncle Robbie! I like that!"

"Darling, dinner's served in half an hour; Ernst will be home from rehearsal. And you'll be happy to know that the early-evening mail arrived just a while ago and a letter for you is on your pillow."

He raced up the steps. The envelope was on the soft blue bedspread, the handwriting bold and large.

> Rob, I am sending this just two hours after you left, and it should come to you Monday evening if it got into the mailbag on the late-morning train. I miss you so and loathe the thought it will be four more nights until you return. Just after you departed, I received a kind letter from Keir Hardie about our book, saying he is cheering for me. Do you remember my talking of him? The Scottish speaker who so inspired me when I went to hear him in London before your exhibition.

But the main thing I must say is that when you left this morning, I had a sort of panic that you wouldn't return. I know you will, of course, forever. I am plotting how I can earn money to keep you here. I don't know why I'm only whole when we're together, but that's how it is for me. Meanwhile I journey on as an unpaid socialist speaker. I'm going to Yorkshire this week and then down to Shropshire, but home waiting for you on Friday. I always hope to be more applauded than heckled, but one never knows. It doesn't matter if they vote Labour or Liberal in any election, though Labour will give more to help the workingman and the old. I have Conservative friends here and hope I can persuade them otherwise. How is Louise? And your work? How is society's darling?

Robbie wrote back at once, without even removing his coat, though he tried to keep his good cuffs away from the ink.

Why do you fuss about me earning the living? It's so easy for me; I paint anyway. You took care of me for years. Louise is utterly joyful. It's only four days until I'm back.... Shall I count the hours? For God's mercy, don't call me society's darling. I will be sick.

Your R.

He was almost late for his Friday train home because his last client detained him talking about her daughter's difficulty in finding a husband. The cab was stuck in traffic behind a fallen horse, and he jumped out and ran the last six streets, pulling open the train's compartment door just as it moved. He sat with other men commuting home from work, reading newspapers.

Over the next many months, he became a commuter.

Sometimes he would glance at those men in their bowlers riding the train with him, large newspapers held up before their faces, pipe smoke of varying pungency filling the compartment. He wondered, going home, what they looked forward to. He wished the train would go faster. When he arrived, he wanted intimacy, sex, talk, food, and walks all at once.

The City Council seat was won by a Labour man.

Anton had supported him but not stood himself. He shook his head when asked why.

Mary came only weekly. Robbie generally brought food for them from a London shop, and they heated it in the kitchen. As they ate, he listened to Anton's stories of the week. Anton had traveled to support local candidates across England. The main subject was always the new People's Budget, with its plans for old-age pensions, decent housing, and medical care for all, to be voted upon by the House of Commons in the London Parliament soon.

When Anton spoke on weekends, Robbie went with him. He sat in a chair to the side of some church or hall, listening to the cadence of Anton's voice. The halls were cold in winter; people huddled in their coats. Christmas was well behind them, and winter lingered. Sometimes there were ten people, sometimes a hundred. Anton's voice was strained. Once he had to shout above heckling. Once someone threw an apple at him. Back at home, he often sat in George's kitchen drinking hot tea with honey and brandy. He said, "I feel sometimes I'm in a war."

Robbie answered passionately, "Sometimes I wish you'd just write and leave the speaking to others."

"Why? I'm good at it."

"Hayes's brother is a doctor and says you have to rest more."

"I can't rest, Rob. Not yet."

When Robbie was in London, they wrote each other daily. Early spring finally arrived. Once Anton called from the village pub, but of course they could say nothing personal. Robbie felt the anxiety seep through his clothes to his skin.

As he hurried into the train one Friday evening, he heard the first shouting of newsboys, which broke into a roar about the cavernous station. He managed to buy the last newspaper. Taped to a wall near the entrance to the men's latrine was a huge sign painted in red letters. "People's Budget voted in Commons."

His train was called. He found a seat past two arguing men. The compartment was filled with old cigar smoke. Another man offered him a drink from his flask. He said, "What do you think? The bloody Budget passed. I guess there go my taxes."

The train jolted along past the squalid warehouses outside the city as he tried to make out the tiny columns of print. He read...*raising money to wage implacable warfare against poverty and squalidness.*

Anton was waiting for him at the station. Robbie saw him and ran shouting across the high grass through the new spring wildflowers, leaping to the gig seat. Anton seemed to burn from within; he breathed so deeply that his chest filled out under his open greatcoat. They looked back to see the train conductor throwing a heap of newspapers in twine to the platform.

Anton coughed several times.

"The news just came by telegram to the club," Anton said. "It's the first step. Now it's got to be ratified by the House of Lords. Those gentlemen have had their seats given them because of their inherited wealth and nobility. What a hurdle! But the king is with us. Edward VII with his mad extravagant lifestyle of twelve-course dinners and twenty cigars a day is with us. Imagine that."

An hour later they sat down to dinner in George's little dining room. On the wall hung many of Robbie's drawings that he had created his first year here, when he still vaguely planned to go up to university. There was cool ale from the cellar in the old glasses, and George's housekeeper, who was a good cook, brought the roast beef and Yorkshire pudding and potatoes. "Still, so far it's excellent news," Robbie said, shaking out his napkin from the ring.

George did not touch his fork. "Lads, I've bit of news to tell," he said. "Though it's such a small thing in the face of all that is happening in England, it's a considerable one for me."

"Oh Lord, are you ill?"

George Langstaff shook his head. "Only the usual aches, Robbie. There's been some talk for weeks with the churchwardens and vestry. Some feel they need a younger man. It's true I'm more tired. I don't want to wait until they try to make me go, so I have chosen the date. It's been coming a time, and you know, my memory's not quite what it was."

Anton leaned forward. "That's not so," he said emphatically.

"I think it is," George said gently. "You both flatter me. Besides, I need to go. My sisters are getting older and won't come here. Since the oldest Matilda went to heaven, they've been nattering at me to come home. I must take care of them; they want to fuss over me. But I've loved it here. Change comes, my lads. We go on thinking it won't, but it does."

Robbie tossed restlessly that night. It seemed inconceivable that his beloved teacher would not walk through his garden each Sunday down the path to the heavy stone church. He would not celebrate the Mass, which sometimes awed and sometimes bored Robbie, candles flickering this way and that on the altar. Robbie remembered God only now and then as if he were someone he'd not written in months; he always felt George had a good enough relationship with the divine to make up for it. The old man held a particular light. Even with the same parish members, the church Robbie had known would be gone.

At seven the next morning, he walked over to the vicarage, where he found George already sorting papers at his desk.

Robbie said, "Don't go away. Move into our house…too much room there. Anton says you must. You can write."

George turned another paper and shook his head. "You're most kind," he said. "But I've long promised my sisters. The diocese has the new fellow coming in already, the new incumbent. His wife was here to measure the rooms for her furniture."

It took days to clear out the vicarage and sort through some forty years of a life. George had kept everything. Others came to help. They took down the pictures; they made decisions about what do with things. "What do you think, George?" they asked. Sometimes the old man was so tired, he simply sat down, looking about, bewildered. He said with a smile, "That clock has always been there. An ordination gift from my cousin, rest in peace."

"This jar of raspberries is very old." Robbie had brought it from the cellar, carefully wiping the dust from the lid to make out the date.

"Ah! My wife preserved that the third year I came here, and to eat the last of the jars seemed too terrible. If you'd known her, you would understand."

"Then we must keep it," Robbie said. He had found a watercolor of the pretty young wife. He also found many typed sermons and older ones written in blue ink.

Robbie wanted to keep all the furniture, but George felt it should go to the poor. The vicar wished to give the piano to the church house. The typewriter he gifted to one of the young women from the church school who was going up to university; George said that it tired him too much to type now, and he would write by hand.

There was the huge unspoken sadness of saying goodbye to a very rich life, and the unspoken thought that the next life would be diminished. The vicar would no longer be the vicar.

Anton cleaned out the attic. For days, old parishioners came to visit.

Anton had bought a motorcar at a good price, so they drove George to his sisters' house with so many books in the car that the back was weighed down. The rest of the possessions would arrive by train. Anton drove recklessly and Robbie finally took the wheel. A friend in the city had showed him how to drive a motorcar.

When they arrived in Yorkshire, George's five elderly, unmarried sisters came fluttering from the door, gathering about him.

Later, as Robbie, Anton, and the old vicar sat alone in the fussy, fringed, feminine parlor, George said, "Before you go, I must say a few words regarding the necessity of prudence. I won't be there to look after you both."

"Well, you know we're prudent," Anton said. He folded his arms over his chest. Robbie said nothing, only running his hand over the lampshade tassels, making them dance. They were as old as a ball dress stored in a trunk.

"No, simply words of caution. Mary knows of course; she has for some time but says it's no one's business. Did you realize that, Anton? You helped her family long ago in bad times. She's very loyal. As for the others about…they cannot imagine you'd have more than friendship. I will miss you both so much. I will pray for you every day. Enough said, now. I think we need to have a glass of two of port."

They had not heard any news while away, but when they drove up to the house, Mrs. Cullen was waiting for them with several newspapers. Her bicycle was leaning against the old stable and her face was grim under her shapeless black hat.

She came forward as they stepped from the motorcar, saying, "It's over. The People's Budget was stopped at the House of Lords so that's the end of it. Why would the people with most of the wealth in the land want it chipped away for some starving creature, some lesser being? Really, it's time I retired from this work. My daughter tells me that every morning. Burrows will never give up. He will die with his boots on."

Anton seized the large watering can and hurled it against the side of the house, where the water splashed down. His face was flushed. "The bastards do what they've always done," he shouted. "What did I expect?"

By darkness, his fever had come on.

Robbie had seldom known Anton to be sick. Even though Mrs. Cullen came to nurse him, Robbie was reluctant to return to work. The local doctor felt Anton's lymph nodes at his throat and said he thought it was glandular fever. He would need weeks of rest. The fever broke in a few days, leaving muscle aches and fatigue. Anton turned, groaning, in bed.

When Robbie finally returned to London, he had to continue his portrait of the ugly Lady Bessell. Every time he took up his brush, he saw her crafty cold eyes; he tried hard to find something lovely in her, but there was nothing. He was late to all sessions; he sat on a bench on the Embankment looking out at the rolling Thames, thinking of the watering can hurled against the house and the water seeping down the brick. He knew very well what her ladyship thought of socialism.

He sent her a letter withdrawing from the work. *I am very sorry to disappoint you, my lady...*

She wrote back, *It is just as well, as I am disappointed in your work.*

She had been the last of three difficult clients. After a few years of rising success, he wondered if his talent were drying up.

30

THE HOUSE NEAR FLORENCE

June–August 1909

He took the train, hunched with anger. Anton was lying on the sofa writing.

Robbie dropped to the floor beside him. "I hate my work," he said. "I'm away from you. Every time I go away, I'm afraid I'll come back and find you talking to crowds in the rain."

"Darling, unlikely." Anton put down his writing board and the pencil. "I'm still too weak to speak well. But I've something to tell you. Sit down by me."

Robbie sat on the sofa edge.

Anton rubbed his finger over his mustache. He said at last, "They'll call a general election soon to try to pass the bill. The king has threatened to make more Liberal peers to flood the Lords and force them to ratify."

"I read it in the papers. Then here's hope."

"A seat in the House of Commons is open. Burrows and others here want me to stand for it."

"Dear God, that means you'd go up to Parliament if you win?"

"No, I won't stand. I said no."

Robbie sat up straight; for a moment, he could not find his voice. "You couldn't have said that," he managed.

Anton shifted, allowing more room for Robbie. He stroked Robbie's back and said, "I did, my darling. They have a second choice, Hendricks. Both the Labour and Liberal parties will join forces behind him. Together they may beat the Conservative candidate, but they'll never get the Budget through the Lords. This raggle-taggle bunch of us meeting in union halls and church undercrofts, waving our handmade signs and banners. It's madness. It always has been."

"They need you. Hendricks has no fire and you've always wanted this."

"Let's go away to Italy for the summer, to my grandmother's house. We went for a day years ago. You can paint landscapes there and I can finish my next book. Take some time away from your work. Can you? Can we afford it?"

"You're not standing for Commons?"

"No."

Robbie stood up and walked about the room with his arms folded tightly cross his chest. He burst out, "Yes, I want to say the hell with everything and go away with you. But I don't understand your decision. You've gone one way so far and now turned around."

Anton's face grew stern. He said, "I won't say more on it. It's done."

On the train to the harbor, Anton leaned back on the red-plush carriage seat, half asleep, his thoughts wandering wearily. He recalled one unhappy day in his marriage when he and Louise had been living in London that he had walked up from the new promenade along the Thames called the Embankment and seen the huge Gothic Houses of Parliament in London rising above him.

He saw their decorative patterns and lancet windows, the spires and finials. That summer day he had walked to them had been unusually clear of any fog, and white clouds drifted through a very blue sky.

Looking up at their magnificence, Anton had thought, Here the laws of the land are made. What would it be like to help change their course?

Now leaning back on the red-plush seat, his face grew stern. Robbie sat beside him with an open book on his lap which he did not read as their train rushed toward the coast to the waiting boat bound for Italy.

They traveled to Livorno and then drove past Florence on a clear day; they reached the countryside and arrived by cart at the house where Anton's maternal grandmother had been born. In the bright sun, the stucco walls peeled away to show flaking layers of different-colored paint. They unlocked the door with the huge iron key from the flowerpot where the neighbor who checked the house had said it would be.

Inside was softer light. The air smelled different, the smell of old plaster and oil. Robbie explored the handful of rooms upstairs and down. He called that he had rediscovered the oval saint painted on enamel embedded in the iron headboard of the capacious bed. He hurried down the steps again, and they stood together on the terrace looking over the valley and green fields below. Anton could feel how the sun entered Robbie, seeping into his muscles and chest. He could sense it enter Robbie's right hand and warm his fingers.

Anton felt the presence in the rooms of his grandmother as a young girl. He had formed a picture of her in his head from an old blurry photograph, about seven years old and barefoot, having just lost some of her milk teeth. He sensed her as she had traveled to England before she was twenty and met his grandfather.

After a few days, he began to write again.

He and Robbie walked farther every afternoon. They found tiny churches, pictures of saints on the sides of houses, small altars to the Virgin on hills and in rock crevices. They explored the local town of San Casciano to buy food and wine.

Robbie grew a beard and heavy mustache.

When they set out to choose a landscape for a painting, Anton braced the easel over his own shoulder while Robbie carried the picnic basket with his paints and palette tucked next to the wine. As Robbie worked, Anton lay on his side and read under the shade of some tree or sat up to write with the notebook on his knees.

At night they ate at the table outside looking down the hill.

Some weeks after they had come, they took the public coach

into Florence, which sat between the mountains, and from there posted the first six landscapes to England.

Three weeks later, there was among others a letter from Robbie's teacher DuChamps which he read aloud to Anton as they returned to Anton's grandmother's house, passing the vineyards and munching bread.

I received your landscape pastels safely two weeks ago and was able to slip them into an exhibition of the work of former students here at the Academy. Three of them were sold, though I am afraid for modest amounts of money. You wrote you have more. Do you want me to send a few to Galeries Durand-Ruel in Paris along with mine?

Mina and the children and I have missed you a great deal, and so many other artists and friends are always asking about you. Annie has told me her aunt has come to take care of her mother, and that she is moving to a new flat with a friend, a soprano at the opera, and is so grateful for the few portrait jobs to which you referred to her.

I was surprised to see that the Guild Hall, where Anton was supposed to speak next week, had the word *Canceled* through his name. Mina and I were planning to come. We both know how tired he has been.

Anton had finished his new book, which he called *Changes in the Life of the Lower Class 1850–1905*. Robbie had typed it in the evenings by oil lamp. By this time, Anton needed only a nap in the hot afternoon and had plenty of energy. Now that the book was finished, he suddenly was faced with time before him. At dusk on a July evening, when they were sitting on the terrace overlooking the fields and hills and churches, he said as lightly as he could, "I miss home, Rob. Do you?"

"You're feeling more than you'll say, Anton. Was there something in your letters today? What did Burrows say about the candidate?"

Anton said lightly, "He said Hendricks is sincere and intellectual in his approach and a bit dull. He'll stand in the general election after Christmas."

He hesitated and then reached for a pipe, tamping down the fragrant tobacco. He had given up smoking but recently started again.

Robbie looked out over the houses. He asked, "Once you promised you'd always be honest with me from now on. Why did you refuse the nomination?"

"I told you; I am tired of throwing my life before something impossible."

"I think it's because you wanted it so much."

"I wish sometimes you didn't know me so well."

"Am I right then?"

They sat holding hands in the falling darkness. "You are. If I tried and failed, I couldn't bear it. It would prove my father was right about me. It's Hendricks now, so no use looking back. I should speak on his behalf. I could help him. I did refuse and he's their man."

"You could go back until the election to speak for him." Robbie stood up slowly. "I think we should go. You need to be part of this. But before we leave, let's carve our names on the kitchen wall. That will be a sign this place is waiting for us."

They found a bit of wall near the large dish cabinet, and both carved their given names. They stood looking at what they had done, arms wound about each other. Robbie looked away because his eyes were full of tears.

They left from Livorno again, taking the boat and then the train to Nottingham. It was odd once again to hear most people speaking English.

Mrs. Cullen came to fetch them in her rattling car. Their own car was parked on the road before the house, with the roof covered with leaves and nuts. She had tended the garden and rabbits which Robbie had bought in the spring. He and Anton fitted the key into their lock and walked into their house.

Upstairs the same papers sat under the brick, a letter to a friend unsent. Robbie had been wretched to leave Italy but now was happy to see their old things: the pipe rack, the sofa. He heard the coo of the wood pigeon, a neighbor's cart from far away; he smelled the damp smell.

Rain began heavily over their small portion of the county of Nottinghamshire. The sound of a motorcar on the wet earth woke Robbie that Saturday morning. Anton was already downstairs.

Voices rose from below. Robbie wrapped himself in his dressing gown and sat down in one of the big chairs with his feet on the hassock, taking up his Italian grammar, but was unable to read. The house door below opened again, and the car drove away over the wet road. He heard Anton's step on the stairs.

Anton stood at the door. "Burrows came with a few men from the Labour and Liberal parties. Hendricks has stepped down as candidate for member of Parliament. They asked me again if I'd stand."

"And what did you say?"

"I said yes. I have to try. The general election's in February. If I win, I'll go up to London. The House of Commons will push the People's Budget through again, and the House of Lords must ratify it this time."

The rain was a patter outside now. The yard would be full of puddles, making a bit of mud of the graveled road from the house. Anton hunched his shoulders; his trimmed beard looked dark against his face. He asked, "What do you think, Rob?"

"You know what I think. You know what I've always thought. It's you who first told them no."

After dinner, Harry came with his horse and cart, quite soaked, to deliver a telegram from London. Louise had given birth to a healthy fat boy and said they *must* both come to the baptism.

31

Words from a Novel

October 1909

The baby was the loveliest and most miraculous creature; Robbie thought he had never seen such a sweet child. After the baptism, everyone left the church and returned to the house on Eccleston Square to celebrate and pass the child around. Louise named him Samuel, after her missing brother. Annie, who had become good friends with Louise, was there as well.

He and Anton returned that afternoon to Nottinghamshire where Anton gave his first speech following the nomination. The cheers that rose up in the old hall were deafening. Walking out after into the night, they allowed the edges of their hands to brush. Above them the sky stretched endlessly with a thousand stars as they had in Italy.

Robbie climbed the steps to his London room, unbuttoning his shirt collar as he went. The soft gurgles of the child from the nursery across the hall made him smile for a moment, but more pressing was his schedule book which he had brought up from the vestibule. So many cross-outs, so many notes received from clients which Louise had tucked inside the pages.

The truth was he was two months behind schedule. Two people had canceled due to his last client's bad reports, but six more had asked him to find time for them. Still, they paid a little less than before he had gone away, and he wondered if his career would recover its bright trajectory, which he sometimes suspected had been more due to his long curly hair and flowing shirts than his talent.

The first few days back at his easel, he missed Anton so much that he couldn't find the soul of the man or woman he was painting. Annie was in love and had little time for him. Louise was utterly absorbed with her baby. He went home after his long days and read and waited for the weekend to go home.

One Tuesday he ran into an old friend at the art supply shop who told him of a studio party of artists that night near Covent Garden, in a building soon to be demolished. It had been a long time since Robbie had spent an evening like that and, as he painted that day, he thought about it with comfort. After he left his client, he stopped to buy wine and cheese, but when he climbed the five flights of stairs, he found no one there. Perhaps the address was wrong.

Feeling foolish, he walked slowly back down again and stood on the street. Motorcars rolled by, people walked together, a man and woman stood close together in a doorway. In the streetlight, he saw her white ungloved hand on the man's shoulder.

He began to walk aimlessly past the windows of bright restaurants. He could sit at one of the tables and order dinner but hated the thought of eating alone. The cloth bag with the wine, bread, and cheese swayed from his arm against his trousers.

Standing on Waterloo Bridge, he put his hand in his pocket for his watch, and his fingers touched a letter which had come a few weeks before. He could sense the brief phrases uneasily through his fingers. *I am in the city again, Mr. Stillman, and hear you are as well. It would be a great kindness of you to visit briefly. I am alone these days.*

He had intended to throw it away.

Under a lamp, he made out the return address. It was not Lord Morris's family home, where Robbie had painted Lady Morris what seemed many years ago. He knew from dinner gossip that Lord Morris was separated from his wife and had moved away.

Then why not give kindness? he thought. Besides, he was lonely.

Robbie descended from the bridge and walked to the street of terraced stucco-fronted houses, many of which had been divided into flats for the upper middle class. Finding the address, he mounted the graceful marble stairs to the second floor and knocked. The baron's not there, he thought with some relief. But just as he was turning to descend, he heard footsteps and Lord Morris opened the door.

His face seemed some years older as if he had been through a very difficult time, and his breath a little labored. At the sight of Robbie, he smiled slightly. "You're gracious to visit me," he said. "Will you come in? I had lost hope of ever meeting you again, Mr. Stillman. I have no butler, you see."

Robbie noticed that his lordship's hands trembled slightly. Behind him, Robbie could see the parlor with a grand piano; over that hung Robbie's self-portrait, framed plainly so as not to distract from the simplicity of his boyish efforts.

He looked away. Why have I come? he asked himself.

His lordship closed the door. "Sit down," he said amiably, ushering Robbie inside. "Will you have port or whiskey?"

"Whiskey, please. Thank you, my lord," Robbie answered formally. "I knew you were back from Paris for some time."

Lord Morris poured the whiskey. He said, "When my wife and I returned, she moved back into our house." His voice broke a little, and he looked away at the piano. He continued, "My behavior has been a heartbreak to her, her disappointment in me extreme. We had to flee to Paris because I couldn't keep from my desires, and even there I fell from my resolve. We fled for her shame. When we returned, she asked me to move away for a time."

He looked up, clearing his throat, smiling with difficulty. He added, "You know, I've collected many pieces of your art. The landscapes from Italy. I love your pastel work; your hand is freer. They comfort me. I like to think I have your art at least since we met that strange night at my house."

Robbie sat carefully in a chair. I shouldn't have come, he thought...but then he looked more at his host's gentle face. He would be all right even if he had drunk the whiskey too quickly. He could leave this place and walk rapidly if unsteadily back to Louise's house. He knew he shouldn't drink anymore and yet he would. "You can't drink, Rob," Anton had said to him after that disastrous dinner so long ago.

His host studied the carpet pattern of spring flowers under their chairs as if they were a map. Then he raised his eyes and looked directly at Robbie. He said, "When you first refused to have anything to do me with me the evening I spoke to you in my library, I was disappointed…for it was you I saw that night long ago."

"Yes," said Robbie. "It was me."

"You could have found love many places other than with strangers in a Charing Cross pub."

"It was despair for me, my lord. And I wasn't sure whom I could trust."

Lord Morris looked at him. "After we spoke and you returned to painting my wife, you barely greeted me. I needed to speak with you. I wanted to know about you: how a boy went from giving himself to strangers to what you've become. I found out what I could about you. I am rather good at it. Your lover is a socialist speaker for the People's Budget. Harrington, as I recall."

"I wish you had not."

"I wanted to know you. You seem happy. How do you find happiness?"

"That is a complicated question, my lord. It comes and goes."

"And where is it tonight?"

Robbie was silent.

Lord Morris sat back, frowning. He wore a dark blue dressing gown trimmed in blue satin over his trousers and shirt. He said reluctantly, "I read Mr. Harrington's book. How strange our country has become what it has become! In what squalor the people live! I have financial interests in many things, and I suppose some of my factory workers should have made something more of themselves. Why don't they work harder instead of letting their children go hungry?"

"Why aren't they paid more?"

"So that others can earn their fair profit."

"Is it fair?"

"Yes, mostly. Such bosh! Your Mr. Harrington and others, Mr. Lloyd George and Mr. Churchill (that mad young man!), thinking that we can mend things just like that! Mr. Lloyd George has spoken of the rapacity of the landlord class, especially the dukes, in language I cannot excuse."

It was a small flat. Through the open door down the hall, Robbie could see a single bed made up, a bachelor's bed with a blue covering. He looked away. On the parlor mantel were framed pictures of Lord Morris's opulent life and the grown children, the angry son at some public school wearing his sport whites.

Lord Morris drank again. He held himself steady and spoke slowly to keep his words clear. He had been drinking all the lonely early autumn evening, Robbie suspected. The newspaper had not been opened.

"Mr. Stillman," he said.

"My lord."

His lordship thought before he spoke. "I own a country estate in Sussex. Used to be a religious house since 1214. Very large, a great deal of land. When I die, my son will inherit it, but if the new laws are ratified, he will have a larger estate tax and have to sell off land and goods. And a long time from now, when he dies, the estate will be diminished again. Does your socialist lover realize that while he's helping the desperate of this country, he's also tearing down England? The country houses, some hundreds of years old, will struggle to sustain themselves. Some will manage to go on. We will last a few generations with good fortune."

Robbie exclaimed, "I'd be sorry to see that happen. I truly want the best for everyone. I want it all to exist: great houses and well-fed workers and no families living ten to a room with no fire to warm them."

"Dear boy, you are a dreamer."

Lord Morris carefully took a book up from the table. "*Howards End* by E. M. Forster," his lordship said. "Just published. It asks some troubling and necessary questions. One is: 'To whom does England belong?'"

"I know the book; I love it. My friend loves it." He wasn't sure he should have said that. He remembered reading it aloud on a damp day one weekend at home recently, the rare weekend when there was not another speech or rally.

Lord Morris put on his glasses. "Forgive me, my eyes are growing old," he said. He held the book up and read.

"England was alive, throbbing through all her estuaries.… Does she belong to those who have moulded her and made her feared by other lands, or to those who have added nothing to her power, but have somehow seen her, seen the whole island at once, lying as a jewel in a silver sea, sailing as a ship of souls, with all the brave world's fleet accompanying her towards eternity."

"I can't answer that, but the passage moves me. My copy's underlined." Robbie put down the glass. "You asked me something once, I think for my forgiveness. I should never have gone home with strangers. I wanted to destroy myself or give myself without anyone knowing me. I never wanted to love anyone again. I don't blame you for not stopping me going; I blame myself. I do forgive you. It seems now a stupid thing to withhold it. I'd like you to be happy." He glanced once more down the hall where he could see the narrow bed through the half-open door It was an unspoken question.

Lord Morris saw Robbie's eyes and asked sadly, "Why did you come tonight?"

"I was a little lonely and you had invited me."

"Were you? It doesn't seem you could be. Well, be that as it may. Your friend reaches for great things. He's likely to fail."

"He will try. I want that for him."

Lord Morris pressed his lips together. After a moment, he said, "Thank you very much, Mr. Stillman. You're a kind man. If I had had the courage, I would have spoken to you that night and treated you well. I think I would have loved you very much, but I didn't allow it. Neither would you have allowed it. Now you're respected and well known. Remember that few of us are entirely safe. But I will use my influence to do something good for you."

Shortly after, they shook hands and Robbie left with his bag of wine and bread.

He ran for the train as fast as he could on Friday evenings, immediately reading the political news. Word was everywhere; there were posters on buildings and lampposts. Men on the train talked angrily or sympathetically. Some said with contempt, "It's madness, these Labour people." All over the country, they were preparing for the election.

At home, over the next weeks, he heard more of Anton's speeches; he knew the cadence of the words. He could tell if Anton was jubilant or discouraged or angry. And then there were always their quiet hours, walking in the woods, reading to each other. He read to Anton sitting on the same sofa, leaning against him.

Colder weather was coming. The newspapers were dated November. The wind blew harder outside the house, and the flying yellow leaves clung to his wool coat like refugees when he walked to the station in the still-dark early mornings.

He was reading in Louise's house, one day midweek, when he heard the harsh ring of the electrical doorbell and ran down the steps barefoot, his shirt half buttoned, his hair unbrushed.

Two boys of about sixteen stood there wearing gold-trimmed scarlet uniforms. Robbie recognized the royal livery; the cipher of the monarch and his queen embroidered on their coats. They were royal court pages. "So sorry, but I think you've rung the wrong house," he said.

"Are you Mr. Stillman?" asked the taller boy. Robbie took the heavy envelope they held out and turned it over. On the back in embossed letters, he read, *Her Majesty the Queen.* It's some prank of my friends, he thought.

"We'll come tomorrow for the answer, sir," said one of the

pages. Robbie glanced at the black motorcar, with its driver also in livery who awaited them.

He closed the door, feeling for the vestibule chair. He reached for the letter knife and drew out the folded paper, so heavy it would serve for several pages of ordinary paper.

A few minutes later, Louise walked from her motorcar to the house, her tiny Samuel wrapped in her arms. Robbie was still in the vestibule when she opened the door.

"Take your nephew," she said, giving Robbie the sleeping bundle so that she could unpin her mauve velvet hat. "Oh, what a terror he was before, and now sleeping and sleeping. They do what they want, the little ones." She was a fussy mother, nursing herself, which was unusual for her class, as he knew.

He held the warm little bundle.

"I'm going upstairs for nappy change," she said.

"No, wait a moment, Louise!" And with his free hand, he picked up the letter from the table. She put down her hatpins in the silver dish and took it up.

Her eyes grew wide. "Oh, darling," she said. "Her majesty Queen Alexandra has requested you paint her portrait. Oh God, your socks won't match. I'll have to inspect you top to toe. I'm so thrilled. You must tell me everything. I've never been to court."

Robbie felt for the marble edge of the vestibule table; he saw their reflections in the oval mirror, a self-possessed, joyful woman and a pale man in his twenties with a mustache. He saw them as she came toward him with her arms out for the baby, still looking at him amazed. "I can't do it," he murmured, turning aside.

An hour later, Robbie walked swiftly on this cool brisk day past the beefeaters guarding Buckingham Palace, almost averting his eyes, to the Royal Academy of Arts where he had first studied as a boy, hurrying down the hall to the office of Augustine DuChamps. Passing through a classroom, he heard whispers of his name.

The office was so crowded with framed work and statues

that there was hardly a place to sit. "Clear the papers from that chair," his old teacher said, shaking both of Robbie's hands. "Good! Word's out already that you'd be asked. Good news travels. I am so proud of you."

"How did you hear? But, Augustine, this is impossible! How do you paint a queen?"

"With dignity and love. Once I painted King Edward. He was formidable and bored and sent a box of expensive cigars with my fee. I painted three of the late Queen Victoria's daughters in her last years." DuChamps passed his hand over his lips as he laughed, throwing back his head. "Robbie! The rooms are so grand there, I felt I ought to be advised on how many times a minute I might breathe."

"Oh God, no," Robbie said, picking up a student's sketchbook to glance through it.

"Don't shake your head. I understand Her Majesty Queen Alexandra is a kind lady, not at all like some you've painted. She'll like you, Rob. Everyone does. And you will paint well. And then you can do just what you want to do for the whole year; you'll be rich enough. Not that this will be a quick painting. They will want every shimmering fold of her dress, every tiny curl of her hair."

He added more seriously, "Be kind to her; her husband sleeps with everyone. She's not had an easy time. Tea, Robbie? Or whiskey, perhaps?"

He could have walked to Buckingham Palace, of course, for it wasn't that far from Eccleston Square, and had a motorcar take his things. He would have preferred to walk to quiet his nerves; but of course, the motorcar was to take him as well. Robbie sat in the front near the chauffer while a servant sat in back with Robbie's easel and paints and brushes and his primed canvas. It would be six feet by eight, a seated portrait, a gift to her family.

The motorcar drove through the gates of the main entrances. A footman greeted him and walked before him, also wearing that splendid red uniform. They passed corridors of paintings.

Here were eight hundred years or more of the kings and queens of the country. Doors opened, and he found himself in a drawing room decorated in fanciful Chinese style with exotic wallpaper of green silk and a collection of antique vases with a great deal of jade. There was a gray-blue fireplace with a Chinese painting above it and a lovely low armchair and a chaise longue.

The servant had gone before him, and there was his easel set on a drop cloth. He looked about the room with its eighteenth-century cabinets and small collection of Chinese cloisonné cups with gold and green slithering Chinese dragons on them. The footman said, "Used to be Her Majesty Queen Victoria's breakfast room. Now called the Luncheon Room."

He would have liked to look at everything closely, but he heard the rustle of skirts and saw that the queen had come in with two of her ladies. The footman bowed and barked, "Her Majesty, Queen Alexandra." Robbie saw a woman of about sixty whose waist was corseted in as snugly as a girl's.

The neckline of her blue silk dress was low-cut but discreet and almost square; she wore several strands of pearls. "Your Majesty," he said, and bowed.

The footman said, hardly moving his lips, "The artist Mr. Stillman, ma'am."

She sat down on the blue chair where he would paint her and looked at him from her lovely oval face. He had already adjusted his easel for the size of the canvas; he saw that the light was sufficient to work and was glad of a fire in the fireplace; his hands and his colors did not work well in cold. "If your ladies would arrange your skirts," he began. "And you must be comfortable, ma'am, if you are to sit for a time in that pose."

But the women did not arrange the folds as he wanted them to catch the light, which would of course change as the day progressed. "If I might," he murmured, and at her nod, he went forward to kneel and move her skirt. This is just a living woman, he thought. Still, he touched with great delicacy; this was, after all, the queen.

Robbie felt her looking down at him with a warm, motherly

gaze. He flushed and stood rapidly, in every way the profession-
al, and returned to the safety of his easel. "If you would turn a
little to the left, ma'am. There."

He studied her politely. The blue silk dress shimmered, and
her skin was very pale, as if she never went in the sun. Two of
her ladies and the house steward watched him.

What a stultifying thing to be a queen, he thought. I wouldn't
be royal for anything in the world.

He prepared the palette, still thinking, feeling her waiting.
She was giving him four hours a day over the few weeks. He
stood back and looked at her. He drew in his breath and said,
"If you would consider it, ma'am, think of something that is
pleasing to you, perhaps when you were a girl."

She looked at him curiously. "Why?"

"Because your face will grow soft with memory. No one will
know what the thought is; it's private to you alone. There...
there's a light in your face."

He went away and returned for the next session. He worked in
silence. The only sound was their breathing and his brush as he
set it down and took up another.

"Do you have children, Mr. Stillman?"

"No, Your Majesty."

"But you have a wife surely?"

"I have never been married, ma'am, but perhaps I will be
soon."

"That's lovely news! I'm so glad Lord Morris gave me your
name. He and his wife are old friends."

Ah, Robbie thought.... But then, he had known all along.
He said to himself, I must send a letter of thanks! Perhaps his
wife has forgiven him, and he has gone home.

For the month during which he painted the queen, he did
little else. Often, she was not there and one of her ladies wore
the dress. He spoke of it effusively on weekends at home. He
was glad when the painting was done; he realized how tired he
was and yet so happy. By this time, he was a little in love with
the woman beneath the blue silk dress. She would forget him,

but she would remain inside him for a time, someone he knew very well and did not know: his queen, the lady of the cups with gold dragons and the ancient decorated vases in her secret world.

Robbie had forgotten to write his letter of thanks.

It was too late.

He was having dinner at Louise's with friends when he heard that Lord Morris had ended his life with his pistol the day before, quite alone. Robbie's eyes filled with tears. In one moment that part of his world came back to him: the burning of his early drawings, his first studies, his desperate waiting to be chosen by someone fairly kind in the smoky tavern on Charing Cross Road and (as he now recalled) a man with some silver in his hair looking wistfully at him.

32

ELECTIONS

December 1909–February 1910

Christmas was not ordinary. How could it be without George in his vicarage? They exchanged pleasantries with this cold, proper new vicar whose wife was redesigning the garden. Months before, Robbie had seen George's worn chairs put out on the lawn to give away. One day they were joined by boxes of books which George had not taken, to be sold to a bookseller. Robbie had felt it a desecration and slipped a few under his coat. He would have taken more, but knew they'd be unread. Too much early church history and so much in Greek, which he had never begun to master.

He and Anton walked down to the woods, where they cut down a conifer. Robbie still wore his city clothes, and pine needles stuck to his polished shoes. At least campaigning had stopped for the few days of Christmas.

On Christmas Day, they went to church from habit and because George would inquire if they had. They stood side by side in the pew singing carols. Everyone after, at tea, was polite to them. Some socialists had left the small congregation, as the new minister himself was a Conservative. Robbie and Anton were known by the older members as vicar's lads: they were aware Robbie had painted their queen (they were hushed with respect) and that Mr. Harrington, who had given his fortune to the poor (everyone knew about that too), was their Labour/Liberal candidate for the House of Commons. They thought Robbie loved a woman in London.

Annie came from the city with a few friends, and they had dinner and laughed a lot. In two days, the campaigning would begin again. They could feel something rising all over the country. Anton went down to the mines to inspect them, and his hair smelled of coal and deep rock for a time.

Robbie would return with his friends to the city. The thought appalled him.

But if Anton won, they would both live in London when Parliament was in session. That was wonderful. But would it be? The race between the candidates was close, and people were angry. "He is campaigning to help end the way of life that has held a thousand years," Hayes said when Robbie met him in Market Square. "He will be a powerful voice. The generous side of me says he's right; the man of business is appalled."

Anton had been cheered by the women when walking into a steamy laundry. One child behind an ironing surface seemed no more than twelve. Robbie could not forget her longing eyes.

The polls had been open for ten days so that everyone could vote. During this period, Anton and his colleagues visited every union and spoke in the cold air and knocked on doors in Nottingham side streets, urging people to the polls.

Robbie stopped painting and came home for the last rally on February 9th before the last voting day.

The farmhouse was full of party members and the yard before the house cluttered with motorcars and bicycles. Ten days of votes were locked away in the City Council Chambers in Market Square; thousands of individual slips of paper lay in darkness inside the locked wood voting boxes.

Anton drove them toward Nottingham. Everyone else would follow. They passed neighbors in wagons, on bicycles, or on foot making their way in the same direction. Some nodded curtly, but others called out, "We're going to your rally, Mr. Harrington." Anton stopped the car to take up a young man who walked with a crutch.

Darkness had come. The familiar roads seemed strange to Anton by the lantern light; it was as if he knew the houses and yet saw them for the first time. He felt both calm and agitated; sometimes he could hardly feel his hands on the wheel. His speech was in his pocket. It was more personal words than he intended; last night he had reworked them at two in the morning. Robbie had heard him and made him tea and eggs.

They rode into Nottingham and turned toward the huge Methodist hall. A post hung outside with the names of the speakers. He descended, and many people came forward to shake his hand. "Very glad," he said. "Happy you could come."

Anton found his place in a small room with a pitcher of ale and cakes; the two other speakers shook his hand. He could hear the pews filling. Slowly, the murmuring grew into a dull roar. A thousand people, someone said.

At eight o'clock, a man in a dark robe came to lead them to the several chairs before the church altar. Every seat before him and in the balcony above was filled. Men stood in the back in two or three rows and along the sides.

There were three speakers; Anton was the last.

He looked up and about, seeing a few people he knew. There in the balcony was the man who delivered his coal. John, who had been his lover when Robbie had left him, looked warmly at him, raising his hand slightly in greeting. He saw Robbie. Hello, dear! he thought. So, here we go.

Anton's name was announced. He rose slowly and stood in the center of the chairs before the podium. There was a rustling of skirts and then a great silence. His voice echoed back from the roof and the balconies.

"Ladies and gentlemen, my words are rather different tonight, not specifically of budgets and bills but the reason behind them. I want to speak to you of why I am here… and perhaps why you are here. This country has been my home for all of my life, though I have traveled a bit and always longed to return.

"Several months ago, I was traveling from France back to Dover by ferry, and I stood on deck though there was a cold wind. I wanted to feel that wind and see the channel. And then I raised my eyes and saw the white cliffs of Dover before me as if I had never seen them before. They rose from the sea like something eternal. All my train ride home to Nottinghamshire, the very train wheels seemed to repeat, *England*. And then I returned and found what I believed here and in all of you.

"We stand in a profound moment in our history. We live in a rich and beautiful country whose heritage of kings goes back perhaps nine hundred years. Every road, every old church, every tree is beautiful. And more beautiful are you who live here and work and are part of this land we love."

Everyone was very still. One old woman was staring at him intensely.

"It's not my voice you hear tonight but the voice of the thousands who have no voice. One day they too will have a voice, and this land will not be divided anymore. My voice will have passed into theirs, and that is what I want with all my heart.

"I can't find any better words to say than those I read in a novel recently published by the great English novelist E. M. Forster. In it, he asks the profound question 'To whom does England belong?'"

At those words, Robbie felt the hand of Lord Morris on his sleeve when they had parted the last time and heard the dead man's voice whispering some of them as well.

"'England.... Does she belong to those who have moulded her and made her feared by other lands, or to those who have added nothing to her power, but have somehow seen her.... To whom does England belong? Who will inherit her?'—my dear friends, we are this ship of souls on that jewel of the sea. England is her people. England is ours. Not the rich and the poor, but all of us."

And then it was over, and the clapping was like rain pattering and then thunder. From the back, a band began to play, and

Anton walked forward into the hundreds of people. He could hardly hear them for loudness of the brass instruments playing "God Save the King."

Rain threatened two days later but did not come, though the clouds seemed to press lower and lower and all the colors of the brick and stone houses in Market Square darkened. Toward midafternoon it was filled with people and the wind bands had begun to play once more. Robbie saw Burrows and several friends. They waited for the doors of the City Council Chambers to open.

Finally, a tall man emerged to the steps and held up his hand. He called, "For the first time in our history, our constituency voted in a man from the joined Labour and Liberal Parties. Mr. Harrington, we congratulate you, sir."

Robbie fell in with the many people who pushed their way down a side street to the Independent Labour Party in the church undercroft. They were shouting and laughing. Someone had ordered food from a tavern; the undercroft smelled of lamb and beef and hot carrots. A great deal of whiskey was passed around. Anton seemed near drunk as he was pulled from person to person.

Robbie had slept uneasily for days, and all the shouts made his head pound. He whispered to Anton that he would see him later and trudged the path home reflectively with a borrowed lantern.

Winter again, but such a winter. He tightened his muffler and brought his hat down lower on his forehead. As leaves crunched beneath his feet, the dark houses set back from the road reflected his loneliness. He had wanted Anton alone if only for a few minutes. One kiss, one moment of enveloping each other as if the world weren't there. Damn the world.

"But he's done it," Robbie said, suddenly joyful under his breath as he approached home, hearing the cold stream rushing under the little bridge as he crossed it.

The house was completely dark; clouds above it covered the moon. He climbed the steps to their rooms, lighting more lamps, which brought out the bright red of pillows and book bindings and a teapot with tea from hours before grown cold. The clock struck midnight; he stared at the hands as the tone ceased and still hung in the air. All the noise of the celebrations and the bands and the singing was far away. Now he was sorry he had left.

Robbie took off his tie and emptied the papers from his coat pocket to the desk, throwing some in the wastepaper bin. He shook his head; he had tossed away his list of clients, who must be rescheduled. Bother! He rummaged for it in the bin, looking at several papers until he found it. Near it was a letter torn in two. He made out some of the writing and stuffed it down into the basket. It wasn't his.

He dropped down on the sofa, and tried to read some Socialist newspaper, but could not stop thinking of the torn letter. He was shivering, though the fire was warm.

The clock read twenty minutes to one.

Robbie walked into the bedroom and in the shadows made out the bed and the wardrobe, the mirror which showed his dim sullen face, Anton's razor and soap on the washstand, and his clothing piled over chairs. It's him I need, he thought resentfully. He doesn't belong to those strangers. What do they know of him really?

It's all stupid, he thought, throwing off his clothes and falling into the bed, pulling the old green quilt over him, finding the familiar pillows. He slept suddenly, as if his mind could hold no more.

He was awakened by the sound of a bicycle on the dead fallen leaves. He heard the unsteady footsteps up the stairs and the study door creak, and then felt Anton's warm whiskey kiss pressing hard against his mouth.

"I'm here," Anton said. "Didn't dare use the car; borrowed a bicycle and fell over twice. I think I bloodied my knee. I didn't want anyone else to drive me; I wanted to come alone."

Robbie drew him closer. He said, "I was so tired and so proud. I wanted to hug you and kiss you until you couldn't breathe. I wanted to shout to everyone, 'He's mine.' I couldn't, of course."

"Kiss me now for a long time. I haven't much use for breathing."

"Ah, don't you?" asked Robbie.

"None. You taste delicious."

"Lots of whiskey, Anton, but so do you."

33

THE HOUSE IN NOTTINGHAMSHIRE

February 1910

Robbie opened his eyes slowly the next morning; he had been so deep in dreams that it was hard for him to focus. He heard Anton humming in the study. In moments, last night returned to him.

He lay contented, looking at the light coming in the window onto the ragged fringes of the worn rug, as he had seen it many times before. He remembered waiting for Anton last night, unable to read, unable to rest. He had taken the papers from his pocket and thrown away his client list. Retrieving it, he had found... No, he hadn't. He had dreamed it. It could never have been real.

This place will stay always the same: the creak of the floor, the wavering of the curtain, and the oak outside, he thought suddenly, even when I'm not here to see it.

Robbie sat up as if pulled. What was he thinking of? The fear had always been there in the back of his mind since they had returned from his disastrous art exhibition dinner, where he had almost told their secret to people he hardly knew. Once, he and Anton had been here and thought they had heard someone below, and Anton had gone down. It was a squirrel, somehow got in, but they had not slept again for a time. Another night a tramp banged on the door. They had thought, What if...and who?

Who had come for Keith? His Irish friend had been dancing around the room, someone said, wearing the shirt of his newest lover, happy...and then. That was how the moral arrests happened, when someone had it in for you or could earn reward money. Otherwise, men spent their whole lives together quietly, happily. Always a little anxious, but sometimes almost forgetting. The brothers in the house with white curtains. The bachelors hoping to find the right woman.

And now there was the torn letter he had found.

But there is this place, Robbie thought, where we can be secretive and happy, talking half the night. We're safe. There was so much to say. There was always another subject. Robbie sometimes burst out about what he wanted to do in art. This beautiful thing growing every day, this thing they called *us*...this *us*, more important than anything else in the world.

Robbie stood, gathering his dressing gown, having trouble finding the sleeve. His feet were cold; he couldn't find his left slipper. Then he stood listening to that half song.

He squeaked opened the door.

Anton was standing at his desk, leaning on it with one hand. He looked up, his eyes shining. Robbie said, "Good morning, Mr. Harrington."

"Good morning, my lover. I prefer you call me 'my lover.'"

"I need to talk to you, Anton."

"My God, what's the matter? Why so serious?" Anton's old way of standing with both hands thrust into dressing-gown pockets, the dark eyes looking at him challenging. "Oh, nothing serious, not this morning! I've hardly slept these past weeks and was up early today, our day alone. No one is coming; aren't you glad?"

Robbie bit his lip. He was silent for a moment and then said, "When you were out last night, I found a torn letter in the trash basket. I was looking for something I'd thrown away." Robbie reached down and found the two pieces, holding them together. Perhaps he had not read it all last night. He had read some, his mind refusing to take it in. But Anton's face changed, and he snatched the papers and strode toward the fire. Robbie shouted, "No," and seized Anton's arm.

Anton's shoulders were hard now. "It came in the mail a week ago or so.... It's trash. It's nothing. Whoever they are, they mean only to make me back off. Whoever it was didn't even sign it."

"You didn't tell me."

"I didn't want to write you in London. You've been working yourself into exhaustion."

Robbie held out his hand, and Anton gave him the letter. Now Robbie forced himself to make the written words come together; there was no signature. *We are aware of the indecencies between you and your artist. If you vote against our interests, watch out. There can be witnesses. The old vicar can't protect you anymore as he did.*

Anton was silent for a moment. "He never told us about anything, I never thought... But he would protect us. Of course he would."

"Do you have any idea who wrote it, Anton?"

Anton replied, "I don't know. I have enemies. We all have enemies in politics."

"But this person is threatening to denounce you."

"He couldn't have seen anything. He can do nothing." Anton threw himself into a chair.

"Anton," Robbie said, "he might. Once, in the woods, we let ourselves kiss. Perhaps other times. He does say that there could be witnesses, not that there are witnesses. But if he does report us, we could be imprisoned."

His voice broke and he dropped to Anton's lap, burying his face on Anton's shoulder. "And then what? Someone might still want my paintings, even if I had to change to landscapes or children's book illustration under another name, but you... It might bring everything you've worked for down. Everything we worked for. Oh, Anton, don't you see? You're going up to Parliament. We can't be together anymore."

His next words were incoherent; he pulled away from Anton, who tried to hold him. He had to make a space between them. He had not expected Anton to win—that was the truth. The race was so close. Was it by a few hundred votes?

His heart was beating so fast.

Anton would need a residence in London. They had doubted they could live together but planned to stay with each other as much as they could. That was the first scrambled plan when they had discussed "if and when." Robbie would stay with

Louise, and he and Anton would creep quietly upstairs at night. They would sometimes stay in Anton's new flat, hoping that any charwoman or neighbor who saw them would pay them no mind.

Even that wouldn't do it seemed. There were people watching. Robbie sprang up and kicked over the trash basket. He threw himself onto a footstool.

"Be reasonable," Anton said for the fourth time, kneeling by him. "Don't push me off." Robbie raised his head and stroked Anton's cheek, stubbly under his fingers. He kissed the scar on Anton's wrist under his dressing gown cuff.

Anton said, "It's one letter, Rob. And remember we agreed once to decide things together. I wouldn't buy a motorcar without asking you."

"This isn't a damn car. This is our whole lives."

"Rob, we can't be apart. Let's go out and talk about it. Now, when you're so pulled by your emotions, I must be the rational one."

"You always put yourself in such a rational role when I'm not."

"What other recourse do we have?"

Robbie nodded blindly. He dressed, though he had to button his shirt twice to get it right. They went downstairs together and packed a basket with bread and cheese and tea in a bottle. Anton knocked over the knife box, which fell open to the floor. The festivities of last night seemed in another life to Robbie. He thought, Who were those people?

"Let's walk," Anton said, not looking at him. "How about the old barn? Don't look at me with love like that after what you just said upstairs." Anton's voice broke. He stood before the hanging iron and copper pots. "You crazy fellow. Dear God, I just won the seat in Parliament and you've decided this is the morning to break my heart again. Why did I ever let you into my life or take you back? You promised not to go away anymore."

"But it's because I love you," said Robbie. "So much."

It was a still day, very overcast but not cold. They ate the bread as they walked and threw the crumbs to the birds. Robbie finally felt that his voice was steady enough to speak. "You can see what's most important for the country but not what's just before you," he said.

He swallowed, tasting the bread. He said, "I'm not very good at praying, but I prayed for your success every night. But we should have understood, of course. You'll have more enemies now. Someone will try to bring you down because you love me."

"They can't!"

"Look up, Anton! There's a golden eagle! I haven't seen him for years. The hares won't be safe, or the ducks; he's descending to the pond that way. Look."

Anton kicked some fallen twigs. He touched the tree bark as he went, trailing his hand against it.

Robbie followed him. He said, "Anton, I saw what happened to Keith. I met another man whom prison crushed. He had three months of solitude for twenty-three hours a day, no visitors for months. For what? For bloody what? What harm did he do anyone?"

"We won't be denounced. Burrows will warn us; he finds out everything around here. He'll come with me to London when I need him."

"Yes, but he's not powerful, not yet." Robbie took Anton's arm and kicked a little at the dirt.

Anton said, "Oscar Wilde had warning and didn't escape. The most brilliant writer in England, and once they sent him to prison, all his successful plays in the West End closed. Perhaps if they came after us, we'd have time. We'd go to Tuscany." He frowned and stopped walking. "But if we had no time to escape and I was sent to prison for two years—"

He stopped between the low bare branches of a black walnut tree.

"I'd help you in any way I could," Robbie said. "I'd call on every ally. But perhaps I'd be the one taken, you know. They'd strike out at you through me. After, we'd go to your grandmother's house. But..."

Robbie fought the lump in his throat by kicking leaves. He

said, "But even if we stayed here, if you were convicted, it would be the end of the dream you have. You could write, but no one would let you stand for the Labour Party again. They'd jeer you when you spoke. Everything we worked toward would be gone. Will you lose that because of loving me? One day you'd resent me. Perhaps you'd hate me. You'll say, 'I came to this because I loved him.' For that thing…"

There was the forest; there had always been the forest—though centuries of English shipbuilding had diminished it; though the cultivation of land had curtailed it and the hunters brought down the fleeing deer, it had been here. We're part of it, Robbie thought, looking at the white sky above the bare limbs of the trees. I could paint it.

They walked the path past a coal mine some mile off to the west, at last intertwining fingers. Across a field they saw the dilapidated barn, the one broken door stuck open, the paint worn off years ago. They slipped inside and smelled the old straw. Robbie looked up.

Anton said grimly, "Sit down; there's no one here. I think I could bar that door. Prison is terrible, and who knows what it would do to you."

"It would end your work. I know that."

"My work isn't worth losing you," Anton said. "Come here—let me hold you. Without you, I wouldn't have gone back to what I wanted to do. Because I did go back, because I listened to you, now you're saying you're leaving me, Rob."

They lay on their backs on the stiff straw-packed dirt floor, looking into the rafters. Anton was silent for a time. He said at last, "So this is what you propose. You take your last sock out of our house and hurry back to Louise. I move to the least expensive flat I can in London and spend my entire life until I am old and wrinkled fighting for the rights of those in need. And thus goes my life. The bill they call the People's Budget will pass this year or in five years. The devil with the bill, Rob!"

He turned on his side and touched Robbie's cheek. "The

devil with all of them, Rob. For whom am I fighting? And of the many people who voted for me and knew about us, how many would turn from me? Those who cheer me now as if in some way I can save them? I can't do this and conceal what I am."

Robbie said, "But this is what you wanted all your life."

"No, Rob—I damn well don't have to go. I could change my mind. Who do I come home to? Taking your hand, telling you everything! You'd find love easily. If you only hadn't ever come back."

They tussled and rolled over; old straw caught in their hair. "That's the end of the subject!" Anton shouted. "Nothing's changing. We're not changing. It's over for me. We're moving to Italy. There's no laws against us there."

"Our lives are here. You're taking your seat in Parliament."

Anton didn't stay long in the house when they returned; he seized another muffler without a word and turned his bicycle toward Nottingham. "I've meetings," he called back coldly. "I'll see you for supper, and I hope to God you won't talk any more nonsense to me."

Robbie stood before the door watching him go. For a long time, he remembered those bent, angry shoulders, that wild dark hair in the wind, the resentful voice echoing back.

He sagged. He thought, But he knows that he won't see me.

He walked carefully from room to room looking at everything he loved and finally sat on the stairs leading to the study. "Anton," he whispered. "How will I bear this?" On the landing, Anton had dropped his leather bag of tools a month ago, the last time he had repaired a door or a shutter or a roof. The whole neighborhood for miles about bore signs of his careful restoration work.

He cried for a long time. It was as if he were a boy again and coming back from the theater to find the study door locked. That was so long ago.

After a long time, he dried his face and stood up. Sitting at the desk in the study, he wrote a letter to Anton, the last he swore he would ever write. He begged him to burn their correspondence. Then he packed his bag and left the house.

He had to calm down during his walk to the train station; too many people would look at him. From there, he called London and then boarded the train.

He couldn't read, of course; he could do nothing on the ride.

The compartment was empty, but there were no more tears. His chest heaved, but that was all. He looked through the window at the coming dusk, seeing his face, a young man he did not entirely recognize as himself.

Who am I now, Anton? he thought. Who am I without you? I must have, as you once wrote me, a purpose and a reason. Without that, you said, we're lost. So how will I live and where will I go? Where will I succeed and where will I fail? I don't know. I can only manage this day with such belief, with such love as is inside me. But without you…every day, every year without you.

The train was pulling into the London King's Cross station. Already he heard the noises of the crowd pulling him. He kept his hat down, jammed as much as he could over his eyes. "Goodbye, my darling," he said under his breath, "for this little while or a great and endless while. Be all you were meant to be."

Then he went forward down the platform to his friends who were waiting for him.

BRIEF NOTES

The People's Budget was passed by the House of Lords in spring 1910. A few years after World War I, the Welshman David Lloyd George formed the first Labour government. Health care, old-age pensions, unionization, and many other programs began to help the poor and lower middle classes. Taxes were levied on the wealthy and their properties. Of course, governments change, and have gone back and forth in the UK since that time.

The political situation was quite complex, and I have simplified it for the needs of this novel.

The Gross Indecency Laws, created in 1885, which sent men to prison for two years for the crime of homosexuality, were finally repealed in 1967; a new bill permitted private intimacy between men over twenty-one. (When Queen Victoria was asked if female lovers should also be considered guilty, she replied, "Women don't do such things.") Over fifty thousand men were sentenced to prison in a period of some eighty-two years. However, most men escaped notice if they lived quietly. Their neighbors often could not conceive that such love could exist among the ordinary people they knew. Or they knew but believed in "Live and let live," and never said a word.

The characters are fictional but so real to me that when I began writing this novel, I traveled to Nottingham "looking" for them in my own way and was grieved that I couldn't find them.

FURTHER NOTES AND ACKNOWLEDGEMENTS

I first had a vision of these characters while walking down outdoor wood steps in a country house in New York State. I passed them descending to the wooded area and the stream. The two young men were real and yet not quite. I left them, and when I turned, they were gone.

It was an old house under heavy trees, with fields and forest walks and streams and, nearby, ruined stone cottages in a field. The two men I had "seen" kept returning to my mind. Who were they?

Sometime later, when I told friends Stephanie Low and Karen Lee Bowers about the beginnings of the story which was haunting me, they challenged me to write it down. I came back with a very short, rough draft, setting it in the English midlands. I was an opera singer then, not a novelist. Shortly after, I left singing for writing. While I published several other novels, *The Boy in the Rain* was slowly growing though the printout remained on a closet shelf. Now and then I would share it with friends. During the terrible isolation of the 2020/21 pandemic when I stayed at home a lot, I knew that if I could write and publish only more novel, this would be it. I finished the final draft and sent it out to Regal House Publishing where it has happily found a home.

A few small notes about history in this novel: The actual date of the passage of The People's Budget in the House of Commons and the publication of *Howards End* have been moved slightly. The name of the village is fictional.

I am grateful to my draft readers/volunteer editors over the years. Thanks to Judith Ackerman, Jacqueline Baird, Bruce Bawer, Vicki Bijur, Robert Blumenfeld, Karen Lee Bowers, Mary Burns, Lauri Carroll, Fiona Claire, Russell Clay, Christina

Britton Conroy, Lauren B. Davis, Michael DiShiavi, Susanne Dunlap, Lindsay Edmunds, Susan Dormady Eisenberg (triple thanks for endless support!), Christine Emmert, David Forrer, Ruth Henderson, Isabelle Holland, Mitchell James Kaplan, Katherine Kirkpatrick, Peggy Harrington, Ros Gardiner, Jane Gardner, Loretta Goldberg, Jennie Mathieu Greenfield, Edna Johnson, Pamela Leggett, Madeleine L'Engle, Bonda Lewis, Judith Lindbergh, Stephanie Low, Shellen Lubin, Michael McGaughey, Amy Jessen-Marshall, James and Viraja Mathieu, Phil Melito, Emily Petit, David Pike, Cathie Phelps, Elsa Rael, Lance Ringel, M.J. Rose, Amy Rosenberg, Rick Rowley, John Russo, Sanna Stanley, Barbara Quick, Susan Wands, Bob Weber, Naomi Weinstein, and Sally Whitehead. My apologies to any I have forgotten.

Particularly deep thanks for my most recent editors in pre-submission drafts: Ali Tufel who lived with various incarnations of this novel for years, Andrea Simon whose patience and editing skills astonish me, and my oldest friend in the world, Renée Vera Cafiero, who brought fifty years of exacting copy-editing skills to this manuscript.

Thanks to my colleagues in my three writing groups past and present not listed above who also have cheered on my writing: Linda Cox Austin, Pat McMann Barry, Amy Baruch, Rhonda Hunt-Del Bene, Karen Finch, Casey Kelly and Kathleen Rodgers. Thanks also to Writer Unboxed and my FB writer friends and my FB groups Fiction Writers' Co-op and Historical Fiction Authors and to the Historical Novel Society, especially Sarah Johnson and Richard Lee. Dearest friends from my Shakespeare reading groups, what would I do without you?

Whatever perseverance I have is due to the love of my family: my son James Nordstrom, the IT guy who keeps a place for me in his old farmhouse, and his wife, archivist Kristina Wilson, and James's two daughters, Hanna who managed to re-organize my books and house while living with me and sharing a great deal of pasta, and Emma, a lovely young woman who is always just a phone call away; and my son filmmaker Jesse Cowell who listens to hours of my artistic angst while walking in the gardens near his home and is creating a TikTok and other social media for this novel; and to his partner animator Erica Langworthy, for love, creative sharing and her graphic support. Much gratitude to my sister and brother-in-law Jennie and Jerry Greenfield, to my stepsister novelist Gabrielle Mathieu and her husband Jerry Mahoney, and my beloved stepmother Viraja Mathieu and to my late father, the artist James Albert Mathieu. And last and always remembered, my late husband poet Russell O'Neal Clay to whom this book is dedicated and who loved it above all my books. Russell, I think of you every day.

Thanks to priests and parishioners and musicians at my former church of St. Thomas Fifth Avenue in New York City and my present parish of St. Ignatius of Antioch. In the earliest days of creating this book, I would run up for dinner and prayers at The Community of the Holy Spirit, the convent where Sister Mary Christabel was a great steady light in my life.

Beloved Madeleine L'Engle, you were also a very great light to me and opened worlds.

Lastly, warmest gratitude to Jaynie Royal, the founder and Editor-in-Chief of Regal House Publishing and her Managing Editor Pam Van Dyk for acquiring, editing, and bringing *The Boy in the Rain* into a printed book. I am so proud to be part of the steadily rising star of this publishing house.